(A Mortal Techniques novel)

By

Rob J. Hayes

For everyone who read Never Die and demanded more. I heard your cries.

Rob J. Hayes

I have commanded armies. I have waged war, true war in all its myriad incarnations. I have come to understand it like none other before me, and none other will after I am gone. People think war is a concept inflicted upon the weak by the powerful. A contest of battles, a push and pull of opposing forces struggling for dominance, searching for that one move that would cut off the head and let the war die. That is a lie.

War is a living thing, unique to humanity amongst the physical and spiritual kingdoms, and it mimics its conceptualists with alarming accuracy. A war starts small. An idea, a thought. A conception. Never quick, it takes time to gestate, to grow, to take form long before it is birthed into the world. And it is always birthed in blood. Violence and screaming and love. No war can take place without love. Be it love for a person, love for power, love for money, love for a nation. Wars grow, expanding beyond the boundaries of their initial conception. As more participants join a war, they add their own purposes to it, muddy its waters and change its flow. Wars grow, and as they grow, they change, consume, spread. They are lonely things, seeking company, spawning smaller conflicts.

Yet they grow tired over time, giving and taking scars that heal into tougher tissue, more callous. And when they die, they die hard, just as people die hard, clinging to every second, every scrap of life. Wars never end when the head is chopped off. That is also a lie. Battles continue, even though their purpose is forgotten, their driving ideal scattered to the wind. Men fight on, far beyond hope and even beyond reason. And when a war is finally laid to rest, as all wars must be, it is remembered by those it has delivered, and by those it has destroyed.

-Xiaodan Wei

Prologue

"All the other gods are waiting, Natsuko," Fuyuko said, his childish voice high and excited. "Hurry up and choose."

Natsuko frowned at her twin brother and went back to her contemplation of the portraits on the walls. She had been in the Hall of Faces for days now, trying to make a choice. Millions of paintings hung from the walls of the vast auditorium, one of each human in Hosa, Ipia, Nash, and Cochtan. Even as she watched, one of the paintings' edges curled up, its parchment yellowed, and its ink faded. Another human had died. They were always dying and in such great numbers, especially in the past hundred years. A century of war and so many lives lost. The parchment crumbled away, the face it once showed gone. Changang, the God of Life, would be around soon to replace the parchment and paint a new face. It was his role in Tianmen to keep the Hall of Faces up to date. But even Changang was waiting for Natsuko now.

"Pick, sister! We don't have all eternity."

"Be patient, brother," Natsuko said defiantly. "We only get one chance at this."

"I know, sister," Fuyuko said, his boyish face crumpling into a frown. "Of all the gods, *I* know!"

Time to make a choice. Natsuko blew out a sigh and plucked one of the paintings from the wall. A middle-aged woman with lines on her face that spoke of easy smiles long since replaced with the tight frowns of guilt and grief. A life of pain, of hardship, of loss. This face, this human, of all the millions around her, might understand. "This one," Natsuko said. She expected it to feel right when she picked the painting she wanted, but she felt nothing. Michi, the god of omens, would probably have something to say about that, but then Michi had something to say about everything.

"Are you sure?" Fuyuko said. He was staring at the painting and pulling that face that meant he thought his sister was mad. Such an easy boy to read. Far too earnest. That was why they were playing the roles they were. It could be no other way.

Natsuko grinned at her brother and nodded emphatically. Then she grabbed his hand and pulled him from the Hall of Faces. They rushed through the halls of Tianmen, sandals slapping against the marble floor, clouds churning to either side and above in place of walls and ceiling. It was oddly quiet. All the gods were gathered in the throne room, waiting to begin the contest. Waiting for her.

The great doors to the throne room loomed out of the clouds ahead, were open and Natsuko slipped through, clutching her painting to her chest, and holding her brother's hand tightly. She would not let him go, not when they were so close. All the gods turned to watch her enter. Hundreds of them, some her friends, others anything but. A few even snarled at her. All the gods had enemies, even child gods like Natsuko. Up on the dais, in front of the jade throne waited Batu, God of War, the tianjun for the past hundred years. For a century he had ruled heaven, and for a century the world below had known only war. But now the gods had a chance to change that. Natsuko had a chance to change it. And she would pay any price.

"Are you finally ready, little Natsuko?" Batu asked, smiling at her. He was not unkind, for a god. He stood radiant, bare-chested, bronze skinned, with not a hair on his head save for curling eyebrows the colour of fire and bushy golden chops. Ceremonial beads hung around his neck, his only ornamentation. He leaned upon his red wood staff, a weapon no other god, mortal, or spirit, could lift. The jade throne was his. For now.

Natsuko strode through the gathering of gods, dragging Fuyuko behind her. "Were you all waiting for me?" she said with a giggle.

Batu laughed. "Well, we can't do this without all of us here. Though I will admit I was about to send Sarnai to drag you here, ready or not."

Sarnai, the goddess of fire, sneered down at Natsuko. She was taller than most gods and half-reptilian. A long tail coiled behind her and scales peppered her skin. Fire dripped from her mouth whenever she opened it, which gave her a terrible lisp that made her insufferably difficult to understand. "I thee you have chothen," the fire goddess said. "May I thee?" She extended a clawed hand and Natsuko clutched the painting tighter to her chest. Sarnai laughed, spraying fire from her lips. She carried her own chosen painting, though the face upon it looked more machine than man.

Batu raised his staff and then tapped it on the floor. The sound was as loud as ten gongs struck at once. He waited for silence and then grinned. "It's time," he said, grinning down at them all. "Gods who wish to challenge for my throne, step forward."

Natsuko stepped forward. She wasn't alone. Thirty-five of the gathered hundreds were choosing to take part. Each carried a painting in one hand, their artefact in the other.

"So many of you," Batu said grinning like a goat. "Has my time as tianjun really been so bad?" He held up a hand before any of them could answer. He knew exactly what his rule had been and did not care. After all, he was the god of war, and war was his purpose. "You all know the rules. And you all know the price." He gazed down at Natsuko, and she saw sadness in his eyes. No other god was giving up as much to take part as she was.

Batu drew in a deep breath, raised his voice, and said with an air of formality, "We have gathered here, we gods of Hosa, Ipia, Nash, and Cochtan, as we do just once every hundred years, to participate in the Heavenly Crucible. To see which of us will sit the throne for the next century. Which of you will try to take my place? Leave your artefacts and I will seed them. Take your paintings and find your champions." He pointed to the sky and the moon sliding across it. "Hikaru?"

Hikaru, the goddess of the moon, stepped forward on slippered feet and bowed her head. For a moment, the moon seemed to shine brighter. "In twenty-five days, the moon will be full again," the goddess said. Natsuko almost laughed to think of how such a thing would confuse the humans. The stargazers took great care to document and predict the passage of moon and stars. Hikaru had just sped up the cycle and thrown all those predictions into chaos.

Batu clapped his hands together. "The contest will start with the light of the new day. Good luck, and…" His grin spread wider, stretching his face into something menacing. "I hope you all fail." Most of the gods chuckled at the joke, but Natsuko did not. She saw beneath Batu's humour and wondered what he might do to bring all their failures about. He would not be the first ruler of heaven to rig the game. "Well, don't just stand there. Get on with it."

Each of the participating gods stepped forward and left their artefacts before the throne. Natsuko went last, struggling to let go of the thing she cherished most in the world. But she had to. It was the cost of entering the contest, and the only way to bring an end to Batu's reign.

"I'll give it a good home," Batu said quietly so no other gods could hear.

Natsuko clenched one hand into a fist, the other still clutching the painting. "Away from your wars?"

The smile slipped from Batu's face, and he gave her a look like cold steel. "There is no such place. After all, I might have just twenty-five days left to rule. I intend to engulf the world in discord like never before, little Natsuko."

9

Natsuko winced, then glared up at Batu. "I'm going to stop you."

The god of war spread his arms wide. "Then stop me."

Natsuko glared at Batu a moment longer, left her artefact on the dais, then turned and strode away as fast as her little legs would carry her. Her heart broke and she struggled to hold back tears. It had to be done. It was all part of the plan. Fuyuko's plan. Only *he* did not have the strength to carry it out. That's why it was up to her. "I hope you're the right choice," she whispered to the painting.

Chapter 1

Yuu watched the old man over the table as he stared at the few pieces left to him. He was a foolish old man who brought a bottle of wine to the table and shared it without hesitation. A cunning tactic that might have worked on a lesser strategist, but she saw through his plan. That and it would take more than one bottle of wine to make her so poor at chess as to lose to the likes of him. He was wrinkled from more years than Yuu cared to count and had a drooping grey moustache. He was chewing on the left side of that moustache, grinding the hairs between his teeth, as he tried to find a way out of the trap she had led him into. There was no way out. Only fools left anything to chance.

"Don't worry," Yuu said, stifling a yawn. "We have all day." It was late morning and white clouds covered the sky. There would be no rain today. Another day of drought.

"Don't rush me," the old man snapped as he stared at his pieces. "Chaoxiang wrote that no war is lost while the will to fight persists." He glanced up at her and winked as though some tired old philosophy could turn the tide. "My will is set. Today is the day I beat you."

He had said the same thing yesterday, and the day before. And the day before that too. He was wrong on all counts. For a start, he had lost after his sixth move, even if he hadn't realised it, and all thirty moves since were just tightening the noose. Also, his interpretation of Chaoxiang was as lacking as his skill at chess. He had lost the game, and he had lost the battle. The war, on the other hand, would indeed go on until his will gave out. He would challenge her again and again, and he would lose again and again. And eventually his will would falter. Until then, Yuu would happily take his money and his wine. She raised her wine cup and sipped happily at it, enjoying the fuzzy edges of her drunk. Five years ago she would have condemned any of her soldiers for being drunk by midday. But things had changed and she had changed with them. The choice between change or death was no choice at all.

The old man placed a finger on his last Thief. He had just three Pawns, his Emperor, a Shintei, and the Thief he was now fingering. Yuu knew his move long before he made it. She had left him with only the one move, the one way out, one way to save his Emperor. He took it and moved his Thief forward two spaces and left one, blocking Yuu's Monk. She waited for the old man to lift his finger from the piece, consummating his loss. Then Yuu plucked her Hero from the board, slid it all the way to the far side, and stood it next to the old man's Emperor.

"Checkmate," Yuu said with a drunken smile. She let the man stare at the board for a few moments. "Pay up."

The old man's eyes twitched about the board for a few moments more, then he sighed and slapped two coins on the stone table. "Can't even win when I get you drunk."

"Nope," Yuu agreed happily. "But I thank you for trying." She bowed her head to him and giggled drunkenly. "Let me know when you want to try again."

The old man grumbled and stood from the table, his knees popping. He walked away with his head lowered. Yuu guessed his wife would be angry with him tonight. The foolishness of people never ceased to amaze her. For the fifth day in a row he'd lost his coin, and this time he lost a bottle of wine as well. Yuu noticed he'd even left what remained of the wine. She tucked a few errant strands of hair behind her ear and poured herself another cup, then went about resetting the pieces on the board in case anyone else was stupid enough to challenge her to a game.

Xindu was a sleepy little village just three days west of Ban Ping. A few dozen families called the place home, and in the relative peace following Einrich WuLong taking the throne and declaring himself Emperor of Ten Kings, it was growing slowly. There were whispers the Leper Emperor was planning a new war against Cochtan, but as yet no officials had come to levy troops. The village had a small square with a tavern looming over it, and in that square stood a stone table perfect for games of chess. It was a pleasant village to hide in, but Yuu had to remember that she *was* in hiding. She would have to move on soon, before the villagers started to ask who she really was. Until then, though, she would gladly beat all challengers, take their money, and drink it away. At a certain point each day, when she'd had just the right amount to drink, she could forget what she had done and who had paid the price. In that moment, her mind would stop analysing the world and find peace.

A new challenger sat down across the table, and Yuu blinked away the fuzziness in her eyes. Her thoughts had been drifting, leading her down the familiar dark path, and any distraction was a welcome one. Her new challenger appeared to be a young girl, maybe only six years old. Too young to remember the last emperor and the war he waged upon his own people. Yuu envied the girl her youth, but it was likely she would grow up to be just as foolish as everyone else.

"I don't teach," Yuu slurred. She plucked the bottle of wine from the table to refill her cup but found it empty. She stared down into its mouth, just to make certain, but it was definitely empty. Another loss to mourn.

"And I'm not here to learn," the girl said in a voice so eloquent it made Yuu reassess her age. She was small, with short black hair and deceptively deep brown eyes. She wore a simple red hanfu with white patterning sewn into it, and a single wooden dragon earring coiled around her left ear. It seemed an odd thing and certainly not any fashion Yuu was aware of. Perhaps she had lost the other earring. She was so young perhaps she didn't even realise it. Her clothes were too clean for a field worker's, and her attitude spoke of nobility. She was out of place here in Xindu, and

13

Yuu didn't like when things were out of place. There was something she wasn't seeing.

"What's your name, girl?" Yuu asked. She had been in Xindu for almost a week and had never seen the child before. The village had no affiliation with any of the clans, and this girl was anything but a commoner.

"Natsuko," the girl said cheerfully. An Ipian name, it meant summer child. There was something unnervingly focused about the girl's eyes.

"You're a long way from Ipia," Yuu said. Three weeks travel at least, much of it over mountains, not to mention crossing a guarded border. She looked around for the child's parents. It was not so much that she disliked children as a rule, only that they served so little purpose until they were old enough to be useful. On second thought, she decided she did dislike children, and with good reason.

"What's your name?" the girl asked.

"Yuu." She was so used to the lie it came unbidden to her now. Five years as Yuu.

"No it isn't," the girl chided. "Your name is Daiyu Lingsen."

Yuu panicked, and a dose of clarity rushed in, sharpening the fuzzy edges of her thinking. She found herself feeling a lot soberer than a moment before and cursed her complacency. She glanced about the village square nervously, searching for lawfolk or bounty hunters. The last she heard, there was four thousand lien on her head, and the royal family of Qing weren't too bothered if the rest of her was attached. She'd pushed her luck, stayed in this deceptively sleepy village for too long. Rumour had it the legendary bounty hunter, the Laws of Hope, was in Ban Ping, and the city wasn't so far from Xindu that he wouldn't make the trip. Especially if four thousand lien was at stake. By the stars, four thousand lien was enough money to turn any of the idiot villagers in Xindu into a bounty hunter. It was time to run again, time to change her name again. Maybe she'd just leave Hosa for good, go live in Nash or Ipia, where no one had ever heard of the strategist the Art of War or her murder of the Steel Prince.

The only other people in the square were two village locals, a goatherd talking to a woman drawing water from the well. If they were there for her, then they weren't doing a good job of penning her in. Xindu's main road ran through the village square, and two narrow alleyways lay behind Yuu. One of them would be streaked with lines of washing at this time of day, which would provide extra cover for her escape. When she glanced back at the girl, she was still staring at Yuu, smiling patiently.

"What is this?" Yuu asked. "A shakedown? I have no money and—"

"No," the girl said quickly. "Nothing like that. I'm here to ask for your help. Let me start again. My name is Natsuko, and I'm a goddess."

Yuu stared hard at the girl and received nothing but impassive confidence in return. She had a passing knowledge of the gods, though there were so many of them only the monks could hope to remember them all. Still, the name rang a bell. "Would that be the Ipian god of the lost?" she asked.

The girl sighed impatiently. "Goddess of missed opportunities and lost things," she said grumpily. "Not *the lost*."

Would a goddess really come down from heaven to torment Yuu? She had to admit it was possible, likely even. What good did the gods serve if not to toy with mortals? The worst thing about it was that a goddess sitting across a gaming table from her was not the craziest thing she had ever seen. She'd seen long dead heroes brought back to life and had also seen them kill an oni. She'd thought she'd left that life behind. "Tell me this then, little goddess," she said. "Why do you gods always appear as children?" She wasn't sure she could run from a goddess, but it seemed far more likely than escaping the Laws of Hope if he came for her. His was a legend that stretched far and wide. No one escaped him.

15

The girl narrowed her eyes. "Always? You've met with gods before?"

A few strands of hair had fallen in front of her face again and Yuu tucked them back behind her ears. "Well, there was a shinigami a few years ago…" She glanced about the square again, looking for danger, but all seemed peaceful.

The girl snorted out a laugh. "Shinigami are not gods. They're spirits. Powerful spirits, true, but they're more akin to common yokai than to gods." She had a flippant tone when talking about the Reapers that went a long way in convincing Yuu she might actually be telling the truth. Not many folk knew the truth about shinigami, and in Hosa far fewer likely knew the truth about an obscure Ipian goddess. "But if it makes you feel better…" The girl trailed off. Yuu squinted at the goatherd still chatting up the woman at the well. Yuu was certain she had seen him around the village before, but he was definitely glancing her way too often for her liking.

The girl's voice slipped into the amused croak of an ancient grandmother. "How's this?"

Yuu snapped her head around, ignoring a blur of drunken dizziness, and the goddess no longer wore the pink-cheeked face of a young girl but the lined and sagging face of an ancient woman. She wore the same hanfu and the same single wooden earring in her left ear. "What is this?" Yuu asked. "Where did the girl go? How drunk am I?"

The old woman shrugged and cackled. "Probably far too drunk for this conversation. However, I don't have all the time in the world, and honestly I was struggling to find a time when you weren't at least one bottle in."

Yuu glanced at the empty wine bottle on the table. She had to admit it was not her first of the day. She had finished a bottle with breakfast, but that was nothing new. She rubbed her eyes and stared again at the old woman. The child was certainly gone, but there was something familiar about the ancient woman. She had the same brown eyes, so deep and wise.

"Are you convinced now?" the old woman asked.

Yuu had heard of tricksters, some with unique techniques, and some with impressive sleight of hand, but none who could change their appearance so quickly and so convincingly. She leaned over the table and glanced down beside the old woman, but if the child was hiding somewhere she was not there. Yuu sat back down and considered. The most obvious answer was that she was being tricked somehow and had not the wit to see through it. Then again, the world was full of stories about gods coming down from Tianmen to play with humans. It would be just her luck. "Can't you, uh, do something to show me for certain?"

The old woman frowned, deepening the lines on her face. "Like what?"

"I don't know." Yuu glanced around. "Refill the wine bottle."

"I'm the goddess of missed opportunities, not the goddess of booze."

"Shame." She was right, of course. The goddess of booze was Zhenzhen, and it was a name on many lips these days. It was, after all, customary to say a prayer to the goddess before the first sip of the day. Yuu failed to observe the custom of late, but then her first sip of the day was getting earlier and earlier, and she could barely remember to pour the wine into a cup at such times, much less say a prayer.

The old woman reached across the table. "Give me your hand."

Yuu pulled back for a moment, suspicious, and glanced about the square again. The goatherd and the water woman were gone now. Yuu and the old woman were all alone. The old woman just held her hand out next to the chessboard, waiting for Yuu. Yuu reached out and clasped the woman's hand. The old woman smiled a grandmother's smile, and for just a moment looked too much like the woman who had raised Yuu back in another life,

when she was known by her old name. Before war made her a
murderer, and before peace made her a criminal. Then the old
woman pulled her hand away, leaving something small and
angular in Yuu's palm.

"This isn't possible," Yuu said, her throat tightening. She
stifled a sob and blinked away tears. In her hand was a small chess
piece. Not one of hers — she carved and chiselled her own chess
pieces these days in various likenesses — but one she knew well.
One she had lost many many years ago. "How?"

The old woman smiled kindly at her. "I am the goddess of
lost things and missed opportunities. This was a gift from your
grandmother. Well, part of the set." It was a single chess piece, a
Pawn, the weakest of all pieces. Yuu rubbed her thumb over the
little Hosan soldier. His spear had snapped off above the hand,
and he had several little burrs along his cloak and helm. Some of
the wood was discoloured from years of use, skin oils seeping into
the grain. It was this exact Pawn Yuu had used to take her
grandmother's Emperor the very first time she defeated her. She
had lost the piece on the road, forced to leave it when bandits
attacked her camp during the night. She'd fled into the forest, the
bandits close behind her. They would have caught her had she not
run face-first into the Steel Prince, had he not saved her by
slaughtering the bandits. It was the same chess piece. But it
couldn't be.

Yuu clutched the Pawn tightly and closed her eyes,
remembering the many times she played against her grandmother.
The many times she lost, and that one and only time she won. She
slipped the piece into a pocket in her patchwork robe, and opened
her eyes to find the goddess smiling sadly at her. Yuu sniffed and
wiped at her eyes again. It was the booze. She couldn't afford to
be emotional now; she needed clarity and a clear head. "Natsuko?
Let's say I believe you. What does a goddess want with me?"

"Have you ever heard of the Heavenly Crucible?" Natsuko
asked.

Yuu shook her head. Beyond a scattering of names, she knew little about the Gods or their rituals. Other than demanding prayer, they seemed to play little to no part in the daily lives of humans, but there was no denying they existed.

Natsuko sighed. "We hide so much from you. Have you noticed how for the past hundred years the world has known only war?"

Yuu shrugged. War was the way of the world, the way of the people in it, and the way of those who ruled it. It was true she hated it, the violence and death, sickness and famine. So many lives were lost to war, and the toll went far beyond those killed in battle. On the other hand, she had made her name in war, as strategist for the Steel Prince of Qing. For a time the position had made her both powerful and respected. Now it made her despised and hunted. She hated war, and yet owed it everything she had and everything she was, good and bad.

Natsuko seemed to wait a moment for Yuu to say something. When she didn't, the goddess continued, "It's all because Batu, the god of war, sits on Tianmen's throne. His reign as tianjun has been bloody and violent. He is the god of war and war is his only purpose. He has brought it to every corner of Hosa, Ipia, Nash, and Cochtan, bathing the world in slaughter. And none of us can stop him," Natsuko said, her wrinkled face contorted with grief.

"Why not?"

"Because he is the tianjun," Natsuko looked at Yuu as if she were simple. "His word is law. His rule is absolute. What laws he makes, we must abide."

"I didn't realise the gods had an emperor," Yuu said, wishing she had another bottle of wine or two. She had a feeling she wasn't going to like where this conversation was going, and bad news always went down better when she could only understand half the words.

Natsuko nodded. "Every hundred years we hold a contest, the Heavenly Crucible. The winner becomes tianjun for the next century."

"It's now, isn't it?" Yuu asked. She could see only one reason the goddess would be telling her about it. "This contest thing." She picked up the wine bottle and stared into its depths again. Still bloody empty.

"Yes."

"And you're looking for a strategist to help you fight a war against the god of war?" Yuu laughed at the idea and shook her head. No doubt a greater war had never before been fought, but she wasn't a strategist anymore. She wasn't the Art of War anymore. "Look elsewhere. I don't do that. I want no part in any wars. I just want to play chess and—"

"And drink yourself into the grave?"

Yuu waved the empty bottle in the air. "My way of paying tribute to Zhenzhen."

Natsuko sighed. "It's not a war. It's a contest."

"Then you would be better off choosing a warrior," Yuu said with another dismissive wave. "I don't know how to fight." It was not entirely true, she had rudimentary skill with the sword, but nothing compared to the heroes who wandered Hosa or the bandits who plagued the outer villages of the empire. Or even the occasional rabid thug with nothing but a rusty blade. Any one of them would be a better choice than a disgraced strategist. She might have won every battle, and even the war, but she had sacrificed her Emperor… her Steel Prince. It was a poor trade.

"Oh, do shut up and let me finish. It is not a war, nor a fight. It is a quest. The gods choose champions. Humans. Divine artefacts are hidden throughout Hosa. The winner is the god whose champion finds and collects the most artefacts by the next full moon. "

Yuu giggled. "Really? The gods choose their emperor by way of a scavenger hunt."

"Yes," Natsuko said cheerily with a clap of her gnarled hands. "That is a wonderful way to describe it."

Yuu placed the empty wine bottle on the table and set it spinning slowly. "Why me?" She was neither a warrior nor a thief, nor particularly good at finding things. As far as she could tell, she had no place anywhere near this contest. She had no place anywhere at all except at a chess board, fleecing old men for coins. She had found her niche in life, and the stakes were exactly what she was comfortable with. No more empires hanging in the balance, no more kings and princes dying on her word, no more sacrificing the lives of hundreds of soldiers for a ploy. No more. She needed to find another bottle of wine before the reality of all she had done sobered her completely.

Natsuko's creased face softened. "Because we want the same thing, an end to war. All war. Because I am the goddess of missed opportunities, and you have missed too many in your life. And because while other gods might choose warriors to take the artefacts by force or thieves to take them by guile, I have decided to employ someone who can see the journey rather than just the next step. Someone who can plan ahead and use resources that go beyond their own skill. I have chosen you, Daiyu Lingsen."

Yuu curled her lip in distaste. "Then you chose poorly because that woman doesn't exist. Daiyu Lingsen is dead— and good riddance to her. Thank you for my chess piece, Goddess Natsuko." Yuu bowed her head. "Now go away."

The goddess' face fell, the lines around her mouth drooped. "Oh, do stop being so pitiful. I am the goddess of missed opportunities, so you will forgive me if I point out what a fool you are being by missing out on this one. I am giving you a chance to bring peace to the four empires. True peace. And you are too busy wallowing in self-pity and drinking away your grief to see it. So how about this. A wager." She gestured to the chess board. "If I win, you help me. If you win, I will give back the thing you most cherish, the thing you have lost."

21

"You can't," Yuu said sadly. "You can't bring back the dead."

The old goddess smiled slyly and gestured again at the chess board.

Chapter 2

Yuu made the first move, claiming the centre of the field with her Emperor's Pawn and freeing both her Hero and the Emperor's Monk to enter the conflict. Natsuko responded in kind, using her Hero's Pawn to stake her own claim to the centre. Yuu leapt one of her Thieves over her line of defence to challenge Natsuko's claim of the centre. The goddess moved her own Thief to protect her Pawn. It seemed the goddess was no stranger to the game. Yuu moved her Emperor's Monk across the field to attack Natsuko's Thief, and the Goddess countered by bringing her second Thief into play, threatening Yuu's Pawn and her control of the centre of the board. It was a classic opening move and the perfect riposte, but the game was only beginning.

Yuu swapped the places of her Emperor and Shintei, allowing the Shintei to take the field and further barricading her Emperor. The move eased the pressure on the goddess and allowed her to start pushing her own agenda on the battlefield, but it was worth it to free such a powerful piece. Natsuko responded by deploying a second Pawn, enabling her to move another Monk forward and claim a spot in the centre of the board, further solidifying her control of the battlefield.

"Weapons are not dangerous," said the goddess as she slid her Monk into place. "Nor is a man with a weapon. A person's skill and intent are the real danger." Yuu knew the line. Chang Lihua, a Hosan philosopher of limited wisdom but boundless popularity.

Yuu moved her Shintei onto the field and struck down one of Natsuko's Pawns, momentarily claiming the centre of the field. It was a trap, putting a high value piece in danger in the hope of luring out the enemy Hero. "Wars are waged by some, yet fought by others," she said, quoting Chaoxiang. "But death makes no distinction." That last bit was her own addition.

The goddess didn't fall for the trap; instead, she moved her Emperor to safety and freed up her second Monk. They traded some more moves, each deploying more of their forces while trying to keep their defensive lines intact and controlling the centre. Natsuko was a cautious player, opting for defence rather than offence, ignoring the Yuu's more obvious traps. She was slowly manoeuvring her pieces into a Hangsu formation. It was a basic defence that relied on layers, each piece guarded by at least one other to form a supposedly impenetrable grid. Yuu picked away at the goddess' front lines, always sacrificing up rather than down in value.

"Wars are not won by heroics," Yuu said, reaching for one of her Monks. "They are won by sacrifice. Every war has a cost, and it is paid in blood." She thrust her Monk deep into the goddess' Hangsu formation, flipped Natsuko's Shintei piece into the air, and snatched it even as she let the Monk settle into the vacated position. That Shintei was the backbone of the formation; without it the bastion would collapse, leaving Yuu to clean up the rubble. She looked up to find the goddess grinning like a wolf. It was unnerving, especially so from someone just five moves away from defeat.

"Knowledge without wisdom often leads to a misuse of power," Natsuko said, this time quoting Chaoxiang herself. She plucked her last remaining Monk, slid it slowly across the battlefield through a gap in the centre that Yuu was certain had not been there before, and slipped it into Yuu's defence, taking one of her Pawns and putting her Emperor in check. Yuu winced, flinching as she pinched her own thigh. The possibility of loss always brought pain. *Focus on the lessons.*

"What?" Yuu said, frantically scanning the board. "What happened to my Shintei?" It was gone. She was certain she had a Shintei guarding the centre. Certain of it. Didn't she? The piece wasn't on the board anymore, and neither was it in the pile of the goddess' defeated enemies. It was gone.

"Oh dear," Natsuko said with a sly grin. "Have you *lost* a piece?"

"You cheated!" Yuu said, gripping the table hard. How had she not seen it? When had the goddess taken her piece?

"Did I?" Natsuko asked, her face the very picture of wrinkled innocence. "Do you have any proof? Are you certain? Perhaps you just misplaced it. Maybe you just do not remember me taking it. Was it a Shintei, did you say?"

Of course the goddess wasn't about to admit to cheating. Codes of conduct and rules of engagement were for soldiers and generals. Strategists had no need for them, nor for honour or morality. Strategists knew the only thing that really mattered was winning, and cheating was simply another tactic to that end. Besides, the game was not over yet, and Yuu could recover. She could salvage the battle. All she needed was to reposition her Emperor and retake the centre of the field… and keep a better eye on her remaining pieces.

"Truth is a bubble of air trapped underwater," she said as she analysed the new state of the board. "It is always looking for a way to the surface, and given even the slightest path, it will escape." She had to leave her Monk in the heart of the goddess' formation and sacrificed her last Thief to get her Emperor to safety. She had gone from mere moments away from victory to dancing along the edge of defeat, searching for a new opening. But Natsuko gave her none. The goddess relentlessly attacked her, chasing Yuu's Emperor around the board, giving her no time to mount any offence. Yuu's agency was gone, her control of the field shattered. This was how the game was lost, by settling in to reacting defensively until the enemy picked your bones clean.

"Do not ask for victory," the goddess said, as if reading Yuu's mind. "Take it."

"But know that someday someone will not ask you for victory." Yuu finished the quote by Dong Ao. She picked up one of her last three Pawns and moved it up to the left of the centre,

25

sitting it on its own, safe from attack and threatening nothing. The move made Natsuko pause. The goddess stared at the piece, frowning as she tried to fathom out the meaning behind the move.

"Interesting gambit," Natsuko said.

Yuu just smiled. Her favourite quote from Chaoxiang was *No bars are ever as sturdy as those we forge for ourselves.* The goddess needed no prodding or coaxing. She would walk herself into the trap whether she meant to or not.

After a few minutes, Natsuko decided to ignore the Pawn, continuing her harassment of Yuu's Emperor instead. Yuu let her think she was winning, running her Emperor from square to square in flight, and at last, the goddess stepped into the noose. Yuu slipped her Emperor into the space vacated by the Pawn. There, he was flanked on two sides, protected for a turn. A single turn. One move, one moment in time, one chance. Natsuko aggressively moved to strip away Yuu's last defences. She raced her Shintei across the board to cut into Yuu's lines. One more turn and her Emperor would have nowhere to run. He was cornered. But sometimes victory can only be seen hanging in the jaws of defeat.

"We are never more vulnerable than in the moment of victory," Yuu said, quoting her own grandmother. She had been holding back her most powerful piece. She unleashed her Hero, streaking across the board, cutting down the goddess' last remaining Shintei and moving into striking range of her Emperor. "Check," Yuu said as she pushed a few strands of hair from in front her face, not taking her eyes off the board lest another of her pieces go missing. "And mate in one more move."

Natsuko looked over the board for a minute then placed a finger on her Emperor's head and toppled him. When Yuu looked up, the goddess was grinning, her eyes twinkling. "And you asked why I chose you to be my champion. You really are as good as your reputation. A master strategist."

Yuu snorted. "You lost the wager, goddess. Give me back what I have lost. Give me back my prince." She already knew it was fruitless. She had known even before the first move of the game. But if there was a chance to right the wrongs she had committed, to bring back the one piece she should never have sacrificed, if there was even the barest sliver of a chance she could bring him back, she had to try.

"Of course," Natsuko said, the smile dropping from her wrinkled face. "I will give you back what you cherish most. What you have lost."

"My prince!" Yuu snapped.

The goddess was silent for a moment, perfectly still. "I cannot bring back the dead."

Yuu sighed and started gathering the pieces, resetting them on the board. "I knew it," she snarled. One of her Shintei pieces was missing. The goddess really had cheated.

"Yet," Natsuko continued, "the shinigami are shepherds and guardians of the dead. They may be merely spirits, but they have no compulsion to obey an obscure god such as me. However, they are bound to obey the tianjun." Yuu glanced up to find the goddess beaming at her. "The Lord of Heaven commands all, gods and spirits alike. Help me. Be my champion in this contest, and I promise I will give you back what you have lost, that which you most cherish."

Yuu shook her head. Hope was such a dangerous thing, requiring only a single thread for a person to hang themselves with. "How can I trust your promise, goddess? You have already proven yourself a cheat."

The goddess harrumphed. "A game. Was is not Dong Ao who said *Rules are for losers to believe they have a chance at victory.*" Yuu couldn't deny the ancient philosopher had said those words, but then she also believed he had been an incomparable arsehole who deserved every one of the sixty-two knives the people of Ganxi used to kill him. "I offer you the promise of a god," Natsuko continued. "We do not swear such oaths lightly and no contract has ever been as binding." Then she shrugged. "Also, what have you got to lose?"

It was the most compelling argument the goddess had yet made. All Yuu had to do was take part in a divine scavenger hunt, and if she won, she would bring the Steel Prince back to life. Perhaps even clear her name, her real name. She could go back to her old life at Prince Guang Qing's side. No more hustling old men over games of chess in obscure villages no one had ever heard of. No more drinking herself into a stupor each day just to forget her past for a few hours. The goddess was offering Yuu her life back, and all she had to do was play a game.

Yuu finished resetting the chess board and placed a finger where her missing Shintei should be. "Do you gods enjoy meddling in the affairs of mortals?"

Natsuko cackled. "It is the entire reason we exist."

As answers went it wasn't one. But Yuu had already made her decision. "Fine. Let us go win this scavenger hunt of yours."

"You will be my champion?"

"Yes."

A bright light flashed above the chess board, a single flare and then gone. Yuu felt a scratching sensation travelling up her right arm and saw words appearing on her flesh as though her skin were parchment. She rubbed at them, but they were indelible, like tattoos. "What is this?" she asked, her voice rising with panic.

"A contract," the goddess said. "One we share." She raised her left arm, and Yuu saw similar text writing itself across Natsuko's wrinkled flesh. It was written in an old language, the Gods' Words, a precursor to modern Hosan. Yuu knew the language, but it would take time to translate, and she'd need her old reference books. But those books were gone now, likely burned by the authorities of Qing, along with all her other possessions. Her entire life burned to the ground. She was a traitor, after all. If she wanted to translate the language, she would need new books.

Yuu watched the text scratch itself onto her skin for a few more moments, then tore her attention away from it. "Now what?"

"Now we start looking for artefacts," Natsuko said perkily. "I can feel some that way." She pointed vaguely west. It made sense, Yuu supposed; to the west lay Ban Ping, the City of Monks. It was the largest city in the Xihai province and home to the grandest temple in Hosa. Where else would she expect to find divine artefacts?

Yuu stood and stretched her back. Sitting still so long had made her ache. "You can feel where they are? Are you some sort of divining rod?"

The goddess stood effortlessly. She was short, no taller than she had been in the guise of a young girl. Her white hair fell about her face and her eyes sparkled. She wore the same white-on-red hanfu as she had as the little girl, and its fine weave made Yuu's patchwork robes seem even more faded. Still, Yuu liked her robes. They were clean enough that she wasn't mistaken for a beggar, but stitched together from a dozen different garments. And they were voluminous enough to keep her warm throughout winter. Also, they had pockets and Yuu loved pockets. She and the goddess made an odd pair, an ancient crone in a pristine robe and a middle-aged woman in rags.

"I can feel a general direction," Natsuko said as they walked away from the stone table. "A sense of where to look, but it is far from exact and I cannot tell which gods the artefacts belong to from so far away. What about your chess pieces?"

Yuu glanced back at the gaming table. The board was carved into the stone itself, and the pieces were crude things. They had been there when she arrived, and she saw no reason to change that, though she regretted the missing Shintei. She shook her head. "It's about time I carved a new set." She would need to pick up some tools and some stone or wood in Ban Ping. Where she would find the lien for such purchases was another matter entirely.

Yuu left the village of Xindu with as little ceremony as her arrival a couple of weeks before. No one noticed, and no one cared. She had arrived with nothing but a few lien and a gourd of wine. She left with a few lien, an empty gourd, and the company of a goddess.

Chapter 3

Dried up rice paddies and rocky fields fit for nothing but goats soon gave way to grassy pastures, home to roaming buffalo, horses, and fields full of tubers, only the leaves visible above ground, as they headed north along the Sword Road. Two days from Xindu, the city of Ban Ping appeared as a dark smudge on the crest of a distant ridge, but as the miles wore on and the blisters on Yuu's feet wore with them, the smudge resolved into the sharp lines of tall buildings and taller pagodas, all shrouded in mossy tiles. On the mountainside overlooking the city, five great statues were carved into the rock, each one a bald-headed monk at prayer, each one dedicated to one of the five major constellations: Rymer, Fenwong, Osh, Ryoko, and Lili. In the late afternoon gloom, Yuu couldn't see the thousands of steps leading up the mountain, but she knew they led past the five statues, high up to the five temples near the mountain peak. She had never made the trek up to the top, but everyone in Hosa knew of Ban Ping's famed temples built to worship the stars.

Despite her apparent decrepitude, Natsuko kept pace easily, and no matter how much dust the traffic on the road kicked up, none of it seemed to stick to her or her clothing. The benefits to being a god, Yuu supposed. Yuu herself was not nearly so lucky; the dust found every little fold, seam, and tear in her patchwork robes, making her itch like she had fleas. At least, she hoped it was just the dust. As roads merged leading up to the city, traffic increased with hikers carrying packs and carts laden with goods. Just a few years ago the empire had been rife with poverty and famine, and people had fled to the cities hoping for handouts. The new emperor of Hosa changed all that, bringing true peace to his lands to replace the peace of a sword waiting to fall. Yuu often wondered how long it would last, whether the rumours of war with Cochtan were anything more than empty words uttered by misinformed gabblers deep in their cups. In another life she would have been by the emperor's side, helping him plan for those wars. Moving troops into position, setting up the board rather than just trying to sneak across it.

"So, what do we do when we get there?" Yuu asked as she skirted a stalled cart with a cracked wheel. The owner was cursing his poor luck and kicking the broken spokes; his cart mule was idly chomping weeds from the roadside and eyeing passers-by with dull eyes. No one stopped to help the poor fellow, and Yuu decided not to change that. There was nothing to gain from charity but an aching back and an empty pocket.

"We start looking for the artefacts," Natsuko said. "Others will be looking also, and you can bet your lost dignity there will be at least one other champion in Ban Ping. Maybe more. It is a big city."

Yuu couldn't deny that. Up until now, she had been avoiding big cities for an exceptionally good reason. There were always far more wanted posters and bounty hunters there than in sleepy little villages. "But how do we find the artefacts?"

"I don't know," Natsuko said with a snort. "That's what you're here for."

"But I don't even know what to look for," Yuu said.

"Neither do I," the Goddess said with a creased smile.

"But you'll know when you see them?"

"Nope."

"What do you mean no?" Yuu stopped in the middle of the road. A farmer carrying a basket of green shoots on his back almost bumped into her. He grumbled something about vagrants, stepped around her, and continued up the road behind Natsuko. Yuu ignored him. "If you don't know what we're looking for and I don't know what we're looking for, how are we supposed to find the bloody things?"

The goddess looked over her shoulder and cackled. "Don't get yourself so twisted up. I was only joking... after a fashion."

"What does that mean?" Yuu hurried to catch up, overtaking the farmer and uttering an empty apology.

The old woman sighed. "I was a little late to the gathering." She glanced sideways at Yuu. "Too busy deciding if I should place my trust in a washed up drunk who was pissing away her gift. Nevertheless, each god must give up a single item to play the game, but I did not see all the artefacts the other gods gave up to enter the contest." She held up a gnarled hand to stop Yuu from complaining. "Lucky for both of us, I have an inherent advantage in this game."

"Lost items," Yuu said. She might have guessed it earlier, but the goddess was still tight-lipped about many of the specifics of the contest.

"Finally using that mind of yours, I see," Natsuko said. "See what a couple of days without any poison will do for you?" Yuu almost grumbled that what a couple of days without booze had done for her was give her cold sweats and a nasty case of the shakes, but it was also true her mind felt a little sharper, if not clearer. Either way, she intended to spend one of her last lien on some wine as soon as they entered Ban Ping. Or possibly sooner.

"But if the items, uh, artefacts are lost," Yuu said. "Can't you just do your thing?" She waved her hands about, not really sure how the gods did what they did. It certainly didn't seem like a mortal technique, and she doubted qi was involved. Actually, she wasn't even sure if gods had qi. Until a couple of days ago she considered them to be little more than abstract concepts that existed somewhere else and only influenced the world in subtle ways. Spirits were undoubtedly real and a plague upon the world, but she had never *seen* a god before Natsuko showed up. Now she had spent two days with a goddess, and she was certain she preferred her preconceptions of them to the real thing. The gods were never anything but trouble.

"No," said the goddess. "Well, yes, I could, but it would disqualify me from the contest, so what would be the point? We pick champions to represent us for a reason. I am unable to directly help you. I can point you toward the items and pat you on the back when you've found them, but other than that I can only watch."

That certainly sounded like something the gods would dream up. Humans do all the work and then praise the divine for their blessings. The gods, on the other hand, receive a reward for merely existing. It was the very definition of religion. "What about lien?" Yuu asked. Every game had loopholes, rules that could be exploited. But it would be much easier to exploit the rules if she knew them to begin with. "You wouldn't be directly helping me if you provide me with coin, and surely people all over the world pray to you to give back the money they've lost."

"Ha!" The old woman barked a laugh. "That's the truth right there. I would probably be a forgotten god if not for thriftless fools. But the worst part of it is that most times they are praying to the wrong god. I cannot count the number of times a day when some dolt sits down in front of one of my shrines and asks me to return the money they have *lost* at mah-jongg. Bloody idiots should be praying to Yang Yang."

Yuu smiled at that. Yang Yang was the Hosan god of gambling, and she had offered him more than a few prayers herself over the past five years. She didn't really believe in luck or divine intervention, but it never hurt to hedge your bets. "So, you can help me out with a few lien?" Yuu prodded.

"Of course I can!" snapped the goddess. "Here," she held up her hand, a small stack of lien between her fingers. "Bo Wan of Shinxei lost these in the marsh outside his home just this morning. Bloody fool taking the coin with him, but it is his own damned fault. He was intending to visit a pleasure house instead of going home to his wife this evening. Serves him right."

Yuu plucked the lien from the Goddess' fingers and sniffed at them. They did have an odd stagnant-water smell to them. She eyed a stall on the roadside. "You sound quite proud of the loss," she said. "Do you ever… facilitate losses."

Natsuko glanced over her shoulder and loosed an inhuman grin that was far too wide and toothy, her eyes suddenly dark and manic. Then she turned back to the road and cackled. "We gods don't exist to provide comfort and answer prayers. We are here to teach people lessons. Some of us may…"

Yuu dropped back into the flowing crowd, slipped around a passing farmhand leading a buffalo, and shuffled to the side of the road. The merchant's stall was little more than a half dozen rickety stools, a plank across two sawhorses for a bar, and a cloth roof that stretched into a tent at the back. The man behind the bar was all pudgy, red-faced smiles, with an oiled moustache and hair tied into a loose braid. A single front tooth was a slightly different shade than all the rest, and Yuu surmised it was false, possibly ivory. A big man stood to his side, hand resting on the hilt of a gleaming dadao. He had long, tri-braided hair in the traditional Nash fashion, and stood as though he was accustomed to riding a horse. Many of the Nash had settled into vast cities, but just as many were still nomadic, choosing to roam across the plains of the Nash empire.

"Welcome weary traveller," the smiling barman said as Yuu slipped onto a stool next to an old man staring into his cup. "The road is rarely kind, but Tsin Xao's House of Refreshment is here to make it slightly less inhospitable. For those with lien, of course." He had an expectant look in his eye. Yuu sized him up in a bare moment. He had a kind face, owing much to the extra flesh on his jowls, and seemed pleasant enough. But the look in his eyes spoke of a shrewd intellect. Given that there were no other stalls along the stretch of road, Yuu also suspected he was far more ruthless than his face suggested. The Nash thug with the dadao certainly looked ready and willing for a spot of violence. In another life, he probably would have been a roaming bandit, but they were all but gone from Hosa now that the Leper Emperor sat the throne.

Yuu slipped a lien onto the bar and pushed it across the rough wood plank. "Two bottles of wine." The man reached for the coin but Yuu kept her finger on it. "And none of the watered-down stuff." She waited until the man met her eyes, then removed her finger and let him snatch up the lien.

"Of course, of course," the man said. He reached below the bar and produced two clay bottles and a little cup. "We at Tsin Xao's House of Refreshment would do no such thing. We provide only the highest quality wine and for a price no establishment in the city can match."

The man sitting beside Yuu sniffed at his own cup of wine, then sipped it and frowned.

"What are you doing?" Natsuko said as she caught up and sat down next to Yuu. The proprietor silently slipped a second cup onto the bar.

"Poisoning myself," Yuu said. "Do you want a cup? Do gods drink?"

The proprietor quirked an eyebrow but said nothing.

Natsuko grumbled as she settled onto her stool. "Of course we do." She poured wine into the little cup until it was brimming and then swallowed it in one gulp. Yuu followed her example and sighed gratefully at the spicy bite, then poured herself a second cup and sipped at it.

"It's not bad," Yuu said with a smile at the man behind the bar.

"We at Tsin Xao's House of Refreshment have travelled far and wide to serve our deserving customers only the finest vintages."

"That would involve lots of sampling, I suppose," Yuu said.

The man grinned.

"We don't have time for this," said Natsuko. She played the part of a grumpy old woman almost as well as she did a little girl.

"The contest has started, and the other champions will not be drinking themselves into a stupor. They will be searching for artefacts."

"All the champions are human?" Yuu asked. A strange buzzing noise like a plague of bees was drifting in from the east.

"Yes."

"Then, as a representative human, I think you might be grossly overestimating our enthusiasm, not to mention our abstemiousness." Yuu raised her cup and sipped a bit more. The buzzing noise was growing louder.

"Uh, boss?" the Nash thug was staring at something in the sky. Now that Yuu thought to look, a lot of people had stopped in the road to stare up at something.

She leaned back on her stool and squinted into the waning sunlight. Something far larger than a bird flew overhead. The buzzing noise came from several spinning blades attached above it.

Natsuko said something in a language Yuu had never heard before.

"Is that a thopter?" Yuu said. She had never actually seen one before, but knew they existed. The Cochtans were an inventive people and never stopped coming up with new engines to inflict upon the world. They were masterful at figuring out how to turn each engine to the purpose of war only moments after creation. With spinning blades both above and behind the engine, Yuu could understand the theory of how such a thing could take flight, but seeing it in action was still somewhat mind boggling.

"The Cochtans are invading!" said the proprietor. "We at Tsin Xao's... ah fuck it. Drink up, we're closing."

Yuu started pouring her second bottle of wine into the hollowed-out gourd she kept for just such an occasion. The other man at the bar downed his cup, and stood up, knocking over his stool. Only Natsuko didn't seem worried. She sipped at her cup as if the thopter were merely a crane. Yuu supposed gods had very little to fear from the threat of an attack.

"It is not an invasion," the goddess said calmly. "Look up again. Do you see any more thopters? One hardly counts as an invasion." She was right, there were no other engines in the sky, and the single thopter was already landing somewhere in the vastness of Ban Ping. No doubt the monks would be there to arrest the pilot. Or perhaps they'd just drown him in blessings from the stars. It was hard to tell with monks.

The man behind the bar stopped hurriedly packing away his bottles of wine and approached Natsuko. All smiles and joviality vanished, he leaned on the bar and stared at her. "What do you know, crone?" he asked. "It could be a scout. There's been whispers of a Cochtan invasion for weeks now."

Natsuko arched a menacing eyebrow. "It is more than whispers. The invasion is coming. Batu will make the rivers run red with blood before his time is through. And when the invasion comes, a single thopter will be the least of your worries." She gave the man that inhuman grin of hers, like a toad had learned to smile. "But that thopter has nothing to do with the Cochtan military. It belongs to the Ticking Clock."

"Fuck!" Yuu said. She suddenly wanted nothing to do with Natsuko or her contest. No prize was worth tangling with the Ticking Clock. She stared at the cup of wine in front of her and then slipped a second lien onto the bar. "Two more bottles."

"You mean the assassin, the Ticking Clock?" said the man behind the bar as he placed two more bottles of wine on the bar.

Natsuko rolled her eyes. "Of course. Who else would I be talking about?"

"I heard he killed the Ipian emperor," said the Nash thug. "Broke into the palace and painted the walls red. Half the Ise royal line dead in a single night, and then he just flies away like it was nothing."

The man behind the bar nodded. "His duel with the Shining Light of Song is legend. I once heard a bard recite it — seventeen verses!"

"I heard he's not even human," said the thug. "He's one of them Cochtan engines, walking about like it's a man."

"That sounds like an even better reason to pack up and move on," said the proprietor.

"Fongsa on the Nash border is a nice town," said the thug. "Far away from Cochtan."

As a rule, Yuu ignored the babbling of foolish men, so she turned to Natsuko. "Why is the Ticking Clock here?" she asked. "Is he another champion?"

The goddess nodded. "Sarnai, the goddess of fire's choice."

"She picked an assassin to find a bunch of divine junk?" Yuu asked. Something didn't sit right, and she had a sneaking suspicion this Heavenly Crucible would not end well for her.

Natsuko pursed her lips and looked away. "The rules to the contest are quite firm regarding the participation of the gods. They are somewhat less so when it comes to how the game can be played by the champions."

Yuu groaned and stared at the wine in her cup. She might have only just sipped it, but she felt a pressing need to sip at it again. To down the cup and pour another, and then another after that.

"One tactic," Natsuko continued, "often used by the more violent gods, is to choose a warrior and have them loot the artefacts collected by other champions."

"I'm out," Yuu said. She hadn't signed up to fight anyone, least of all a legendary assassin.

"The contract is binding," Natsuko said firmly, waving her inscribed hand for emphasis.

"You never told me the other gods would send the Ticking Clock to kill me." Yuu doubted there was anyone in Hosa who hadn't heard of the Cochtan assassin. Rumour had it he was well

over a hundred years old. He replaced his body parts as they
withered away, gradually turning himself into one of the engines
he loved so much. Some said it was he who had killed Iron Gut
Chen — the first time — and that was over sixty years ago. Since
then he had proved time and again that no one was safe from him
or his infernal engines. He had a kill list that boasted some of the
greatest heroes the four empires had ever known.

"I heard he killed Ting Lao the Unbreakable last year," said
the Nash thug. "Shattered every bone in his body."

The man behind the bar nodded. "He's resurrected the Blood
Engine as well. That's why Cochtan is amassing for war. Hard to
beat any army when killing a man don't guarantee he stays killed."

Yuu gave up resisting and knocked back another cup of
wine, then quickly poured a replacement to stare at. "What if I just
leave?" she asked, "choose not to take part in the contest?"

Natsuko shrugged. "You could. No guarantee the Ticking
Clock or any of the others won't find you, though. Champions like
the Ticking Clock do not care if you have artefacts or not. If you
are in the contest, you are a threat."

Yuu picked up her cup and downed it, then poured another
measure. "I guess I missed my opportunity to back out," she said
bitterly. She should have asked for all the details before agreeing
to this insanity. She'd spent too long scamming old men out of
their pocket money. Lost her edge. She may have won the chess
game, but it was nothing but a distraction. Natsuko had played her
and won before Yuu even recognised the game they were really
playing. The Art of War should never agree to anything without
knowing all the details. Yuu winced at the pain she always
expected from a loss. "Well, what do I do now?"

Natsuko finished her cup of wine and slipped from the stool.
"Head into the city," she said. "Preferably before you get too
drunk to see straight. Find somewhere to stay. I must return to
Tianmen for a bit. I'll find you later." Without waiting for a reply,

she turned and sauntered toward the road, a cart passed in front of her and when it had gone, so too had Natsuko.

"Lovely mother you have there," said the man behind the bar. He seemed to have stopped packing up his wine, though he kept glancing warily at the sky.

Yuu tried to smile but couldn't quite find the enthusiasm. "Tsin Xao, is it?"

The man laughed. "No. I'm not stupid enough to put my real name on the business. Call me Wen."

"Wen," Yuu said. She leaned over the bar and slipped another lien between them. "Where can I find the most disreputable goons in the city?"

Chapter 4

As night settled over Ban Ping and the initiate monks scuttled about the city lighting the hanging lanterns, Yuu walked through the archway into the open garden of the Jasmin Eye. It was a dingy tavern, full of raucous laughter, flowing booze, and bustling gaming tables. It didn't look like a hive of scum and villainy, but Wen had assured Yuu it was the favoured hangout of any thief, thug, or murderer with a name even half worth knowing. It was possible he thought her unable to handle herself so had directed her to a less violent establishment, but judging by the dozen-or-so brutish thugs standing in the shadows, Yuu had a feeling she was in the right place.

The building was a square with the garden in the centre. That garden was open to the sky, and Yuu could see the stars twinkling down at her, which seemed fitting given that Ban Ping was a city dedicated to the worship of the stars rather than the gods. The grass was well trodden all around, in some places nothing more than bare mud. Rickety wooden tables were scattered around at haphazard angles, each one with a couple of benches running alongside it. If there was any order to the layout, it escaped Yuu. At the far end of the garden a pair of musicians strummed out a melody on an enlarged guzheng. At first glance they appeared to be identical twins, though Yuu had to admit that might be from the makeup the two women were wearing. A few sets of eyes turned Yuu's way as she passed by, but most dismissed her outright. In her patchwork robes she looked a vagrant at best and a pauper at worst, but either way not worth robbing.

There were no free tables. Many were occupied with groups of people chatting and drinking, some performing contests of strength. One table held several men playing mah-jongg with impressive piles of lien strewn about. Yuu assessed her options and settled at a mostly empty table opposite a large man noisily spooning noodle soup between his flabby wet lips. He sucked down a noodle and pulled his bowl a little closer but said nothing. He was tall and broad and his gut bulged against his blue tunic. He had a jowly face, a scraggle of beard, and a wild growth of wiry hair that made his head seem larger than it was. He seemed the type of person who sometimes passed out from forgetting to breathe. Yuu pulled out her carving knife and little block of wood she purchased at a stall outside the city walls and set about making the first piece of her new chess set. She swept the wooden shavings into a pocket in her robes.

The fat man finished his soup and unleashed a belch that wrinkled Yuu's nose even across the table. "You serve yaself here," he said, wiping his mouth with the back of his hand. "Go there." He pointed to where a thickset woman wearing an apron stood behind a bar, next to a blackened board with a list of food and booze and prices scrawled upon it in what might have passed for legible handwriting for a two-year-old.

"How quaint," Yuu said. "That's how the Nash do it, I believe."

The fat man sniffed loudly. "Horse stickers never sit still for two minutes."

"The Nash don't actually fuck horses," Yuu said. There were several used cups on the table. She snagged one with a finger, spat in it, and wiped it out with her sleeve.

"They don't?" The fat man frowned. "Everyone says they do." It was a common insult thrown at the nomadic people, but a baseless one.

Yuu reached inside her robe, retrieved one of the bottles she had purchased from Wen, and poured herself a portion. She downed that first mouthful in one gulp and sighed appreciatively, then poured a second and sipped at it. "Sheep are belligerent creatures who must be herded with great care and skill. People, on the other hand, are stupid and will line up behind any old fool with a loud voice. Have you ever seen anyone from Nash sticking it to a horse?"

The fat man's mouth hung open as he considered. "No," he said eventually with a shake of his wiry-haired head.

"Then it is highly likely they don't. In fact, the Nash tend to respect horses far more than they do people. They would be far more likely to stick it to the likes of you than a horse." Yuu held up the bottle to the fat man. He pushed his own cup in front of her and she filled it. It was always wise to make allies in a seedy establishment like the Jasmin Eye, pawns that could be thrown in front of more dangerous pieces to protect oneself. And few things made friends quicker than free booze.

Yuu went back to carving her little block of wood, starting with the hem of a robe. She pictured a new Hero, far less resplendent than the piece was usually depicted. A vagabond Hero perhaps. The thought made her smile. The fat man stared at her, his eyes occasionally dropping to the wine bottle and then rising again. Yuu wondered what she would do if he attempted to take the bottle. She was no warrior, and she very much doubted the man would agree to a game of chess for the bottle. Eventually, he reached down, picked up a large chui from under his chair, and dropped the mace on the table between them.

"I am Li Bang, Falling Moon," the fat man said. He truly was an odd-looking fellow. The scraggly hair on his chin rushed up his sideburns to join the wiry mess on his head, framing his chubby face in a way that made him seem more kindly than thuggish. He was sweating heavily despite the chill air, and was squinting at her like he was too drunk to see straight.

"Well done," Yuu said and went back to carving her new Hero. Li Bang sighed, his shoulders slumping, and removed his chui from the table. Ever since Einrich WuLong claimed the throne, new heroes seemed to crawl out of the woodwork by the day. Unfortunately, with peace the new reality and the military clearing out bandit camps all over Hosa, there was also little for them to do. A lot of the folk who once called themselves heroes were now turning to crime just to feed themselves. How little it took to flip the coin.

An old woman shuffled onto the bench beside Li Bang. "Move up a bit, Lump. My old bones need more space than your saggy arse."

Li Bang opened his mouth as if to argue, then sighed and shuffled over to give Natsuko room to sit. Yuu smiled and kept working on her Hero's robes, moving her knife deftly, carving out the details in small strokes.

"I see you found another deluxe establishment," the goddess said. "What are you doing here?"

"Drinking," Yuu said without looking up. "Waiting for you. Contemplating the futility of some men fighting baldness."

Li Bang raised a hand to his head, patting at his hair.

"Hmm," Natsuko grumbled and glanced at Li Bang. The fat man was squinting at them both, a scared look on his face like one of them might bite him at any moment. "Who is the lump? A hireling?"

Yuu shrugged. "I was just hoping he wouldn't kill me for my wine." She couldn't help but feel more confident now that Natsuko was around again. There was something quite bolstering about having a goddess as one of your pieces.

"I'm looking for work," Li Bang said, smiling as he glanced between them. "Nothing else for me to do. The recruiters are here in Ban Ping, so I was gonna join the army, but—" he sighed "— they don't want me."

"Why not?" Yuu asked. The Art of War needed to know the strengths and weakness of each piece to use them to their full potential. Of course, any strategist knew that some pieces were only useful as shields.

"I can't see in the dark," Li Bang said, explaining the constant squinting.

Natsuko cackled and the fat man sighed and scratched a dirty fingernail at the wooden table.

"That would make you a liability much of the time," Yuu said. "An army must be ready to fight on any field, lest an ambush make their deficiencies manifest."

Li Bang sighed again, reached down for his chui, and stood.

"What's your rate?" Yuu asked before he could leave. "Four lien a day?"

Li Bang's eyes lit up. He held up a hand, counted on his fingers, then nodded eagerly.

Yuu glanced at Natsuko. "Give him ten lien now." Then she pinned Li Bang with a stern stare. "We'll call the extra six a signing bonus. Then five more a day until I release you from my service."

The goddess arched an eyebrow. Then she waved a withered hand over the table, leaving ten lien twirling in place. "Ju Shiwen lost these on her way to the market forty-five years ago," she said. "Tripped over a stone in the road and did not realise her purse had come loose until it was too late. Her family went hungry that day and her youngest son turned to crime because of it. He was hanged two years later for killing a baker over a flat bread. Every lost item carries a history."

Li Bang scooped up the coins and nodded, though Yuu doubted he understood. A smile lit his face and heat flushed his fleshy cheeks.

"You protect me," Yuu said. "Crack heads when I ask you too. Fetch drinks."

Li Bang bowed, his gut hit the table and nudged him backwards, and he tripped over the bench to sprawl in the grass. A roar of laughter complete with some pointing fingers circulated the garden.

Natsuko rolled her eyes and groaned.

Li Bang disentangled himself from the bench and used it to heft himself back to his feet. "Protect you, I can do that, boss. What about the crone?"

Natsuko glared up at the man. "Who are you calling 'crone', Lump?"

Yuu smiled. "The crone can look after herself. Don't forget the fetching of drinks."

Again, Li Bang nodded happily and trotted off up to fetch another bottle of wine.

"Well, I suppose a half blind lummox might prove useful," Natsuko scoffed. "Though I can't see how."

Yuu smiled and went back to carving, labouring over the folds in the robes, the places where patches were sewn together. The piece needed to be perfect. They all would need to be perfect. "You gave me the idea," she said as she worked. "Besides, at the very least he might slow the Ticking Clock down." All pieces, even the lowliest pawns had a use, as long as the player knew when to sacrifice them. *The Art of War always knows when to sacrifice a piece and never hesitates.*

"I doubt it," Natsuko said stared into the distance a moment. "There are five artefacts in Ban Ping."

"I thought you said there were three."

"Well, now there are five," the goddess said testily.

Yuu made the connection. "The Ticking Clock brought two with him. The contest only started a few days ago and he's collected two already?" That put Yuu and Natsuko far behind. The goddess was right. They had no time to waste. Not if she wanted to bring the Steel Prince back to life.

Natsuko pulled a sour face. "He did not *collect* any. Three of the gods are out of the contest already — their champions are dead. Sarnai is not taking any chances. The Ticking Clock may take artefacts from those he kills, but he is not hunting the artefacts. He is hunting you. Easiest way to win is to kill everyone else."

"Easiest way for him maybe," Yuu said. She couldn't imagine trying to kill all the other champions. Well, actually she could, but she also imagined her head tumbling down the streets of Ban Ping without her body attached.

"Precisely."

"Can he find me?" Yuu asked. Even surrounded by an army with her prince at her back, Yuu would be scared to know the assassin was after her. "Like you can sense the artefacts, maybe?"

"I don't know," Natsuko said. "Not that I know of. I have no way of identifying any of the champions or the other gods unless they are wearing forms I am familiar with." Li Bang came back carrying three bottles of wine and three fresh cups. He set them down on the table with a ruddy-faced grin. "For all I know, Lump here could be a champion."

Li Bang frowned. "I'm a hero."

Natsuko poured herself a cup of wine and groaned, "Of course you are, dear." Yuu didn't think the Goddess could feel the effects of the stuff, but that didn't seem to stop her from drinking it.

"What will Sarnai do, if she wins and becomes tianjun?" Yuu asked.

"She is the goddess of fire," Natsuko sneered. "What do you think?"

Yuu could well imagine. For a hundred years the four empires had been embroiled in war, sometimes against each other, and sometimes against themselves. After all, it was only twenty-five years ago when the Emperor of Ten Kings unified Hosa with the sword. A hundred years this Batu, the god of war, had been tianjun and the world hadn't known a moment of peace. If the goddess of fire were in control, how much of the world would burn? How many would die? Numbers. Only numbers. *The Art of War thinks only in numbers.* They were not people, not lives, only pieces. She had to focus on what was important. If she won, Natsuko could bring back her prince. Stopping the goddess of fire from setting the world aflame would be a happy coincidence. "So, we start now," she said. "Where can we find the first of these artefacts?"

"The closest one? Aye." The goddess cracked a wide smile. "It is quite close actually."

Yuu poured herself another quarter cup of wine and downed it. "Hesitation is the key to many strategies," she said. "It breeds."

"Huh?" Li Bang squinted at them as he downed his own cup.

Natsuko cackled. "She means get off your rump, Lump. We have a divine artefact to procure."

Ban Ping at night was quite pleasant. The hanging lanterns kept it well lit, and most of the prowlers on the streets were monks, courtesans, and people like Yuu who were up to no good. Natsuko led Yuu and Li Bang unerringly onward, and Yuu found herself struggling to keep up with the goddess despite her short stature. Of course, her feet were not as sure as she would have liked. Too much to drink. But it wasn't a problem. She wasn't *so* drunk that it would be a problem. She almost managed to convince herself.

Li Bang shuffled behind Yuu, his chui resting against his shoulder, and his laboured breathing loud in her ear. He drew a few stares, certainly more than an old woman racing through the streets with a patchwork vagabond staggering behind her, but he was far from the most conspicuous individual out that night. Besides, many of the whispers Yuu overheard were focused on one Cochtan assassin who had shown up in rather spectacular style.

They stopped in front of a two-story pagoda with a sign outside that identified it as a bathhouse. Judging by the two thugs playing dice near the entrance, there was more than just steaming hot water on the menu. "In there?" she asked Natsuko. A seedy bathhouse seemed an odd place to find an artefact of divine origin.

The goddess grinned at her. "Chaonan, the god of punishment's most cherished possession, a ring, is in there somewhere. That is as much as I'm allowed to tell you."

In Yuu's opinion, the goddess had told her next to nothing so far. "Each of you had to give up the thing you cherish most," she said. "And Batu has hidden them throughout Hosa. What did you give up, Natsuko? What does the god of missed opportunities cherish most?" She doubted she'd get a straight answer, but it couldn't hurt to ask.

Natsuko chewed on her lip for a moment, glanced up at the sky, then snorted. "The artefact inside is a silver ring, a wide band with an amethyst in the centre, a sleeping dragon coiling its way along the outside length," Natsuko said. "It belonged to Chaonan's wife."

Yuu had never heard of the gods marrying. "A human?" she asked.

Natsuko nodded. "The people of Cochtan are not fond of techniques and often deem those who possess them to be witches or demons. Punishments are cruel and most often fatal. Dawa was a young woman who loved to tinker with Cochtan engines. She had an understanding of machines, an instinct of how they worked. But she also spoke to them. She knew they were not alive, of course, but it made her happy to think of them as such. She might tighten the gears of a timepiece, all the while whispering to it: *It's all right, little one. I'll be finished soon, and you'll be better than new*." Natsuko smiled and sighed. "The people of her town did not care that she made their lives easier by improving the engines upon which they relied. They only cared that she appeared to have a technique they did not understand. They dragged her before the town enginseers and laid their claims, and the enginseers found her guilty of witchcraft. Which is to say, they thought she had a technique, which is against the law there. She was sentenced to death, to be fed to a Blood Engine, as was the practice at the time. But luckily for Dawa, they prayed first to

Chaonan, seeking his approval. I do not know what Chaonan saw in Dawa. Maybe it was her love of little things with no life of their own. Or perhaps her kindness towards the people, even as they meant to kill her. Or it could have been her willingness to accept her punishment. I do not know. What I do know is that he found something in Dawa, and rather than let the Cochtans feed her to their Blood Engine, he took her away to live with him."

"In Tianmen?" Yuu asked.

"Heaven?" Li Bang asked.

"No," Natsuko snapped. "Do not interrupt. Humans are not allowed in Tianmen except once every hundred years. No, Chaonan took her to the mountains between Hosa and Cochtan. They lived there, happy together, all her life. But humans die, and gods do not. Now, all Chaonan has of her are his memories and that ring. A ring he has given up to win the Jade Throne." She smiled. "Or try and win, at least."

Li Bang scratched at his cheek. "I don't understand," he said.

Yuu smiled at him. The point of the story was obvious. "She's trying to impress upon us *how much* she has given up, without telling us *what* she has given up." It was a classic move, an evasion. But the Art of War would never fall for such a distraction.

"I still don't understand." Li Bang said with a shake of his head, then squinted hard. "Are you really a goddess?"

"Yes!" Natsuko snapped. "Stupid lump. Now get in there and find the ring. And I warn you, Batu has a wicked sense of a humour and a vicious streak deep enough to hide all the bodies his wars have created."

"Who's Batu?" Li Bang asked as Yuu started towards the bathhouse.

"The god of war," Yuu said. "And the tianjun, Lord of Heaven."

Li Bang scratched at his wiry black beard. "I don't understand."

"That makes two of us. Just stick close and watch my back."

"*That* I do understand, boss."

The two guards looked up from their dice as Yuu and Li Bang approached. Yuu had been watching them play and was convinced that one of the dice was weighted to land more regularly on Water. She wondered if both thugs knew it, or if one was cheating the other. The ugly thug nudged the uglier one in the ribs and said, "She's a bit worn out to be looking for work here."

They shared a laugh and the uglier one said, "Take your whore elsewhere, big man."

Li Bang hefted his chui from his shoulder, but Yuu held up her hand. He might be able to take both guards, but the Art of War did not rely on mights and maybes. Also, she doubted they'd find a warm welcome in the bathhouse if he made a bloody mess of the front stoop. "What if I'm just looking for a bath?" she said coldly.

"Uh," the ugly one looked at his friend. "I guess that would be fine. We don't get many women coming here for, um, that."

"With that attitude, I can't say I'm surprised," Yuu said with a smile so sweet it was poisonous.

"One lien each," said the ugly one. "And no weapons inside."

Li Bang hung his mace on the weapons rack on the wall and squinted hard at the two guards, though Yuu wondered if that was because he was struggling to see them in the gloom or because he was trying to threaten them. Either way, it looked quite menacing. "I don't carry any weapons," she said as she fished out two lien. "Unless you count my charm." Judging by the stony silence, they did not. She pointed at one of the dice. "That one is weighted." The uglier one's brows rose halfway up his forehead. Apparently, he had not known about it.

Inside, the bathhouse was moist and thick as goat milk. Even in the entrance foyer, sweat trickled down Yuu's back, and the smell of a hundred different herbs made her nose itch. A woman dressed in a respectfully cut golden hanfu with green, leafy patterning gawked at them as they entered, but quickly recovered and smiled prettily. Her makeup made her skin look a shade too pale and her lips two shades too red. Her onyx hair was pinned in a bun on top of her head with no less than five silver pins, and she carried a small chalkboard in the crook of one arm. Yuu spied several names scrawled on the board, but none she recognised.

"How may we serve you today, masters," the woman said as she glided close.

Yuu cringed. "You can never call me that again for a start," she said.

Li Bang shrugged. "While we're here…"

"No," Yuu turned an angry glare on him. "You can do whatever you want on your own time, but right now you're working for me." It was important to establish professional boundaries. He was a hireling, not a friend. A pawn to be sacrificed when the time arose.

The woman coughed politely and lowered her head into a slight bow. "We have baths and a private steam room if you're not looking for company. We also offer a wide range of massages and have women from Hosa, Ipia, and Nash."

"How multicultural of you," Yuu said dryly. The woman was being careful to keep her expression neutral, but her fingers were trembling as they tapped on the chalkboard. "We'll start with the baths and then check the steam room."

"We can supply you with towels and drying robes," the woman said, gesturing to a wall of shelves with several small square cubbyholes built in. Each of the squares held either a neatly folded robe or hastily stuffed-in pile of clothes. Still the woman did not look up to meet Yuu's eyes. There was something Yuu was missing here, something that scared the woman.

Yuu could feel herself sweating underneath her own tattered robes, but the idea of stripping out of them here was not a comfortable one. For a start, she'd miss the numerous pockets she had sewn into the folds. It was somewhat comforting knowing that she had access to everything she owned at a moment's notice, and not at all depressing that everything she owned could fit inside a few pockets. Li Bang sauntered over to the shelves and quickly began stripping off. Yuu hesitated.

The woman coughed again. "This establishment is owned by Flying Sword." She said it with a significant weight to the name, as if it should mean something to Yuu, but Yuu had never heard it before.

"The bandit?" Li Bang asked. He was standing in nothing but his underwrappings, and Yuu had to admit she may have underestimated the man. Some people grew fat and wore it poorly, ambling about like opiated bulls. But Li Bang had a healthy girth of muscle underneath his fat and a lot of it. He shoved his dirty trousers and tunic into one of the shelves and pulled on a white robe that barely managed to cover his bulk.

The hostess gaped at them wide-eyed and bowed her head again. "No, no, no. Flying Sword is a businessman." No wonder she was scared. She was working for a criminal, one who didn't like to be labelled as such. "He operates a number of fine establishments within Ban Ping, each one sanctioned by the monks of Hushon Temple." Yuu had heard of Hushon Temple. It was dedicated to the worship of the constellation Fenwong, the drunkard. If the rumours were true, the monks of Hushon would sanction just about anything for the right price. Not very devout, but practical.

Li Bang tugged at his scraggly beard. "Bandit turned triad when the emperor brought peace to Hosa." The woman was staring directly at them now, frantically waving a hand across her mouth. "The monks can't get any crimes to stick on him, even though they know what he is. Stupid form of law keeping if you ask me. Unless there's proof and witnesses of a crime, they can't do a thing about it."

Yuu nodded. "I would imagine a man like that is hard to find witnesses against."

Li Bang nodded sagely. "Living ones, anyhow." The woman's eyes were darting about frantically, and she was breathing so rapidly Yuu thought she might faint.

"What does this have to do with the bath robes?" Yuu asked.

The woman hurried over to the shelves and plucked a robe from one of the holes. She held it out toward Yuu. "It is suspicious enough that a woman would come here not looking for work. It would be more so if you insist on remaining dressed in such a way." She all but thrust the robe into Yuu's arms. "Whoever you are, you shouldn't be here." A warning seemingly offered in earnest. Unfortunately, it was one Yuu had no choice but to ignore.

Yuu let out a weary sigh and stripped off. The intricate writing on her arm travelled all the way up over her shoulder and onto her back. Unfortunately, she still couldn't understand what it said, and doubted she'd be able to translate it any time soon. She donned the proffered robe. It was clean and far more comfortable than she expected, made of good cotton. But she missed the comforting weight of her patchwork robe. She reached into its pockets and pulled out a handful of wooden shavings before she stuffed the robe into the shelf. They walked through a corridor with doors on both sides. Yuu infused the wooden shavings with her qi and scattered them to the corners. Neither the hostess leading them, nor Li Bang noticed. Yuu hoped she wouldn't have to use them.

There was no mistaking the noises coming from the rooms to either side of the corridor. The place posed as a bathhouse, but the massages they offered were clearly more erotic than therapeutic. The woman led them to a large, open room with several benches around the walls and a large public bath in the centre. Steam curled up from the bath, and the scent of lavender hung heavy in the air. Yuu counted six men in the room, clustered together in small groups. A man with an impressive amount of nose hair and another with saggy breasts lounged in the bath, naked under the water. In the corner, near a steaming stove, a baby-faced fellow was playing Go with an ancient man who had as many animal tattoos as he did wrinkles. She wondered if any money was being wagered and how much could be made by a woman willing to feign ignorance of the rules. Men often thought women knew nothing about games; it was an ignorance she preyed upon many times. On the far side, by a rack of hooks holding unused robes, a one-eyed crook was telling his dull-eyed comrade a story about his latest whore. All eleven eyes turned to watch as she and Li Bang entered the room, and though most only mildly regarded them, the two men in the bath stared hard at Yuu. One had a dragon tattoo winding up one arm, across his shoulders, and down the other arm. For a moment Yuu feared they had recognised her, but that was impossible. The Art of War had always worn a mask. None but the Steel Prince ever knew what she looked like, and he had taken that secret to the grave. It was the only reason she escaped capture for so long despite the substantial bounty on her head.

"This was a bad idea," Li Bang whispered. He wasn't wrong. But they couldn't risk another champion finding the ring before they did. They were already behind in the contest, and with the Ticking Clock in Ban Ping searching for Yuu, the sooner she got out of the city the better.

"Just find the ring," Yuu said, walking around the bath. She was looking at fingers, though some of the men's hands were under the water, making it difficult. She looked suspicious, she knew that, but could see no other way about it. It was apparently suspicious enough that a woman had wandered into the bath house, and Li Bang was large enough to draw attention of his own. Yuu nodded politely to anyone who looked her way and refused to meet anyone's eyes, trying to appear demure, though feminine wiles had never been her speciality. Most men seemed to find her aloof at best, and downright hostile at worst. The saggy breasted man in the bath was leering at her, though, and that gave her an uncomfortable feeling that crawled between her shoulders like lice. Some of the men were wearing jewellery, but nowhere did she see an amethyst stone, and to be honest, the ring Natsuko described sounded more like a woman's wedding ring. She thought it quite unlikely any of the men here would be wearing it, but there were no others in the bath house except for… Yuu stopped and groaned. The only other people in the place, and those far more likely to be wearing a woman's ring, were the prostitutes.

Yuu completed her circuit of the bath and found Li Bang waiting near the entrance to the steam room. His face was flushed from the heat and his wild mop of hair had gone flat. "You might get your wish after all," Yuu said. "It's time to meet some of the women."

The fat man grinned wildly and poked his head inside the steam room. Yuu couldn't see much from behind him, but the smell of jasmine-scented steam was strong enough to make her eyes water. Li Bang sighed and pulled his head back. "As much as I'd like to pretend I haven't seen it," he said, "take a look, boss."

Yuu had no wish to know what was going on in the steam room, but squeezed by Li Bang and stepped into the room, trying not to inhale too much of the pungent cloud. Li Bang followed, his huge belly nudging her forward. Through a passing gap in the steam, Yuu saw what Li Bang had. "I hate the gods," she said wearily. And none more so than this Batu. Natsuko warned her that the god of war had an odd sense of humour and a vicious streak, but still she had underestimated the warning. At the far end of the little steam room, flanked by naked men on both sides, sat a mountain of a man easily as large as Li Bang. And piercing his left nipple was a silver ring with an amethyst stone in the centre.

Chapter 5

Yuu assessed the situation and decided it was bordering on complete shit. The silver dragon ring hung from the nipple of a giant with arms as thick as Yuu's thighs, and the other three men sitting beside him were only slightly less intimidating and slightly more sweaty. Given that the ring bearer had swords tattooed over his arms and chest, it was entirely possible that he was the owner of the establishment, Flying Sword himself, and that meant he might have some technique to back up his towering muscle and superior numbers. There was little else to help Yuu. Three wooden benches, one on each wall of the room, and in the centre was a basket full of coals with a metal pan hanging above it. Water dripped from the roof into the pan, and when the pan filled sufficiently it would tip, emptying its scented contents onto the coals releasing a plume of odoriferous steam.

Li Bang stepped up beside Yuu and waited, his hands balled into fists and his eyes darting around the room. Unfortunately for him, he was the only piece Yuu had to play, and she would have to sacrifice him to win the game.

The man with the ring looked at them through a drifting patch of steam and narrowed his eyes. Yuu noticed one of his sword tattoos was positioned so the amethyst in the ring looked embedded in its hilt. He ran a hand over his head, pushing back sweat, and leaned forward to peer at them. "What do you want?" he demanded.

Perhaps Yuu did have a play after all. If all three men had been in the hot steam room for a while, such oppressive heat might make them sluggish. Additionally, all three were naked, and naked men were always quicker to cower to shield their vulnerable parts. A dozen different strategies rushed through Yuu's head. She needed to get close. She could try to seduce the ring bearer, but it seemed unlikely given she had no idea how to even start the process. She had some skill with sleight of hand if she could get close enough, but taking a ring from a person's finger was likely vastly different to removing it from their nipple. It seemed to be pierced through the flesh much like an earring, but it had no clasp. She could send Li Bang in with fists swinging, but there was no guarantee he could take Flying Sword, let alone three men at once, and the noise would likely draw reinforcements from the bath area. None of her plans seemed to have a chance. Yet sometimes—not often, but sometimes—the simplest plan could succeed where none other could hope to.

Yuu glanced over her shoulder at Li Bang. "Remember why I hired you," she said. "Do your job and follow my lead." She turned to the massive giant on the bench. "Flying Sword?" she asked, taking a few steps forward to stand in front of the coal basket. The water in the pan above reached its tipping point and a small stream tipped over the edge, hitting the coals and sizzling in a plume of steam that billowed up into Yuu's face. She coughed. Whoever had scented the water clearly had never heard of subtlety.

"Who wants to know?" said one of the men to the right of the ring bearer. He stood and stepped in front of the man with the ring, blocking Yuu's view. Of course, he was also giving Flying Sword a close-up view of his arse, which, judging by the girth of the man, was likely not a pleasant view.

"My name is Yuu. This is my bodyguard, Li." She took a step to the left, away from the coals, and bowed far lower than was strictly customary. She hoped the show of respect would help give the men the idea she was harmless. "I have come with a business opportunity." She was making it all up on the spot now, piecing together information from Li Bang's conversation with the woman at the front of the bathhouse. She hated to be so unprepared, but sometimes there simply was no other choice. Her grandmother's voice whispered in her mind, *Never approach a situation without ample knowledge of the environment, the adversary, and the objective. The Art of War should always be utterly prepared for any scenario, including alternatives and secondary measures. Prepare to such a level it seems like foresight.*

The man who was probably Flying Sword grunted, and his fat-arsed guard stepped aside and sat back down on the bench. "Odd place to come to me with business," said Flying Sword.

Another small stream of water poured on the coals, raising another plume of steam. Sixteen seconds since the last plume. Yuu stood up from her bow and took another step forward. "Not at all. Here we are entirely safe from prying eyes and ears, and what place would be more secure than the heart of your budding business empire?"

"Empire…" Flying Sword rolled the word around in his mouth as though tasting it. People really were so simple. Ambitious men like Flying Sword were so easy to manipulate. He waved a languid hand, and Yuu took another step forward. She was surrounded by Flying Sword's naked guards now.

Yuu readied herself. She had taken bits of information from different sources and stitched together a lie. Now she hoped it would hold together long enough. "My master, Wen, runs a number of profitable establishments under the name Tsin Xao's House of Refreshment."

The pig-nosed man to Flying Sword's right snorted. "That slimy fuck out on the Sword Road?" he said. "Sells wine on the roadside, boss. Undercuts the licenced traders in the city." Steam plumed as another little trickle of water hit the coals.

Yuu bowed her head slightly. "That man is merely an employee. He and that particular establishment are just one of many. There are hundreds of Wens across hundreds of Tsin Xao's House of Refreshments across all Hosa. From Fongsa at the Nash border all the way up to Shinxei in Shin. Every city has at least one Wen and one Tsin Xao's House of Refreshment. And many *many* customers. Farmers, mercenaries, merchants, soldiers, everyone drinks at Tsin Xao's House of Refreshment. All the wine is watered down and sold for a fraction of the price city taverns charge. This, of course, is all sanctioned by the monks of Hushon Temple." She had Flying Sword's attention now. No doubt his mind was boggling at how many lien such an enterprise would pull in. If it weren't a complete fabrication, he would be right in thinking it was substantial.

"What does your master want with me?" Flying Sword asked. The water poured onto the coals and the scented steam plumed behind Yuu. Exactly sixteen seconds since the last time.

"A partner," Yuu said with a sickly-sweet smile. "His establishments are profitable, but only as long as they are protected. You have connections to, uh, courageous men with the will to see things done." That was certainly the politest way anyone had ever described a bandit. "He has the infrastructure to give you a foothold in cities beyond Ban Ping. Beyond the province of Xihai. All of Hosa."

Flying Sword smiled for a moment, his eyes goggling. Greed was an adequate lever to move most men. Chang Lihua wrote, *Never fear the greedy man. Greed makes them predictable and malleable. Instead, fear the righteous man. Their faith makes them intractable and temperamental.* Flying Sword grimaced and stood. "And he sent *you* to negotiate? If he was serious, he should have come himself." He took a step forward to tower over Yuu, close enough to touch. Of course, that also meant he was close enough to strangle her with little effort.

Yuu forced herself to look up and meet the bandit's dark gaze. She kept the smile plastered to her face. "Well, I can be quite forceful, when the situation calls for it." She reached up quick as a snake, hooked a finger through the ring, twisted and pulled.

Flesh tore free with a spurt of blood and Flying Sword screamed in pain. Pig Nose was the first to react. He leapt off the bench and reached for Yuu. She ducked his clutching hands, spun about, jumped over the basket of coals — the heat was intense but passed quickly — and landed on the other side in a sprawling heap. Pig Nose rushed on, but Yuu had timed everything perfectly. A stream of water dribbled from the pan and hit the coals, sending up a blinding plume of steam. She kicked at the basket of coals, scattering searing rocks over the steam room floor to a chorus of unmanly screams and burned feet. Not waiting to see the damage she caused, she clutched the ring in her fist and rushed past Li Bang into the bath room beyond.

Yuu realised she may have underestimated the number of the bathhouse's customers who were actually working for Flying Sword. It was all of them. Definitely all of them. His guards, the men playing Go, and those enjoying the bath were all advancing toward the steam room. Some had knives, others just wielded looks that felt like knives, but any one of them would be more than a match for Yuu.

Li Bang sniffed loudly from behind her. "What now?"

Yuu tucked a few errant strands of hair behind her ear. "Earn your lien. Crack some heads."

Li Bang bellowed and charged toward the one-eyed thug. He would never win the fight, not against six men with reinforcements likely to arrive at any moment, but if he fought ferociously enough, he just might draw enough attention for Yuu to escape. She sacrificed her pawn to secure the centre of the board.

The two guards who had been playing Go rounded the bath and were close. The baby-faced one was holding a throwing knife. In the bath, one of the men, the slim goon with more nose hairs than teeth, was wading toward Li Bang. The other bather, the man with drooping breasts, was just in front of Yuu, already heaving himself out of the water. She had only one way out, one way past all the fighting and certain death. She slipped out of her robe and let it fall, took two steps forward and leapt over Drooping Breasts as he struggled out of the bath, dived into the shockingly hot water, and kicked hard toward the other side. Even through her blurred underwater vision, Yuu saw the throwing knife hit the water just ahead of her and drift toward the tiled bottom of the bath.

Yuu broke the surface as she reached the other side, hauled herself out, and rolled to her feet in one mostly fluid if not entirely graceful motion. Behind her she could see Drooping Breasts was back in the water and wading toward her. The two Go players had turned around and were fighting each other to be the first to reach her. Li Bang was struggling with Nose Hairs and One-Eye. The dull-eyed brute was already down behind him blood pooling on the wood plank floor. Yuu turned and slipped, falling back onto her arse. She swore and struggled back to her feet, then ran into the corridor toward the exit.

She could see the entrance foyer, the double doors leading out to the streets of Ban Ping, the hostess with the painted face, hand over her mouth and eyes wide with shock. Then Yuu felt a hand clamp hold of her shoulder. It dragged her to a halt and spun her around to face one of the men who had been playing Go. It was the ancient thug with animals tattooed all over him. Yuu felt for the connection to her qi, the shavings of wood she had scattered along the corridor, and ordered one to life. A replica of the wood shaving but a thousand times bigger erupted from the ground in an explosion of wooden splinters and slammed into the man, smashing him against the wall with such force he was unconscious before he hit what was left of the floor. The effigy of the wood shaving crumbled to dust and debris almost as quickly as it had formed.

Yuu turned toward the entrance and lurched on, but a door to a side room burst open and another man rushed out. He was tall and rakishly thin, with muscles like thick ropes. Clearly he had heard the commotion and didn't care much about the specifics. For all he knew Yuu could have been one of the bathhouse's women fleeing from the struggle. It didn't matter. He wrapped his bony

63

fingers wrapped around Yuu's throat before she could react and slammed her against one wall, then dragged her across the rug and slammed her against the other wall. Bright white spots flared in her vision. She was wrenched sideways again and felt her head bounce off the wall. All struggle fled from her.

She heard Li Bang shout, and the pressure released from her neck. She crumbled to the floor in a heap, sucked in a couple of breaths, and shook her head until the spots cleared. Li Bang had the smaller man by the neck and was punching him in the face probably more times than entirely necessary. He had several small cuts and a bruise on his chin but looked remarkably well for just having fought his way through half a dozen men. He tossed the unconscious thug to the floor, and held out a hand to Yuu. She took it and he hauled her to her feet like she weighed no more than a paper fan.

Flying Sword and three more of his thugs charged through the door at the far end of the corridor. His chest was bleeding heavily from where his nipple had once been, and the flesh of his feet was bright red, probably from the spilled coals. "I'm going to kill you, bitch!" he screamed as he stomped forward, his men at his back.

Yuu glanced at the hostess cowering near the shelves. "Get our clothes, please." She backed up a few steps and waited while Flying Sword advanced. Just a few more steps. She reached out for her qi and activated the dozen-or-so remaining wood shavings. The corridor erupted in chaos. Giant shards of stone, wood, and ratty rug burst from the floor and walls. One of them pinned Flying Sword against the wall, and several others blocked the corridor nearly completely. They would crumble soon, malformed things as they were, but she might have just enough time to escape.

Li Bang struggled into his trousers, and the hostess was holding the rest of his clothes and Yuu's patchwork robes, but they had no time to dress. "Go!" Yuu hissed, pointing at the door. She grabbed the clothes from the hostess as Li Bang ambled to the entrance. "Thank you," Yuu said with a slight bow. She slipped a hand into one of the pockets in her robe and retrieved nine lien. It was all she had left. "Find somewhere else to work." She slapped the coins into the woman's hands and followed Li Bang out onto the streets of Ban Ping.

The two guards at the main entrance were standing back from the doors, gawking. They probably weren't expecting Li Bang to charge out half dressed, nor Yuu to come out in nothing but her underwrappings, dripping from her brief time in the bath. They recovered just in time to watch Li Bang snatch up his chui from the rack and jab it into the ugly one's stomach, curling him over into a wheezing heap. The uglier one rushed forward, but Li Bang flipped the mace around and rammed the butt of it into his face, which would no doubt accentuate his unfortunate features. With both men down and not getting back up any time soon, they made their escape.

"This way," Yuu said as she rushed into the street. There were few people about, and those that were stopped to stare, but it was late and dark, and most respectable people were probably in bed. She glanced back to see Li Bang still standing at the entrance to the bathhouse, squinting into the street. Apparently, he wasn't joking about his night blindness. Yuu considered leaving him. She had already committed to sacrificing the piece to achieve her victory. But he had saved her life in the bathhouse, probably more than once. It was a foolish sentimental attachment, unworthy of the Art of War. However, he was useful and might be so again. Adapting to fortune was often as important as learning from mistakes. Then again, her grandmother always said there was no such thing as good fortune, only the propitious mistakes of others.

Yuu shook the thoughts free before she got into a philosophical debate with the ghost of her grandmother, and rushed back to Li Bang's side. She grabbed his free hand and pulled him into motion. "Follow me!"

"Are we going back to the Jasmin Eye?"

"Do dragons fly? Of course we're going back. I need a drink!"

Chapter 6

When they got back to the Jasmin Eye, Natsuko was not there. Yuu assumed the goddess had gone back to Tianmen. Unfortunately, this left her flat broke as she had given the last of her lien to the hostess at the bathhouse. Li Bang stepped in to save the day. He bought them a bottle each with some of the wages Yuu had paid him. Yuu fell asleep on a bench in the tavern garden with a cup of wine in one hand and Chaonan's ring clutched tightly in the other.

The next morning Yuu woke in a panic, scared someone might have robbed her during the night. It was a foolish thought, of course. She had nothing worth stealing. Her only possessions were an empty gourd, a half-carved block of wood and a carving knife… and a god's ring. She uncurled her fingers to find the ring sitting in her palm. It was crusted in blood and Flying Sword's nipple was still attached. Bile rose in her throat and she swallowed it down. She scraped the lump of flesh away with her carving knife and threw the mangled nipple on the floor. Then she secreted the ring into a pocket of her robe. She really did hate the gods.

The sun was bright to the east, bathing most of the garden in shadow. The Jasmin Eye was mostly empty save for a few other patrons who either couldn't afford a room or had nowhere else to go. Where the twin musicians had been the night before, a small red fox lay curled into a tight ball. Yuu didn't remember the little beast from the night before, and that meant it hadn't been there. Details never escaped her. She had been taught not to let them. No one else seemed to remark upon the fox's presence, and it was soundly asleep. Perhaps it was someone's pet. Her mouth tasted like a beggar's shoes and her stomach rumbled. She tried to remember how long it had been since she had eaten. A full day maybe. She hadn't eaten anything since she arrived in Ban Ping.

No wonder it felt like a tengu was trying to claw its way from her stomach.

Li Bang was laid out on the garden beside the table, snoring softly. One hand lay across his chest, the other splayed out to his side, resting atop his chui. His knuckles on both hands were bloody, and the welt on his chin had blossomed into a swollen purple bruise. He had served his part well at the bathhouse, saving her life and returning to her side even after she had sacrificed him. Not all pieces could be equated to chess, Yuu admitted to herself.

Yuu poked at one of the bottles rolling about on the table but found it empty. Her stomach rumbled again. She needed food and needed a drink, and had no lien to pay for either. "Natsuko?" she said, her voice barely more than a whisper. When the old woman didn't appear, she said it a bit louder, "Natsuko?" It was too much to hope the goddess could be summoned at will. The little red fox did look up though, staring at her through mismatched eyes, one gold and one green. Then it turned its back on her and curled up into a tight ball and dropped off to sleep again.

Li Bang woke himself with a rattling snore, blinked groggily and wiped drool from his face. Then he rolled over on his giant belly, yawned, and heaved himself up onto the bench opposite Yuu. "We're still alive then?" he asked.

Yuu nodded. "Flying Sword will be looking for us."

Li Bang chuckled. "You ripped his nipple off."

"He wasn't using it," she said with a shrug.

"How did you make those things come out of the floor?"

Yuu's stomach growled again, and she glanced over at the bar. "Fetch us some breakfast and I'll tell you."

Li Bang didn't grumble about buying breakfast, and in a few minutes they each had a bowl of rice with a fried egg on top. He brought them a jug of water as well, though Yuu would have much preferred wine. She couldn't remember the last time breakfast hadn't involved some sort of booze. But maybe it was time to try a morning sober for once. They set about demolishing the food, and by the time they were done, the old woman reappeared. Natsuko had a grumpy pout on her wrinkled face and sat down with a huff.

"Did you get it?" she asked without a word of welcome.

Yuu reached inside her robes and flashed the ring at her, then pocketed it again. "Did you know?" she asked. "Where it was."

The goddess jabbed a gnarled finger into Li Bang's belly and he shifted away from her with a long-suffering groan. "In the bathhouse. Just as I told you," Natsuko said.

Yuu glared at the goddess, but she showed no indication she was making fun of them.

"There is only one artefact left up for grabs in Ban Ping," Natsuko said. "Unless you are willing to take some from another champion."

Yuu scoffed. "I'm staying as far away from the Ticking Clock as I can. If not for Li Bang here I'd have been killed by a triad thug last night. Legendary assassins are a little out of my league."

Li Bang sniffed. "And mine."

The goddess' jaw writhed like she had gristle between her teeth. "It's not the Ticking Clock. Another champion found an artefact last night, which means there are at least three of you here in Ban Ping."

That made things a little more complicated, though also a little safer. If there was another champion searching for the artefacts in the city, then there was another champion for the Ticking Clock to hunt. Of course, it also meant there was competition for the final unclaimed artefact in Ban Ping. It would be helpful if they knew who it was. "Whose champion?" Yuu asked.

"Yang Yang," Natsuko said. "The god of gambling and the goddess of lies."

"I don't understand," Li Bang said.

"Already I find that unsurprising," Natsuko said. She jabbed another finger at his belly and Li Bang shifted again, half falling off the end of the bench.

"Yang Yang is the dual god," Yuu said. "Two halves that make up a whole. You don't know who Yang Yang's champion is?"

"No," Natsuko said. "I'm not omnipotent."

Li Bang frowned and scratched at his cheek. "Om... huh?"

They had just two choices in Yuu's estimation. Either they made a move on the other artefact as soon as possible, or they fled the city and let the other two champions squabble over it. "What can you tell us about this other artefact?" she asked.

"You won't like where it is," Natsuko said with a sly grin. She tilted her head to the south and looked up at the sky.

"The temples?" Yuu said. She felt her spirits sink like a scuttled ship. "Wonderful."

"Nowhere in Ban Ping is more heavily guarded by monks," Li Bang said, entirely unhelpfully.

"Do we at least know what we're looking for?" Yuu asked. "It might help."

The goddess pursed her lips and rubbed her wrinkled chin. "When I get closer, I will know."

"They allow people up there to see the temples and pray to the stars," Li Bang said. "But only during the day. I've never been there myself because... well, it's a long way up."

"Yes, you would not want to lose a few rolls of fat, Lump," Natsuko said with a vicious cackle.

"Leave him alone," Yuu snapped. "He saved my life last night, Natsuko. What did you do?"

The goddess fell silent but sent a scathing glare Yuu's way.

They gathered themselves quickly after that, and Yuu snuck away with a few lien to buy herself a bottle of wine, congratulating herself on managing breakfast sober at the very least. Before the sun reached its zenith, they were on their way to the ten thousand steps of the Ascent of Stars.

The city was bustling with news, and the telling of it spilled out into the streets, so it was impossible to escape the rumours swirling about. The Cochtan army had invaded the Shin province with thopters, legions of riflemen, and even the newly resurrected Blood Engine. According to the whispers on the streets, the capital had fallen in one day, but Yuu wagered that was an exaggeration. Even with the aid of thopters, such a thing would be impossible. The capital of Shin was built atop several massive rocky plateaus. It would be difficult to defend effectively, true, but far more difficult to attack effectively. She saw no way either the riflemen or the Blood Engine could reach the city, let alone bring their considerable force to bear. Some rumourmongers even claimed the fighting had spread to Sun Valley, and the wushu masters there were holding the line as only the masters of Sun Valley could.

They stopped briefly to buy rice balls from a street vendor who proudly displayed a sign indicating he was sanctioned by Hushon Temple. The rice was overcooked, but Yuu devoured it all the same. The vendor chatted happily and claimed the legendary bounty hunter, the Laws of Hope, was asking for information on a number of thefts that had occurred the previous night, including a ruckus at a bathhouse, though no one seemed to know what had been stolen. Yuu had heard many stories of the Laws of Hope and his ability to chase down bounties. She also had no doubt he had not forgotten the substantial bounty attached to the Art of War. The sooner she left Ban Ping, the safer she would be, whether anyone knew her true name or not.

The beginning of the Ascent of Stars was a temple in and of itself. A large building with five shrines arranged around the interior sat at the foot of the mountain. Monks were out in abundance, decked out in fancy, colourful robes and wishing *May the stars shine favourable upon you* to everyone who passed. There seemed no guile in the monks, though the Steel Prince had often expounded upon the military aspect of the spiritual ranks. He told Yuu that the monks were wushu masters who could almost challenge the masters of Sun Valley, and their knowledge of qi was near unrivalled. Unfortunately, the monks took no part in the wars of Hosa or conflict of any kind outside enforcing the laws of Ban Ping. The Steel Prince had been the leader of the rebellion against the previous Emperor of Ten Kings. He was a prince by blood and true heir of the Qing province, a hero, fighting an oppressive rule that had brought nothing but misery, famine, and death to Hosa. Yet the monks politely refused every request he sent them, always wishing the stars to shine favourably upon him, but offering no aid. They called themselves pacifists, but Yuu scoffed at that. The monks of Ban Ping were cowards, willing to let a corrupt ruler crush Hosa under his heel rather than take a stand.

Li Bang returned the monks' greetings and well wishing, but Yuu stormed past them toward the rear of the temple. A portly monk waited by the curtained doorway, a bundle of incense sticks in her hand. Yuu ignored yet another wish for the stars to shine favourably but snatched one of the proffered incense sticks. She had no intention of lighting it at any of the temples and thought as little of the stars as she did of the gods, but who knew when a smelly stick might come in handy. She whisked it into one of the folds of her robe and stepped onto the first step.

Legend had it there were ten thousand steps leading up the mountain to the temple, and each one was named after a star. Yuu wondered how many of the names were repeated.

"You seem in a foul mood," Natsuko said as she drew up next to Yuu. Despite the goddess' apparent senectitude, she seemed far more capable of climbing the seemingly endless steps than either Yuu or Li Bang. "And I am finding it hard to maintain my own grump when you are doing such a better job of it."

"Bloody monks," Yuu said. "If they had just joined the war when Quang asked them, we would have won it without... Before the shinigami got involved. My prince would never have died."

"*Might* never have died," Natsuko said. Yuu shot her a glare, but the goddess only returned it. "It's true. You might have won the war, but your prince may have choked on an aggressive fly the next day. Stop projecting your anger at yourself on others. Monks will do what the monks will do. If they wish to play at peace and worship big balls of fire in the sky, so be it. Let them be fools. The fact is they were never going to join your war, so blaming them for not joining it is about as useful as blaming yourself for the hero you loved being a hero and getting himself killed over it."

Yuu continued to glare at the little woman as they climbed step after step. The stone steps were carved directly into the mountain in a winding path from bottom to top. There were a few people far ahead of them, little more than dots struggling up the grey path, and a couple were just starting on the first step. So many tourists come to pay pilgrimage.

"What are you staring at," the goddess asked with a sidelong glance.

"I'm debating throwing you off the mountain," Yuu snapped.

Li Bang spoke up from a few steps behind. He was already panting and they had barely even started. "You fought in the war?" he asked.

Yuu felt the old panic rise inside her and fumbled for her wine gourd. If Li Bang knew she had fought in the war and also knew her technique, he might make the connection. "A lot of people fought in the war," she said.

"Does that… make you… a hero?" he asked between puffing breaths. "If you fought in the war… and have a technique."

Natsuko was a few steps ahead, but she glanced over her shoulder with that goddess grin of hers. "You used your technique? Dangerous."

Yuu tucked a few strands of hair behind her ear. "What about you, Li Bang?" she asked, trying to change the subject. "When we met you called yourself Falling Moon. Not many get a name like that without a technique to back it up."

Li Bang looked crestfallen as he slogged his way up the steps. "Nope. No technique. I thought…" He sighed. "I gave myself the name. Hoped it might spread and maybe if enough people knew me as Falling Moon, I'd get a technique."

Natsuko cackled like a crow. "Stupid Lump doesn't even know how techniques work."

"That hardly makes him unique," Yuu said. "Nor deserving of mockery. Honestly, you're a goddess, shouldn't you know better?"

Again, that inhuman grin over the shoulder. "I know to have a good laugh when the opportunity presents itself."

Yuu sighed and waited for Li Bang to catch up. He was huffing and puffing up the steps but made no request to rest. "Techniques rarely spontaneously manifest, Li Bang," she said. She remembered when her grandmother sat her down and explained the same thing to her. And how she had told Yuu she would not pass her own technique onto any of her natural grandchildren, but Daiyu Lingsen was a different matter, deserving not only of the unique technique, but also of a legacy. "There are three forms of technique. First, I should explain innate technique. It is… Everyone can use it. From the pig farmer to the wushu master to the emperor. Innate technique is the ability to use your qi to strengthen your body. Some people use it without even realising it. The man who lifts a fallen rock off his wife's leg. The woman who carries twelve buckets of water from the well each day. They tap into their qi and use it to make themselves stronger or faster, or even to heal themselves quicker. Innate technique is the ability to push your body beyond its normal physical limits.

"Some heroes specialise in it. The wushu masters of Sun Valley strengthen their qi and technique to such levels that they can use innate techniques all the time, permanently making themselves – superhuman. But most heroes can use it in bursts, whether they realise it or not, temporarily making themselves stronger, faster."

"Can you use innate technique?" Li Bang asked.

Yuu chuckled. "Not very well. You may have noticed I'm not particularly useful in a fight."

"That's an understatement," Li Bang scoffed. "Uh, sorry, boss. What about that technique you used to… um, make things come out of the floor?"

"I'm able to infuse objects with my qi and cause enlarged effigies to manifest from the substrate around them. What you saw was a crude rush job. I had to infuse the wood shavings with qi on the spot, which is quite draining. It also leads to malformed effigies that lack the necessary cohesion to stay in one piece."

Li Bang wiped sweat from his forehead. "Huh?"

Yuu decided to press on. She fished her half-carved chess piece from her robes. It had tattered robes much like her own, but that was about as far as she had gotten with it. "I usually use little statues like this that I can infuse with qi as I carve them. That allows me to animate them and even give them simple commands. Much more useful than enlarged wood shavings erupting from the ground."

Li Bang frowned and Yuu could see his mind chewing on the information. Perhaps she had given him too much. He was certainly no scholar, but it would not take a genius to connect her to a famed strategist who had the exact same technique. She rushed on with the lecture before he could reason out the truth. "It belongs to the second group of techniques — learned techniques. These are techniques that, theoretically, anyone could learn, given the proper instruction and training. They are… extremely varied. I have seen people make their sword leave trails of fire, men who can step through the world to appear somewhere else, women who secrete crippling toxins from their skin. I have seen a man control his hair like a rat does its tail and a woman freeze a lake with nothing but her breath. In theory, learned techniques are as endless as one's imagination and dedication to learning."

"Ha!" Natsuko scoffed and turned around to face them. Evidently, she had been eavesdropping. She walked backwards up the stairs, without missing a step. "That would be Master Han Sholieu's theory. He was an idiot. There are a limited number of mortal techniques, but that is not to say humans have discovered them all." She turned and continued up the steps.

Yuu glanced at Li Bang. "There you have it, from the mouth of the gods."

"Does that mean it's true?" Li Bang asked.

Yuu sighed. "I wouldn't count on it. If there's one thing to remember about the gods, Li Bang, it's that they lie."

Yuu drew her wine gourd from her robes and unstoppered it, took a large swig and sighed gratefully. Then had another sip before passing it to Li Bang. "Regardless of just how many learned techniques there are, they can be taught." She took the gourd back and sipped at it again, plugged the stopper back in, then slid it back into her robes. "There are, in fact, dojos that specialise in teaching specific techniques to those with the will to learn and enough lien to pay for the teaching."

Li Bang stopped and bent over panting, hands on his thighs. "Can you… teach me… your technique?"

"No!" Yuu said perhaps a bit too sharply. "It is…" A technique she swore only to pass on once, along with the name and the legacy. "It's my grandmother's technique. It-It's not my place to teach it to others."

Natsuko chuckled softly but said nothing. Yuu glared at her back.

Li Bang sigh and started climbing again. "What about the third form of techniques?"

"Inherited techniques," Yuu said. "Sometimes called bloodline techniques, though that term was all but discarded about a hundred years ago when the Cochtans unleashed their Blood Engine on the world. Nobody wanted the association. Inherited techniques are unique to families. They cannot be taught in the traditional manner. They tend to be immensely powerful and extremely rare. Even within a family, the technique is not always passed down. Sometimes it skips generations, seeming to manifest randomly in some children but not others.

"For example, the Usami clan, an Ipian bloodline. They famously had a technique which allowed them to grow jutting spurs of bone from their skin. It provided them with armour and weapons both, but at a heavy cost to their qi. The clan was all but wiped out in battle when the Ipian emperor, Katsuo Ise, ordered them to spearhead an invasion of Nash. The Nash vhargan…"

"Huh?"

"It is the Nash equivalent of an emperor," Yuu said. "Though it would translate better as Lord of Lords. The Nash vhargan, Chotan Khourlas, learned of the impending invasion and set an ingenious trap. She sacrificed the entire town of Naaglii, knowing it would be impossible to hold against the Ipian emperor's forces, but she hid a thousand soldiers nearby, buried in the sand. When the main force of the Ipians thought they had secured the town as a new supply line, they moved on. The Nash soldiers then emerged, destroyed the Ipian supply lines, and burned their own town to the ground, giving the Ipian forces no possible way to retreat. The Ipian force pushed on, they could no longer turn back and the emperor had ordered them to take the Nash capital of Darbaatar. The Nash forces harried them, making them pay in blood for every day they marched. By the time the Ipian army reached Darbaatar all they found there was an abandoned city, its wells poisoned. The Nash were always nomadic, so rather than wait for the Ipians to attack, they abandoned their largest settlement. With their supplies cut off, the last of the Ipian forces starved to death in the ruins of a city they had been ordered to take."

Yuu found both Li Bang and Natsuko staring at her and realised she had been lecturing them on ancient history.

"Sorry," Yuu said. They probably thought her a fool, veering off on a tangent about a battle none but a strategist or historian would still care about. "My point is that the Usami clan was all but wiped out, only those without the ability to use their bloodline technique were left behind. But thirty years ago, the technique manifested once more in a descendant of the clan."

"So, I might have an inherited technique?" Li Bang said squinting at Yuu and rubbing his wiry beard. He had sweated through his tunic, which was now stuck to his hanging belly.

Yuu smiled at him. "Probably not. Unless you know of any ancestors who did?"

Li Bang shook his head. He was struggling up the stairs, labouring with each breath. "Nope. My family never done anything but herd buffalo. I'm the first one to leave the village in… forever, I think. Apart from my father. He was conscripted by the Emperor of Ten Kings and died at the battle of Jieshu. An army officer told us he was killed by the Steel Prince himself. Gave my mother five lien for the trouble and that was that."

"I'm sorry," Yuu said quietly. No doubt Li Bang thought she was just being polite, but there was more to it. If his father had died at the battle of Jieshu, then it was her fault. Daiyu Lingsen, the Art of War, had led that battle. It had been her plan, her orders. She might not have swung the sword, but she was responsible nonetheless. She had killed Li Bang's father. Just as she had killed thousands of others. Sent them to their deaths just like her prince. She fumbled for her gourd and took another deep swig, desperately trying to reach the level of drunkenness that washed away guilt.

"You missed one," said Natsuko. Of all of them she was the only one not struggling with the climb. "There is another form of technique in your list. Spontaneous manifestation."

Of course the goddess was right, but Yuu hadn't missed it — she had omitted it. "Because it's so rare," she said. "And usually involves the intervention of a god or a powerful spirit such as a kami."

Li Bang looked up from his contemplation of the next step. There was hope on his pudgy face.

They came to a turning where the stairs snaked around and doubled back on themselves. It was a small plateau, but a way station all the same. A single bench sat at the rear of the plateau, overlooking the city of Ban Ping. Next to the bench stood a monk holding a ladle, and a large wooden bucket full of water strapped to her back. At least it was probably water. Too much to hope the monks might provide free wine to anyone devout enough to make the trek up their damned mountain. Natsuko barely even broke stride as she turned and started up the next set of steps, but Yuu and Li Bang stopped in front of the monk.

"May the stars shine favourably upon you," the monk said as she reached over her shoulder and spooned a ladle of water into a wooden bowl and held it out to them.

"Uh huh," Yuu panted as she accepted the water. She sank down onto the bench. She couldn't even find the breath to snap at the foolish monk. Li Bang plumped down next to her, red faced and breathing hard. He tipped the water over his head and slouched. It seemed they had come such a long way, yet still had so much further to go. Even so, the view was spectacular. Ban Ping spread out before them, and Yuu could see to every corner and beyond to the fields and rice paddies. She saw people moving along the roads, smoke rising from restaurants, the sun glinting off a thousand windows.

Natsuko turned around and saw them sitting on the bench. She plodded back down the stairs toward them. "Yes, yes, it is a lovely view. It will be even more grand up top."

"May the stars shine favourably upon you," the monk said, holding out a bowl of water to Natsuko.

The goddess scoffed. "The stars are nothing but gas and fire, young lady. You should be praying the gods smile down upon you. Or better yet, that we ignore your insignificant existence entirely. Would you like to know what happened to that mouse you kept when you were a child? The one you lost in Sochon Temple." She grinned that goddess grin of hers. "Master Io found it and—"

Yuu stood, stepped between Natsuko and the monk, and silenced the goddess with a glare. She had no love for the monks, nor the stars they worshipped, but neither did she wish cruelty upon them, and it didn't take an oracle to figure out where Natsuko's story was going. "Thank you for the water," she said, still glaring at Natsuko. She placed the bowl on the bench and started up the stairs. Li Bang repeated the blessing of the stars to the monk, got back to his feet with a groan, and followed. Natsuko snorted and started walking, quickly overtaking Yuu.

"Are all the gods so cruel?" Yuu asked.

Natsuko didn't answer.

Chapter 7

Three more times they stopped at plateaus to catch their breath and each time a monk was waiting for them with a barrel of water and a blessing of the stars. Yuu could only assume the unfortunate souls had to carry the barrels up the mountain each morning. Tiring work, but also an excellent way to strengthen both body and qi. The view became both better and worse the further up they travelled. The city grew smaller — the people turned to ants scurrying through their hive — but the majesty of Xihai province was revealed: rolling plains once green but turned yellow by drought, and roving herds of animals all reduced to hazy smudges of indistinct colour. The air became colder and thinner as they ascended, and Yuu was glad of her voluminous robes keeping out the worst of the chill. Natsuko skipped up the steps, much of the old woman giving way to the child she had been when they first met. Something about the altitude, Yuu guessed, being closer to heaven. Li Bang continued to struggle, falling behind them, his feet plodding and his breath misting in front of him.

It was late afternoon by the time they reached the summit. The sun was hot on the skin, but still could not chase away the chill of the mountain top. Two monks stood guard at the top, but these were not like the monks down in the city. Despite the cold, their orange robes were lighter and hung over only one shoulder, leaving their left arms exposed, and they wore colourful trousers. Their feet were wrapped in linen, and their wrists and hands were tied with bandages and leather straps. They were entirely bald, not a hair on their heads or even their faces. People without eyebrows always seemed to look both surprised and menacing all at once, Yuu thought. Both monks held heavy staffs of several lengths of bamboo banded with iron all along their lengths. Yuu knew full well that a staff like that was just as deadly a weapon as any sword, perhaps even more so for its reach and versatility. Even more telling, these monks did not offer the blessing of the stars. They barred the way past the temple arch.

Beyond the monks, Yuu spied a rocky plateau, paved with stone slabs, large enough to be considered a small town in its own right. Five temples far grander than any in the city below were arrayed around the plateau in a deliberate pattern, though its intent escaped her. Yuu quickly counted a hundred monks going through training katas in the centre of the expanse between the temples, and closer to the archway, another fifty were sitting in some form of silent meditation upon prayer mats. They were all a far difference from the soft star-worshipping monks in the city below. This was the true strength her prince had coveted. The true strength the monks of Ban Ping had held back, refusing to let the world see. This was an army of martial artists.

Li Bang reached the last of the stairs, puffing noisily, and all but dropped onto his knees when he realised there was no more climbing to do. "Never… again," he said between heaving breaths.

The taller of the two monks barring their way stepped forward. He towered over Yuu and Natsuko and wore a dangerous smirk. "Thank you for your pilgrimage," he said, flicking his eyes between the two of them. "Three lien per person if you wish to see the temples." He held out a cloth-and-leather wrapped hand, the other tightening around his staff.

"That's extortion," Yuu said. "I thought the temples of the stars were open to all who wished to pay respect."

The smirking monk said nothing, hand still extended. His partner kept his eyes focused on Li Bang as the big man struggled back to his feet. Li Bang had brought his chui with him, but Yuu had no doubt it would be useless here. These monks were not the kind to be beaten into submission, but rather the kind that did the beating and really didn't care whether you submitted or not. After which they probably looted the broken bodies and pushed what was left down the mountain with a hearty *May the stars shine favourably upon your mangled corpse.*

The board shifted — all the playing pieces jumped and settled into new positions — and Yuu suddenly saw Ban Ping for what it truly was. A city dedicated to the worship of the stars, yes, but also a city ruled by the most ruthless criminal organisation in the entire empire, its grip so tight even the Emperor of Ten Kings had been forced to allow the monks to operate the city as they saw fit. If a business wanted to operate in Ban Ping, it had to pay Hushon Temple for the privilege, or the blessing as they liked to call it. Merchants and farmers coming to sell their wares were *advised* to pay a fee to Lenshin Temple to ensure the stars shone favourably upon their dealings. Any criminals who hadn't paid to be sanctioned were charged a hefty fine to pay penance to the stars. The people who lived in Ban Ping had to pay Gong Ang Temple just to live in their own houses. And on top of this, the temples were always asking worshippers for donations. Here, up at the pinnacle, where they were closest to the stars, Yuu saw the monks for what they really were. Thugs demanding protection money. They had created both the danger and protection from it, and charged visitors an extortionate amount for the privilege of being oppressed. The triads in the city below were children playing at banditry compared to the monks. The monks of Ban Ping were undoubtedly the most successful criminal organisation Hosa had ever seen, and even worse, they had legitimised the venture by creating a religion around their syndicate. No wonder they refused to take part in the Steel Prince's war against the emperor, they had no stake in it one way or another. The whole of Hosa could burn, and Ban Ping would stand, and the monks would no doubt charge the people for that privilege too.

"Pay them," Yuu said, gesturing to Natsuko.

The goddess shot Yuu an odd look, then shrugged. She whisked her hand and deposited nine lien into the monk's wrapped hand. "Take good care of those," the goddess said. "Make sure you don't lose them."

The monk smiled viciously and stepped aside to let them pass. "May the stars shine favourably upon you," he said smirking.

Yuu flashed a smile just as menacing. "May the gods take notice of your efforts here."

They started walking towards the centre of the plateau where the monks were going through their training routines. There was tiled stone beneath their feet, dusty from the gusting wind. The whole plateau had obviously been flattened by countless hours of hard labour and then the centre laid with the tiles.

"What was that about?" Natsuko asked.

Yuu grimaced. "Don't you have a god of disingenuous worship or something?"

"Ahh, you've noticed."

"How long have we worshipped the stars?" Yuu asked. "Where did it all start? Was it here? Was the entire religion built to fund a criminal empire of… monks?"

"Yes," Natsuko said with a cackle. "Though they were not monks at the beginning. I think it was an… evolution."

"And you let it happen?" Yuu asked. "The gods just rolled over and let an entire religion grow around a lie?" She couldn't fathom why they hadn't crushed it early on, or why they didn't take offence to it now. The entire empire worshipped the stars, while the gods were often forsaken, their shrines crumbling under the weight of time and irrelevance.

Natsuko stopped walking and turned to look at Yuu, a frown creasing her face. "How is this lie any different to the one that structures your empire? These monks collect taxes and convince idiots to worship the stars. Your laws, the very foundation your empire is built upon, collect taxes and demand other idiots worship an emperor. I mean, what is a kingdom but a collection of people who don't need to be ruled by a person who has no idea how?"

"But..."

"You cannot fight something this big," the goddess said in the cadence of a kindly old grandmother calmly explaining the world to a child. "And the gods have no desire to. We have something far more important to be about anyway. So, come along and stop looking for an unwinnable war to wage. Honestly, are you trying to bring your prince back or join him?"

Natsuko turned and started walking past the monks bowed in their prayer positions, towards the temple at the western end of the plateau. Yuu stood still for a few moments, Li Bang at her back, and watched the other group of monks training. An army of criminals dedicated to the worship of false deities. And the legitimate deities didn't care. They were slowly being replaced by false worship, by a lie, and they were too busy squabbling amongst themselves to give a crap. Fighting over who got to be Lord of Heaven, even as the gates were locking them in. Yuu shook her head and started after the goddess. Every time she thought she had a handle on the world, it surprised her, usually by proving that everything she thought was a lie.

The whole world is nothing but a fiction, her grandmother used to say. *A pretty little lie told to distract everyone from the truth. The only truth. There are rules to the game, and the...*

Li Bang sniffed loudly and Yuu realised she had stopped and had been staring off into shifting patterns of wispy clouds against the darkening sky. She smiled at him and hurried to catch up with the goddess.

The temple Natsuko led them to was dedicated to Ryoko, the One that is All, the largest of the constellations. Two more militant monks stood outside it. The one on the left was a woman with a ji resting in the crook of her arm. Its haft was as long as she was tall and the blade at its top was a pair of outward facing crescent moons with a snaking spear tip between them. The monk on the right was a short man with several sheathed daggers hanging from his belt. Though the monks in the city below rarely carried weapons, it seemed all those up here were armed. This was the heart of the criminal empire.

The woman stepped forward, holding her ji to bar entrance. "Three lien each to enter."

Yuu glared at her, but the monk just smiled in return. Natsuko handed over six lien and then stepped back. "I think I will rest my weary bones out here and watch the young men and women play. My son and daughter would like to see the temple, though." She turned and whispered to Yuu. "You are looking for Katashi's artefact. He is the god of truth. It is a lantern with a single burning candle that never goes out, though the lantern may be shuttered. It is black iron with edges gilded in the shape of sleeping dragons." She lowered herself cross legged to the ground with a groan and stared at the monks performing their katas. "Ooh, look at them dance. So pretty."

Yuu exchanged a glance with Li Bang, but he just shrugged at her.

"May the stars shine favourably upon you," the two monks said in unison as Yuu and Li Bang mounted the steps into Ryoko's temple.

The interior of Ryoko's temple was gloomy and cavernous and so thick with incense Yuu had to wade through it. Along the walls were works of art dedicated to the constellation. Paintings of the stars with those in the constellation made to glow more brightly. Statues of monks in the Ryoko prayer pose. Depictions of Ryoko as a beautiful woman on the edge of obesity and heavy with child. Ryoko, the One that is All, the Mother, the Giver, the Nurturer. Of course, she also had another name, a far older one: the Devourer. Yuu's grandmother taught her the original names of the constellations long ago as part of her education, her training. Ryoko was nothing but a great maw, poised in the act of consuming all the other constellations. A monster hoping to devour the world. The monks conveniently seemed to forget the older, less wholesome version of their false deity. No doubt it was far easier to convince people to worship a loving mother than it was an insatiable monster. Below each work of art was a collection plate, many of which were piled high with donations. Yuu could see just how ingenious the monks truly were. They might squeeze the citizens of Ban Ping for every lien they had, but they also made the city an attractive tourist spot and a worthy destination for pilgrimage. They convinced an entire culture to worship their false deities and then convinced the poor dupes to hand over their money to do so. Was it criminal if the people being robbed were willing participants? The idea made her head spin.

The monks inside the temple were moving about cleaning statues, sweeping the floor, waving incense around as though in some form of prayer. Were they believers? Had they bought into their own delusion? Or perhaps it was more likely that most of the monks had no idea their deities were false and the religion they practised was the most cunning and seditious protection racket ever created. Maybe only those at the very top of the criminal empire knew the truth.

Li Bang was squinting into the gloom. His night blindness really was a problem. In daylight or a well-lit room, he was an excellent brawler, but if the light dimmed just a little, he might be more hindrance than help. "Go back outside and wait with Natsuko," Yuu said.

"But what if you need me?"

Yuu glanced around at the monks. They were as well-armed as those outside. "I don't think we're going to start a brawl this time," she said. "Go outside and wait for me."

Li Bang nodded and walked cautiously back toward the light. Yuu focused on an ascending stairway up at the far end of the room. It was probably too much to hope the lantern was just hanging around lighting up one of the art displays, but at least she wasn't likely to find it attached to someone's nipple this time.

The second floor of the temple was given over to worship. A dozen monks knelt in prayer in front of a shrine. Among the monks were other supplicants, most likely visiting and begging for the favour of the stars, and of Ryoko. It was not uncommon for women to pray to the Mother in the hopes it would help them conceive, though they would be better off praying to Changang, the god of life, or Fuyuko, the god of children. Yuu scanned the room, but it seemed lit only by sconces with candles. She saw no lanterns anywhere. Why Natsuko couldn't tell her exactly where to find it was a mystery. It would not be directly helping Yuu, only giving her a gentle nudge in the right direction. The rules of the contest were clearly made by the gods themselves and, thus, beyond any sort of rationale. Arbitrary rules conceived by entities that could not understand how their whimsical nature affected the people who lived in the world. Humans suffering under the rule of foolish gods. Yuu wondered if what the monks were doing was really so bad. Their religion demanded constant tributes, keeping the people who worshipped the stars as poor as possible so they could keep praying for better lots in life, but at least they made no other demands. Worship of the stars was optional, and there were no vengeful spirits waiting to fuck up the lives of anyone who forgot to pray.

The stairs that led up to the third floor were guarded, the monks armed and watching her with unblinking stares. When Yuu drew close, the guards huddled together to block her path. There would be no getting to the top floor from inside, not without a bout of violence she would quickly lose. She flashed a smile as fake as their religion and backed away toward the stairs down to the first floor.

Natsuko and Li Bang were sitting side by side on the ground, watching the monks spar. Yuu saw them pass a bottle of something and felt a familiar longing. "Time to go," she said as she hurried past them.

Natsuko all but shot to her feet, regardless of how old she looked. She held out a gnarled hand to Li Bang. "Up you get, Lump. No sense in dawdling if we want to see the city before midnight."

Natsuko caught up with Yuu just past the first step down. "You didn't get it," she said angrily. "It is still back up there. I can feel it."

Yuu sighed. "There's no getting that lantern without an army, Natsuko. I searched as much of the temple as I could and didn't see it. There are three armed monks guarding the stairs to the third floor. I suppose I could have attacked them, maybe I'd even have managed to bleed on them a little before they skewered me like chuan."

The goddess opened her mouth.

"Neither can he," Yuu said quickly, thumbing over her shoulder at Li Bang. "We're not getting in."

The goddess narrowed her eyes and her curled her lips into a menacing sneer. "That is not acceptable."

"I thought you might say that," Yuu grumbled. "There are other artefacts. Is this one important?"

Natsuko shook her head. "No more than any other. But we are already lagging behind and it is here. Find a way in!"

Of course a god would ask the impossible. Yuu shook her head. "I can't. At least not by myself." She was already forming a plan, had been since the moment she stepped foot onto the plateau. It was a crazy plan, but they were often the ones with the best chances. Certainly, no one would counter it. No one would see it coming. But before she could put the plan to work, she needed another piece. She tucked a clump of hair behind her ear. "We need to hire a thief."

Chapter 8

It was full dark by the time they approached the bottom of the mountain. Yuu was leading Li Bang down each step, his chubby, sweating hand engulfing hers. The monk waiting for them at the shrine below bowed to them and gave them yet another blessing of the stars. Yuu waved the benediction and the woman away, utterly sick of their impotent blessings. She was now certain the majority of monks had no idea their religion was a sham. The monks down in the city were willing dupes, spreading their idiotic delusion to others. Passing on a sickness of the mind that robbed people of their senses along with their purses.

As soon as they were out onto the streets of Ban Ping, Yuu pulled Natsuko aside. "I need you to do something," she said quietly, making certain no one would overhear.

Natsuko sighed and opened her hand, producing ten more lien. "Wei Chu lost these just yesterday," she said. "Dropped in the evacuation of Shin Yen as the Cochtans scorched the ground to ash and churned up bodies in their infernal Blood Engine. Batu is keeping his promise. He is drowning the world in war. It is spreading. The two sides of the Ipian imperial family are at it again; the Ido family have sent an army to western Ipia and the Ise family have turtled up behind their walls. The Nash vhargan was murdered in her sleep and half the clans are fighting amongst themselves, while the other half are raiding western Ipian. All four empires are at war with themselves and each other."

Yuu pushed the information aside for the moment. It was not her war to fight. None of them were. She left it all behind along with her mask. "No," she said as she took the lien. No sense in wasting the offering. "I need you to return to Tianmen and tell the other gods, everyone you can find, that the Art of War is your champion."

Natsuko snorted so hard she stirred the dust beneath her feet. "You are mad, girl. You might as well walk around with a sign that says *Kill me for a free artefact*."

Yuu sighed. "You recruited me to be your champion because I'm a strategist, not because I'm a warrior. So, let me strategise. If you want us to get that lantern, then we need a plan. And I have one."

Natsuko narrowed her eyes and stared hard at Yuu. "What is it then?"

"Well..." Yuu paused. She couldn't tell the goddess her complete plan. Natsuko would never agree. She'd claim it was foolishness, and she would be right. "I don't have it all worked out yet, but it's, uh, coming to me. Just trust me. Go back to Tianmen and brag about your champion, the Art of War. Do it subtly if you can."

Natsuko grimaced. "*I* know how to be subtle."

"I'll be fine," Yuu insisted, trying to convince herself more than the goddess. "No one knows *I* am the Art of War... was the Art of War."

Natsuko's hard lines softened. She reached out and patted Yuu's hand. "You still are. Just because the mask is gone, doesn't mean the hero went with it."

Yuu opened her mouth to argue that she was never a hero. That it was always the Steel Prince who was the hero. She was only the idiot who got him killed and then disgraced his name. But Natsuko shook her head and turned away, muttering something to herself as she stepped around the corner of the shrine. Yuu waited a moment then glanced around the corner, but the goddess was gone. Like it or not, the plan was in motion now. She turned back to Li Bang to find him squinting at her despite the light of the nearby hanging lanterns.

"Back to the Jasmin Eye," Yuu said, trying to hide the nervous quaver in her voice. *The Art of War is never apprehensive. Bold attitude delivers bold strategies.* The lessons

91

of her old life, delivered harshly. "We need to find a thief with a death wish."

A crowd had gathered outside the Jasmin Eye and not a small one. Yuu stuck to the shadows and pulled Li Bang with her. She didn't think anyone would recognise her as the legendary strategist, the Art of War, but just a night ago she had ripped the nipple from a triad boss, so it was entirely possible her enemies were looking for a woman in a patchwork robe, not a figure in a mask. A cluster of people were blocking the entrance to the drinking house, and Yuu recognised some of them as patrons she had seen drinking there before, but most were new faces. There was a lot of grumbling, and plenty of demanding to be let into the tavern. It appeared something was happening, but no one knew what.

Yuu's gaze was drawn by a slim man of middling years with a warrior's braid that hung down to his waist. He wore a light suit of ornate ceramic armour painted white over a bleached bone linen tunic. In his left hand he held a shield, far larger than any normal man or woman could wield with ease. It was as tall as him and twice as wide, half a hand thick and made of fire-hardened ironwood embossed with a metal depiction of an open book. In his right hand he carried a long segmented dao, a weapon half sword and half whip. Yuu had seen its like only once before. This was the Laws of Hope, a bounty hunter who had brought to justice many of the worst bandits Hosa had seen in the past few decades. He had chased the Silent Sisters all the way from Shin to the Ipian border and brought back all eight of their heads in a millet sack. He alone had determined the true identity of No One, the serial murderer famed for having no pattern and leaving no clues. He had walked into the bandit camp at Hunshowei and walked out dragging the indomitable Thunder Chu in chains. Rumour had it he only went after the largest bounties these days, so Yuu could see no other reason he would be here than to finally bring her to justice. After all, the Art of War had a bounty large enough to buy half the city.

Beside the Laws of Hope stood another man, smaller with short cropped hair dusted with grey and a thick moustache oiled to droop at the ends. He was wearing the uniform and ceramic armour of a Hosan soldier and when he stepped up onto a nearby chair to address the crowd, Yuu recognised him. His name was Hua Shi. He had been one of her lieutenants during the war. She had thought he died, along with so many others, during the battle of Jieshu when they threw down the old Emperor of Ten Kings and installed the Leper Emperor in his place. Part of her was glad to see Hua Shi still alive and wanted to go talk to him. He had a keen mind, was no stranger to the chess board, and knew his way around an argument. But he wouldn't recognise her without the Art of War's mask, and even if he did, it would not end well with the Laws of Hope standing beside him. Yuu sunk further back into the shadows and arranged a few strands of hair in front of her face just in case.

Hua Shi raised his hands to the crowd and called for quiet. More people were joining the gathering now, hundreds of faces waiting to hear what he said. It gave Yuu hope, for there was no better place to hide than in a crowd. "I am here by order of Emperor Einrich WuLong," Hua Shi shouted over the murmur of the crowd. "The Cochtan army has invaded Hosa. Shin has fallen…"

The murmur rose to a tumult as the crowd shouted back.

"How can a whole province be lost?"

"Do they truly have a Blood Engine?"

"Are they coming here?"

Hua Shi waved his hands in the air, desperately trying to quiet them to no avail. Then the Laws of Hope raised his shield just a little and slammed it to the ground with a crash that cracked stone and silenced the rabble. The Laws of Hope looked up at Hua Shi. "Continue, representative Shi."

Hua Shi looked nervous as he chewed over his next words. "Sun Valley burns, many of its masters lay dead in their fields. The survivors have fled into the Cliffs Unbreakable, where they weather relentless assaults by Cochtan thopter crews." Before the crowd could erupt again, he held up his hands and continued, shouting, "Emperor Einrich WuLong has marshalled an army in Qing to take back Shin. He is leading it himself. He has enacted a new conscription law. Any man over the age of fifteen must report to the nearest recruitment centre. Emperor WuLong's mighty general, Roaring Tiger, is gathering a second army in Ning and will soon march north to strike into the heart of Cochtan territory. Under the emperor's glorious command, our most hated enemies will perish."

Yuu knew Roaring Tiger. He was more bully than strategist. His tactics favoured the teachings of Dong Ao. They were like performing surgery with a hammer. Yet his brother, the Crimson Tide, was a warrior almost without equal and had single-handedly turned the tide at Sengfai and the skirmish at the Bridge of Peace. Together, they might indeed lead a deadly strike into the heart of Cochtan. Still, it seemed too obvious an attack. The Cochtans would have their own strategists, and they would see this coming. Yuu shook her head and reminded herself that this was not her war. She had given up wars.

"Ban Ping doesn't allow conscription!" shouted a man in the crowd. His cry was taken up by several others.

"True," Hua Shi cried. "But the Sochon Temple has sanctioned the order. As such we have set up a recruitment station on the road north. The emperor demands... I ask that all able-bodied men come and enlist. We must strike back at Cochtan. They threaten not only Shin, but all Hosa." The crowd was shouting over him now, and he raised his voice even louder. "Even Ban Ping!"

There was dissent among the gathered masses. Some agreed and took up Hua Shi's plea, claiming they needed to fight for their homes. Others shouted at Hua Shi to leave the city and never come back. The crowd surged back and forth, a milling mass of flesh and confusion on the edge of violence. Chaoxiang wrote that any mass of people is no different from a field of poppies, they sway whichever way the wind blows.

The Laws of Hope slammed his shield to the ground again, sending chips of stone scattering. The tension of the crowd leaked away and all eyes turned to the bounty hunter. "Representative Shi has spoken his piece. Those of you who wish to enlist can do so on the north road. But the monks have assured me there will be no forced conscription inside the city limits." He turned his steely gaze on Hua Shi. "The laws of Ban Ping stand."

Hua Shi nodded and stepped down from the chair.

The Laws of Hope banged his shield on the ground a third time with a crack like thunder. "Disperse!" No one argued with the bounty hunter, and the crowd thinned as people walked away.

Yuu ducked into the alley alongside the Jasmin Eye toward the rear entrance to the drinking house. Li Bang followed slowly, squinting against the gloom of the alley. "Should I go?" he asked slowly. "If they're conscripting, then they'd take me, even with my poor eyesight."

Yuu shook her head sharply. "No. You're working for me until I say otherwise. After that, you can go and join as many doomed armies as you wish." It was for the fool's own good. The chance he would die in her service was high, but the chance he would die fighting the Cochtans was a certainty.

They slipped into the Jasmin Eye to find it almost empty save for a yawning serving woman and a couple of drunks who likely never left unless they were kicked out. Yuu claimed the table farthest from the entrance, gave Li Bang five lien, and told him to fetch them some drinks. She could feel herself shaking, and the sobriety had left her feeling raw and tender. Her mind wandered through strategies and battle reports she had memorised as a child. The first time the Cochtans invaded Hosa, their desire for war fuelled by their engines, they had attacked Ning province first, establishing a foothold within Hosa. They were following the same pattern, but this time they invaded Shin province first. It made sense. Ning was mostly flatland, easy to navigate and difficult to defend. Shin was mountainous, full of treacherous passes and lethal drops. Any invading army would need to slog up steep mountain paths or scale crumbling cliffs before they could wage an assault, and siege weapons were impossible to transport. It was easily defensible. So it made sense to take Shin first before the Emperor of Ten Kings could raise his armies to defend it. Shin gave the Cochtans a foothold in Hosa they could hold for eternity. They had easy access to Qing province and to Sun Valley, and could bring in supplies with their thopters.

But it was not her fight! Not her war. Yuu pinched herself on the arm. The pain made her wince and focus her mind. It was not her war. She had her own battle to fight, her own strategy to plan. She had to concentrate on Natsuko's contest. She watched the patrons filter in through the main entrance now that the crowd had dispersed. Her fear of seeing the Laws of Hope saunter in was unfounded, as most fear was in her experience. The night waged on, and despite the large crowd that had gathered outside, the Jasmin Eye was far less busy than the night before. Yuu downed her first cup of wine, sighing happily at the bite of it, then poured another and sipped. By now, Natsuko would be playing her own part back in Tianmen, Yuu hoped. It was time to find a thief skilled enough to sneak past the monks and stupid enough to try.

A few subtle enquiries of the nearby patrons turned up one name again and again. Zuan li Fang, a thief of passing notoriety, much of it owing to brazen confessions of every crime he ever committed. Apparently he turned up at the Eye most nights, often closer to morning than not, and more often already stinking drunk. He had a pet fox, a little red beast, mostly tame, that followed him almost everywhere. Yuu remembered seeing the fox the previous morning, but not the master.

There was no mistaking Zuan li Fang when he entered. His fox preceded him, slinking in low to the ground, mismatched eyes scanning the garden, nose twitching. Zuan li Fang walked in as though he owned the place, a confident swagger drawing every eye. "I did it," he all but shouted. "I stole Lady Oolong's jade hairpin. You all said it couldn't be done. Well, I fucking did it!" He grinned victoriously and sauntered over to the nearest table, shooing another man off the bench and claiming his seat. He wore plain black trousers, a matching tunic and red waistcoat with a lotus in black on the back. His hair was short and oiled, and a thick mat of dark stubble graced his chin and cheeks. He was handsome, but knew it, and in Yuu's eyes that lessened the impact. He draped himself over the bench, rather than sat, and waved for wine. In an establishment where patrons were required to fetch their own drinks, Zuan li Fang was the exception.

"He's an idiot," Li Bang said with a deep frown. They had been discussing qi and Yuu was instructing him on feeling the flow of it through his body. He was not getting it. And Yuu kept finding her attention drifting to the flamboyant thief.

"Yes," she said. "He's perfect. Assuming he can actually steal things and not just boast about stealing things."

Li Bang sniffed and closed his eyes again, trying to feel his qi. "I think I got it," he said. "It feels like fire but inside."

Yuu downed the last of her cup of wine and scooped up a fresh bottle. "Keep practising."

She strode over to the table Zuan li Fang had appropriated, keeping her eyes on him. His little red fox watched her approach. It was curled up by his feet and didn't move. Yuu sat down on the bench opposite Zuan li Fang, forcing a smaller man to scootch over to make room. She placed the wine bottle on the table between them and waited until he looked at her. "You're a thief?" she asked as casually as she could.

Zuan li Fang laughed and looked around the table, some of the others joined in, though it looked like they had no idea what they were laughing at. "Lady, *I* am the Prince of Thieves." He raised his hands as though accepting adulation. No one applauded. "The great Fang, Lord of the Night. Thief of gold, jewels, trinkets…" He leaned forward, smiled, and winked at her. "And hearts." He held her stare for a long while, his eyes darting about as though searching her face. "Has anyone ever told you, you are beautiful?"

Yuu snorted. "Only liars and one long dead prince."

Zuan li Fang held up a two fingers. "Two princes now."

Yuu shrugged. "I was counting you in the first category."

He leaned back and clutched at his chest. "You wound me." He grinned. "I like it. The name's Zuan li Fang, but my friends—" he paused again and grinned at her "—and my lovers— call me Fang. And you are?"

"Yuu."

"Nah," Fang rubbed at his stubble. "You don't look Ipian. I'm going to call you Ling."

Panic crashed over Yuu like thunder. Could this thief know her real name was Daiyu Lingsen? Or was it just a coincidence? Ling was a common enough name, she supposed. But what if he knew?

The thief frowned. Had he expected a witty retort, a continuation of their banter? Yes. He had no idea who she was, he was just trying to flirt, and now Yuu was making him suspicious by acting suspicious herself. She grabbed the bottle of wine she had brought as a way to stall the conversation. There were no cups around, so she swigged straight from the bottle, pouring as much wine down her chin as into her mouth. If Fang wasn't suspicious before, he certainly would be now.

"I like a girl who's not afraid to get messy," he said, taking hold of the bottle and swigging from it himself.

Yuu was done being playful. She wiped her chin with her sleeve. "I have a job," she said. "I need a skilled thief to do it, and I hear you're the best." Nothing like a bit of flattery to get things started. Men like Fang lived through their egos. *Knowing your opponent is the first step to winning any battle*, her grandmother used to say. *When you know what moves a man, you can move him to distraction. When you know what drives a man, you can drive him to victory. When you know what scares a man, you can scare him to madness. When you know all three, you will know how to destroy him.* Fang was clearly a man driven by his ego, willing to fluff himself when no one else would. He would be simple enough to manipulate. A bit of flattery, the temptation of a challenge that would put his name in the history books, and he'd do anything.

Fang's demeanour changed instantly. His smile vanished and he leaned over the table toward her. Yuu noticed his hands were gloved in supple brown suede, thin enough that he could feel through the fabric. "You heard right. They don't call me the Prince of Thieves for nothing."

"Prove it," Yuu said. "You claim you stole a jade hairpin. Where is it?"

Fang smiled again, but it was not the flirtatious smile; it was a self-assured grin. "You're new to Ban Ping." He rolled his eyes over her seeming to take in every detail and came to rest on her right hand. The hand where the goddess' contract was scrawled. Yuu tucked the hand away into her sleeve. "Let me explain how things work in this here city," Fang continued. "The laws here aren't like the laws in the rest of Hosa. For a crime to be punishable there must be proof. Simply knowing who did it is not enough. The monks would never act upon it, especially if the suspected criminal is sanctioned by Yi Temple. I confess. I stole Lady Oolong's jade hairpin. I've stolen from every major lord and lady in the city. I've stolen from merchants and from peasants. I confess to every crime ever committed within the city limits or without. But if there's no proof, there's nothing anyone can do about it. So maybe I could produce the jade hairpin and give you proof I am as good as I say I am, but then I'd also be providing you with proof of the crime. For all I know you're a bounty hunter come to collect on the great Fang." He leaned back, grinning, and the little fox leapt up onto the bench next to him and sat, staring at Yuu with accusing gold and green eyes.

"How could there be a bounty on you, if there is no proof you've committed a crime?" Yuu asked. She knew the rules about posting bounties. She knew because there *was* proof of her crime. The body of the Steel Prince rotting in his old camp. The body of the impostor that the Art of War had sent to battle in his place. The royal family of Qing needed no more proof to post their bounty.

"Well, there isn't actually a bounty on me," Fang admitted.

"So there's no proof of a crime, but also no proof that you're a thief without peer?" Yuu shrugged. "Perhaps I should find the King of Thieves instead."

Fang chuckled. "You're smarter than the usual lot we get in here," he leaned forward again and lowered his voice. "I'm listening. Why do you need a thief?"

Yuu brushed hair out of her face and tucked it behind her ear, lowering her voice to match his. "Have you ever stolen from the monks?"

Fang snorted. "Of course not. No one steals from the monks."

"Why not?"

"You don't bite the hand that feeds you, lady." Fang shook his head. "Truth is, the monks' strict adherence to the idea of *no proof no crime* is a protection for those of us in my profession. We pay the Temple of Yi a cut to sanction us as purveyors of rare goods, and they look the other way when some lord or lady says we're guilty of whatever we are almost certainly guilty of. They protect us from retribution as long as we're good enough not to get caught. But steal from the monks themselves? Do that, and no donation to the Yi Temple will stop them bringing their full monkish fury down on you. I know they look peaceful with their robes and blessings, but that's a show, lady. The monks here mean business and those who know anything know this rule above all others — don't fuck with the monks."

"Ah," Yuu said with feigned sadness. She had already stroked his ego and now it was time to challenge it. "You really aren't the man I thought you were." She shuffled to the edge of the bench and stood.

Fang lurched forward and caught hold of Yuu's right hand. He stared at the writing scrawled over her flesh. He had such a light, delicate touch. She pulled her hand free and hid it inside her robes again.

"Sit down," Fang said. "Please."

Yuu slid back onto the bench and waited. Fang swigged straight out of her wine bottle again and leaned over the table. "What sort of job are we talking about exactly?"

Yuu leaned forward herself, hands resting on the table, close enough to smell his wine scented breath. "The sort of job that involves making a pilgrimage up the mountain and coming down a very rich man."

Fang lowered his voice to a conspiratorial whisper. "You want to steal something from the temples?" A grin spread slowly across his face. "I assume you have a plan?"

Yuu did have a plan. She just wished she had a better plan.

Chapter 9

Natsuko bounced along the halls of Tianmen, enjoying the freedom and vigour of youth again. The problem with wearing her old woman's aspect, was that she had to act like an elder. No one expected an ancient crone to start skipping along and rejoicing in the way the breeze fluttered her hair, so seeing it made them suspicious. Worse still, it tended to make mortals angry, as if it were somehow an affront to them that an old woman might take joy in the simple act of being alive while they could not. Humans were unfathomable creatures. But that is what made them so much fun. Besides, she quite enjoyed playing at being the old woman occasionally. Being the curmudgeon was oddly liberating.

Her part of the Art of War's plan was done, whatever that plan was. She had bragged to every god who would listen, and a few who would not, that she had secured the services of the famed strategist, the Art of War, as her champion. The news had rightly caused a bit of a stir. Even the most ignorant of gods had heard of the Art of War. How could they not? Some even foolishly believed the strategist was immortal, no different than the Ticking Clock. They had both fought in the old Cochtan-Hosan wars, after all. The truth was rather more pedestrian, but truth often was. That was why so many people preferred to believe the fiction — it was more fun. But in this case, it really did not matter what anyone believed.

One moment Natsuko was skipping through gilded halls surrounded by clouds, carefree as only a child could be; the next she was trudging along, weighed down by countless years and loose, sagging skin as she stepped out of the shadows onto the streets of Ban Ping in front of the Jasmin Eye, a disastrously human establishment. It lacked any semblance of grace or artistry, but did exactly what it set out to do, got people drunk and gave a space to those with nowhere else to go. A haven for the forgotten and for those who wished to be forgotten. No wonder her champion had chosen to make it home.

It was early in the day and the garden was empty save for those too drunk to leave. Quite why they called it the garden was a mystery to Natsuko. There were no flowers, the grass was patchy in most places and covered over with mouldy wooden floorboards in others, and the benches were full of drunks snoring their lives away. A garden by virtue of simply not having a roof. The Lump was sitting cross-legged on the floor, his eyes screwed shut and his palms held out and up before him. As Natsuko approached, she heard him making a strange sound, as though he were humming to himself. Her champion was nowhere in sight, but she was close, Natsuko could feel it.

She sat down opposite the Lump and stared at him for a moment. He seemed utterly oblivious to the world around him. Natsuko kicked him in the shin.

"Argh!" The Lump opened his eyes. He squinted for a moment against the light and stared at Natsuko until recognition dawned. He rubbed his leg and frowned at her. "What was that for?"

Natsuko shrugged. It was no more appropriate for mortals to demand answers from the gods, than it was appropriate for gods to supply answers to mortals. "What were you doing?"

"Practising my qi," the Lump said.

Natsuko cackled. "Idiot Lump. You do not practice qi. You train with it. Learn to feel it, to use it, to strengthen it."

"That," the Lump said with a nod that set his flabby cheeks jiggling. "I'm doing that."

"Why?"

The Lump looked down at his hands. "I want to be a hero. Can't be a hero without a technique."

Again, Natsuko cackled. The fool honestly believed he could develop a technique just by wanting it hard enough. "You really are a foolish lump."

"And you really are a bitch," the Lump said. "Goddess or not."

She reached out and patted him on his leg. "You have no idea. Where is my champion?"

The Lump grimaced and nodded up at the Jasmin Eye's second-storey balcony where the rooms were. He said nothing else but went back to *practising his qi* with a frown on his face. So Natsuko decided to meditate with him. He might never know how lucky he was to have spent such peaceful time so close to a god. Humans were so simple she envied them.

When her champion finally roused herself and made an appearance, she was not alone. Yuu opened the door on the second floor and staggered out onto the balcony that overlooked the garden. While she yawned and stretched, a young man walked out behind her. He was handsome enough for a mortal, full of a confidence that the world and the gods had yet to beat out of him. He placed a hand on the small of Yuu's back, but she shrugged away from him and made for the stairs.

Natsuko sniffed. There was an odd scent on the air, something she could not quite place. She followed her nose and found a small red fox near the far corner of the garden. It leapt up onto a table, heedless of the sleeping fool drooling onto the wood, and sat. Then it shoved its muzzle into a cup and lapped at whatever drink was souring there.

Yuu brushed away Fang's fawning attempts at contact and focused her attention on Natsuko. The goddess had returned; now all the pieces were in place. She made her way to the ground floor, the thief she had so recently bedded stumbling behind her with none of the bluster he'd shown the night before. Perhaps he thought there was more to their encounter than she did. The truth was they were drunk, he was handsome, and Yuu gave herself as much chance of dying as succeeding with her plan. If she was going to die, then at least she should have a good night before she did. And it had been a good night.

Natsuko grinned at Yuu as she joined her and Li Bang in the garden. It was not the inhuman smile of the god, but a knowing smile nonetheless. Fang sat down on the nearby bench, and Natsuko cocked an eyebrow at him. "Who is the new boy?" she asked.

"Boy?" Fang asked with a snort. "I think you'll find I proved myself a man well enough."

Natsuko glanced at Yuu.

Yuu considered the unspoken question for a moment and then shrugged. "Well enough, I suppose. Lots of enthusiasm at the very least."

Fang frowned and glared at the goddess. "And just who are you, grandmother?"

Natsuko turned her god smile on the thief. "I'm the one with the money, dear. So respect your elders."

"Speaking of money," Fang said, tapping the table with a single finger in a pattern Yuu couldn't quite grasp. "We, uh, got distracted before we actually discussed pay for this insane plan of yours… which you also didn't describe in any detail."

"Too busy, were you?" Natsuko asked.

"Fifty lien," Yuu said. It was a small amount really, but she had no idea how much a thief would actually want for the job and nor did she know how much money the goddess could conjure at will.

Fang snorted. "For going against the monks?" he said in a whisper. "A hundred lien."

"Done," Yuu said, glad that part of the discussion was over.

"Really?" Fang asked. He narrowed his eyes at Natsuko. "Where are you hiding the coins, grandmother?"

"Nowhere you will ever get your pinchy little fingers." Natsuko slapped a hand on the table and when she raised it a stack of twenty lien was there. "Just a little taste of Lord Fung Na's lost fortune."

Fang leaned forward and snatched the coins up. "Why are they wet?"

"Because his ship sank," Natsuko said. "All hands were lost along with his treasure. His sons and grandsons have been searching for the wreck for generations." She grinned that god grin again. "But they're looking in the wrong places."

Fang stared at her as he leaned back and pocketed the lien. "Riiiight. I'll still need eighty more."

"So, what's the plan?" Natsuko asked.

Yuu sighed. This was it. Time to lie to them. The pieces never needed to know the strategy, only the parts they needed to play. Otherwise, they might realise when they were being sacrificed to win the game. "It's actually quite simple. Li Bang and Fang will enter the Ryoko Temple and proceed to the second floor to *pray* to Ryoko. You'll wait there until the monks leave. Then you proceed to the third floor, find the lantern and steal it. Simple."

"Why do I need him?" Fang asked with a sidelong glance at Li Bang.

"Because there may be a few monks on the third floor, and you might need someone to beat the crap out of them," Yuu said.

"Not very heroic, beating up monks," Li Bang said.

"Sorry." Yuu patted him on the shoulder. "If it helps, they're actually all thugs running the greatest protection racket the world has ever seen."

Li Bang opened his eyes and sighed. "It doesn't. And why do I need him?"

"Because there's a good chance the lantern will be kept under lock and key, and it might require a thief's touch to open it. Without knowing exactly where it's being kept, I need to plan for as many situations as possible with as few resources as possible."

"How are you going to empty the temple?" Fang asked. "I've been up there, and it's filled with monks all praying to the stars or just standing around looking all menacing and monk-y."

"I'm going to cause a distraction," Yuu said.

"What type of distraction?"

Yuu sighed and stared up at the bright blue sky and the wispy white clouds drifting across it. "The type that will draw every monk on the mountain top out of the temples and into the open. Once it's done, you and Li Bang will take the lantern down the mountain and wait for me at the western entrance to Ban Ping. You'll get the rest of your pay, I'll get the lantern, and then I'll leave this corrupt city and its false faith as far behind as I can."

Chapter 10

Yuu sent Li Bang and Fang on ahead. She was certain the two wouldn't get along, but it shouldn't matter. They didn't need to be friends as long as they did their job, and Li Bang seemed the sort of man who could put aside differences for the cause. She respected that. It took someone of surpassing integrity to let insult slide, especially when he had the strength to do something about it. Of course, Li Bang also seemed determined to have his name in the hero books. A valiant dream to chase, but one that could easily be corrupted in the wrong hands. Yuu glanced down at her hand, tattooed with the goddess' contract, and the sentiment rang all too true.

By the time Yuu and Natsuko reached the top of the mountain, the sun was past its zenith and slogging towards the horizon. Two armed monks waited for them as expected and demanded four lien per person for entry. It did not escape Yuu's notice that it was more than the day before, and she wagered they were lining their own pockets as well as the temples.

Natsuko said little on their climb, but now that they were at the temple, she looked like she had much to say. "Now what?" she asked once they were out of earshot. "You still have not told me how you intend to distract these bloody monks." There were close to fifty of the robed figures training on the plateau and another hundred or so in prayer. Yuu wagered there would be another hundred in the various temples. Two hundred and fifty monks, if they were lucky. It was an army. A well-armed, well-trained army.

"I need you to do me a favour, Natsuko," Yuu said.

"I cannot help you," the goddess snapped. "I told you before. I cannot assist you in obtaining any of the artefacts. It is against the rules. In fact, it is *the* rule."

Yuu smiled. There was always something fun about subverting the rules of the game. She remembered a time with her grandmother, sitting around outside of the house while her adopted family worked the fields for the magistrate. Some glared at her in anger, others in envy that she was so favoured by their grandmother. None of them liked her. None of them were kind to her. Yuu had lost focus and winced at the pain as she focused on the game her grandmother was playing, the lesson she was trying to teach. There were three cups and one ball, a simple game with simple rules. Her grandmother placed the ball under one cup, then whisked the cups about slowly, telling Yuu to keep her eye on the ball. A simple game with simple rules. Except it wasn't. Yuu tried to pick the cup with the ball underneath it, and when her grandmother raised the cup, the ball was not there. Yuu winced at the pain of the loss. Her grandmother would snap at her to *focus on the lessons*. They tried again. Yuu concentrated intensely on the cup with the ball, letting the world around her fade to almost nothing, a background haze and muted hum. All that mattered was that she followed the cup, saw through her grandmother's trick, and found the ball. She was sure she'd found it this time. Her grandmother lifted the cup and — no ball. Yuu rubbed the sudden pain from her shin. She had to focus harder. They tried again. She failed again. She always failed and her grandmother was never pleased. That was what her adopted brothers and sisters did not understand. She was favoured by their grandmother, but she disappointed her too often. They tried once more at the game, and Yuu failed again. She couldn't understand it. She had followed the correct cup, all her attention bent upon it. Frustrated, Yuu knocked over the other two cups and found them all empty. The ball was nowhere to be seen. The lesson was one Yuu learnt and remembered for the pain of its losses. The best way to win a game, any game, was to know the rules. Once you did, you knew not only how the game was played, but how those rules could be exploited. Her grandmother had said, "*break the rules within the rules.*" Yuu winced again at the memory.

"Should I assume you also cannot directly hinder another god's champion?" Yuu asked.

Natsuko grumbled and nodded.

"Is there anything in the rules about hindering your own champion?"

The goddess barked out a laugh. A couple of nearby supplicants praying at a shrine glanced their way, but quickly went back to their worship. "Of course not. Why would anyone hinder their own champion? You don't win a race by stabbing your horse in the leg."

"Good," Yuu said. This was it. This was everything she had been running from for the past five years. All the lies she had woven and the identity she had forged, she was about to bring it all crashing down around her. She had to steel herself with a deep breath and even then her voice trembled. "Go back down the mountain. The quick way. Head to the temple of law. Tell everyone who will listen, the Art of War is at the temples of the stars. Specifically, make sure the Laws of Hope hears you."

"Are you mad?" Natsuko asked. "He will arrest you. Or maybe just kill you if he's in the mood."

Yuu nodded. "I'm hoping he'll try. For four thousand lien, I'm hoping he and every other bounty hunter in the city will flock here as fast as they can. They might even get here in time."

Natsuko just stared at Yuu, her mouth hanging open slightly. Yuu was somewhat pleased to know how easily she could confuse a god. "You know it is not your fault, right?" Natsuko asked with a deep frown that pulled all her skin into such a collision of wrinkles that she seemed beyond ancient. "You did not kill the Steel Prince. You do not have to atone for his death."

The goddess was wrong there. Yuu might not have actually struck him down, but it had been her decisions that put him in harm's way. And Daiyu Lingsen had done something far worse than just murder her prince. She killed the Steel Prince's name and legacy. She put another man in his armour to lead the prince's army. Because of her, the Steel Prince, a truly just hero, would forever be known as an impostor. A fake. A charlatan. Yuu knew she deserved the justice the royal family of Qing demanded. She deserved it not for the murder of the prince, nor for the insult to the royal family. She deserved it for killing his legacy. For tarnishing his name, the name of the man she loved.

"I don't intend to die here today, Natsuko," Yuu said, wondering if it was a lie even as the words passed her lips. "I intend to leave this mountaintop with a second artefact and a way out of the city that no one will be able to follow. But I need you to trust me and do your part. Head down to the city and tell everyone who will listen that the most wanted criminal in all Hosa is here."

Natsuko drew in a deep breath, then shook her head and started walking towards the mountain stairs. "I really do know how to pick them." She passed behind a shrine and was gone.

Yuu strolled along the tiled stone of the plateau to the where the monks were praying out in the open and found a spot out of the way of those on pilgrimage to the temples. A few of the monks paused in their prayers to give her a look, likely unused to people joining them out in the open. That was what the temples were for, after all. Yuu ignored them and knelt on a prayer mat in the centre of one slab of stone. She pulled out the two sticks of incense, one from today and one from the day before, wedged them between two small cracks in the stone, and lit them. Then she pulled out her carving knife and block of wood and started on a new chess piece. This one would take the place of the Shintei, a rock, a fortress as strong as the earth but rigid in its movements. A powerful piece, but difficult to deploy without the skill and knowledge of how best to use it. Wood shavings scattered around her, taken by the breeze and blown across the plateau. Some caught in the folds of the monks' robes; others nestled into cracks that snaked their way through some of the stone tiles. The wooden block started to take shape. A large man, rotund but strong, with a scraggly mane of hair, a chui in one hand, the haft resting upon his shoulder. Hours passed, but no one ever said justice was swift, and not even heroes could defy gravity. Villains, it seemed, were another matter.

The whirring buzz of a thopter in Yuu's ears drowned out the drone of the monks' prayers. Her hands trembled and she fumbled the carving, accidentally gouging out a piece of its ample belly and burying a splinter of wood in her thumb. She whisked both carving and knife into the folds of her robes and stuck her thumb in her mouth, sucking at the little wound. The tourists on the plateau had all stopped to watch the thopter hover overhead. Even the monks at martial practice and devoted prayer stopped to gawk at the wondrous machine. It was not often one got to see humans bend the laws of nature with a mechanical engine. It was a wood-and-metal contraption about the size of two oxen with a plow attached, with six fan-shaped blades turning in unison to keep it aloft. A figure was leaning out of the thopter, the last rays of the waning sun glinting off glass goggles. Yuu felt herself trembling with fear. The Ticking Clock had come to kill her.

Part of the plan or not, it really didn't matter. Yuu didn't want to die. And the assassin could be here for no other reason. The thopter started descending, far faster than Yuu would have thought safe. Monks scattered as the engine landed at the centre of their training area. The thopter blades slowed, and the Ticking Clock stepped down from the engine's pilot compartment. He was tall and slim, wearing tailored grey trousers, a black waistcoat over a white shirt, and a long brown coat that draped to his knees. Unmistakably Cochtan. He wore boots and gloves, and a gilded mask with two shiny glass goggles for his eyes. There was no opening in his mask for mouth or nose. It was as featureless as the Art of War's had been, though her mask had been white and made of ivory and his was black iron and gold. No skin, Yuu realised.

Not a patch of skin showed anywhere on his body. The Ticking Clock hid whatever humanity he had left.

Yuu stood and stretched the knots out of her back. She would not be killed on her knees; she would face it on her feet. She had to admit, though, it would be nice if her knees would stop shaking.

"I have come for the Art of War." The Ticking Clock's voice was tinny, like the ring of a struck gong fading away. He took a step forward and looked around at the gathered monks. He moved like a bird, even the smallest movement a sudden jerk. There was no fluidity to the man, no smooth edges, no life. As he stepped forward, his coattail billowed in the wind. Yuu saw a long, thin sword buckled to his waist and small pistols holstered on either side of his hip. Ranged weaponry. More accurate and with greater range than any bow, but far slower to load and shoot.

One of the monks, an elderly woman who had been leading the wushu practice, stepped forward. She was wrinkled but matched the Ticking Clock for height and, despite her age, had arms any smith would be proud of. "You are not permitted here, Cochtan," the monk said. "This is a place for worship of the stars. Your engines have no place here. Please, I must ask you to leave."

The Ticking Clock ignored the monk. His head continued to move in small jerky motions as he looked at each of the monks. Then his goggles turned toward Yuu, and her breath caught in her throat. The Ticking Clock stared straight at her. Somehow, he knew. She couldn't fathom how he knew, but he knew.

They were all of them nothing but pieces in a never-ending game. Yuu and the Ticking Clock were pawns in the game the gods played. And the monks were in turn pieces in a game being played by Yuu and the Ticking Clock, whether the assassin realised it or not. Whether they all realised it or not. And it was time for the pieces to be sacrificed for the win.

Yuu focused on a wood shaving clinging to the crack in a flagstone near the monks and activated it. A spire of crumbling rock erupted from the earth to the left of the Ticking Clock. The assassin's hand shot out in a blur of motion, and the elderly monk's head tumbled off her shoulders in a fountain of blood and gore. The plateau erupted into a glorious distraction.

Chapter 11

The Ticking Clock snatched a dagger from inside his coat and threw it at Yuu. Yuu focused on a wood shaving trapped against a small stone on the plateau floor, and a shard of crumbling rock jutted up in front of her. The dagger shattered it and hit Yuu's hip, tangling in her robes. Yuu felt a sharp pain where the razor-sharp blade nicked her skin. She pulled the knife out of her robes to find it stained red.

Even as the elderly monk's headless body hit the floor, the other monks closed in and a furious melee began on the plateau.

A hulking monk swung a heavy staff at the Ticking Clock's head. He blocked the blow with one arm and the clang of wood striking metal echoed off the shrines. He brought his other arm around, drawing his jian, and sliced the staff in two, then pivoted toward the monk and stabbed him in the gut, punching his arm back and forth in a blur of motion. The hulking monk crumbled to the ground and curled into a ball, twitching and bleeding out. The Ticking Clock took another step toward Yuu.

Two more monks ran at him, one with a pair of short blades, and the other with sword. The short knives clanked against his metal chest, barely cutting his tunic. He dodged the sword thrust and clamped a hand down on the blade, his grip shattering the metal. The assassin caught a falling shard and slit one monk's throat then buried the shard in the other monk's eye. He took another step toward Yuu.

Monks charged the Ticking Clock. He weathered some blows, blocked others, and edged around more. He moved like a puppet with half its strings cut, his limbs bending back upon themselves, his torso whirling completely independent of his legs. A dozen monks fell around him, throats cut, stab wounds bleeding, necks broken. And still the Ticking Clock took step after step toward Yuu. First twenty steps away, then fifteen, now ten.

Yuu staggered back and almost tripped over her own feet. She had underestimated the assassin, miscalculated his prowess, and now he was going to kill her.

Another dozen monks fell to the Ticking Clock's relentless, methodical savagery. The plateau ran red, blood flowing through cracks and crevices in the rock. Yuu had not expected the cost to be so high. She stepped back as the assassin approached. A holding pattern, staying one step ahead of the enemy. Too frightened to strike back. This was how people lost games, when they stopped considering how to win and bent all their thought and energy on simply not losing. At which point, they had already lost whether they knew it or not. But Yuu had no other choice. All she could do was play for time and hope.

Despite their losses, monks poured from the surrounding temples. This was what Yuu had planned on. She just hoped the Temple of Ryoko would be clear enough for Fang and Li Bang to make their move. She had done her part; now all she needed to do was survive long enough to escape. It sounded so easy when she put it like that. When she ignored the cost the monks were paying for her. *They are numbers. Not people.* Her grandmother's words. Yuu flinched at the pain of them.

The Ticking Clock skewered a snarling monk through the gut, pulled out his dripping jian, and continued toward Yuu. He was just eight paces from her now, so close Yuu could hear his joints clicking as he moved. The Steel Prince had once told Daiyu Lingsen that the monks of Ban Ping were a martial force to be reckoned with. That their participation might have changed the outcome of the war. But they were nothing to this Cochtan assassin. The Ticking Clock was a one-man army. And the monks realised it too. Their attacks faltered and Yuu saw some of the robed figures running for the safety of their temples, others stepping back and dropping their weapons. She could hardly blame them for their cowardice

Yuu felt for her wood shavings and activated one. A stalagmite thrust out of the ground to the right of the Ticking Clock. The assassin leapt, placed a hand on the rock, and flipped over it, landing unharmed on the other side. Yuu activated another shaving. This time the assassin casually backhanded the rock, shattering it to dust. Yuu thrust hands into her robes, searching for something, anything that could help. All she had were a couple of half-formed chess pieces, two knives that would never pierce his metal hide, and her grandmother's Pawn. The one she had lost and Natsuko had returned. But she couldn't use that. If she animated that piece and the Ticking Clock destroyed it, she would lose it all over again. She couldn't. It was her last memento of her grandmother. Yuu winced as the inevitability of loss dawned on her.

She had lost. Despite all her planning, she had lost. *The Art of War does not lose.* The Art of War never loses, always has another card to play, another piece to sacrifice, another plan already in motion! The Art of War *never* lost. A lesson delivered in pain. Yuu realised she was pinching her arm, fingernails digging into the soft flesh of her bicep. Hard enough to bruise. Hard enough to draw blood. Hard enough to remind her that losing was not acceptable unless it was part of the plan. That winning was all that mattered. All that ever mattered. *Focus on the lessons.*

Yuu took another step back and her foot hit something hard. She tripped and sprawled backwards, landing on her arse with a yelp. The Ticking Clock paused. There were no monks between them now. Some robed figures were standing nearby, weapons ready, but not moving. Her pieces had failed her.

"You are the Art of War," the Ticking Clock said in a voice like a broken flute. "Hand over your artefacts."

It did not escape Yuu's notice that he did not offer to let her live. She scrabbled to her knees and tried to stand, but her legs had no strength left. Nevertheless, she forced a grim smile to her lips. "You'll have to take them from my..."

The Ticking Clock reached down quick as a lightning strike and drew both his pistols. He aimed them at Yuu and pulled the triggers.

The weapons flashed and Yuu's vision went grey.

A moment later she realised she wasn't dead. The grey blur resolved into the back of a man wearing white ceramic armour and carrying a grotesquely oversized shield. Her final piece had arrived just in time. The Laws of Hope had protected her from the shots, saving her. And now as he held up his shield, sheltering them both, he smiled at her. "Daiyu Lingsen, I assume?"

Yuu almost nodded. Then her brain kicked in and she realised that was the last thing she should do. The Laws of Hope chuckled and shook his head. He reached out a hand and gently snapped something around Yuu's left wrist. Then he stood up to his full height, still sheltered behind his massive shield, and stared down at her, the smile still on his lips. "Daiyu Lingsen, the criminal known as the Art of War. You are under arrest for the murder of the Steel Prince. I claim your bounty and will protect you until such time as you are delivered to the authorities of Qing to face justice for your crime." He lowered his voice for her alone. "Please don't run. The authorities of Qing care not whether you're alive or dead as long as you are delivered, but I hate getting blood on my armour." He said it so sincerely Yuu almost believed him.

She looked down at her wrist. An iron manacle attached to a chain, leading to a metal ball the size of her head on the ground. She tugged on it a little, but it weighed enough to crack the stone beneath it. There was no chance she was moving it. She could hardly believe the bounty hunter had moved it.

The Laws of Hope turned, showing her his back, and faced the assassin. "Cochtan citizen known as the Ticking Clock," he said in a loud voice. "There is no bounty on you. Leave."

A gangly monk with no chin stepped toward the bounty hunter. "The Temple of Fenwong places a bounty of one thousand lien on the criminal the Ticking Clock."

The Laws of Hope glanced at the monk. "I don't work for free, monk."

"The Temple of Ryoko matches the bounty," said another monk who was clutching at a broken arm. Yet another stepped forward proffering a matching bounty from the Temple of Lili. Within moments the Ticking Clock had gone from no bounty to five thousand lien. Yuu had to admit it was a both annoying and reassuring that his bounty now exceeded hers.

The Laws of Hope smiled and reached for his sword with his left hand. "Cochtan criminal known as the Ticking Clock," he called out, the smile evident in his tone. "I hereby claim your bounty."

Chapter 12

Li's back ached from sitting in prayer position for so long. His gut rested on the mat below him and his knees were on fire from being bent beneath him for so long. Yuu told him to come and pretend to pray, but she hadn't said it would take so achingly long. He groaned, then clenched his teeth to stop any other noise from escaping. A glance to his left showed the thief, Fang, was asleep. Slumped over in something vaguely resembling prayer position, his eyes were closed and a thin string of drool leaked from his open mouth and pooled on the mat. How he could be comfortable enough to sleep was a mystery to Li. Some people had all the luck: skill, looks, a body that didn't ache like swords were jabbing into his bones.

There was some shouting outside, vague noises without form or meaning. Li hoped it was Yuu's distraction. By the stars, he hoped it was the distraction. Actually, he was now fairly certain that belief in the stars was false worship if what Yuu and Natsuko said was true. So, he decided to pray to the gods instead. Unfortunately, he only knew the name of one god, and she was an ancient bitch. Still, she was a god, so Li prayed to Natsuko, the god of the lost, that the noise outside was the distraction *finally* taking place. Because if he didn't move soon, he might never move again. Minutes passed. Agonising minutes. Or maybe it was only seconds, really. It was difficult to tell when he focused on it. The shouting outside continued, and Li tried to ignore the pain in his back and knees, and focus on the noise. He felt his qi flowing throughout his body. Now that he knew how to look for it, he could feel it so strongly. Li's vision doubled and for just a moment he was staring into the prayer room, and he was also outside, watching Yuu stand frozen in place while a clockwork man slaughtered monks. Then it was gone, leaving him wondering if it had been real or a delusion brought about by the cramps torturing his thighs.

Footsteps pounded on the stairs and a breathless monk appeared. "We need help outside," the monk shouted. "A Cochtan is attacking us."

A few of the praying monks exchanged glances, then all ran for the stairs down to the first level. One of the guards at the ascending stairs left as well. So too, did the two praying civilians, drawn by the promise of a spectacle. That left only Li, one guard standing at the stairs, and Fang, still snoring softly in a patch of his own drool.

Li uncoiled and felt his back crack like bamboo bent too far. His knees popped, and relief and pain mixed into something akin to having his feet licked by the puppy he'd had as a... He shook the thought from his head. He would have loved nothing more than to take a minute or two to let his body adjust and relax, but they had no idea how long Yuu could keep up the distraction. He shuffled over to Fang and nudged him with the toe of his boot. A loud snore escaped his lips.

"Wake up," Li said, nudging him again. Another snore ripped through the silence of the temple, so loud the guard glanced their way. Li was just about to try again when he saw Fang's eye open and fixed on him. The thief winked, then produced another echoing snore.

Li walked over to the monk. "My friend won't wake up," he said as he approached.

The monk frowned and glanced at Fang. "What do you want me to do about it?"

Li shrugged. He was no good at lying and hated having to do it. Luckily, he was close enough to drop the act, and though lying made his skin crawl, knocking the heads of criminal monks did not. He leapt at the monk and grabbed his arms, then head-butted him with such force he heard the monk's nose break even as he felt the warm spray of blood across his face. The monk swayed on his feet, his eyes rolled back in his head, and Li let him fall to the floor.

"Good work, little brother," Fang said as he uncoiled nimbly. "I never doubted you for a moment."

Li shrugged. He liked the thief, the way he was so generous with his compliments. They had spent a few hours together walking up the mountain, and Fang hadn't mocked Li's struggle up the stairs even once. He wasn't too sure about the nicknames though.

Fang stormed past Li and up the stairs. "Time to go to work," said the thief. "My considerable skills, all to steal a lantern. Tales may not be sung of this, but you can be sure I will embellish it. Don't worry, little brother, in my telling you will defeat a hundred monks."

The third floor of the temple was dimly lit. Li squinted, but he could barely make out anything but a few patches of light in the murky darkness. There were no windows, and the candles the monks were burning flickered listlessly, giving off no real light. He took a couple of steps into the darkness, then turned back and stared back down the stairs to the second floor. The brightly lit prayer room looked so inviting.

"Well this is certainly a treasure trove," Fang said from somewhere in the darkness. "And if I knew what I was looking at, I could probably make a fortune."

"We're just here for the lantern," Li said, trying to make out the thief. There was no sense taking anything else. They were here because Yuu and Natsuko needed the lantern for some reason. He hadn't bothered to ask why. No doubt it was something to do with the gods and heroes.

"Uh huh," Fang said. "Lots of scrolls on this desk. Numbers, numbers, more numbers. Oh!" Li heard the rustle of parchment. "This one is a poem." Fang laughed. "It's awful."

The thief cleared his throat. "*By moonlight I watch the light in your eyes. Fair brother your hair is like oiled steel. We dance, we dance, we dance. To feel your arms is to feel my own.*" He chuckled.

"We're not here to read bad poetry!" Li hissed. Although he had to admit, he quite liked it.

"There is always time to read bad poetry, little brother. It's the good stuff that's a complete waste of... Ah ha! A safe. No point in having a safe unless you have something to put in it. That's the first rule in the *Great Fang's Book of Stealing Shit.*"

"You don't have a book," Li said.

"I could have a book!" Fang sounded truly wounded by the accusation. "Some enterprising young scholar could have heard of my great deeds and sought me out to chronicle my life and my advice. A role model to budding thieves. You don't know. Have you read every book?"

"You don't have a book!" Li insisted.

"No, you're right," Fang admitted. "It was adapted into a play instead."

Li sighed. "Can you open the safe?"

"Can I..." Fang laughed. "I am the Great Fang, Prince of Thieves." He sighed. "I'll certainly try my best."

Li heard the thief grunt and then grumble something, then heard some clicking noises. In the darkness Li could see none of it, so he kept watch on the stairs in case anyone came up to check on the monk they had incapacitated. His heart raced and his skin felt clammy. Nerves and... something else. Something he couldn't place. He breathed out a steadying breath and focused on his qi again, hoping it would calm him.

Again, his vision doubled. He was staring down the stairs at an unconscious monk leaking crimson onto the floor from what used to be his nose. He was also outside, under the stars, watching the Ticking Clock advance on Yuu while the monks stood by and watched. The assassin drew something from under his coat. There was a flash, and then the Laws of Hope was there, sheltering Yuu with his shield. He snapped a manacle around her wrist, then turned to face the Ticking Clock.

Li blinked away his double vision and turned back to the gloom of the temple. "Yuu is in trouble," he said, not sure where to look.

Fang cursed. "Wonderful. I really need to concentrate on this."

"But she needs help," Li said. She was caught between an immortal assassin and a legendary bounty hunter and both wanted her dead or in custody. And if his vision was true, the Laws of Hope had chained Yuu to a metal ball she had no hope of moving.

"So, go help her," Fang snapped. "But unless you want it all to be for nothing, leave me the fuck alone to get this damned safe open. Wait! I've got it. No. No, I don't."

Li had no idea what to do. He was not good at making these sorts of decisions. That was why he always worked with others, why he tried to join the army. Making decisions like this, with lives on the line, was just too confusing. Yuu told him to stay with Fang in case the thief needed help. But Yuu was in trouble and needed help. So, he had to help her. It seemed to make sense.

"I'm going," Li said.

Fang sighed loudly. "Great. Go!"

Li started down the stairs, past the unconscious monk. He felt for his qi as he went, trying to summon up the visions like he had before, to check on Yuu and see how she was faring. He had almost reached the temple door when his vision doubled again. This time it was not Yuu he saw, but Fang. The thief was running down the stairs to the second floor of the temple holding an ornate lantern with dragons curling around its edges in his hand. He turned away from the stairs down to the first floor and ran instead to the window at the rear of the temple. He was taking the lantern and running. Li's vision faded and he was staring at the temple door. He had another decision to make. Did he go back and stop

Fang from taking the lantern? Or did he help Yuu escape? Being a hero was very complicated.

The Ticking Clock charged the Laws of Hope, drawing his sword. The bounty hunter blocked a thrust with his oversized shield, and the assassin drove his blade into the wood, somehow forcing it through. The tip of the sword poked out behind the shield and the Laws of Hope froze, staring at the shining edge. Then he jerked the shield back, pulling the sword out of the Ticking Clock's hand.

Yuu watched in horror as the two titans fought to decide her fate. Either one would be her doom. She tugged on the metal ball attached to her manacle and managed to make it roll a little, but it was ungainly. She knelt and got her weight behind the ball, pushing it, rolling it, making her way inch by inch toward the thopter. The monks around her paid her no heed. There was a battle going on and judging by the clanging of steel, the grunts of effort, and the furious clicking of the Ticking Clock's joints, it was quite the spectacle. She glanced up to see the two legends clashing in a flurry of blocked strikes, impossible athletics, and lightning-fast attacks. It was a level of skill Yuu hadn't seen since the last battle of the war when the fake Steel Prince had led her army against the Emperor of Ten Kings at Jieshu.

The Ticking Clock moved like nothing human, his limbs twisting into impossible strikes, his body seeming to shift around parries and jabs. The Laws of Hope was an unassailable bastion, his defence impregnable. He knocked away a thrust by the Ticking Clock with a wave of his shield, then swung his sword around the edge. The segmented blade extended, each bladed segment connected by wires, and lashed across the Ticking Clock's arm with a clang of steel. The Laws of Hope then pulled his sword back and the segments slotted back into place perfectly. How the man could move so easily carrying such a large shield was a wonder. It must have weighed as much as a horse!

Yuu turned her attention back to the ball and pushed at it again, rolling it over once more. It was moving, but far too slowly. The fight wouldn't last forever, and it didn't matter who won. She looked at the manacle around her wrist, wondering if she could remove it somehow. It had no lock that she could see, but no matter how hard she tugged at it, it wouldn't open.

"I'm here," Li Bang said as he slid to a stop beside her. Yuu looked up at him in surprise and felt her spirits soar a little. With his help she might be able to escape this crucible she had wrought. Fang was nowhere to be seen.

"The lantern?" Yuu asked.

Li Bang grimaced and shook his head. "Fang stole it."

"That was the plan," Yuu said.

"From us, I mean. I saw you were in trouble and thought it better to help you. No sense in having the lantern if you're not around to appreciate it." A smile stretched across his face. "I have a technique!"

"That's nice," Yuu said as she pushed the ball again. Unless his technique could shatter metal or move something as heavy as a particularly obese buffalo, she didn't really care at that moment.

"I can see things," Li Bang continued.

Yuu glanced up at him and frowned. "Can you see me trying to move this… damn… ball?"

"I mean I can see things even when I'm not there to see them. I was in the temple and I saw you out here in trouble."

Yuu sighed and sagged. The metal ball was in a rut and she couldn't shift it. "So, your technique is that you can look out a window. Well done. Very impressive. Are you going to help me or not?"

Li Bang frowned. "There was no window," he said as he stooped down and wrapped his arms around the ball. Even with his strength he struggled to lift it. Sweat beaded on his forehead and his face reddened from the strain. How had the Laws of Hope carried this damned thing up the mountain with such ease? Along with his shield. How had he moved so quickly while carrying both?

Dozens of monks stood between them and the thopter watching the two legends fight. Yuu started toward it again, but Li Bang moved a different way, toward the stairs down the mountain. The chain snapped taut and Yuu found herself dragged along. "Stop," she hissed. "We're getting on that thing." She pointed at the engine with her free hand.

Li Bang's mouth gaped. "How does it fly?"

Honestly, she didn't have the first clue. Nor could she see a way to start it and take off without the Ticking Clock and the Laws of Hope noticing and stopping her before she got off the ground. They needed to sneak away, not attempt some grand exit. But she had failed. She winced, expecting the pain that always accompanied a failure, a loss. A pinch or punch, sometimes even the kiss of a knife. But the pain didn't come. She squeezed her thumb where the wooden splinter had sunk into her flesh, and the sharp bite of it made the failure a reality. It also helped to clear her mind. She had failed, but she could salvage something from the situation. Stealing the Ticking Clock's thopter seemed the only thing left. But Li Bang was right, she had no idea how to operate it and no time to learn. They had to flee while they still could. Indecision paralysed her. *Indecision is the death of the strategist,* her grandmother told her long ago. *The Art of War never hesitates. All gambits, possibilities, and outcomes must be considered before the first move is made. The failure of one plan means the activation of the next.* But Yuu was out of moves, just like she was out of time. She squeezed the splinter into her thumb once more and changed direction. Chain clinking, she and Li Bang stumbled toward the stairs.

Yuu looked over her shoulder one last time to see the fight still raging. The Laws of Hope raised his shield and smashed it down, shattering the stone tile and sending a wave of force that knocked over everyone nearby. Even the Ticking Clock was thrown backwards and crashed to the ground. He sat up and flipped back to his feet, then clutched his left arm with his right, pulled it from its socket, and dropped it on the ground. It slithered away like a snake, threading between the legs of the clambering monks where Yuu lost sight of it.

The Ticking Clock sprinted at the Laws of Hope, eating up the ground between them in long, mechanical strides. The Laws of Hope whipped his sword out in a horizontal arc. The Cochtan assassin dropped, slid below the steel blade, lurched upright and leapt into the air, aiming a kick at the bounty hunter. Metal foot hit wooden shield as the Laws of Hope hunkered down behind his protection, the stone beneath him cracking from the force. Then he heaved upwards. The Ticking Clock flew into the air, spinning, and unleashing a half dozen throwing knives with his one hand. Two of the knives thwacked into the bounty hunter's shield, and the others stabbed into the stone at his feet. The Laws of Hope whipped his segmented sword up around his shield and wrapped it around the Ticking Clock's leg. Yuu had no doubt the steel would have severed a normal person's leg, but the Ticking Clock was not a normal person. Still, the assassin was caught in mid-air. The Laws of Hope jerked his sword back and slammed the Ticking Clock down on the stony ground, sending stone shards and dust pluming around him.

As the dust cleared, the Ticking Clock rose jerkily to his feet. His coat was torn, his left arm missing. The Laws of Hope dashed at him so quickly Yuu barely saw it. He hit the Ticking Clock with the full force of his shield, sending the assassin tumbling metal limb over metal limb across the rubble-and-body-strewn plateau.

Yuu realised everyone was standing still, watching the fight. Every monk and every tourist there to pray to the stars stood transfixed. Even she and Li Bang had stopped to watch. She willed her body to move, tried to tear her eyes away, even as the Ticking Clock lurched back to his feet again. One leg was bent the wrong way, his arm was hanging by what looked like a copper tendon, his neck twisted at an angle any normal person would consider broken— were they not already dead. The assassin clicked his leg straight, wound his arm back up the copper tendon and into his shoulder, then pushed his head straight with a clang. He crouched, readying himself again.

The two combatants, legendary bounty hunter against immortal assassin, stared at each other across an expanse of slowly clearing dust. Then the Laws of Hope screamed in pain. The Ticking Clock's snaking left arm had slithered up behind the bounty hunter and was stabbing one of the assassin's knives through the back of his ankle. The Laws of Hope collapsed to one knee. He wrenched the metal arm from his ankle, dropped it on the ground, and crushed it with the full force of his shield. But the damage was done. The Ticking Clock marched across the rubble, leapt over the shield, and dropkicked two metal feet into bounty hunter's face.

"Shit!" Yuu said as her senses returned to her, realising it really didn't matter who won. Unless the two killed each other, she was screwed. "Definitely time to go." She nudged Li Bang in the ribs and he nodded, slowly at first, then more vigorously. They ambled to the stairs leading from the plateau, Li Bang carrying the metal ball, and Yuu carrying a weight far heavier in her conscience.

The city was a long way down. The light was fading fast, and Yuu would have to lead Li Bang soon or his night blindness could send them both tumbling down the mountain. Though at least they would make it to the bottom faster that way.

Night fell and Yuu lead Li Bang even as he carried the metal ball she was attached to. About halfway down, she heard a distant buzzing like a swarm of bees. The Ticking Clock's thopter whirred overhead, descending into the city of Ban Ping. The idea that not even the Laws of Hope could best the Ticking Clock was a terrifying one. If he couldn't, what hope did she have? And she was certain she would meet the assassin again.

They reached the bottom of the mountain sweaty and exhausted. Li Bang was trembling with the effort of holding the metal ball, and Yuu was sick with worry. She half expected to find the Ticking Clock waiting for her, but only monks greeted them at the base of the stairs.

"May the stars shine favourably..." the woman fell silent when she saw the manacle and the big metal ball.

Yuu waved the woman away with a gesture she hoped would be considered intensely rude and dragged Li Bang westward toward the city's edge.

"Natsuko?" Yuu said as they stumbled onto the dusty street. "Now would be a good time for you to suddenly appear." If the goddess was watching, she did not show herself.

There was a stable near the eastern entrance to the city and they staggered into it, startling the boy tending the horses. The beasts themselves did not appear to be the slightest bit surprised by their entrance. Li Bang dropped the metal ball and slumped to the ground in a pile of hay. He was panting and looked to be on the edge of passing out. Yuu could not blame him. He had saved her life for a certainty. Of course, she was now imprisoned in the middle of the stable by the ball and chain.

"Uhhh," the stable boy gawked at them, a bucket of water hanging from his hands.

"Is that clean?" Yuu asked. The boy nodded. "Bring it here."

The boy edged forward and put the bucket down just out of Yuu's reach. She had to get her weight behind the ball again to roll it enough so she could reach the bucket. Once she did, she scooped up a handful and slurped it down. It was glorious, though she wished it were wine. She pushed the bucket towards Li Bang, collapsed onto the floor, and closed her eyes.

Chapter 13

Yuu opened her eyes to find an old woman standing over her, holding an ancient jian with rust spots on the blade. Her simple brown hanfu was dusted with flour, and her hair was grey as an autumn storm. "Who are you?" the old woman rasped. She gave Yuu a light poke with the dull blade to make her point.

Yuu groaned as she struggled to wake up. How long had she slept? It couldn't have been long. She was exhausted but… Where were they anyway? She tried to rub at her face, but her left hand pulled taut against the chain. The memories flooded in and she winced as she realised the truth. She had lost. She had trusted the wrong piece, and he had taken the prize and fled. If she ever saw Fang again, she'd make damned sure to sacrifice him properly. She sighed and glanced over at Li Bang snoring softly, splayed out on a pile of hay. Two horses, one brown and one grey, were watching as well, their heads hanging over the doors to their stalls.

"My name is Yuu," she said. "I'm…"

"A criminal?" the old woman asked. She lowered the point of her sword towards Yuu's chest. Yuu couldn't help but notice how steadily the woman held it. This old woman was no stranger to the blade, though the blade seemed a long-time stranger to a whetstone.

"We are all criminals in the eyes of our enemies," Yuu said. It was one of Dong Ao's teachings, and a more insipid statement might not exist.

The old woman looked far from satisfied. "I don't have any enemies."

"Tell that to the Cochtans," Yuu said. She was looking around for something to break the manacle off her wrist. "Natsuko?"

The old woman narrowed her eyes in suspicion. "Who else is here besides you and the oaf sprawling on my hay?"

Yuu waited for a response from the goddess. It didn't come. "No one apparently. Is this your stable?"

The old woman nodded.

"I need two things. First is a hammer and chisel or something to get this manacle off. Second, I need a horse." Yuu tried to smile disarmingly. "I'll pay for both."

"Or I could turn you in to the monks."

Yuu crossed her legs and buried her head in her hands. She really needed a drink. "You could," she admitted. "They would probably pay you for your trouble as well. But you would be committing me to death."

The old woman lowered her sword and took a step back. Yuu spied a young boy at the far end of the stable, watching around a crack in the door. "What are you running from?" the old woman asked.

Yuu shrugged and kicked Li Bang's leg to wake him. "A Cochtan assassin and a legendary bounty hunter. Mostly though, my past."

The old woman narrowed her eyes and clicked her tongue. "Are you violent?"

Yuu shook her head. "No. Just foolish."

"Hmm. Five lien to free you from the chain. Fifty for the horse. And the only animal we can spare is the old, half blind one."

"It'll fit right in," Yuu said. She fished into her robes with her free hand and pulled out a pouch containing all the money Natsuko had given her. It was only twenty-five lien, but hopefully enough to convince the old woman she was serious.

The boy disappeared and returned with tools. Li Bang took a hammer and chisel from him and went to work on the chain. He was not confident enough to try his luck at the manacle. The band of metal chafed at Yuu's skin, but when the chain fell away she felt elated to be free again. To prove it, she stood up and paced away from the metal ball, hoping she would never see the damned thing again.

"You don't get the horse until I see the rest of the money," the old woman said. It had not escaped Yuu's notice that she still held the sword.

This was a problem. Yuu had been counting on Natsuko showing up and giving them more lien. Without her, she couldn't afford the horse. She could walk out of Ban Ping easily enough, but wanted to get as far away from the city as quickly as possible. Again, she lamented that she hadn't been able to steal the Ticking Clock's thopter.

"Here," Li Bang stepped forward and placed his own money purse on the floor in front of the old woman. "Should be enough to cover the rest." Yuu wanted to tell the fool to take back his money, that he'd need it for himself and she had no way to pay him back. But her desire for a horse was greater.

A few minutes later they were walking out of the stable into the night air with a mangy old horse between them. The woman had gifted them a few days' worth of feed for the animal, but no saddle. Yuu wasn't sure the beast would get her to the next town, to be honest, and she certainly wasn't going to risk making it run, but at least it would save her feet the ache of walking.

There wasn't much in the way of traffic on the road, only a few people here and there getting a head start on the next day's work. The monks were out in force though, patrolling the streets. It was rare to see them with weapons in hand down in Ban Ping, but news of the events at the temples had clearly spread. It didn't matter, they weren't stopping people from leaving the city. The monks had always been far quicker to eject criminals than punish them. Far better to make them someone else's problem.

"Why only the one horse?" Li Bang asked as they approached the arch that signalled the city limits.

Yuu had been waiting for this conversation, going over it in her head again and again, trying to find the best way to approach

133

it. There wasn't one. However she said it, it would sound like a betrayal. "Because you're not coming with me."

Li Bang pouted. "I can still help," he said sulkily. It was a token argument at best.

Yuu shook her head. "You don't understand. You can't leave Ban Ping. The Hosan army will have recruiters everywhere, Li Bang. They're conscripting men. If you come with me, you'll just end up marched north to fight the Cochtans. Stay in Ban Ping. You're free here."

Li Bang was silent for a while. "What else am I going to do? If I go with you, I might get conscripted. If I stay here, I might as well go and sign up. I'm not good for anything else. I need to earn a living somehow."

Yuu stopped the horse and ducked under its head to stand in front of Li Bang. It made a lazy snap at her with its teeth, but it was clear the beast's heart was simply not in it. Poor animal probably just wanted to go back to its cosy stable and live out the rest of its dwindling life in relative comfort. It was a sentiment Yuu could empathise with.

"Do you know who I really am?" Yuu asked.

Li Bang was silent for a moment, then nodded.

"I have led armies," Yuu said. "I have fought wars. People like you… Strategists put people like you on the front lines, Li Bang. You will not be expected to survive. You will not survive. And the last thing you want is to fall to the Cochtan Blood Engine. Nobody should have to suffer being fed to that abomination."

"What else can I do?"

"Anything," Yuu said. "You have a technique now. You can see things, a form of clairvoyance. It's a useful technique to have. You can be a real hero now."

Li Bang looked like he'd just sniffed a sewer. "Heroes have useful techniques. Being able to see things even when I'm not there won't help me fight better."

Yuu tucked a few errant strands of hair behind her ear. "Not all heroes swing a dao... or a chui," she said with a smile. "Practice your technique. Learn to control it. I think you'll soon find your services in high demand."

Li Bang nodded. He didn't look happy. Then he lurched forward and wrapped his big arms around Yuu so swiftly she squeaked in his crushing embrace. "Thank you," he said as he released her. "And thank the crone for me when you next see her."

"Good luck, Li Bang," Yuu said with a deep, respectful bow. She really was sad to leave him behind. He may have been a piece on the board, and she certainly tried to sacrifice him a couple of times, but he stayed loyal, and she had forged a bond with him. It was foolish. Strategists should never form bonds. It made their choices harder. *The Art of War should always remain aloof and detached*, her grandmother's words. It was one more reason why she had to go on alone.

Yuu left Ban Ping the same way she arrived. Alone. But at least she had an artefact now. One of the divine artefacts. It was not enough... but one was better than none.

Chapter 14

Yuu rode through most of the night on dirt roads that were uncharacteristically empty. The horse smelled like mouldy oats and piss, and snapped at her whenever she got too close to its head. Luckily, he was as blind as Li Bang, so he missed more often than not. Still, Yuu found a few new bruises where the beast had snagged her. She didn't really like horses, but the Art of War had learned to ride them and ride them well. She had also learned to sleep in the saddle, and right then she counted that as one of the most valuable skills in the world, practically a technique in itself, even if she didn't have a saddle. Her grandmother might have taught Yuu just about everything she knew about strategy and playing by and against the rules, but none of those things mattered a damn when you needed to sleep and run away at the same time. The horse did not move fast, barely quicker than a lumbering ox, but he was old enough and wise enough to stick to the beaten paths even without guidance from his rider. A couple of times Yuu was startled awake by calls from passing travellers, but none seemed of a violent mind, and she quickly dropped back to dozing again. She was so tired. And she really needed a drink.

Natsuko found her as the sun came up. The first rays of brilliant light woke Yuu, and the goddess was kneeling by the side of the road at a small wooden table, and appeared to be playing mah-jongg. Yuu slipped from the horse's back and felt all her aches and pains anew as she hit the ground. It took a few gasps and a lot of agony for her to straighten her back, and her legs felt like soup noodles. Middle age seemed to have snuck up on her overnight and given her the ass-kicking she so rightly deserved.

"Are you an idiot?" Natsuko asked as Yuu led the horse near. The glassy-eyed beast sniffed at the goddess in a way Yuu recognised as preparing to take a bite. Then he clearly thought better of the idea, no doubt deciding the old crone would taste like vinegar and bile and probably prunes. It stepped to the side of the road and found some grass to chew. Its tail flicked around happily as it ripped up a few green blades.

Yuu buried her hands in her robe and pinched herself on the arm. Failure was always due to a lack of focus. With enough attention and preparation, no outcome could not be predicted, and no situation could not be overcome. The pain helped her mind focus. It always had. "No," she said slowly. There really wasn't any way to answer the question. At least not one that would satisfy the goddess.

"Then why are you trying to kill yourself?" Natsuko was serious, not even a hint of a smile on her wizened face. "Did you really think that was a good plan? Putting yourself in between two of the strongest warriors in Hosa? On one side death and on the other side prison, all for what? So you could pay penance for the death of your prince?"

Yuu shook her head. Confronted by the goddess' anger, she had difficulty ordering her thoughts. But Natsuko was right, it had been a stupid plan. "Only those willing to lose, can taste victory."

"Pah!" Natsuko spat. "Dong Ao was an idiot, and do not for a moment try to convince me you think otherwise. Your own beloved Chaoxiang wrote: *Only a fool marches to war knowing they might lose.* There is more at stake now than your measly life. I do not care how much misplaced guilt you have rattling around in that vacant head of yours, do not try to kill yourself again."

Yuu could think of no way to answer the goddess, so she said nothing. Maybe Natsuko was right. Maybe Yuu had been trying to sacrifice herself, end the game, pay the price of her failures. She'd known the plan was dangerous, but now that she thought about it, it was foolish and poorly thought out, too. If Li Bang had not come back for her, she would be either dead or in the hands of Qing, which was as good as dead. She rubbed at the chaffed skin around her metal manacle.

137

"Did you replace Lump with this new Lump?" Natsuko asked, pointing to the horse.

"I left Li Bang behind in Ban Ping," Yuu said. She sank down across from Natsuko and studied the game. It appeared to be mah-jongg, but she didn't recognise any of the pieces.

"That was foolish. I thought his technique would prove useful."

Yuu looked at the goddess. "Was that your doing? Spontaneous manifestation of a technique. The blessing of a god."

Natsuko smiled, her attention on the game in front of her. She scooped up a couple of pieces, clapped them together, and put them in a little leather pouch. "Did you get the lantern?"

Yuu sighed. "No. I trusted the wrong thief."

"I could have told you that," Natsuko said with a snort. She was frowning now, and not at the game.

"Well you didn't," Yuu said. "Fang stole the lantern while Li Bang was saving me. I don't know if he thought he could get a better price for it elsewhere, or if…" It was a possibility she had been trying to ignore.

"Or if he is another god's champion?" Natsuko asked. "Did you not see a contract on his skin when you fucked him?"

Yuu looked away from the goddess and felt heat rush to her cheeks. "We didn't actually undress. Too much of a rush, I guess."

"So, you got screwed by the enemy, and sent away your only ally," Natsuko said. "Truly such a strategist. What would you call that move?"

"A mistake? A tactical misapplication," Yuu said. She reached into her robes and pinched her arm again. Then she pulled out the little chess piece she had been carving and set to it with her knife. It resembled Li Bang and was almost finished. It felt good to be doing something with her hands, something she knew how to do.

"Mistakes are like wrinkles," Natsuko said as she snapped together the last few pieces of the game and put them away in her pouch. "The older we get, the more we have, and we forget them until we look in a mirror." She threw the pouch behind her into the grass and stood.

Yuu looked at the little table by the roadside. There was a single mah-jongg piece on it showing a black lotus flower, a dozen identical petals overlapping. The goddess had left that one piece out of the collection and thrown the rest of the collection away. She wondered if Natsuko even realised she had done it. Had it been on purpose, or was creating lost things just what she did? Could the goddess be separated from her icon? Or was she as bound by her name as humans were by their pasts?

"Where to next?" Yuu asked, pocketing the carving of Li Bang. She stood and dusted off her robes.

"North," Natsuko said. She whistled at the horse and led him onto the road. The beast swished his tail and blew out his lips, but didn't snap at her. He would need to rest soon enough. An old beast like that had limited stamina. "There is an inn on the way to Ning province, close to the standing stones. There is an artefact there."

"Ning is on the Cochtan border," Yuu said. "The further north we go, the more likely we are to encounter the war." Deep down she almost wanted to find the front. Meet up with the Hosan forces and reveal herself, take command and lead the armies to victory. She had been trying to ignore it, deny it, but now that she was playing the game again, the possibility of war was a siren's call. A foolish fancy. She was a wanted criminal. They'd slap her in even more irons and send her back to Qing to be executed. Besides, it wasn't her war to fight. She was done with war. It had only ever led her to misery.

"Pah!" Natsuko spat. "It is just like Batu to make war where he has hidden the artefacts. But we will go nowhere near the actual fighting."

Yuu stood and joined the goddess and the horse on the road. The morning sun was slowly warming the world around them, but there was a definite chill in the air. Along with the drought, it made for a dry, dusty, washed out expanse of road, rock, and brush. "Batu has been tianjun for the past century," Yuu said. "Who was tianjun before him?"

"Mira, the god of the harvest and crude jokes," Natsuko cackled. "Well, just the god of the harvest really, but she had a mind so full of smut you wouldn't believe. She once told me a joke. What do you get if you cross a man and a horse?" She stared at Yuu a moment. "A good time!" She cackled in appreciation of the terrible joke. Yuu's horse snorted. "Oh, not you, Lump," Natsuko said, patting the horse's neck. "You have been gelded. Poor fellow."

Yuu couldn't claim to be an expert on the gods, but had never heard of Mira before. "I thought the god of the harvest was Bianzwei?"

"He is now."

"What happened to Mira?" Yuu asked.

Natsuko was silent for a moment, then said, "Same goddess, different name. The Cochtans, Nash, Ipians, and Hosans might all have their own name for the god of storms but that does not make him four different gods. Just one. Nir. And he is an arrogant, loud bastard with no regard for anyone smaller than him." She grumbled out a few words Yuu couldn't understand. "And he is a terrible dancer."

It made some sense, Yuu supposed. There were many languages and many myths. It seemed obvious that different nations would name their gods differently. "It was a time of prosperity," she said, thinking back to her grandmother's history lessons. The old woman's natural grandchildren had hated listening to those lessons at the feet of their grandmother. *Useless stories*, they called them. Not Yuu. She had loved sitting there, listening to her grandmother talk about old kings and heroes of legend, great deeds and villainous acts. Dragons that once roamed the skies, now rarer than peace.

"Well of course," Natsuko said. "Mira was the god of the harvest. When she was tianjun, all four nations prospered, had plenty of food and a long, monotonous peace." Yuu glanced sidelong at the goddess. "Oh, don't look at me like that. I don't agree with Batu in the slightest. War is not exciting. But Mira certainly made the world a boring place. Everything was eating and rutting, eating and rutting. Humans spread out all across the nations and beat back the natural order. Boring. When did you last see a dragon in the world? Or a pixiu? Or a xiao?"

Yuu could only shake her head. She had only ever heard of them in stories.

"They are not gone," Natsuko continued with a shrug. "Just lost."

"Is that why you want to be the next tianjun?" Yuu asked. "To bring them back?"

"Hah!" Natsuko said. "That is part of it, sure." She lowered her voice. "But only part of it. I am the god of missed opportunities, but the truth is I hate it when people miss opportunities. No one ever thanks me for it, just like no one ever thanks me when their dog goes missing. They only ever pray to my shrines to bring back what they have lost. *I lost my favourite shoe in the mud. Please give it back to me. Give me another chance to woo the woman I love.* No one ever thanks me when they find their lost earring. No one ever thanks me when they take a risk and do not miss an opportunity. I hate missed opportunities, just like my brother Fuyuko hates orphaned children... I mean, children being orphaned." Yuu had heard of Fuyuko, the god of children and orphans, but had not known he was Natsuko's brother. She hadn't even realised the gods could have siblings. Did they have parents also? Children? Was that how new gods were born?

"Nothing creates more missed opportunities than war," Natsuko continued. "Nothing creates more orphans than war. I want to take the throne to stop Batu. To end his century of bloodshed. He has done nothing but pit nations against each other, turn brother against brother and son against father. What Mira achieved in spreading the people far and wide with prosperous harvests and swelling populations, Batu has perverted. More people means more soldiers, more food means better supply lines, allowing those soldiers to strike further into their neighbours' lands. He has turned the world into his own personal shrine with every nation, every emperor, every soldier praying to him in blood whether they realise it or not. My brother and I have spent half a century waiting for this contest. Waiting to bring Batu down."

Natsuko paused and sighed. "Now that I have answered your question, it is about time you answered mine. Why would a renowned strategist such as yourself do her absolute best to avoid war? Why run and hide, and change your name, and spend your days cheating old men out of their money when you could sit at the head of the army trying to protect this nation?"

This was not a subject Yuu was comfortable with, so she offered up half the truth. "I have a bounty on my head."

"For murdering the Steel Prince, yes I know. But we both know you did not actually kill him. You could not save him, so you put someone else in his place to lead your necessary war. But that is not the point." Natsuko stared at her with those bottomless brown eyes. "You could have asked the emperor to pardon you, traded your service for your freedom. You could have gone before what is left of the Qing royal family and explained, begged for mercy. Instead, you wallow in grief, misplaced guilt, and self-pity."

"And you pretend you don't know the truth," Yuu said. How could the god of the lost and of missed opportunities not know everything about Yuu's life? "I hate war. I spent half my life dedicated to it. My childhood was spent learning tactics and terrain, weapons and armour, troop movements and fortifications. My grandmother, bereft of any willing decedent of her own, thrust her legacy upon me. And I revelled in it. I excelled at it. And then, when the time came, I used all I learned from her and became her legacy incarnate." Yuu shook her head. Perhaps Natsuko was right, she was wallowing. But damn, it felt good to wallow out loud for once. "Batu is the god of war. Well, I have spent most of my life in his service," she said, her voice cracking. "I have given him everything, and he has taken everything from me.

"Even as a child, he was taking everything from me. My father died to war." Yuu hadn't thought about him in years, but still she missed the sound of his voice, the smell of old leather that clung to him. "When the Seafolk invaded Nash, my village was one of the first to fall. The men were taken as slaves, our homes burned, the women and children slaughtered. My mother and I only survived because we were collecting nuts for the evening meal. I saw them take my father, whipped bloody and barely able to stand, and I saw them set fire to my home. And then my mother dragged me away.

"I lost my grandmother to war, too, to the famine the emperor created by taxing the people of Hosa to starvation. She ate less so she could feed me, and eventually she just faded away. I was an orphan when she took me in and raised me, taught me everything I know. And in the end, she died so that I would live." Yuu sniffed and shrugged. "And then her dull-witted family kicked me out."

The goddess snorted. "And do not forget, you lost your prince to the war," she said with a shake of her head. "I am well aware of all of it. It is why I picked you. Well, that and your skills, I suppose— though they seem somewhat less effective than advertised. You see, you are an orphan, so you had my brother's blessing. You have lost everything, and I will not even get started on the opportunities you have missed. Trust me, there is a lot of them."

Yuu suddenly felt uncomfortable. The goddess knew too much about her. She knew everything about her. Not just the things she had done, the crimes she had committed, the lives she had sacrificed. No. The goddess knew *everything*. Everything that had happened to Yuu, everything that might have happened to her. All the opportunities she had missed. Could her prince have lived? Was there a risk Yuu could have taken, a decision she could have made, an opportunity she had missed to save the Steel Prince's life? Had she been too stupid to see it? She winced at the pain and realised she was dragging a fingernail down her arm, scraping away the flesh. She wanted to change the subject. To talk about something else. That, and she really needed a drink. "Is your brother in the contest too?"

Natsuko grimaced. "No. Only one of us could enter."
"Why?"
"We have the same artefact. Could not enter it twice."
"And you're still not going to tell me what it is?"
The goddess shook her head.
"Shouldn't we try to find it?" Yuu asked. It seemed to her Natsuko would want to find her own artefact most of all. The goddess didn't reply.

Chapter 15

They turned off the western road and headed north towards Ning province. Natsuko vanished without a trace and left Yuu to travel alone. Yuu was glad not to continue their uncomfortable conversations. The goddess wasn't bad company most of the time, but there was something about her Yuu couldn't quite name. A strange tension whenever she was around. The world seemed a sharper place in the presence of a god. Without the distraction, Yuu went back to her wood carving and finished the little statue of Li Bang. Perfect except for the accidental gouge she'd sliced out of his belly back on the plateau at Ban Ping. Then she pulled out her own piece, the little Hero with patchwork robes, still just a block of wood above the waist. She couldn't quite bring herself to finish it. Instead, she pulled out another block and started to work on a new chess piece. She needed a Thief, a piece that could move in an abnormal pattern, hiding its true strength, but able to leap over even the most stalwart of defences. Of course, she already had a depiction in mind: Fang. He was without a doubt worthy of the Thief piece. He had not only stolen the lantern from the monks, but also from Yuu. He betrayed her, and Suazon Lee taught that *Only a fool trusts twice.* No! Fang did not deserve to be one of her pieces. She would not place her trust in him again.

The grassy plains soon gave way to a rockier landscape and Yuu could see the blur of forests on the northern horizon. She passed a few farms, but many of them seemed empty, fields scorched yellow by the drought and unrelenting sun. Natsuko didn't appear again that day, and when night fell Yuu led Lump off the path and found shelter wedged in between two large boulders just far enough from the road where she wouldn't be seen. She gave the horse some of the grain and one of the shrivelled apples the old lady had provided, skilfully dodging his gnashing teeth, and then sat down and chewed on some dried fruit and a strip of meat that might once have belonged to a buffalo. All alone and with no protection, she didn't want to risk a fire. It was unlikely there would be any bandits about — they had been all but wiped out since the new Emperor of Ten Kings took power — but some things weren't worth risking. With no bed roll and no fire, Yuu pulled her robes tight and curled into a ball with her back against one of the boulders. Sleep came quickly and fitfully.

Yuu woke to the sunrise, aching and shivering. The vague impression of a disturbing dream still echoed in her mind like a peal of thunder fading into the distance. Lump was lying on his side in the grass and for a moment she thought the beast had died until his chest rose in a great, rattling snore and fell again in a quiet *humph*. She placed a handful of grain and another withered apple in front of the creature and stood back quickly as he snuffed a couple of times, then leaned forward to scoop the food into his mouth. Finally, his eyes opened, and he laboriously heaved himself back to his feet with a groan before shooting Yuu a stare that looked far too accusing for her liking. Still the goddess did not appear. Yuu and Lump set off again long before the rising sun burned the mist from the ground, not because Yuu was eager to be underway, but because she had nothing else to do. And the sooner she had a drink in her belly and another in her hand, the better.

She alternated between riding Lump and walking alongside him to give him a much-needed rest and let him graze on the yellow grass at the side of the road whenever he wanted. It had been a long time since she had been so far into western Hosa, but Yuu thought the Forest of Bamboo should be coming into view soon. Rumour had it the place was infested with spirits and anyone who didn't stick to the path marked out by shrines was likely to never be seen again. Her newest chess piece was coming along well, though she was struggling to capture the attitude of the subject. It irked her to have not one, but two unfinished pieces, but what else could she do?

Another night passed and still Natsuko did not show her wrinkled face. Yuu would almost believe the goddess had abandoned her, but the writing still scrawled on her left arm convinced her otherwise. She spent a while staring at the graceful lines and tried to translate some of it. Her God's Word was far too rusty, and she could only pick out occasional bits. There was something about a contest written on her wrist, and then some text about being linked together between her fingers, then a bunch of stuff Yuu couldn't make out for the life of her. Around the knuckle of her index finger was a letter that might mean *battle*, but the style was slightly wrong and she was far from certain. For all she really knew, it could mean *potato* and the whole thing could be an elaborate recipe for ramen.

Yuu didn't really believe the goddess would leave her. Natsuko was committed to the contest, and Yuu was her chosen piece. She wouldn't abandon her. But her prolonged absence was worrying. Without the goddess' guidance, Yuu could see no way to continue her efforts. She could walk right past an artefact and be none the wiser. She drifted off to sleep and dreamed of fires raging out of control, armies turning the world barren in their wake, fields of bodies, and rivers running red. Nightmares, no matter how she looked at them.

She woke that morning to a campfire she had not started and the smell of something cooking over it. Natsuko sat on the other side of the flames, her gnarled face frightful in the flickering light. Yuu hadn't really paid attention to where she camped last night, but taking it in now she could see a craggy cliff to her left, nestled in a field of tall, yellow blade grass.

"I didn't know you could cook," Yuu said as she uncurled and felt all the aches once more. She was not made for this style of life. She needed beds, hearty meals and booze on hand whenever she wanted it. In the Steel Prince's service, she'd had all those things and more.

"I'm a god, not a fool," Natsuko snapped. A small pot was hanging above the campfire, its contents bubbling merrily. The goddess stirred it with a spoon and sniffed. "Almost ready."

"Where did you get all that?"

"You would be surprised what people lose," Natsuko said. "The pot was one of Takagawa Toshi's favourites. It had been in her family for three generations, passed down from mother to daughter. A lot of love and great care went into the preservation of it, and it has seen more meals than you have seen days. A true family treasure. But war has consumed Ipia as well. The Nash horselords raid the western border, and the Ise and Ido families are both fighting over the Serpent Throne. Takagawa Toshi's village became a battlefield, and though she survived, she lost everything. Yet another of Batu's schemes come to fruition."

"What about the contents?" Yuu asked. The pot seemed to contain a watery broth with many chunks floating in it.

Natsuko shrugged. "You decided to sleep not a few hundred paces from a farm. I stole a few vegetables. Honestly, why did you not you go and ask for a bed for the night?"

Yuu said nothing, not willing to admit her mistake. She hadn't realised there was a farm so close. She had seen no lights and heard no noise. *The Art of War should always be aware of her surroundings.* Another of her grandmother's lessons. Yuu had been on the cusp of puberty at the time, and the old woman had woken her early one morning and dragged her out to a field that had once grown carrots. The carrots had been torn up and taken away by a passing tax collector for the Emperor of Ten Kings, leaving the family with a few measly leftovers smaller than her fingers. The weather had grown too cold to grow anything else, and they were forced to suffer another lean year of dwindling rations. That Yuu was another mouth to feed and not truly related to them was a matter her adopted family never let her forget.

There was a series of obstacles arranged in the field. Some barrels, some crates, a plow, and some rakes. Even the old family ox, long past useful for anything but atrocious smells. There was talk of eating the poor beast but no one seemed to have the heart to put him down. Yuu was given ten minutes to look at the field and the obstacles it contained, with no clue as to why, and then her grandmother slipped a thick black scarf over her eyes, cinched it tight, and told her to walk from one side to the other. The first time she tried, she stepped on a rake, and the haft shot up, smacked her in the collarbone, and knocked her on her arse with a cry of pain. *Focus on the lessons*, her grandmother said and pulled her back to the edge of the field to try again. The second time, Yuu stubbed her toe on a crate and winced at the pain. Grandmother dragged her back again. The third time, she stepped on another rake, the same offensive tool as before. This time the pain was accompanied by raucous laughter, and she pulled the scarf away to find two of the three of her adopted siblings laughing and pointing at her. They never missed an opportunity to ridicule her, but it rarely slipped into violence. At least, not when her grandmother was watching. Her grandmother tied the scarf back around Yuu's eyes and hauled her back to the edge of the field. *The Art of War should always be aware of her surroundings. You have seen the layout, girl. You know it. So, remember it.* Yuu remembered it had been a particularly painful day, and hurtful too. She could still feel her grandmother's disappointment like it was yesterday.

They ate in silence. Yuu demolished two bowls of the broth, and Natsuko fed Lump. The beast seemed to like the goddess, as far as a dull-minded creature could. It nuzzled against her and followed her about the little camp, picking up the seemingly random items she dropped and giving them back to her. Natsuko took them happily, patting the beast on the muzzle with a few kind words, then promptly threw them away again immediately. A spoon here, a lien there, a pair of dice, a dagger with intricate etching down the blade. Yuu never saw where the items came from, but all were left scattered about in the grass. Lost.

"I have some bad news," Natsuko said eventually. "And some good news, I suppose. Yang Yang, the god of gambling and goddess of lies, has managed to secure five artefacts. Sarnai and her Ticking Clock have four. We have only one. And the assassin has killed four of the other champions."

"The Laws of Hope?" Yuu asked.

"Is not a champion."

"Did he survive?"

The goddess scoffed. "Don't know. Don't care. The numbers are thinning. Eight gods have dropped out due to their champions dying, and two more have given up for reasons entirely beyond my understanding. They sacrificed something precious to enter, and they just give up when the going gets tough? Fools."

"Maybe their chosen champions refused to participate." Yuu said. She'd be lying if she hadn't considered it herself. Especially since she had seen the Ticking Clock in action and felt the kiss of his knife. She rubbed the spot where it had nicked her skin and then found the knife still hidden in her pockets. She'd give it back to the assassin pointy end first if she ever had the chance, though in truth she would much more happily never see him again.

"Then they should have made better choices," the goddess continued. "The bad news is we are lagging far behind." Natsuko poured the last of the broth into a bowl and put it down in front of the horse, then picked up the pan and hurled it into the undergrowth. Lost again. "The good news is we should reach the tavern before night, and the artefact is still there." The horse finished off the broth and started licking at the bowl, but Natsuko whisked it away and threw it, too, into the brush. The horse swished its tail and stalked away, rummaging through the long grass. It came back to the campfire with the bowl between its teeth.

Piece by piece, Natsuko scattered the spit, bowls, spoons, and everything else. Each bit lost just as it had been before she conjured it out of nowhere.

The goddess was a whirlwind of activity and noise, bringing life and chaos to what had been a cold, dreary camp. The company was good, it reminded Yuu she was still part of the world and not some yokai just drifting through it from place to place with no real substance. When had she become so detached? So... lost? "What is it?" she asked, trying to escape her own thoughts. "The artefact?"

"A coin," Natsuko said, grabbing at the bowl between the horse's teeth. They wrestled over it for a few moments, and then the goddess gave up. The horse backed away a couple of steps, victorious, and dropped the bowl on the grass. Then he bent down to lick at it some more. The goddess nodded approvingly. "I like this new Lump. He has spirit."

"A coin?" Yuu asked. "Just a lien?"

"No, of course not. It is far more valuable than a lien. And also worth nothing at all." The goddess cackled. "It belongs to Yang Yang, his male side anyway, and it is not any sort of currency recognised in Hosa, Nash, Ipia, or Cochtan. It is made of jade. On one side is a picture of the sun; on the other is a picture of the moon."

"Yang Yang is the god of gambling," Yuu said. "Why is this coin special enough to be his artefact? Is it the first coin he ever won? Given to him by a lover? Did it fall from the stars?"

Natsuko scoffed. "Nothing so dreadfully romantic." The horse's ears twitched and it looked up toward the farm. The goddess took the opportunity to steal the bowl, licked so clean it likely couldn't even remember the broth it once held, and threw it into the brush on the other side of the beast. "Time to go," she announced and rocked to her feet, already walking north.

Owning nothing she didn't keep hidden within her robes, Yuu had nothing to gather but the horse, and he needed little encouragement, dutifully following along behind them. Natsuko plodded happily along the dirt road that apparently led to a tavern, which Yuu hoped was close by and not just because the artefact might be there. "This coin," Yuu said as she caught Natsuko up. "What is so special about it?"

"It never wins," the goddess said with a smirk. "Yang Yang had it made by Tuck, a jeweller, dead, oh, six centuries now at least. Had a skill like none other, and with Yang Yang's blessing he could work strange properties into his art. That coin is unique. Flip it in the air and call Sun. It will land on moon. Flip it and call Moon, and it will land on sun. It never wins."

"Why would the god of gambling want a coin that always loses?" Yuu asked.

"For such a smart woman, you are remarkably deaf," the goddess snapped. "I said it never wins, not it always loses."

"Is there a difference?"

The goddess seemed to think about it for a few moments, then shrugged. "I don't know, but you still heard me wrong. Anyway, the problem with being the god of gambling, I suppose, is that he always wins. It is really quite frustrating for him as well. So, he had that coin made. A coin to remind him that even he can lose when the conditions are right."

Yuu considered the idea and decided it was a load of crap. All that coin meant was that Yang Yang could lose when he chose to, not when the conditions were right. That wasn't gambling. But then neither was winning all the time. It seemed an odd curse that the god of gambling couldn't actually gamble.

They passed a few travellers on the road. None said anything and most looked weary and wary and hurried past Yuu like she might try to stop and rob them. Not only that, but they didn't look to be travelling light. Some of them seemed to be carrying everything they owned on their backs or in rickety carts, and there were no men save for the ancient or boys too young to count. The emperor's conscription was obviously in full effect.

It was late afternoon by the time they reached the tavern. It stood just off the beaten path, nestled between a couple of tall trees at the foot of a bumpy hillock. The sun was low and cast the tavern in a morbid light. Barely more than four bamboo walls and a thinning roof of old straw, it appeared out of the gloom like a mirage and stood dark and silent, a lonely silhouette against the setting sun. All three of them, woman, goddess, and horse, stopped to stare at the building, and Yuu felt an icy anxiety creeping through her gut. Something was wrong. Something in the air, a foul smell coupled with ill omen. The clouds in the distance only added to the effect.

"Are you sure about this?" Yuu asked.

"It is in there," Natsuko said. "Somewhere."

Yuu scratched at an itch on her neck, then pushed her matted hair out of her eyes. "How about you go in first?" she said. "Check it out."

"I cannot help you directly." The goddess stared flatly at Yuu. "Imagine if you had someone with a technique that could see places without actually being there?"

"Point taken," Yuu said. She realised then she had sacrificed one of her most powerful pieces. By protecting Li Bang, she had sacrificed him as surely as if she had gotten him killed. But at least he was alive. "A jade coin?" She walked toward the inn's entrance.

Natsuko didn't join her. "Good luck."

The stink became overpowering as Yuu approached. The sickly sweet of rot mixed with the foul stench of faeces and metallic tang of blood. She was no stranger to battlefields, nor the aftermath of slaughter, and she knew the smell all too well. That was why she knew just what to expect when the door swung open at her touch, the rotting hinges creaking.

Bodies littered the floor, dried blood staining the straw and floorboards. Some of the corpses had flies buzzing about open wounds, others were crawling with maggots. The slaughter had been done a while ago, and Yuu hoped the danger had passed. Whoever or whatever had done it had been quick and methodical. Some of the bodies were collapsed on the floor, others were still at the tables. A few bodies still held their cups, as though they had died instantly.

Yuu coughed and held a sleeve over her nose, then stepped into the inn. She picked her way through the bodies, stepping over them as often as around. Some appeared to have been killed by blades, others had smaller wounds. Arrows perhaps, the hafts snapped off, but the heads left in the decaying flesh. Rats gnawing on the dead flesh peered at Yuu as she moved further into the tavern, their eyes dark as night. How was she supposed to find a coin amidst this slaughter? The answer was obvious. She'd have to desecrate the dead, go through their pockets like some looting bandit.

Yuu nudged a gooey body with the toe of her sandal and a cloud of flies swarmed into the air, buzzing angrily around her. She flailed at them impotently, but they soon lost interest. She was living, and they much preferred the rotting flesh of the dead. The body at her feet was a man, tall and dressed in the faded uniform of a Hosan soldier. His hair was matted with blood, which did nothing to hide the gaping hole in the back of his skull that had killed him. Yuu wasn't immune to such a grisly sight, but had seen its like and worse many times before. On the battlefield, in the thick of the fighting, it didn't matter how a person died, just as long as *they* did, and *you* survived. Death was always messy. She patted down the body and found a coin purse in a trouser pocket. Upon opening it, she found three lien, but no jade coin. For a moment she considered putting the money back, but the dead had no need of coin. She pocketed the lien and moved onto the next corpse. She counted thirty-two bodies in the main room alone and prayed to the gods she wouldn't have to search them all.

She held her breath as she checked the next body. He was propped up against a chair, both hands on the table, one holding a cup of soured wine, and the other holding a card. He'd been gambling at the moment of death, and Yuu took that as a good sign. He had been burly in life, but his flesh was sagging and grey in death, and the stink coming off him was somehow worse than the others, worse than anything she'd ever smelled. His throat had been cut and blood had run freely onto his tunic. An eyepatch covered one eye, and Yuu saw something wriggling beneath it. Yuu pulled his coat aside to check for a coin pouch, and the dead man's hand reached over and snapped hold of her wrist.

Chapter 16

Yuu's scream startled the rats and set a crow cawing and fleeing to the rafters. She fell back, batting at the dead man's hand around her wrist, around the manacle the Laws of Hope had put on her. Despite being dead, which until now Yuu had considered a physical disability, his grip was like iron. Slowly, the corpse's head turned to stare at her, his sole eye milky white. Yuu tugged and screamed again, hoping Natsuko would hear her and come in, or send the horse in, or do something. The dead man dropped the cards in his other hand and raised a single finger to his rotting lips.

"Shhhh," he said. "You scream loud enough to wake the dead." The laughter that escaped him was nothing human and started a chorus of chuckles among the other corpses. Yuu glanced around to see several of them trembling with laughter, puss and other fouler fluids leaking out onto the floor.

Yuu's mind couldn't quite register the idea that she had found a talking corpse amidst the slaughter and it had just cracked a joke. It was a poor joke, but the rest of the dead seemed to find it exceedingly funny. "Let me go!" she hissed, tugging her wrist around and beating on the dead hand with her other fist. Her heart was pounding in her ears like an army in quick march.

At last, the dead man released his grip, and Yuu lurched back a step, turned and ran. Another corpse reached out a skeletal hand, the flesh all but gnawed away, and grasped her ankle. She tripped and went down hard on another corpse, which oozed something foul and ejected a squelch of gas that made her retch. She pushed away from the body and vomited on the floor. The other corpse still had hold of her ankle and she kicked at it, screaming, "Get off. Get off. Get off!" She looked for the exit, but the door had closed behind her and the body of a gutted man, his guts trailing on the floor, now lay in front of it. She had the sinking feeling she had walked into a trap. But set by whom?

"Batu," Yuu said. The corpse holding her leg released its grip and she stumbled away. She didn't run toward the exit — she had a feeling the corpses would stop her — but crept back toward the corpse sitting at the table. The one that had awoken first. "Batu killed you?"

"The Cochtans killed me," said the corpse at the table, his voice like a whetstone being dragged along a rusted blade.

"And me," said another corpse, a woman's voice gurgling around the decay in her mouth.

"And me!" All the corpses started talking over each other. A chorus of death.

"Seven days ago?" Yuu asked. "That would be when the contest started." The decay of the bodies was roughly in line with that. Batu must have hidden the coin here after the Cochtans had slaughtered everyone. A divine artefact protected by the dead.

"Time loses meaning when you're dead," said the corpse at the table. "One day, seven days, eternity." His eye swivelled in its socket.

She stopped behind the chair opposite the corpse and looked down at the cards on the table. There was a lot of lien strewn about, Yuu estimated at least fifty coins, but none of them were jade. If the corpse had died while playing cards, who had been his opponent?

"I'm looking for a jade coin," she said. The corpses were still again, no movement but the flies and rats returning. "It's in here somewhere."

The corpse opposite her twitched and a maggot wriggled out from underneath its eyepatch. The fat thing dropped onto the table, and the dead man's milky eye rolled to regard it. He moved his hand slowly, placed a finger on the little creature, and crushed it onto the table.

"I have your coin," said the dead man across from her. He grinned and one of his teeth fell out and bounced off the table. A fat black fly flew out of his mouth and buzzed around for a moment before flying off to another corpse. "I'll play you for it."

Yuu glanced down at the cards on the table again. She flipped over the ones in front of her, a green dragon, a four of swords, and a black fire. Assuming the game was Kami, it was a losing hand any way she looked at it. With just one more card left to receive, the highest possible hand would be a pair of dragons. She looked across the table at the cards in front of the corpse. A red fire, a red earth, and a red dragon. A winning hand already. The game had been moments from its end, and the corpse would have won.

"If I win, I get the coin?" Yuu asked.

The corpse nodded slowly. Another maggot wormed its foul head out from under the eyepatch. "And if I win, I get your life. Even trade."

The stakes seemed more than a little unfair. Then again, she doubted the corpses would let her leave without playing the game. She glanced over toward the exit again. A second body had somehow moved and was propped up against the door. She hadn't seen it move, nor heard it.

"How many of you are there?" Yuu asked.

"Thirty-six bodies," the corpse opposite her said.

"That's not what I asked," Yuu said as she pulled out the wobbly wooden chair and sat down at the table. "How many living dead are here, in this inn."

The corpse rolled his milky white eye up at her, and she could see something wriggling in the depths of it. "Just me," it rasped.

Yuu reached inside her robes and clutched the knife that the Ticking Clock had almost killed her with. If this corpse was controlling all the bodies, then she could try to kill it. Then again, even if she destroyed the body sitting there with maggots crawling around within its skull, and she was far from certain she could, that did not mean it would vanish. If it was not just this one corpse but all of them, then another would surely take its place. It seemed her best bet was to play the game and win the coin.

"Prove you have it," Yuu said. There was no sense playing if the stakes weren't real.

The corpse flipped up its eyepatch to reveal a wriggling mass of maggots. Pale flesh writhed against pale flesh and dozens of little mandibles opened and closed around nothing. The corpse dug into the putrid mass and spilled wriggling bodies onto the table. Then it pulled out a small jade coin and flipped the eyepatch down again. Yuu was glad of that. She really didn't want to play a hand of cards while staring at a tangle of larvae chewing on the man's brains. The corpse set the coin spinning on the table.

"Deal," the corpse rasped.

Yuu split the pile of lien in the centre of the table, pushed half toward the corpse, and gathered the other half to herself. Then she collected the cards and dealt two to each of them. A glance down at her hand told her she was right to make a large opening bet. A red forest and a green sun made for a decent start. If she pulled a lake of any colour or a white moon, she would almost certainly win. She pushed ten lien into the centre of the table and waited for the dead man to make his move. The corpse lifted the corners of his cards, and his eye rolled down in its socket. Whatever was in that milky orb writhed about like a fish in a bowl. Then the eye rolled back up to meet Yuu, and he pushed a handful of coins in to match hers.

The next cards went down. Yuu got a three of spears. It didn't help at all, but it was her bet. She could either bluff and represent a high hand or bet low and show weakness. She glanced up at the corpse to find him still as the grave. It didn't help that he was dead, making him hard to read, and it also didn't help that the corpse had so much less to lose than her. Yuu heard a shuffling behind her and glanced over her shoulder. One of the other corpses had somehow moved and was leaning against the wall not an arm's reach from her. Its expression was slack in death and something foul and yellow leaked from one nostril. Its gut had been slashed open and a trail of ropey intestines followed it across the tavern.

"Are you trying to cheat?" she asked the corpse.

The corpse opposite her glanced at his cards again. When he looked back up, his jaw dropped from his face into his lap. His fat brown tongue hung dry and limp like cracked leather. "Your bet," said one of the other corpses from deeper within the inn. A male voice, strained as though spoken through clenched teeth.

Yuu pushed another ten lien into the middle, leaving her with five. The corpse didn't hesitate to match her bet. Either he had a winning hand already, or the stakes meant nothing to him.

She dealt them each another card and glanced at her own, careful not the let the corpse behind her see it. A white moon, just what she needed. It was far from unbeatable, but a strong hand nonetheless. Worth betting on. Was it worth betting her life on though? There were still five different hands capable of beating her and twenty-six combinations of cards to achieve those hands. The odds felt worse every moment she considered them. She fought the urge to check the cards again. It's not like they could have changed.

"Your bet," a woman's voice gurgled.

Yuu reached for her lien. She'd have to bet it all on this one hand. A good hand. A winning hand. Her life on the line. Perhaps Natsuko was right. Perhaps she was trying to sacrifice herself, to pay for the things she had done, for the death of her prince. But like this? Murdered by corpses for a single coin. This was not how she wanted to die.

"Your bet," yet another voice. A man's voice high and nasally and closer than the last. A body lying at her feet. It hadn't been there a moment before.

Her fingers fidgeted across the five lien remaining to her. Her heart pounded in her ears. Never before had she felt an anxious terror like this during a game. Not chess, not mah-jongg, not Go. No, the only other time she had felt this anxious was during the battle of Jieshu. When the emperor's forces had sprung their trap, and their army closed in from all sides. When she had played the last of her pieces and given everything over to a glimmer of victory, knowing the odds were against her and failure would mean certain death. She had won, of course. Back then she had been the Art of War, and the Art of War never lost.

"You're yokai," Yuu said as it all clicked into place in her head. The yokai were vengeful spirits who clawed their way back from death. They formed when someone was wronged, like a bride murdered on her wedding day. From unfinished business, such as dying with an act of vengeance unfulfilled. Or from a missed opportunity, like being killed mere moments from a victory. She thought about all she knew of the spirits. It was widely believed yokai only formed from people of exceptionally strong will, or sometimes those who could simply not let their grievances go, even in death.

"Your bet," this from the corpse behind her against the wall, his rancid breath tickling the back of her neck.

Yuu took her hand from her lien. "I fold."

That was how Yuu could win. Not by winning, but by losing. She had to give the yokai what it wanted, what it needed in order to rest. She had to give it the victory it had been robbed of when the Cochtans slaughtered everyone at the inn. Then again, if she was wrong, she was willingly throwing away her life to the spirit. A win might get her the coin, but there was nothing to stop the yokai from murdering her and taking it back. A loss would forfeit her life by the rules of the game, by the bet she had made and the terms she had agreed to. But hopefully it would exorcise the spirit before it could claim her. At least she hoped it would. Chaoxiang may have said: *Only a fool marches to war knowing they might lose.* But it was Yuu's own grandmother, the first Art of War who said: *The first step toward winning is knowing which game you are playing.*

The corpse reached out and pulled the pile of coins toward itself. Then it gathered up the cards in its rotting hands and dealt again. Her cards were awful. A two of swords, a black dragon. The corpse pushed five lien into the centre of the table. If she wanted to win, she should fold. Get out of the hand before she lost it all. But if she wanted to lose, she would likely never get a better chance. She thought she understood the rules now. She hoped she understood the rules.

Yuu pushed her last five lien into the centre of the table. The corpse flicked over its cards- two dragons, a white and a red. An excellent hand. Yuu flipped over her own cards. The corpse against the wall started laughing.

"Your life is mine," said the yokai through the mouth of the body behind Yuu. A hand brushed against her shoulder and she gasped in fright.

"Two more cards each," Yuu said quickly.

"You can't win," slurred a man's voice. Yuu heard shuffling. Three more corpses had moved while she wasn't looking. She was surrounded, and they were closing in.

"Deal the cards!" Yuu hissed.

The yokai laughed, a haunting sound, the dry tongue dangling from its jawless maw.

"The game isn't over," Yuu snarled. "Two more cards. Deal them!"

The corpse leered at her through its milky eye and slowly dealt them two more cards. It didn't matter. Her hand was a loser from the start. The corpses were closing in around her, shuffling across the floor, drawing close. This was not how she wanted to die, buried beneath a pile of clawing corpses. All because she misjudged a yokai, misplayed a hand. She winced, squeezing the meat of her thigh so tightly it hurt. Pain and loss went hand in hand. Pain reminded her not to lose again. *Focus on the lessons.*

"You win," Yuu shouted over the noise of shuffling corpses. "That was why you came back. Unfinished business. You died before you could win this money. Well, now you've won it. Now, you can rest! Please."

The shuffling ceased. Yuu glanced over her shoulder. Two bodies, each with its mouth open, congealed blood and bile dripping like saliva, hovered over her. Others were all around her, hands reaching for her. All frozen a mere moment before tearing her apart.

The yokai chuckled again, tongue dry and cracked, flapping against its ruin of a mouth. It leaned forward across the table; its milky eye fixed upon her. Then the eye popped, and its head crashed down on the pile of lien on the table. All around her, corpses crumpled to the floor, in piles, crashing over chairs, limbs dropping off. Yuu snatched up the jade coin and fled.

Chapter 17

Yuu slammed the inn door closed behind her and leaned against the bamboo wall, breathing heavily, listening to her heart drumming in her ears. She was trembling, her hand clenched so tight around the jade coin it hurt.

Yuu peered into the darkness about the inn. Natsuko was nowhere to be seen. The goddess had a habit of vanishing whenever things got intense. Yuu couldn't decide whether it was because she couldn't help directly, or if she was up to something. She had a feeling the goddess wasn't telling her something. Probably a lot of things. The whole contest seemed... off, but Yuu couldn't put her finger on it. She knew if she could just read the contract scrawled over her skin, it would reveal everything.

The first step toward winning is knowing which game you are playing. Her grandmother's lesson, perhaps her first. Yuu had been starving, alone, a grubby little orphan girl. Her mother had abandoned her to join the Emperor of Ten Kings' harem. Well, that was part of it. The last words her mother had ever said to her were *Why do you look so much like him?* Yuu had fallen asleep on the side of a dirt road leading nowhere, sobbing as quietly as she could while her mother stared at her with such pain in her eyes. She woke up alone. She never saw her mother again. She had wandered around Song province, begging for scraps, stealing whatever she could and running before anyone could catch her. Then one day in a little village called Schuan an old woman caught her eye. The woman was sitting at a wooden table outside a bustling house, a bowl of rice porridge steaming before her next to a chessboard. Her eyes were closed and she rocked back and forth with the gentle rhythm of sleep. Yuu thought the bowl of porridge would be the easiest theft so far and crept closer, clinging to the shadows, mouth watering at the thought of food. It had been days since she had last eaten, and her stomach was a twisted knot that felt like it was trying to devour itself. The old woman was snoring so softly, when her eyes flicked open just as Yuu was reaching for the bowl, Yuu almost peed herself in fright. She dropped the bowl and made to run, but the old woman's hand shot out and grabbed her skinny arm. Yuu expected her to call for help or cry *thief*, but instead the old woman gestured at the board and pieces on the table and simply asked: *Do you know the game?* Yuu shook her head and the old woman tittered. She made a deal then: if Yuu played and won, she would earn herself a full meal of meat and rice and vegetables. Such a bounty over so little a thing as a game; how could Yuu refuse? Of course, she had lost. She hadn't known the rules, and the old woman was teaching them to her as she went. That was when she said, *The first step toward winning is knowing which game you are playing.* Despite the loss, the old woman fed Yuu and let her sleep on the floor at the foot of her own bed. Yuu drifted off that night to the snores of the old woman and for the first time in so long she felt safe. The next day they played again. Yuu lost, but the old woman fed her again. And before Yuu knew what was happening, she had a home. She had a family, though most of them didn't like her much. But she still didn't understand the rules of the game they were playing until her grandmother pressed that damned mask into her hands and told her she was the new Art of War.

It started raining while she was inside the inn. A light drizzle, but the roiling, grey clouds heralded a storm waiting to break. Hosa had been in the midst of a drought for a couple of months; the rain was much needed, but it would turn the surrounding roads and fields to mud. She could remain dry by staying on the porch of the inn, but that meant staying on the porch of the inn. Close to the corpses. She was still trembling from her close call with the yokai. By the stars or the gods or whoever was real and listening, she needed a drink.

Yuu pushed open the door to inn and stared into the gloom. The corpses were unmoving, silent, stinking of rot. "Move," she said, unsure whether she was talking to herself or the bodies. "Move!" she said again. This time it was definitely to herself.

She inched inside as quietly as possible. Three corpses were piled near the door. One was a wriggling mass of maggots and papery skin. Another's head was flopped to the side, a gaping wound where a neck should have been. But something had changed. The tension had faded from the inn. Now, it was just the sight of a massacre. Still horrifying, but the fear had gone, the sense of foreboding fled. She stepped over bodies and made her way to the bar. The Cochtans were thorough in their slaughter, but must have moved on quickly. There were still several bottles of wine. She selected a few that smelled less vinegary and picked up a chair too, then turned to flee once more. Hanging next to the door she spotted an old bamboo douli. No doubt the owner was dead now, and the hat would help keep the rain off her head. She snatched it from the wall and took her looted items out onto the porch, closing the door behind her. Lump stared at her, chewing lethargically on a clump of grass, caring nothing for the drizzling rain.

"Say what you want," Yuu said. "Going back inside was heroic!" The horse glanced at her, predictably said nothing, then swished its mangy tail and went back to chewing grass.

Yuu settled down in her chair on the porch, swigged some wine, then released a contented sigh. Then sipped again. It was a day from souring at best, but that was fine because Yuu didn't intend to give it the day it needed. The storm clouds opened and the drizzle turned into a downpour. Lump knickered in annoyance as the rain pelted him, soaking his patchy hide. Yuu clicked her tongue and pointed beside her, and the horse mounted the porch, found a dry spot to lie on, and flopped onto his side. The porch kept the worst of the storm at bay, but water dripped through the thatch roof here and there.

Yuu watched the rain and considered the coin she had just won. Yang Yang's coin, the god of gambling's most precious possession. A coin that, according to Natsuko, never won. Yuu flipped it into the air and let it fall back down into her hand. It landed moon side up, a crescent sliver like the lopsided grin of a fool. She flipped it again. This time it landed sun side up, a blazing jagged ball. She flipped it a third time and called out *sun* while it was in the air. It landed in her palm and the crescent moon grinned up at her. Yuu repeated the process another two dozen times between swigs of wine, and each time the coin landed with the losing side up.

Natsuko told the truth about the coin, it seemed. That such items existed was a wonder to Yuu. The coin held no technique, nor any qi. It was a mystery. She couldn't imagine how such a thing might work. The first wine bottle ran empty while she was considering the artefact, and she placed it off the porch to collect rainwater, then opened a second bottle.

She continued to examine the artefact. It was light as jade, and its depictions of sun and moon were intricate and beautiful. An undulating dragon chased its tail around the coin's edge. But there were no clues as to how it worked. The coin had to function by a set of rules. All things had rules. The world was full of them. The sun and moon moved across the sky, each sharing the world, sometimes bathing it in light, other times shrouding it in darkness. Gravity was another rule of the world, a constant pull to the earth. People were born, grew up, grew old, and died. All functioned within the laws of the world as set down by… Yuu had to think about that. Who made the rules? The gods? The stars? Were the laws of the world older than the gods? These were questions philosophers had worried themselves grey over for generations upon generations. People had gone mad trying to reason them out. Yuu's grandmother had made a study of rules, claiming there was nothing in the world so important. But even she had been confounded by the grand laws. She had said: *Know the rules of every game, great and small, and you will never be surprised. But do not concern yourself with the unyielding laws of nature. Focus, instead, on the rules you can bend or break. When you know those rules, when you understand them, you will know how to win.*

Yuu flipped the coin again and let it land in her palm. Without looking at it, she quickly covered it with her other hand. "Sun," she said, and pulled away her hand to reveal its moon side. She repeated the process another two dozen times with the same result. A game of chance destined to lose by some mechanism she couldn't understand.

Yuu finished the second bottle of wine and was feeling quite fuzzy around the edges. It was a pleasant drunkenness that made everything softer, quieter and more peaceful. Even the pouring rain and the crack of thunder seemed a welcome comfort. She placed the coin on the wooden floor of the porch, sun side up and staggered out of her chair. She concluded she was, perhaps, slightly more drunk than she had first thought. No matter. Drunk was drunk was drunk, no matter how much drink had been drunk. She giggled at the thought and placed the second empty bottle out in the rain. "Sun," she slurred and turned quickly, as if hoping to catch some little spirit changing which side the coin showed. She tripped and landed awkwardly on the wooden floor. The coin still showed its sunny side to the world.

"You tricksy little bastard," Yuu slurred at the coin. "How do you work?"

The coin did not answer, even when she poked it. Yuu clambered to her feet, rubbed the pain from her arse, and slumped down into the chair again. Then she contented herself by glaring at the coin while she opened the third bottle of wine. She knew she should ration it, and also knew she was already more than drunk enough. But it had been a tough few days and she just wanted to get entirely drunk. Tits-over-arse drunk! No, that wasn't right. Arse-over-tits drunk? She couldn't remember, but the saying definitely had something to do with arses and tits. She giggled again as she considered the words and wished she had some company to get drunk with. After all, the horse was asleep, and the coin was a sullen conversationalist at best, even with its sunny side up.

She was well into that third bottle of wine, and still giving the coin an icy glare, when three young girls appeared out of the pouring rain, walking up the muddy path toward the inn. Yuu squinted until the three resolved into one, then groaned. "I wondered when you would turn up."

The girl stepped up onto the porch, and then suddenly she wasn't a girl anymore, but an old crone, heavily wrinkled and somehow entirely dry.

"You found it then," Natsuko said as she stepped around the coin and knelt in front of the doorway to the inn.

"Yes, I won it," Yuu said, her voice slow even to her own ears. "Or maybe I lost it. Bloody coin. You could have told me there was a yokai in there." She waved a hand toward the inn.

"I see you found some wine too," Natsuko said.

"Well it *is* an inn," Yuu giggled. "Thish coin. How does it do… the thing… the trick." She sighed. "How does it work?"

The goddess rolled her eyes at Yuu. "I told you. When you flip it…"

"No no no no no no no," Yuu said, shaking her head until the world was a sickening blur. "No. I know what it does, but how? How does it do it? What are the rules?"

Natsuko shrugged. "I don't know. It's not my coin."

Yuu groaned again as she leaned forward and struggled to pick the coin up, mostly because there were suddenly three coins and she couldn't decide which was real. She found it on her second grab and flipped it into the air. It landed moon side up. She flipped it again and it landed sun side up. "Call it," she said as she flipped again.

"Sun," the goddess said, reaching over and pulling the third bottle of wine away from Yuu. That was fine. She'd had enough already. Though there was some left and it seemed foolish to waste it. The coin landed in her hand and the blazing sun glinted up at Yuu.

"Huh," she said. "You win."

"Lucky me."

Yuu flipped the coin again. "Call it," she said.

"Moon," Natsuko said. This time Yuu missed the catch, snatching at air, and the coin clattered to the wooden floor. The moon grinned up at her.

Yuu flipped the coin once more. "Again."

The goddess sighed. "Sun."

"Sun," Yuu repeated. The coin landed in her palm, moon side up. "Interesting." She was certain it was interesting, but not certain *how* it was interesting. "Rules…" Yuu said and let the word trail off into nothing.

Natsuko was watching her through narrowed eyes, the bottle of wine now beside her. "Get some sleep, Daiyu," she said. "We have a long way to go yet, and you need the rest."

Yuu tried to push a few strands of hair from her face but missed and slapped a hand against her eye socket. "You don't get to tell me when… how... um…" The goddess was right. Yuu was exhausted. Too many long days, too many long nights. She clutched the coin in her hand for a moment, then slipped it into the same pocket as the ring. She may not have figured out how it worked, but she was certain she had figured out the rules of the coin, and that was something. Maybe. Unless it was nothing.

Just before she drifted off to sleep, she heard Natsuko say, "I am sorry."

Chapter 18

The next day was made miserable by pouring rain and a hangover that felt like five armies going to war in Yuu's head, none of which had the vaguest semblance of a plan. Also, she woke to find a familiar, if somewhat soggy, chubby face staring down at her.

"What are you doing here?" Yuu asked. She groaned melodramatically and considered closing her eyes again, wishing it was all a dream.

Li Bang shrugged. "Thought you might need my help."

"The Lump wants to help," Natsuko snapped. "Let him help."

The horse looked up at that. The beast was standing out in the rain, its feet sunk deep into the mud, but it squelched closer and snorted at Natsuko.

"The other Lump," the goddess said. The horse tried to mount the porch of the inn, but there really wasn't enough space with three people already sitting on it. "Fine!" Natsuko said, shooing the beast away. "You can be the only Lump." She patted the horse on the nose and looked at Li Bang. "You can be…"

"I told you to stay in Ban Ping," Yuu said a little more sharply than intended. Her hangover was making everything hard. She felt raw and on edge, tired and grimy. The pain in her head and lethargy in her limbs was exposing the worst of her, and she wanted no one to see them. She didn't even want to see them herself.

Li Bang nodded. Water was dripping from his wiry hair onto his face, rolling down his cheeks almost like tears. "I, um, saw you. Knew you'd need help. I thought it would be worth the risk. After all, if I get conscripted, I get to fight. Now that I have a technique, I can make a name for myself." He smiled so innocently. He had never known war. He didn't know that death was far more likely than heroism. She'd seen innocent men like him. Seen them die. Seen the innocence die in those that lived. She couldn't decide which was worse.

"Bulge!" Natsuko said with a snap of her fingers. "That is your new name."

Li Bang turned a surly stare on the goddess. "My name is Li Bang," he said. "Unless you want to call me Falling Moon."

Natsuko harrumphed and leapt off the porch into the rain. The water bounced off her, somehow not touching her. "Nope. Bulge, it is."

Yuu was missing something. She had that familiar itch. The back of her mind had pieced something together and was trying desperately to force the knowledge through the haze of her hangover. "How did you find me?" she asked.

"I saw you," Li Bang said far too quickly, not meeting her gaze. "With my technique. Why aren't you in the tavern? Why are we outside? What's in there?" It was a lot of questions from a man who didn't usually ask many.

"You don't want to know," Yuu said, still trying to force her mind to think through the stabbing pain.

Li Bang's gaze went distant for a moment. Yuu got the distinct feeling he was here and also somewhere else. Then he focused again, shuddered, and stared at Yuu with eyes as wide as rice bowls. "Did you do that?"

Yuu stared at him. "Do I look like I could do that?" She rolled her eyes. "The Cochtans passed through days ago and slaughtered them. The yokai was Batu's doing though."

"Oh," Li Bang looked lost. "I don't understand." Yuu didn't have the patience to explain it all to him.

"You couldn't have caught up with me," Yuu said slowly as the pieces of information squeezed through the fog and assembled into something approaching a coherent thought. Even if Li Bang had seen her, his vision was not clairvoyant, he must have known he would never arrive in time to help. Besides, he couldn't see in the dark, and she had a head start on him. He could never have found her, could never have caught her up unless… unless someone led him to her.

Yuu rounded on Natsuko. "You led him here." It was not a question.

The goddess shrugged. "You might be willing to throw away your strongest ally, but I was not."

Yuu staggered off the porch into the pouring rain and trudged through the mud to the ancient little goddess. Of course, she didn't understand. She thought Yuu was just throwing away a piece that could still be useful. She had never even considered what it might cost Li Bang. Yuu glared down at Natsuko. "You undermined me!"

Natsuko's lip curled and she glared up at Yuu. "I corrected your idiotic decision."

Yuu shook her head sending water droplets flying from her messy tangle of hair. She pushed it behind her ears. "You don't make the decisions here. You chose me to be your champion because I am a strategist. How can I do the job you've hired me for, if you change my orders?"

"*Your* orders?" Natsuko scoffed. "Do not forget who you are talking to, mortal. I am not some weak-minded bulge you can push around, nor some foolish old man you can bully at chess." All around them raindrops froze in the air and shattered into a hanging mist. It was an impressive display of power. "I am the god of all things lost, of all opportunities missed." A light like a million campfires flamed in the goddess' eyes. Her wrinkles deepened and cast dancing shadows across her face. "You are not in charge here. You work by *my* will!"

Yuu was trembling, and it was not from the hangover or even the cold or rain. She had known Natsuko was a god, true, but this was the first time she had seen her angry, seen the power she could wield. There was menace in the goddess' words, and Yuu was not foolish enough to believe she was beyond the reach of it.

Champion or not, Yuu was dealing with a god. She had forgotten that. She had been duped by the appearance of an old crone and the pleasant, if occasionally grouchy demeanour. She clenched her hands tight, nails dug into her palms. Pain to learn the lesson.

The rain resumed as if it hadn't just stopped and exploded in mid-air, the other-worldly lights in Natsuko's eyes flickering out. Yuu gasped in a breath, felt her pulse pounding in her ears like a cavalry charge. The goddess' face softened. "I am trying to help you, in the only way I can," she said in a kindly voice that reminded Yuu of her grandmother. "I am trying to save you from yourself."

Yuu stood trembling, unable to find her voice. She couldn't tell if the water streaming down her face was rain or tears. She tried to move, but her feet were frozen, sandals sunk into the mud. Her breath came in short, ragged gasps. The memories of another life pressed in close and she was struggling to hold them at bay. Then Lump was there. The old horse poked Yuu with its muzzle, snorted hot breath into her hair, then snuffled about her robes searching for something sweet to eat. Yuu patted the beast, and for once it didn't try to bite her.

She realised Natsuko was watching her, an entirely blank look on her face. Li Bang stood near the door to the inn, silent and almost forgotten. They were waiting for her. Waiting on her orders. *The Art of War should always be in control.* Her grandmother's words. *The truth about people is they are all, without exception, looking for someone else to be in charge. To take the responsibility and the consequences of decision away from them. Command is about confidence. Show no fear, no hesitation, no indecision. And in that certainty of self, men, soldiers, generals, and even kings will follow you without question.* Yuu couldn't help but wonder if the same could be said of gods.

She swallowed hard and took a deep breath, willed her feet to move and pulled them free of the sucking mud. "Time to go," she said. Neither man, nor horse, nor god argued with her.

The douli she had taken from the inn kept the worst of the rain off her, but the water still soaked into her sandals and the outer layers of her robes, and that made it far from pleasant. Also, wet horse was a special type of musty scent she would never get used to. The rain bounced off Natsuko, never actually touching her, leaving her bone dry, which made the matter even more unbearable. Only Li Bang was more miserable than Yuu and that was because he was entirely soaked through.

They were heading north-west. Deeper into the heart of the Ning province. It was a prosperous region full of farms that grew root vegetables, and famous for a twice-yearly festival dedicated to the musical arts. Bards, house musicians, and even old farmers claiming they could play a whistle flocked to Ning for the festival. It was said everyone was given a chance to play, and some of the greatest musicians in Hosa had been discovered there. Even during the last emperor's violent reign, and despite the rampant banditry of the region, the festival continued to run. A beacon of hope in a time when there was no rarer commodity. But it seemed even that wonderful tradition could not survive Cochtan's war.

The field they passed showed all the evidence of a festival cut short. Banners proudly proclaiming names and accolades hung soaked and miserable in the rain. Instruments, from flutes to guzheng to simple drums, all lay discarded on the wet grass or trampled into the mud. The field had been churned to muck, tents broken and fluttering in the breeze. No bodies though, Yuu noticed. She realised then that, while the Cochtans might be to blame, this wasn't their doing. This was the Hosan army recruiters. What better place to conscript hundreds— perhaps thousands —of new soldiers all at once? A thing of beauty, dedicated to the arts and to bringing people together in peace, destroyed by a senseless war.

"Do the Cochtans even want anything?" Yuu mused. "Or is war just in their nature?" Perhaps they weren't really so different. War was in her nature too, no matter how much she tried to avoid it.

"Eh?" Natsuko shouted over the driving rain. "What's that?"

"Where are we going?" Yuu asked, changing the subject before she could ruminate on it.

"Anding," the goddess shouted. It was the old capital of Ning province, a large city built upon a hill surrounded by sheer cliffs on three sides. Yuu's grandmother said there was no more defensible city in all Hosa, and she would know. She held it for two hundred and twelve days against a relentless Cochtan assault. The place of her grandmother's first battle, the birthplace of the Art of War.

"What are we looking for?" Yuu shouted through the hissing rain.

"Somewhere out of the rain for a bloody start," the goddess grumbled, despite being dry save for the mud squelching over her sandals.

"Yes please," Li Bang said. His hair was flat and sodden, and his trousers splashed with stinking mud.

Natsuko stopped to gaze at the festival field. "So many lost things," she said, shaking her head. "Already people are praying at shrines for me to return them." She trudged toward a wooden flute lying half buried in the muck. "This belonged to Jian Wei, a talented young man who makes eyeglasses for a living. He loves helping people see again almost as much as he loves lifting spirits with lively ditties. He carved this flute himself, and it has always been a little out of tune, perfectly matching his skill with the instrument." She paused and sighed. "He was going to meet the love of his life here, two souls coming together in song, a voice to match Jian Wei's playing. But that opportunity is gone now."

"Can't you return it?" Yuu shouted over the rain.

The goddess stared down at the flute for a few more moments, then stepped over it and continued walking. Yuu and Li Bang hurried to catch up. Lump followed behind, his hooves squelching in the mud, his nose to the ground as though searching for something to eat amidst the sludge. He was always looking for something to eat.

"There are two artefacts in Anding," Natsuko said, staring to the north-west. "Guangfai's mirror and Khando's sword, or what's left of it at least. Getting them might be difficult."

Yuu laughed. "Because getting the ring and coin were easy?" But of course, the goddess would think it was easy. She might point the way and tell Yuu what the artefacts were, but the moment any actual work needed doing, she vanished. No doubt she took the opportunity to return to Tianmen and watch from the safety of heaven while Yuu risked her life for the goddess' cause.

They slogged along the road in silence for a while after that. The goddess seemed deep in thought. For Yuu's part, she was left wondering why the goddess did not consider returning the flute. She had seemed so impassioned talking about it, so mournful about the opportunity the owner had missed. Whenever she spoke of the items people had lost, it seemed to come from her heart and there was pain there. She could return items if she wanted to. Yuu reached into a pocket of her robe and rubbed her thumb over the chess piece the goddess had returned to her the day they met. Why did she not return the flute then? Why did she not return all the items that people prayed to her shrines for?

By afternoon, the rain had slowed to a depressing drizzle and the sky had lightened to a patchy blanket of greys. They crested a hill and Yuu got her first sight of Anding. And of the army camped outside it. Even from half a league away, Yuu could see thousands of tents down in the valley, arrayed around the road at the foot of another hill leading up to the city. It was the beginnings of a siege, soldiers building reinforcements and digging in, preparing to starve out the inhabitants of the city. But the odd thing was they were flying Hosan banners. The WuLong family crest, two mountains with a golden dragon between them, was stitched into many of the tents, and hundreds of banners showed the symbol for spirit, the new emperor's chosen emblem. Yuu saw other banners too, evidence of soldiers and nobility from all over Hosa. She saw the river symbol of Ganxi, the hope symbol of Lau, the ice symbol of Sich. She even saw the raven symbol on a flag fluttering in the breeze and it sent a chill down her spine. The raven was the chosen symbol of Qing, which meant that at least one of the royal family was in attendance. Yuu had no wish to encounter any members of the family who had placed so large a bounty on her head.

"Perhaps we should leave," Yuu said. The Hosan army was laying siege to its own city, which meant Anding had fallen and was occupied by the Cochtans. Which meant both sides of the battle would happily see her dead. She very much doubted there would be any chance to retrieve the artefacts.

"Nonsense," Natsuko said, catching Yuu's arm even as she turned to head back down the hill. "We are lagging behind in this contest and there are two artefacts here."

"And two armies between us and those artefacts," Yuu said, pulling her arm free. "How do you expect me to get in there and find them?"

The goddess shrugged. "You are the strategist."

"And as the strategist, I'm telling you it's impossible. Look at them, Natsuko." She pointed to the encamped Hosan army. "They are set up and dug in to prevent anyone entering or leaving the city. It's a fool's tactic, but it prevents us from getting in there."

"A fool's tactic?" Natsuko asked. "How so?"

"Against any other nation, it might work," Yuu admitted. "Surround the city and prevent supplies from reaching the defenders. Starve them out. It's not a quick victory, but as long as you can supply your own troops and keep them from deserting, you will eventually force your enemy into surrendering or assaulting your entrenched position."

Again, the goddess shrugged. "The Hosans haven't surrounded the city."

"They've surrounded the only part that matters. Anding has sheer cliffs on three sides and only one road up the hill to its gates. It's as defensible a city as any I've ever seen. Unassailable even." Though it looked as though the southern wall had suffered some catastrophic damage. A large section of it had tumbled down the cliffside and lay strewn at the bottom in piles of broken rubble. Yuu could not see any battle damage though, and she suspected a part of the cliff had eroded, taking the wall with it. "But the Cochtans possess a unique advantage the Hosan general clearly has not considered. They do not require supplies to be brought up the mountain. They can have them delivered by thopter. They can hold the city indefinitely, and the Hosan force will eventually disperse. More than that, the Hosan force is also vulnerable to attacks from behind while it is laid out so rigidly."

She pointed to the Hosan army. "This Hosan army was originally intended to march north into Cochtan and strike at the enemy while the emperor's own force to the east freed Shin. See how the general has arrayed his forces? Horses and tents to the north, ready to march as soon as the city is retaken. But…"

Natsuko was nodding along, though her eyes were wide. "It all sounds quite complicated."

"It isn't," Yuu said. "It's bloody brilliant. By the Cochtans, I mean. Whoever planned this assault knew exactly what they were doing."

"How so?"

"They're splitting the Hosan forces by taking the most defensible cities in the north, forcing the Hosans to split their armies and fight without the advantage of numbers, something they have always relied on. Here the Cochtans have taken Anding, the most defensible city in all Hosa. In Shin, they have taken the capital, another city that is all but unassailable due to its position across several rocky plateaus. They have also taken Sun Valley, the path between the two capitals of Ning and Shin. This secures supply lines between the two and limits the scope of possible engagements."

"Sounds like the Hosans need a good strategist," Natsuko said. The wrinkled goddess was staring at the walled city ahead of them.

"No!" Yuu said emphatically. She was done with war. Left it behind as surely as her old name. That part of her had died with her prince.

"We need to get into the city," Natsuko said, spreading her hands as though the entire thing were out of her control. "For that, we need to help the Hosans retake the city, and quickly. *You* are the greatest strategist in all Hosa. Tell me you don't have at least a few ideas of how they can do it."

Yuu shook her head at the goddess. "Even if I did." And they both knew she did. "What makes you think the Hosans would listen to me? I can't just walk into an armed camp, demand to see the general, and start handing out orders."

Natsuko turned that inhuman grin on her. "Not as Yuu, no." The goddess reached into the sleeve of her hanfu and pulled out a plain mask, ceramic and white as snow. A large crack ran down from the right eye to the chin. Damage taken during the battle of Jieshu.

Yuu shook her head. "Where did you get that?" It was the Art of War's mask. She had worn it for years, through every battle at the Steel Prince's side. She had been wearing it the day she failed, when she lost her prince. It hurt then and it hurt worse now. Losing is pain. She pinched the back of her hand, her fingernails tearing the flesh and drawing blood. Then she took a step back still staring at the mask.

"I am the god of lost things," Natsuko said. She took a step forward, holding the mask before her, demanding Yuu take it.

"I didn't lose it," Yuu said with a savage shake of her head. "I left it behind."

The goddess followed her, still holding out the mask. "There is little difference but the words. Consequence is rarely shaped by intention." She took another step forward. "This mask belongs to the Art of War. It belongs to you."

"Just a few days ago, you were admonishing me for putting my life at risk. For trying to get myself killed as a way of atonement. What would you call this?" Yuu asked with a wavering voice. She had given up that mask the day the war was won. Even as the imposter Steel Prince was revealed and his body spat upon by the very soldiers he had died fighting alongside, Yuu had thrown the mask away and melted into the streets of Jieshu. She liked to think the Art of War had died that day. Daiyu Lingsen had died that day along with the memory of the Steel Prince. Yuu had been born. And Yuu had nothing to do with war. All Yuu wanted was to play chess and drink each day away until she could forget.

"I would call this *stop being such a damned child and own up to your past and your responsibilities*!" Natsuko rushed forward and caught Yuu's tattooed hand with her own. She pushed the mask into her hand and stepped away.

"You don't understand what you're saying," Yuu snapped. "There are soldiers from Qing province down there. Someone from the Qing royal family. If I go down there as the Art of War... as me... they will kill me for the murder of the Steel Prince."

"A murder you did not commit," Natsuko said.

"It doesn't matter. I knew about his death and I covered it up. And I sent a fake Steel Prince out in his place." Yuu wanted to scream. "As far as anyone is concerned, I am responsible, and I've already been convicted."

"Then do not let them kill you," the goddess said, her lips quirked up into the hint of a smile. As though such a thing would

181

be easy. "Give them something they want more than you. Trade your expertise for your freedom."

"What?"

The goddess sighed and threw up her hands. "You are the strategist! Think of something. There are artefacts we need in that city, and if we don't get them some other champion will and I will lose my chance to dethrone Batu and all the world will know another century of war. This army also wants that city. Our interests align. Make them see that!"

The goddess had a point. Roaring Tiger was in command of the Hosan army. He was a blustering old fool who knew how to shout troops into line, but hadn't the subtleties required to strategise his way out of a bathtub. But he knew the Art of War did. They had been on opposite sides of more than one battle, and he had never beaten her. But that was then. So much had changed. She stared down at the mask in her hands. She really hated the gods, and was more certain than ever this damned goddess was going to get her killed.

Chapter 19

Yuu donned her old mask and strode down the hill into the valley and towards the encamped army with Natsuko, Li Bang, and Lump just a step behind. It did not take long for her to remember how uncomfortable the mask was. It pushed against her nose and only had holes in it for her eyes. Moisture from her breath pooled at the little lip underneath the chin. She had been used to it before. She had worn it every day for almost seven years; it had become as much a part of her as her hair or nails. It offered anonymity and carried with it a legacy and a responsibility both. Yuu had failed the responsibility and tarnished the legacy. She didn't deserve to wear her grandmother's mask.

Li Bang sniffed loudly, then said in a lilting voice, "They're coming." Yuu realised he was being led by Natsuko, his eyes distant and clouded.

Half a dozen soldiers rode out to meet them each carrying a spear and dressed in black lacquered ceramic armour, their horses' hooves tearing up muddy clumps of earth as they galloped up the hill. Yuu walked on toward them, head held high. It was important to present an air of confidence. She might need General Roaring Tiger to believe her, but she needed the soldiers of this army to believe *in* her. Of course, she had to consider that if the soldiers were from Qing province, they might just spear her in the chest and drag her body back to their army. That would certainly put a quick end to the Art of War's tremulous resurrection.

"Halt!" called one of the soldiers as they drew close. These were no provincial troops; they were the elite soldiers of Wu. They formed up around Yuu and Natsuko and Li Bang, surrounding them. If she played this wrong, they would all die. Well, except Natsuko. The old goddess would likely laugh off a spear in the chest.

"No," Yuu said. She tilted her head so the lead soldier could see under her douli, so he could see her mask. And she continued her determined pace, ignoring the spear levelled at her chest and stepping to the side to move around the big stallion snorting mist in her face. Natsuko was blessedly silent.

The lead soldier looked to his comrades. Yuu could not see much of his expression under his helmet, but she could tell some of the confidence leaked out of him. It was important to appear in control, even if everything was going to hell around you. The soldier wheeled his horse around as Yuu walked past it, and manoeuvred in front of her again.

"I said halt!" He held the spear tip inches from Yuu's chest.

"And I won't repeat myself," Yuu said. Her voice had changed, taken on the air of command, the confidence she had once been so proud of. The change had not been a conscious decision. It had come naturally. She gently pushed the spear tip out of her way and continued walking. "I'm here to see General Roaring Tiger. He will want to meet with me."

"Are you really her?" asked a beardless soldier, his horse drawing level with Yuu.

Yuu looked up at the man, and his eyes searched her mask, featureless save for the crack running from the right eye.

"Our prayers are answered," the beardless soldier said. "I fought for you, strategist. I fought for you and the Steel Prince." He fell silent for a moment, but Yuu could sense him chewing over his next words. "Did you do it?"

Yuu turned her gaze back toward the army encamped at the bottom of the valley, on the trampled road leading up to the city. Project confidence. Never let your enemy see you waver. Never let your troops see you uncertain. Inside her robes, she pinched her arm so hard it hurt. The Art of War should always lead and expect others to follow without question. "I did not kill the Steel Prince." They were words she had never said to anyone. They were the truth, and yet they tasted like lies on her lips. "But I did replace him. To win the battle, to win the war, I did what was necessary."

The beardless soldier nodded. "We'll escort you to the general, strategist."

The lead soldier kicked his horse on and gave the beardless soldier a hard shove in his saddle. "I'm in charge here, soldier."

"This is the Art of War, sergeant. If anyone can figure out how to take back the city and save our people, it's her."

Yuu ignored the argument and kept walking, stepping around the horse in front of her. She had no idea if Natsuko was following, or if the goddess had done another of her vanishing tricks. Or if Li Bang and Lump were being held at spear point. She couldn't afford to look over her shoulder and check.

"If that's true, then she is a criminal and a traitor," said the sergeant.

"That's not for you to decide, sir. Only the general can make that decision."

The sergeant wheeled his horse around again, walking it alongside Yuu. "Go!" he snarled. And just like that, she had an escort into the Hosan army.

Hosan soldiers gawked at Yuu as she strode into their camp with her head held high, and whispers slithered like serpents behind her. The camp was remarkably well organised with neat rows of tents all around. The sounds of a hammer striking anvil rang out, the shouts of a sergeant taking troops through manoeuvres joined it. The smell was an atrocious mix of wet smoke, mud, and shit. Some soldiers were oiling their spears, reworking the leather grips on their swords, or sleeping; they were the veterans. Others were joking in groups, shifting about in their ill-fitting armour, or pacing nervously in the mud; the raw recruits who had yet to see battle. It was all so familiar to Yuu, like coming home and finding nothing had changed.

Her escort showed her to what had once been a crossroads at
the foot of the hill, but thousands upon thousands of booted feet
had long since churned the road to a sucking quagmire. The
soldiers led her to a tall wooden inn at the centre of camp. A sign
hung outside, but there was nothing but a dark smudge on it. It
was spacious inside, with only a few chairs, a battered wooden
table nestled against the far wall, and a staircase leading up to a
second floor. Deep scrapes in the floorboard were evidence there
was once furniture aplenty, but it was long gone. This was
General Roaring Tiger's command centre, and the man appeared
to have austere tastes. Yuu approved of that much at least.

"The general is touring the troops, strategist," said the
beardless soldier with a bow. "We've sent word you're here." The
man stood beside the door. The significance was not lost on Yuu.
She was under guard, awaiting the general's verdict. She
maintained her posture, refused to show any anxiety. The mask
helped.

Natsuko strolled past her with a grumble and sank down into
a chair by a window that looked out toward the besieged city. "It
seems everyone is interested by your sudden appearance," the
goddess said. "I heard more than a few proclaim you the Saviour
of Anding."

"Seems a bit early to save that," Li Bang said as he sat down
on the first step of the staircase and tried to wring the water from
his tunic. A puddle quickly formed beneath him. "I thought they
were gonna kill us."

Yuu leaned her shoulder against the wall next to the goddess
and stared up the hill toward the city. She spoke in a hushed voice.
"They're not talking about me. My grandmother was the Saviour
of Anding."

Li Bang sniffed. "Huh?"

"You don't know about the Siege of Anding?" Yuu asked.
"Must be seventy years ago now. The first time the Cochtans
invaded Hosa."

Li Bang just shook his head, but Natsuko grumbled, wringing her gnarled hands. "I was a little busy listening to prayers for the lost at the time. Didn't pay attention to all the details."

Yuu smiled. She never thought she would have cause or opportunity to teach history to a god. "That time, as with now, Anding was one of the first cities hit by the Cochtan invasion. It's the capital of Ning, and as you can see highly defensible. A high value prize, it would serve as a base to launch offensive strikes further into the heart of Hosa." Yuu pushed her douli off her head to hang against her back, then reached into her robes, pulled out the little statue she was working on and began carving. "The king of Ning was a proud man. He refused to give up his city and brought most of his force behind the walls. Even so, the Cochtan forces were overwhelmingly superior, and he knew his calls for aid from the other provinces would take time, if any came at all. He knew it was only a matter of time before Anding fell, and he would fall with it."

"You are enjoying this, aren't you?" Natsuko asked, her eyes narrowed to slits.

Yuu grinned, knowing the goddess wouldn't see it behind her mask. "It makes a refreshing change from being lectured by you. The king of Ning's grasp of tactics and strategy was, by his own admission, lacking. His advisers were in unanimous agreement that he should flee. But there was a lady in his wife's employ who was renowned for her skill at chess, and her consumption of philosophy. It made her something of an outcast among her peers. Well, that and her ability to reduce almost anyone to tears with nothing but the blade of her tongue."

"I like her already," Natsuko said.

"Yes, you probably would have. But regardless of his failing at strategy, if there was one thing the king of Ning was good at, it was spotting talent, and having the wisdom to defer to it. He came to her for advice again and again, consulting on all matters regarding the defence of the city. All in secret, of course. It wouldn't do for the king to be seen seeking the guidance of a woman. Before long, it wasn't enough to have her close. As the Cochtans intensified their assault, he needed her by his side at all times.

"Unfortunately, back then women were neither soldiers, nor scholars, nor advisers in Hosa," Yuu said. She was glad how far things had come in just seventy years. "So, the king of Ning gave this woman a mask and bid her wear it at all times. To stay by his side always. Soon the soldiers and officers all realised where the orders were truly coming from. And so, the Art of War was born. My grandmother, a young woman who previously had known nothing but a wealthy, privileged life behind the walls of a great city, quickly earned respect from some of the strongest, most experienced soldiers in Hosa. And it was through her direction that the city of Anding held out long enough for its allies from Sich, Long, and Lau to arrive.

"They called her the Saviour of Anding, never knowing she was a woman. It was only the start of the war, of course. My grandmother was instrumental in turning back the Cochtan invasion all over the Hosan border. By the end of the war, she was in command of the greatest army Hosa had ever seen, an alliance of seven of the ten provinces. And when the Cochtans finally retreated and the war was won, my grandmother took off her mask in secret, and the Art of War simply disappeared."

"Until you picked up the mantle?" Natsuko said.

Yuu stared down at the floor, her carving knife halfway through peeling off a small shaving. "Not by choice," she said. She never wanted to be the Art of War. Never wanted to be a strategist. Never wanted the burden of her grandmother's legacy. Well, that wasn't entirely true. She hadn't wanted it at first. But she had grown to need it eventually.

The goddess reached out and took Yuu's hand, gave it a gentle squeeze. "Whose choice was it?"

The door burst open, startling them all and none more so than the soldier standing next to it whose spear fell to the floor with a clatter. A greying old man whose battered ceramic armour barely constrained his girth barrelled into the room. He had a face like thunder and a voice like lightning. "This had better not be some sort of joke!" he snarled. "Because it's not funny. Those Qing bastards are already breathing down my neck." His armour was a dull, rusty red and the bulging tunic underneath was black. His pauldrons were shaped like crashing waves.

"General Roaring Tiger," Yuu said. She stepped away from the wall and bowed low at the waist. He was due that much respect at least. A strategist, he might not be, but a good commander didn't always need to be.

"Oh shit," Roaring Tiger growled, his voice dropping to a low rumble. "I really hoped it *was* a joke."

Behind the general came another man. Taller and younger, though undoubtedly related judging by his flat nose and dimpled chin. He looked a man in his prime, standing straight, his skin glowing with health. His armour was deep red, perfectly maintained where his brother's had been left to dull. Yuu regarded him with a little trepidation. Here walked a true hero. The Crimson Tide had a reputation as bloody as his name. Twin dao hung from his belt, and a spear was slung across his back. Rumour had it the Crimson Tide had killed enough men to populate a city with ghosts, and Yuu had to admit there was certainly something menacing about the fire in his deep black eyes. He leaned against the wall close to the door, his arms crossed, and glared at Yuu.

"It can't be you," growled Roaring Tiger, striding across the room and squinting at Yuu.

"It is, general," Yuu said. "I apologise for the inconvenience." *The Art of War should speak eloquently, never in a hurry, certain that everything, no matter how unexpected, is according to plan.*

Roaring Tiger snorted and took to pacing in the centre of the room. "Prove it. Take off that damned mask."

"What would that prove, general?" Yuu asked. "You have never seen my face. We have never met before today."

"Take it off anyway," the general hissed.

Yuu considered it. It didn't truly matter if he recognised her face. She was here, and her fate was entirely in his hands. "No," she said quietly. The Art of War had never been unmasked, and that was one thing she would uphold if she could.

Roaring Tiger stopped pacing and stared at her hard, hands clenched and eyes wide with anger. "I could order it stripped from you."

"I am not here to fight you, general," Yuu said softly. *The Art of War should always speak softly. Forcing others to listen puts them at a disadvantage.* It surprised her just how easily she slipped back into the role. A role she had left behind five years ago and hoped never to play again. "I'm here to help you."

"Help me?" Roaring Tiger scoffed. "By bringing chaos into my camp? Already, half my soldiers want you to save us, and the other half wants to string you up. You have brought dissension into the ranks, strategist. Tell me how that is helping!"

"Because I intend to save you." Yuu smiled even though she knew no one would see it.

"We don't need saving," Roaring Tiger spat. "We need to take that damned city." He narrowed his eyes at Natsuko. The goddess sat still and silent on her chair, surprisingly restrained, content to watch and not get involved. The general flicked his gaze at Li Bang and the still-sodden aspiring hero went pale as goat's milk.

At last the general looked back at Yuu, eyes narrowed and teeth clenched. "You can't be her," he growled. "You're not a ninety-year-old woman." He looked back at Natsuko and a smile crept across his face. "I think I understand now."

Yuu doubted that very much, but if the general wanted to believe Natsuko was the real Art of War, let him. It didn't matter as long as he agreed to follow her orders. "General," Yuu said. "Let me see if I have a full grasp of the situation. Emperor Einrich WuLong is marching the bulk of the Hosan forces from the east into Shin to deal with the Cochtan forces that have taken the province and camped there. The emperor is expecting you and your army to retake Ning and then strike into Cochtan to disrupt their supply lines and split their attention."

General Roaring Tiger grunted and started pacing again.

"The masters of Sun Valley are currently trapped on the Cliffs Unbreakable by overwhelming Cochtan numbers. That Cochtan army has the Forest of Bamboo at its back and is therefore insulated from attack from the south due to the spirits who infest the forest. Therefore, the masters of Sun Valley are unlikely to receive aid and will eventually fall, leaving the Cochtan army free to march west and attack you from the east."

Roaring Tiger grunted again.

"This leaves you," Yuu continued, "in the perilous position of being stuck here and entirely unable to execute the emperor's stratagem. And if the rumours are true and the Cochtans have resurrected their Blood Engine, there is no guarantee the emperor's forces gathering in Qing province will be enough to repel the invasion from Shin." Yuu stepped away from the wall and approached the general, following his back-and-forth pacing. "And I assume this is a situation entirely of your own making?"

The General stopped pacing and turned to Yuu. A vein throbbed at his temple and his eyes goggled at her. It was enough to convince her she was correct.

"You visited Ning just a few days ago. No more than five judging by the state of this camp," Yuu said. "Your army conscripted every able-bodied man into service. Then you left the city all but undefended in your haste to march north into Cochtan. A separate force of Cochtan soldiers then swept in, probably from the east, split off from the force assaulting Sun Valley. They took Anding unimpeded, cutting off your own supplies and putting an enemy at your back, which dragged you back here. You were outplayed, general."

The general's right eye twitched, his fists clenched so tight they were trembling. Then he sighed. "Correct on every account, strategist. I need to take Anding. Now! And I need to do it with minimal losses, or it doesn't matter how quickly I can get to the Cochtan border because I won't have enough men to do anything but piss on their walls."

Yuu bowed her head just a little, her gaze never leaving the general's eyes. "It sounds like you need a strategist."

"And I should trust you?" Roaring Tiger snorted. "Need I remind you, we fought on opposite sides of the last war, strategist."

Yuu shrugged. "That war is over, general. Need I remind you, I fought on the side of the current emperor. I knew him when he was named Death's Echo."

The general barked out a laugh. "Not many know that. I suppose you really are her." He peered over Yuu's shoulder at Natsuko sitting idly against the wall. "You have a plan to take this city?"

"Not yet," Yuu admitted. "I need a map of the city and surrounding area, accurate and up to date information about the defences, and a list of forces you have at your disposal."

The general's face curdled for a moment as he considered, then nodded once and strode to the side of the room. He grabbed hold of the battered table there and dragged it, feet squealing, into the centre of the room. "Fetch the map," he growled at the soldier by the door.

No sooner had the door opened and the soldier fled when another soldier, this one wearing the green armour of Hangsu province, entered. He bowed low and waited for Roaring Tiger to notice him. "What is it?" the general growled.

The soldier straightened and his gaze flicked to Yuu. "The prince of Qing is on his way here, general," the soldier said. "He has two dozen of his personal guard at his back."

Roaring Tiger hissed through his teeth, shook his head, and waved the soldier away as the man carrying the maps re-entered and spread them over the table. " You have minutes at best, strategist," Roaring Tiger growled. "Come up with a plan to take that damned city before the prince gets here, and I will extend you my protection. Otherwise, he can damned well have you."

It was impossible, and they both knew it. Anding had never fallen to a siege. Her grandmother had held it against a force five times that of her defending army. It was renowned as the most defensible city in Hosa, maybe even the world. And the General wanted her to come up with a plan to seize it in mere minutes. He was setting her up to fail.

Unless he wasn't. There was a tension to the general, like a rope pulled so taut it was fraying and about to snap. Yuu considered all she knew about the man, rummaged through her memories of the past. She had studied him when he was her opponent, learned everything she could about him and his brother in an effort to counter them at every turn.

Roaring Tiger wasn't nobility. He had no royal blood from any of the ten provinces. He was born in the gutters of Kaishi in Lau province. He joined the Hosan army willingly when he was still just a child and brought his younger brother, still just a babe, with him. He earned his rank and the name Roaring Tiger when he took command during the Ipian campaigns. His commander was murdered by a shintei in a duel. His brother rushed forth and killed the shintei, but Roaring Tiger took command of the Hosan forces and led a fighting retreat beset on all sides. It was only through his strength of will and the volume of his roar that he kept the Hosan forces from breaking. After that, his rise through the ranks had been meteoric, and Henan WuLong offered him the position of general in the unification wars. He became the supreme commander of the Hosan army, but was demoted when the Leper Emperor took the throne. He was no politician. No diplomat. His strength lay in the respect he earned from his troops and his ability to hold forces together through an unbreakable will. His courage and the strength of his command had earned him everything.

No. Roaring Tiger wasn't setting her up to fail. Devious cunning was simply not part of his ethos. He was giving her the only chance he could to earn her safety. He couldn't countermand a prince of Qing's claim on her life without a good reason, so she had to give him that reason.

"What forces do the Cochtans have at their disposal?" Yuu asked, approaching the map. It was up to date, a bird's-eye representation of the city along with the crumbling southern wall and the Hosan encampment at the bottom of the hill.

Roaring Tiger huffed as he joined her at the table. "We believe they have about one thousand soldiers. A mix of infantry and archers. Or whatever those damned fire tubes they use are."

"Rifles," Yuu said. She had seen them before. The Leper Emperor carried one back when he was known as the assassin Death's Echo. They were destructive contraptions that used explosive black powder to propel balls of metal at frightening speed. Superior to bows in every way except for the time it took to reload them.

Roaring Tiger leaned on the table, his fingernails digging into the wood. "Horrible range on them, and downhill they have us completely beat in that regard. They also have at least three of those flying engines. Everything else is footmen. Spears and swords mostly, metal armour. The Cochtans don't have techniques, but their soldiers are equipped with some sort of personal engine that makes them stronger. I've seen one bend a sword with his bare hands." That was new. Yuu had never heard of such an engine before, but the Ticking Clock had also seemed far stronger than he should have been without any technique to back him up.

"What about your forces?" Yuu asked.

"Two thousand footman, five hundred archers, two hundred heavy cavalry, not that they'll be much good here, and one hundred and fifty Lotus Guard." The Lotus Guard was a welcome advantage. Since assuming the throne, the emperor had been diligently training his Lotus Guard to be the most elite soldiers Hosa had ever seen. Trained hard in innate techniques and given armour and weapons of the finest quality, each one was more than a match for ten regular soldiers. They were second only to the heroes who travelled the empire.

Roaring Tiger grunted and nodded toward his brother, leaning against the wall by the door. "We also have my brother, the Crimson Tide. I'm sure you know all about him, strategist." She did. The Crimson Tide had often been the one factor Yuu could not plan for. His prowess on the battlefield was legendary, and even the Steel Prince had been hesitant to engage him in pitched combat. "And the archer, Dragon Flight." That name was new to Yuu.

"Tell me about him," she said as she scanned the map. She was already weighing up possibilities, troop formations, feints and counter attacks.

"Bloody good archer," Roaring Tiger growled. "Never misses. Somehow manages to out range even those Cochtan contraptions. He's been keeping their heads down as much as he can. Seems to have a technique to alter an arrow's path once it's left his bow."

Yuu studied the map silently. She couldn't see any way to assault the city without substantial losses. The types of losses that would break the back of an army, even one led by Roaring Tiger. There had to be a way. Something. An advantage she was overlooking. A weakness in the defences that could be exploited.

Perhaps something her grandmother mentioned in her old stories. A rule to break that would allow her to cheat the game to victory.

"There's the matter of the people of Anding as well," said the Crimson Tide in a voice like razor blades wrapped in silk.

Roaring Tiger grunted. "The people we left behind. Women, children, the infirm, city officials too cowardly to enlist hiding behind royal exceptions."

"They're not dead?" Yuu asked.

Roaring Tiger shook his head. "When the Cochtans took the city, there was some brief fighting, but we'd left behind no one capable of defending the place. They took the city in less than an hour and are holding it, but they haven't slaughtered the inhabitants."

"They might, though," said the Crimson Tide, "if we attack."

Another piece on the board. A weak piece with no value except as a hostage, maybe, but another piece all the same. But whose piece was it?

A hard knock sounded at the door. A burly soldier stepped quickly into the room. "Sir, the prince of Ning is here. He has quite a following, sir."

Roaring Tiger waved the man away and set to pacing again. "You're running out of time, strategist. Find me that plan." He nodded to his brother, and the Crimson Tide stepped in front of the closed door, leaning his back against it as though he wasn't nonchalantly barring the entry of a Hosan prince.

Someone banged the door. "General!" a deep voice shouted from outside. "Open the door, general. I know who you have in there, and I will have justice for the murder of my cousin." Again, the banging on the door. Someone clearly threw their weight against it, but the Crimson Tide leaned against it looking smug, and it seemed that was enough to stop the prince and all his men from forcing entry.

"What about the southern wall?" Natsuko asked. The goddess sounded worried, which did nothing to calm Yuu.

"The weakest point of the defences, it's true," Roaring Tiger growled. "But my men can't climb the cliff face without taking fire from the Cochtans. Maybe if we had a full week to build a siege tower, but I need this city taken now."

"Break it down!" the prince shouted from outside.

"Big brother?" the Crimson Tide asked.

Roaring Tiger slammed his fist on the table and growled. "You're out of time, strategist. Let them in."

The Crimson Tide shrugged and stepped away from the door. It slammed open, and a soldier in the silver armour of Qing stumbled over the threshold and sprawled on the floor. Behind him stood a tall, handsome man with a face so like the Steel Prince's, Yuu felt her heart ache. She looked back to the map, her mind racing as it brought up and discarded yet another plan that would only serve to get thousands of Hosan soldiers slaughtered. There had to be something. There was always some way. No defence was unbreakable, no attack irresistible. *The Art of War should never work in stone,* her grandmother had said. *No plan is solid enough to withstand both the cunning of one's enemy and the ineptitude of one's allies.*

"General," the prince shouted as he stepped over his sprawling soldier. "That woman is the criminal known as the Art of War, and I claim her life in the name of Qing."

Roaring Tiger intercepted the prince, stood between Yuu and the man and used his considerable presence to demand attention. "How dare you storm into my command centre and make demands, Prince Qing! *My* authority is granted to me by the Emperor of Ten Kings himself, and that makes my word law here." The general's voice was the low growl of a wild animal about to strike. Even the prince quailed in the face of such anger. "If you have a grievance with one of my advisers you should have taken it up through the correct channels. Through the chain of command."

"I am—"

"*Not* in command here," Roaring Tiger snarled so loudly even the rain outside quieted in fear.

Silence held the room for a moment. Something else Yuu's grandmother had once said came to her. *When defending a city, there is no greater advantage than the city itself and no greater defenders than those who know the city best. Those with the most to lose.*

The Prince of Qing coughed and bowed only as low as was necessary, given that he was technically of a much higher station than the general. "The warrant for her arrest is signed by Emperor Einrich WuLong on behalf the royal family of Qing. She is a fugitive, General. A criminal. A murderer and a traitor. By the very authority upon which you now call, she is condemned. I, as the representative of Qing, have a right to her head!" The prince wasn't backing down. And he was right not to. Roaring Tiger was buying her as much time as he could, but unless she gave him a reason, he simply didn't have the authority he was claiming. Her life was forfeit.

Yet Roaring Tiger did not step aside. "You are aware of who she is, Prince Qing," he growled. "So, you know what she is capable of. There is no greater strategist in Hosa, and the fate of the empire may well lie on the outcome of this siege. He turned his head a little to speak over his shoulder. Do you have a plan, strategist?"

If only there were a way into the city. A subtle way. A way to sneak in just a handful of people. She glanced back at Li Bang sitting happily forgotten on the tavern stairs. Maybe they didn't need to sneak anyone in after all. Maybe they had everything they needed already.

Roaring Tiger deflated with a sigh. "Prince Qing…"

"I have it," Yuu said. Damn, she needed a drink. But even if there were ten bottles of wine on the table, she'd have to take off her mask, and the Art of War never took off her mask.

"No!" the prince hissed. Roaring Tiger quieted him with a raised hand and a threatening stare.

"Truly?" the general snarled. "This is not just a ploy to extend your life, strategist. You have a solid plan to take the city?"

"I do," Yuu said, her voice wavering just a little. Perhaps her grandmother's wouldn't have wavered, but Yuu had never quite lived up to her legacy.

Roaring Tiger smiled wide. "Then it pleases me greatly to extend Emperor Einrich WuLong's protection to you, strategist."

"I will not allow it!" Prince Qing said, drawing his jian. It was a nobleman's sword ornately decorated without so much as a burr on the blade or a smudge on the gilding. A blade that had never seen combat.

Roaring Tiger took one calm step toward the prince so his sword point was scraping the general's ceramic armour. "A duel, is it? Well, of course I accept. But my duelling days are behind me, Prince Qing. My brother will take my place."

Prince Qing glanced at the Crimson Tide to find the hero wearing a sly grin. He returned his sword to its scabbard quickly. "The emperor will hear of this, General!"

Roaring Tiger growled. "Either from you or me, I agree, Prince Qing. But if the strategist's plan is sound, my protection is the emperor's protection." He turned to Yuu and the smile fell from his face. "But if her plan fails, assuming any of us are still alive, she's all yours."

Chapter 20

"We cannot take the city by force," Yuu said. It was a fact, pure and simple.

"Bah," Prince Qing shouted. He had found a chair from near the far wall. "She counsels cowardice."

Roaring Tiger shot the prince an angry glare. "You are here under sufferance, Prince Qing. Shut up and let the strategist talk. She's smarter than both of us."

Yuu nodded to the general and continued. "The defences of Anding are too great, and the Cochtans could use the Hosan people still trapped inside the city as hostages." Yuu drew in a deep breath and thanked her grandmother and the old king of Ning for making the Art of War wear a mask. It was the only thing keeping her together, the only thing keeping the others from seeing her fear and anxiety, and the only thing keeping her own doubts from crushing her. "Our one advantage lies not in our own numbers, but in the Cochtan's. Their force is small, relying entirely on the cliffs and the city walls, and the power of their rifles over our archers. They cannot hold the city against a determined assault."

"You just said we can't take the city by force," Prince Qing said. "You speak in circles, woman. Make up your mind and spit it out so we can do away with this farce and separate your head from your shoulders."

Roaring Tiger did not admonish the prince this time. "He has a point, strategist."

Yuu glanced first at the prince, then at the general. Finally, she turned to Li Bang. He did not look happy to suddenly be the centre of attention and fidgeted on the step. Yuu approached and knelt in front of him, lowering her voice to a whisper so no one else could hear. "Can you scout the city?"

Li Bang let out a nervous squeak of a giggle. "I don't know. I…"

"I'm not asking you to see every part of it," Yuu said. "I am simply trying to save Hosan lives. To help them end a war before it spreads so deep into the empire that it consumes both Hosa and Cochtan. I cannot do it without you and your technique." Li Bang frowned. His lip trembled. But this was what he wanted. A technique. To be a hero. Well, Yuu knew better than most, that not all heroes wielded blades. Some fought from behind the front lines with guile and strategy, though rarely ones as large as him.

Li Bang ran a hand through his messy nest of hair and sniffed. "I'm still figuring it all out, but, uh, maybe. What do you want me to see?"

"The people," Yuu said.

"What is this?" Prince Qing bellowed. "Who is this fat peasant? Why do you ask him for a plan to take the city?"

"Quiet," Roaring Tiger snarled. He was choosing to believe in her because they knew each other. Not directly, nothing so immediate. They had fought against each other countless times through the crucible of war, they had come to understand each other better than they could have through friendship.

"Find the people of Anding," Yuu said quietly. "Women, children, the elderly. Find them. Nothing more. Just find them. Find where they are hiding and tell me."

Li Bang frowned again and nodded uncertainly. "I'll try." He took a few deep breaths, and then his gaze went distant, his eyes clouding over.

"What's he doing?" Roaring Tiger asked.

Natsuko cackled and waved a lazy hand in the air. "I will be going now," she said as she stood and approached the door at the back of the inn. "Places to be, gods to mock." She pulled open the door, stepped through, and closed it behind her.

201

"There's nothing back there," Roaring Tiger growled. "It leads down to the cellar." Yuu sighed. Of course, the goddess had chosen the worst moment possible to play her games.

Prince Qing stormed over to the door and all but tore it from its hinges. Natsuko was gone, of course. "What is this?" the prince hissed. "Some kind of trickery?"

Yuu ignored the prince and returned to the table and the map. "We cannot take the city by force," she repeated. "A full assault on the city will result in a victory for the Hosan forces, but the cost will be too high. We would no longer have the numbers to mount an assault on the Cochtan border, or anywhere."

Roaring Tiger grunted. "Neither can we leave the Cochtans here. If we march north, they'll hit our rear before we can make it to the Cochtan border. While Anding is in their hands, we do not have secure supply lines and an army can't march without supplies."

"But that's exactly what you're going to do, General," Yuu said. "Not march north, but retreat to the east."

"Are you deaf?" Prince Qing snapped from his chair. "He just said…"

"Send a small force to the southern wall now," Yuu said quietly, ignoring the prince. "Have them attempt to climb the cliffs tonight under the—."

"My own people have already inspected those cliffs," Prince Qing said. "They are precarious at the best of times, and the Cochtans have guards stationed above. We lost one soldier just in the scouting. Any attempt to climb is suicide."

"Yes," Yuu nodded to the prince. "The Cochtans will be watching and they will punish any attempt to climb the cliffs. But that is exactly what we are going to attempt. A small force, general. Have your men attempt the climb but pull back as soon as they take losses."

"You don't want them to succeed?" Roaring Tiger growled.

"They cannot succeed," Yuu admitted. "But they must be seen to try."

"How does that help us?" Prince Qing asked.

Yuu suppressed a sigh and was glad all over again for the mask hiding her face. "Wars are won by information far more regularly than by the sword, Prince Qing. Misinformation will win us this battle."

Roaring Tiger grunted. "You say that, strategist, but I'd wager one of us is still going to have to get our sword wet before the Cochtans go home."

Yuu turned her gaze on him and drew in a deep, steadying breath. "They're not going home, General. Not one of them will leave Hosa."

A damning silence descended on the room. Roaring Tiger and Prince Qing stared at Yuu. Then the general said, "You want us to kill all of them. No survivors? No prisoners?"

"So cold," the Crimson Tide said. His lip curled into a sneer and he shook his head.

Yuu snapped her gaze toward the hero, and then back to the general. This was the true burden of the strategist, being the one to make the plans. The weight of that responsibility had driven her to lose her mask once already. "Would you like to know the difference between you and me, General?" Yuu asked. Roaring Tiger just stared at her, so she continued. "You are a leader of men, a commander. You must be hot, and you must use that heat to inspire in your troops both confidence in your unwavering certainty and passion for justifiable murder." Roaring Tiger shifted uncomfortably, but he did not argue the point. "I, on the other hand, am a strategist. I must be cold. I cannot consider the lives of individual troops. To me, troops are numbers. Do we have more or fewer? How many and where? To deliver victories in battle and war, I must detach myself from the consequences. Every Cochtan soldier in that city *must* die. Not just to liberate the city, and not just to win this battle."

Roaring Tiger glanced down at the map quickly. "You're talking about the war?" He barked a laugh, but there was no humour in it. "Damnit, strategist. I asked you to help me take the city, and you've been considering how to best crush the entire Cochtan invasion?"

"Yes," Yuu said. She smiled ruefully, though she knew no one could see it. "Why do you think it took me so long to come up with a plan?"

Roaring Tiger shook his head. "On with it then." He gestured to the map.

Yuu turned her attention back to the table and swallowed the nervousness constricting her throat. Her heart was racing. This was what it was like, commanding armies, developing strategies that planned several moves ahead of both the opposition and her own allies. This was what she had given up five years ago. And by the gods she had missed it! The pride of reasoning out the winning strategy. The heady rush of power when soldiers and heroes move to her command. The excitement of pitting her mind against an opponent in a game where the stakes weren't just high, but everything. The thrill of battle, of seeing it play out before her just as she had seen it in her mind. The anxious waiting as the outcome hung in the air. The joy as she proved herself the better strategist, as her tactics vanquished the opponent. Win or lose, live or die, all depended on her knowledge. No skill, no qi, no techniques. Just one intellect against another. Yes, she had missed this. She was raised for this, trained for it. She had a legacy to uphold.

"Once our small force has been repelled from the southern cliffs, the survivors are to return here," she said, barely able to keep the tremor of excitement from her voice.

"Survivors?" asked the Crimson Tide. "You intend to sacrifice our own people at the southern cliff?"

Yuu nodded and met the hero's gaze, hating the disgust she saw there. "There will be casualties. There has to be for it to be believed." Her decisions, her plans, her strategies. Other people's sacrifice.

The hero scoffed and shook his head. He didn't understand. He couldn't. But that was why he was a hero.

"As soon as the survivors return, we strike camp and march east toward Sun Valley," Yuu continued.

"We leave the city in the Cochtans' hands?" Prince Qing asked.

"Exactly what I said we couldn't do," Roaring Tiger added. "And the emperor ordered me to march north into Cochtan."

"Yes," Yuu said. "The Cochtans don't want the city, General. It is a distraction and nothing more. They took the most defensible city in Hosa to pull your attention here, knowing they would have to give it up when you lost your patience, and knowing that every Cochtan in the city would die. They are here to make you pay for every step you take toward Anding, or to make you pay for every step you take away from Anding. They have driven a wedge through the centre of Hosa, splitting your forces into two parts with inferior numbers. It is a genius strategy, and if it succeeds, the Hosan Empire will fall. We cannot allow that to happen." She stared at the general. "*You* cannot allow it to happen."

"But how can we win by doing exactly what they want us to do?" Roaring Tiger growled.

"Wars are won by information, General," Yuu repeated. "It is only what they want us to do if we don't know they want us to do it."

The Crimson Tide scratched at his hairless chin. "You cannot counter an attack without an attack to counter."

"We pull away toward Sun Valley with as much haste as we can muster," Yuu continued. "At the same time, we make it as uncomfortable for the Cochtan forces in Anding as possible."

"How?" Roaring Tiger asked.

"By getting the Hosan people still inside the city walls to make it uncomfortable," Yuu said. "We don't want them to take up

205

arms against the occupiers, but we do want them to sabotage their supplies, stage protests, everything short of violence. Everything they can get away with without serious retribution. Between the unrest inside the city, and the speed with which our army will be making for Sun Valley, the Cochtans will be forced to leave Anding and follow us. They'll have to. If they don't, your army will take the Cochtan force assaulting Sun Valley unawares, and then continue to trap the larger Cochtan force in Shin province between your army, augmented by the wushu masters of Sun Valley, and the emperor's forces coming from Qing province."

"Flipping the advantage," Roaring Tiger growled. "They've put us in an unwinnable scenario where we have no choice but to do what they want. And you're intending to turn it around and give them no choice."

"Precisely," Yuu said. "A thousand battles may be won behind the walls of a castle, but no war has ever been won on the defensive."

"How do we get the citizens of Anding to do their part?" asked the Crimson Tide. "We have no way to contact them."

"We have Dragon Flight," Yuu said looking from the hero to his brother. "If he is as skilled as you say, General, he can use his bow to get word to the people, as long as we know where they are."

"And once we have drawn them out of the city?" Prince Qing asked.

"We set a trap," Yuu said, not even sparing the prince a glance. "We lure them in to attack our rear along the eastern road to Sun Valley, just north of the Forest of Bamboo. We hide our strongest forces: the cavalry, the Lotus Guard, and the Crimson Tide in the Forest of Bamboo. The baggage train will be the bait, an inviting target, but we will hide a large force of foot soldiers in amongst the wagons. As soon as the Cochtans engage, we close the trap. The hidden foot soldiers will hold up the Cochtans while the Lotus Guard emerge from the forest and hit from the side. At the same time, the cavalry ride around and hit the Cochtans from the rear. We trap them on the east road between the cliffs to the north, the forest to the south, and three separate forces of Hosan soldiers. No survivors. No one to report back to the main Cochtan forces that their plan has failed. Separate them from their information, and their invasion will flounder against superior Hosan forces."

"What if they dispatch scouts north to report back before they engage our force?" Prince Qing asked.

Yuu finally looked at him. "We send Dragon Flight north as soon as we are out of sight of the city. Have him find an advantageous position and watch the roads out of Cochtan. He's the only one who can attack the thopters."

Everyone considered the plan. But only Roaring Tiger mattered. He was no strategist, but he was in command. If he liked the plan, Yuu would live. If he didn't, the prince would have her executed by nightfall. The old general balled his hands into fists and cracked his knuckles against the table. He wasn't staring at the map, he was staring through it, trying to see what Yuu saw. Trying to play the plan out in his head.

"We should just storm the city," Prince Qing said. "She said it herself, we have the numbers to do it. Yes, we'll lose people, but that's what war is. Soldiers should be proud to give their lives for their empire. Execute this traitor, storm the city, and then we can be marching toward Sun Valley by nightfall without the fear of an army at our backs." Yuu could have pointed out that they'd be marching with a few hundred troops at best, leaving behind a host too injured to go on, but she knew further argument would only weaken her case. She had laid out her plan, and Roaring Tiger knew all the factors. She watched the general as he struggled to make the decision.

"Tell me something, Prince Qing." Roaring Tiger pinched the bridge of his nose. "Putting aside your need for vengeance, which option would you choose?" He stared at the prince. "Not just for the sake of the people in this army, or the people in Anding, and not just for the sake of the people of Sun Valley and the emperor's forces who are relying on our aid. For the sake of all Hosa, which option do you think is the right one?"

The Prince of Qing shook his head and said nothing.

Roaring Tiger grunted. "We'll follow your plan, strategist," he said. "I hope for all our sakes, as well as yours, it works."

"I can't do it," Li Bang said with pitiful sigh. His eyes cleared and he sagged against the steps. He was still dripping wet and looking dreadfully sorry for himself. "I'm not a hero. I'm just — useless."

Yuu glanced about the inn. The prince of Qing was watching her, eyes narrowed to slits. Roaring Tiger was gone, delivering his orders. Well, her orders really. She sat down beside Li Bang and shifted her mask a little to try to make it more comfortable. It was perhaps the one battle both Art of Wars had never been able to win, but comfort was not necessary.

She would love to let Li Bang go, escape the whole situation while he could, and figure out the limits of his technique on his own. Unfortunately, Li Bang was pivotal to the whole plan. The population of Anding had to make the occupation of their city uncomfortable, and quickly. The Cochtans could not be allowed to even consider staying holed up behind its walls, or it was likely they would never leave.

"I know the feeling," Yuu said quietly. "Techniques are hard. You see all those heroes parading about Hosa, performing impossible acts, and it looks easy. They make it look easy." She sighed. "But the truth is they have practised for years, strengthened their qi through discipline and hard work."

Li Bang sniffed and shook his head. Yuu really wished they had a bottle of wine to share. "Did yours take time to learn?" he asked.

"You have no idea," Yuu said with a smile. She lifted the side of her mask just enough to let him see it. "It was my grandmother's technique first of course." Everything Yuu had and everything she was belonged first to her grandmother. "I have no idea where she learned it. She was always much better at it than I am. With barely more than a touch, she could bring a statue to life. I once saw her bring the great statue of Lili at Mushon Temple to life. She made the statue dance just to piss off a monk who had refused her entry."

Li Bang chuckled. "She sounds fun."

Yuu opened her mouth to agree but couldn't bring herself to say the words. "As for me? I have to have made the thing myself. I have to infuse it with qi every step of the way or it just falls apart. She might have taught me her technique, but even now, after twenty years, I still haven't mastered it."

"What about the other things you make come out of the ground?" Li Bang asked. "Like in the bathhouse."

"Those were my own iteration of the technique," Yuu admitted. "And my grandmother would be beyond disappointed that I use her technique in such a poor imitation."

Li Bang shifted his bulk to try and get more comfortable on the step. "We don't have twenty years for me to figure out how to use it, do we?"

Yuu shook her head. "You don't need twenty years. Your technique is different, Li Bang. I have sat at the head of armies and waged wars. I have seen dead heroes rise from the grave to seek retribution and justice. I have stood in the presence of shinigami and yokai. And do you know how many times I have seen someone with a spontaneously manifested technique?"

"None?" Li Bang asked.

"Once," Yuu said. She nudged him with an elbow. "Just once. And you know how you got it?"

"It was the crone, wasn't it?"

Yuu chuckled at that. "She wouldn't have given you the technique without a reason, Li Bang. The god of missed opportunities has handed you the greatest opportunity she could muster, the thing you said you wanted the very first time we met. To be a hero. A real hero with a real technique. A unique technique. And you are a hero. A hero saves people, and you've already saved me — I don't know, a dozen times?"

"I wasn't counting, boss." He nodded, and water shook from his scraggly mane, splashed onto Yuu's mask. "Do you think they'll call me Falling Moon if I manage it?"

"I'll make sure of it," Yuu said. "So, concentrate. Feel for your qi and let it flow freely. Don't think about the city. Think about the Hosan people trapped inside. Desperately hoping the Cochtans don't use them as hostages, wanting the Cochtans to leave their city and let life return to normal. Some are probably hiding in basements or have barricaded their homes, hoping against hope they will be ignored. They're hungry, scared, cold. They miss their husbands, their brothers, their sisters, and fathers."

Li Bang's eyes had clouded over. His face was slack, mouth hanging half open. Then he smiled. "I found some! Two women and an old man."

"Don't look away. Stay focused on them." Yuu took his hand as she had in the darkness on their way down the mountain at Ban Ping, and pulled him slowly to his feet. She led him to the table and the map. "Now, where are they, Li Bang? Point them out."

Chapter 21

There was always something exciting about strategising. Analysing all the possible moves and counter moves. Deliberating over the potential costs and rewards. Considering which pieces were expendable at what point of the game. The theory was exhilarating. Putting that plan into practice, when it was no longer a game, when lives were on the line, was neither exciting nor exhilarating. It was gut churning, terrifying, and guilt-ridden.

Yuu stood at the foot of the hill leading up to Anding, surrounded by thousands of Hosan soldiers. Roaring Tiger sat astride his horse to one side, and Prince Qing sat on the other. There was no sign of her own tired old stallion. She hoped they had Lump stabled somewhere and not in a cook pot. Yuu was under no illusions. They might not have taken her mask or clad her in chains, but she was still a prisoner. Rain drizzled down, soaking them all; it ran down her douli and dripped from the rim in a steady stream. Mud soaked into her sandals and she fidgeted from foot to foot to stop sinking ankle deep into the sludge. Yuu watched twenty soldiers ride off toward the southern side of the cliff surrounding Anding. She wondered how many of them would be sacrificed for the feint she needed to sell the next feint. She shook her head. They weren't people, just numbers, just pieces of the game. They couldn't be people. They had to be pieces.

Li Bang did his job well. He found a few different clusters of Anding citizens gathered in basements, homes, warehouses, and even a few chained to posts in the market square, unwilling to succumb to the Cochtans' occupation, she assumed. There were thousands of people left in the city, thousands of pieces waiting behind enemy lines. Dragon Flight had his arrows ready. Each one carried a vague message, in case it was intercepted once it landed. One word scrawled in Hosan on a strip of parchment wrapped tightly around the shaft. *Resist.* Yuu hoped the people of Anding would do so peacefully. She hoped they wouldn't lose heart once the Hosan army marched east. But there was no way to give them the full plan without the possibility that word of it would reach the Cochtans' ears. She needed to trust they would wait out the plan. That sort of trust never came easily. There were factors she couldn't account for.

Even if everything went according to her plan, Yuu would be dragged along to Sun Valley, and once the Cochtans were defeated, she would need to slip away without the Prince of Qing noticing, and make her way back to Anding to find the artefacts Natsuko wanted.

The goddess waited just a step behind Yuu, grumbling at anyone who dared venture too close. Roaring Tiger still clearly believed she was the real Art of War, and as long as he did, Yuu was certain they would not be separated. "Are you regretting forcing me to come here yet?" Yuu asked her quietly.

Natsuko snorted. "A little. I didn't expect you to put yourself in this situation."

"It's the only way into the city," Yuu said.

"We do not have time for you to fight this entire war for the Hosans," the goddess said. "This city is not the last stop. We need more artefacts yet, and we must also reach the pinnacle of Long Mountain. Sixteen days left in case you needed reminding."

Yuu shifted uncomfortably. She was well aware they would be cutting it close. "We'll make it," she said, hoping it was true.

The first of Dragon Flight's arrows rose into the air. Even from a distance, Yuu could see the Cochtan riflemen duck behind the city walls. The heroic archer stared after his arrow, the fingers of his right hand flicking as the arrow changed course, subtle adjustments that altered its path. It arced high over the wall, and Yuu lost sight of it. Dragon Flight stood, still moving his fingers, sheltered from the rain by the soldier holding a parasol over his head. Then reached for the second arrow. Yuu pulled one of her little carvings from her robes and set to carving it, as much to calm her nerves as finish her new chess piece.

"She has a knife!" Prince Qing hissed.

Roaring Tiger turned lazily in his saddle. Despite his girth and the way it strained his armour, he sat a horse so easily he looked almost elegant. He regarded Yuu with a cold stare, then turned away. "Prince Qing," he growled in a quiet voice. "Stop embarrassing yourself."

Yuu grinned and continued carving her new piece. She wondered if she could get the armour right and deliberated over what expression to give the man. Roaring as his name suggested, or caught in a moment of quiet contemplation? In the past she had thought him a bluff dullard, but now that she had met the general, Yuu realised her mistake. He may not be strategically minded, but he was no fool, nor did he suffer them in his company.

Dragon Flight shot another whistling arrow into the air and directed it with his technique. Nervous tension held the camp in a tight fist. The soldiers were formed up in ranks at the base of the hill, making it look as though they were about to attack. As far as they were concerned, they *were* about to attack. Yuu could hear it in their voices and see it in the way they shifted their feet in the mud. A soldier with a loud voice and quivering laugh boasted of how many Cochtans he would kill with his spear, another spat angrily on the muddy ground and said he would kill them all for what they had done. A tall woman with ill-fitting armour tugged at her helm, loosening the strap then tightening it again. A heavily bearded officer put a hand on his sword, pulled the blade two fingers out of the scabbard before sliding it back in. A soldier near the back of the lines burst into a nervous giggle and clapped a hand over her mouth. Yuu had seen it all dozens of times. The lull before the storm. The way people about to throw their lives away deal with the tension, the terror. The way they justify what they were about to do. Some strategists shied away from this, distanced themselves from the men and women whom they would sacrifice.

Not Yuu. She was not her grandmother, able to remove her actions from their consequences. Yuu was not the first Art of War, who sent thousands to their deaths to slaughter thousands more, and never once considered what the loss of life would mean to those connected to them. No matter how hard she tried to be her grandmother, how much she struggled to see everyone as just a piece on a board to be sacrificed in a game played by strategists, she couldn't. She saw the people, their fear and pain, and their deaths. She saw them, and she hated what she forced them to do. Just like she had hated dressing an impostor in the silver raven armour of the Steel Prince.

There was the truth of it. The Prince of Qing demanded her head for his cousin's death, and he deserved to have it. Yuu may not have killed him, but she had slain his legacy. And perhaps worse than that, she had also killed the name and legacy of the man she had dressed up as the Steel Prince. He had been a hero, too, yet the people of Qing had not cared. They had stripped his corpse, paraded it through the streets of Jieshu, desecrated it. They had taken out their anger and grief on a man who had given his life to their cause. And it was all Yuu's fault. Her strategy at the battle of Jieshu made the streets run red, had freed an empire from a tyrannical reign. She had sacrificed the legacy of two great men on the altar of victory. Worst of all, the damnably worst part of it all, was knowing all the consequences, knowing what it had cost her. If she had a chance to do it all differently, she would not. Could not.

Dong Ao wrote that *Victory is worth any cost.* Chaoxiang wrote that *If the cost of victory is too high, then it is no victory at all.* They were both absolutes and in direct opposition to each other, but both were invariably wrong. Life was never so easy as that. Life always found the middle ground. Some victories *were* worth any cost; others were not worth *any* cost.

Sharp pain lanced through her thumb. She glanced down to see blood staining both her knife and the little statue of Roaring

Tiger, and a gash in her thumb. Her grandmother had trained her to separate feeling and emotion from tactical planning. *Focus on the lessons. The pain is nothing but a tool to remember.* She squeezed the bleeding thumb. Lessons learned in pain were indelible. How many times had Yuu...

Natsuko coughed and Yuu glanced down to find the wrinkled old goddess holding out a bandage. "Are you all right?" The drizzling rain still didn't touch her. Though everyone else was soaked, Natsuko stood there bone dry, and no one seemed to notice except Yuu. She took the bandage and wrapped it around her wounded thumb, wincing at the stinging pain.

"It's just a scratch," Yuu said quietly. The Art of War didn't show pain or concern. She showed nothing. That was why her mask was plain white. Yuu resisted the urge to run a finger along the crack in the mask. A crack she had put there. She had tried to destroy the damned thing, but she couldn't go through with it.

"I did not mean your thumb," the goddess said quietly. Yuu glanced at her again and then away, glad her mask hid her face.

Dragon Flight sent up another arrow. By now the Cochtans on the city wall would be wondering why he was aiming so high. Perhaps they might even find one or two of the arrows. It didn't matter. The message wasn't meant for them and would give away nothing of the larger plan. The climbers would have reached the southern cliff face by now. In just an hour the sun would drop behind Long Mountain, its last rays fading from Hosa, and the soldiers would start up the cliff face to be sacrificed.

Three hours after sunset, the survivors came limping back to the encampment. Twenty soldiers had ridden out; five returned, two of them unconscious and bleeding into their horses' hair. In the grand scheme of things, fifteen lives meant nothing. A small sacrifice the Art of War would make without hesitation. Yuu forced herself to watch them ride up and dismount, help their injured comrades off their horses. The captain, a swarthy man with blood running from a cut above his eye, stopped by Roaring

Tiger to report. The cliff face was unclimbable, and the Cochtans were watching it. Ten of the squad had died to Cochtan rifles, five more to falling rocks, and the crumbling cliff. Roaring Tiger nodded and ordered the wounded to the infirmary, then turned to Yuu.

"Now?" the general growled.

Yuu nodded. "Now."

Roaring Tiger grunted and turned to his troops at the base of the hill, then gave the order. By morning, the camp was struck and the Hosan army was marching east toward Sun Valley, leaving the Cochtans in possession of Anding.

They returned her tired old horse, and Lump struggled to keep the pace the vanguard set, but he didn't give up and Yuu was grateful for that. She patted him on the head once or twice, but he simply blew air out in a rush and gave her a half-blind stare. Yuu road ahead with the heavy cavalry with the Lotus Guard at their backs. The elite soldiers could set a grueling pace, such was their training. The conscripted troops and baggage train were following more slowly, a day behind. The pace was unsustainable, but also necessary to convince the Cochtans to abandon Anding sooner than they would have liked. One day passed into the next, and Yuu's Art of War mask felt more and more uncomfortable.

The Forest of Bamboo appeared on the horizon as a green smudge. The old dirt road they'd been following vanished as soon as they entered the dense clutch of trees. Yuu could see small stone shrines set up at regular intervals. It was said those who lost sight of the shrines lost sight of themselves, and the spirits were always happy to take them. Yet, into the forest they went, deep enough that they couldn't be seen from the road to the north. After they set up camp, Yuu, Roaring Tiger, and the prince of Qing rode north out of the forest, past the road and into the craggy slope up the mountain. There they would wait, hidden from view as the foot soldiers and baggage train of the Hosan army passed, and until the Cochtans arrived. Yuu would then signal the forces in the forest, and spring the trap. She would have preferred to be alone, so she could take off the mask, but the prince insisted on keeping an eye on her, and Roaring Tiger wouldn't allow the prince to kill her while no one else was watching. Such a mess, but like it or not, it was all her fault.

They found a little clearing, mostly level and hidden from the road by a rocky outcropping. There they could keep a watch on both the road and the forest. Roaring Tiger wedged himself between two rocks and wiggled until he was comfortable. They couldn't afford to light a fire, so they were cold, wet, and miserable, though judging by the general's half smile he didn't seem to mind. "Too long in comfortable beds," Roaring Tiger growled. "I've gone soft."

Natsuko cackled as she climbed on top of a boulder. "Getting fat will do that to you as surely as getting old."

The prince and Roaring Tiger both startled at her sudden appearance. Yuu smiled beneath her mask and shook her head.

"Who are you, crone?" Prince Qing asked. "And how in the stars did you get here so fast without us seeing you?" He had secured a green parasol from somewhere and was huddling under it, sitting on his folded cape.

Natsuko stared at the prince for a long moment, then cracked that wide, inhuman grin of hers. "I am the god of missed opportunities and lost items, boy."

The prince scoffed. "Fools and traitors, General."

Roaring Tiger watched through narrowed eyes, ignoring the stream of water running down his helm and dripping onto his breastplate. "She's the Art of War, Prince Qing."

"What?" the prince snapped. "The Art of War is Daiyu Lingsen." He pointed a finger at Yuu. "A young woman."

"Thank you," Yuu said with a bow of her head. It was not often people called her young these days.

"Yes," Roaring Tiger said. "And she was a young woman when she commanded the armies of Ning and held Anding against the Cochtans seventy years ago. The benefits of wearing a mask, I suppose. They are both the Art of War. Or at least one was, and the other is."

"What?" Prince Qing shook his head. "Then how will I know I'm executing the right woman?"

"You won't," Yuu said. "So, you probably shouldn't try."

The prince glared at her. "Or I'll just execute both of you."

Natsuko cackled again. "I would like to see you try." Yuu glanced at her and the old goddess winked back. Yuu suppressed a giggle at that.

"Get some sleep," Roaring Tiger said as he wriggled again and closed his eyes, crossing his arms over his straining breastplate. "The Cochtans won't be here until morning at the earliest."

"Close my eyes and let the fugitive escape?" Prince Qing asked. "I think not."

Yuu turned toward him and smiled, though she knew he couldn't see it through her mask. "Suit yourself, Prince Qing," she said with a slight bow of her head, then found a rock to lean against, pulled her douli down a little over her eyes, and drifted off to sleep.

Chapter 22

By the morning, the rain had stopped yet the sky remained grey. It was fitting. The Hosan foot soldiers passed by on the well-worn trail below the mountain and the baggage train followed, churning the wet earth to mud. Yuu peered out from her position hidden in the rocks above the trail. She could not see any of the cavalry or Lotus Guard waiting in the Forest of Bamboo, but knew someone would be there, watching and waiting for the signal. The last of the Hosan carts passed, and again Yuu, Roaring Tiger, and Prince Qing settled down to wait. Midday passed to afternoon with barely a word spoken. Yuu started to worry. If the Cochtans did not follow, if they remained in Anding, would Roaring Tiger consider her plan a failure? Would she be given to Qing for execution? She hated her life being in someone else's hands.

A noise on the trail below drew her attention. Yuu peered over the rock to see Cochtan soldiers running quickly along the trail, leaning forwards into the run, arms trailing behind. Each of the soldiers wore engines attached to their backs, metal tubes glowing with an inner light, small puffs of steam escaping from an external exhaust above their shoulders. The engines extended down their arms and legs, attached at various points to their Cochtan metal armour.

"Now?" Roaring Tiger growled, peering over the rocks beside her.

"Not yet," Yuu said, watching the Cochtans pass. Some carried rifles, others carried single-edged swords that glowed with the same inner light as the engines strapped to their backs. Yuu realised then that all the Cochtans' weapons were attached to the engines on their backs. She'd never seen anything like it.

"Have you ever captured any of them, General?" Yuu asked.

Roaring Tiger grunted and shook his head. "The damned Cochtans have a habit of exploding when caught."

Yuu glanced at the general, then back at the Cochtan army. She was missing something, something vital, and she was certain it had to do with the engines strapped to their backs. But she didn't have time to figure it out. They had to spring the trap now, before the Cochtans passed them and caught up with the Hosan army.

"Now!" Yuu whispered.

Roaring Tiger clutched his red flag and stood, waving it in the air. A moment later, another red flag flashed back from the depths of the Forest of Bamboo. It would take a few minutes for the Lotus Guard to reach the Cochtan front, longer for the cavalry to ride around and engage them from the rear. One of the soldiers glanced at them and slowed to a stop, staring up at Yuu and Roaring Tiger. Yuu slipped back but the general was too slow in clambering back down between the rocks.

"I think they might have seen us," Roaring Tiger growled. "Draw your sword, Prince Qing." The general backed into their little rocky clearing and picked up his spear. Natsuko sighed and hopped up onto a rock, crossed her legs, and waited. Yuu crept back up the rock to watch the Cochtans.

Ten soldiers had stopped now and were picking their way through the steep incline of rocks and scree toward them. Two more had rifles trained on their position. One of them aimed at Yuu and pulled the trigger. The rifle let out a loud pop and steam hissed out just as something struck the rock Yuu was peering over, sending shards flying into the air.

"Get down, strategist," Roaring Tiger growled.

Yuu stared down at the approaching soldiers a moment longer. The rifleman was already reloading. He appeared to be venting steam from one side of the rifle, while he slipped another projectile into the other side. The pipes connecting the engine on his back to the rifle glowed more brightly, casting a shimmer on the bamboo trees behind him. Someone grabbed the back of her robe and pulled Yuu back down into the clearing. Roaring Tiger pushed her back next to Natsuko and took up position in front of them, the Prince of Qing at his side.

"You're still no good in an actual fight, I assume, strategist?" Roaring Tiger growled.

Yuu shook her head. The Steel Prince had taught her to swing a sword, but she had neither the strength nor skill to be anything but a liability. "I'm afraid not, General."

Prince Qing snorted and pulled his jian from its scabbard. "Do you really expect me to protect the traitor who killed my cousin?"

"I expect you to protect yourself, and me," Roaring Tiger snarled. "If they get to her, then we're already dead."

A Cochtan soldier with bright blue eyes scrambled over the rocks, and Roaring Tiger darted forward with his spear. He had skill, that much was clear, and his thrust was steady, but he was slowed by age and excess. The blue-eyed soldier parried the strike with his sword, its blade glowing as it cut through the wooden haft of the spear. Prince Qing darted forward. He stabbed the blade of his jian into the Cochtan soldier's neck and withdrew with a splash of blood. The soldier collapsed, clutching at his neck, blue eyes wide with horror. Dead, even if he didn't realise it yet. The prince and Roaring Tiger backed up and awaited the next assailant. Roaring Tiger threw away the split haft of his spear and drew his sword, a weighty dao with an edge that would likely crush rather than cut.

Yuu stared down at the fallen soldier. Blood leaked from his neck, puddled on the dusty floor of the rocky clearing. The engine attached to his back began to pulse with wavering light, and his sword pulsed with it, heat haze rising from the edge of its blade.

Two more Cochtan soldiers crested the rocks, another behind them, and combat was joined once again. The prince's jian pierced the first soldier's heart in a practised strike. The soldier was dead before he hit the ground. The engine on his back *popped* as the glass cracked. Steam and viscous liquid sprayed onto the ground, and its light faded.

Roaring Tiger snarled a curse as he staggered back under the pressure of two Cochtans wielding glowing blades. He parried an overhead strike with his dao, sending up a shower of sparks and blackening the edge of his blade. The engines on their backs weren't just augmenting their strength and speed somehow, they were also heating the swords.

Another Cochtan launched himself forward with a wild swing of his glowing blade. The prince ducked underneath the attack and gutted the Cochtan, spilling blood and intestines all over the rocky clearing. Three more Cochtan soldiers clambered over the rocks toward them. The prince pulled back and blocked a strike. The Cochtan sword sparked and shattered the blade of his jian. The prince leapt forward and buried the jagged metal near to the hilt into the soldier's chest, then leapt back away the others. He and the general drew together in front of Yuu and Natsuko, and Roaring Tiger handed the prince his dao. "You'll do more with this than I can," the general growled.

The sound of shouting echoed around them, the clash of steel and screams of the injured. The Cochtans faltered, pausing and glancing back down the rocky incline toward the pass. It could mean only one thing, the Crimson Tide and Lotus Guard had arrived, striking out of the Forest of Bamboo. Prince Qing took advantage of the distraction and darted forward with the general's sword in hand. His first strike crunched into the leg of a tall Cochtan soldier, pulverising flesh and shattering bone, almost taking off the soldier's leg at the knee. The soldier fell to the ground, clutching at his ruined leg, and Prince Qing slammed his blade down on the engine on the soldier's back, crushing tubes and cracking glass, and somehow lodging the sword in the tangled contraption. The engine hissed steam and boiling black liquid spewed from its cracked tubes. The Cochtan soldier screamed something Yuu couldn't understand, dropping his sword and frantically reaching for the straps that held the engine on his back. The prince turned with the soldier, trying to wrench his dao free. A high-pitched whistle escaped the engine. The other Cochtan soldiers leapt away, diving behind rocks and scrambling back down toward the pass.

Yuu darted from behind the rock and grabbed the prince by his shoulders. He was far larger than her, but off balance and not expecting an assault from behind. She dragged him backward and kicked the flailing, screaming Cochtan away. She and the prince went down in a tangle, his armour pressing her wrist and knee painfully into the ground. A moment later the Cochtan soldier exploded in a gout of fire, steam, and bloody chunks.

"Get your hands off me, woman!" Prince Qing shouted as he rolled free of Yuu. He staggered to his feet. Yuu's ears were ringing, and she felt nauseous from the sight of blood and body parts. The prince shouted at her. "You dare touch me? Was this how you murdered my cousin?"

"Enough," Roaring Tiger snarled. He had been knocked down by the explosion as well and struggled upright, leaning against a rock for support. His helmet had fallen off and was nowhere to be seen, and blood dripped down from his hairline into his left eye. He held out a hand to Yuu and she let him pull her up. The general was old and slow and fat, but he had an indomitable strength she admired.

"Well, that was exciting," Natsuko said with a clap of her gnarled hands. The goddess hadn't moved from her perch on the rock, and was the only one not spattered with Cochtan blood, though the rock she sat on was practically painted red. If either of the men thought that odd, they didn't mention it.

"*Exciting* is not the word, crone," the prince hissed. "That man exploded!"

"It was his engine," Yuu said. She looked down at the bent metal and shattered glass on the ground, and then at the other bodies strewn about the rocky clearing. The soldiers were dead, their engines no longer glowing, but the damage to one of the engines had caused it to explode violently. Yuu approached the outcropping of rock over the pass and stared down. The battle had started, loud and chaotic. This was the worst part of war, when the fighting was everything and all she could do was watch and hope her plans succeeded. This was when men like Roaring Tiger were far more useful than any strategist. His ability to lead soldiers, to command, would make the difference between victory and defeat. And even now, Yuu could see the battle was leaning toward defeat.

The Lotus Guard, the most elite soldiers in Hosa, were being slaughtered. Despite the element of surprise, they were not prepared for the enemy or their engines. Their armour was useless against the Cochtans. Rifle shot tore through breastplates, and the Cochtan's heated blades cracked ceramic armour as if it were glass. Everywhere Yuu looked the Lotus Guard were falling, outmatched both at close and long range. Their innate techniques made them strong and fast, but the Cochtans' engines did the same. The only advantage the Hosans had was the Crimson Tide. He swept through the Cochtan forces, a spear in each hand, leaving broken and bloody bodies sprawled in his wake. But with each kill, with every body stepped over, he penetrated further into the enemy lines, and the Lotus Guard could not follow.

"General, you need to get down there and take command," Yuu said as she watched the situation worsening by the moment. The plan relied on the Hosan forces being superior, capitalising on the element of surprise to cut the enemy in half before they even realised they were under assault. But the Lotus Guard were outnumbered. Even when the cavalry arrived to reinforce them, they would be outnumbered.

Roaring Tiger grunted and started down over the rocks toward the trail. "With me, Prince Qing," he growled.

"We can't leave the traitor here," the prince said.

"The battle supersedes your petty vengeance. Now come on." Roaring Tiger headed down without looking back. The prince glared at Yuu, then scrambled over the rocks toward the battle.

Yuu watched them slam into the Cochtan forces from behind and push through to join their own troops. Roaring Tiger, true to his name, began bellowing commands, and the Lotus Guard pulled together, forming lines as the general reminded them of their training. Still, it was chaos down there, and far from a quick, decisive Hosan victory. They were losing.

"Well that's that then," Natsuko said with a cackle. "Time to head back to Anding and find those artefacts."

Yuu looked west. They could scramble over the rocks, ignore the pass and the battle, then find the road and be back at Anding by dusk the next day. Without a horse it would be a two-day journey, but safer than heading back into the forest to find Lump. She would be condemning the Hosan forces and Roaring Tiger to death, though. Her brilliant strategy of luring the Cochtans out of the city had worked, but she underestimated the Cochtan's strength, and their new weapons. She winced, expecting pain. *Focus on the lessons.* Her first battle in five years was a decisive loss. And it was likely Sun Valley and maybe all Hosa would pay the price. But Yuu could just walk away from it all. It was the smart choice, the easy choice. She wasn't a warrior — she was a strategist. Her part in the battle was done. It was up to the general and the heroes and the soldiers now. Win or lose, it was on Roaring Tiger's head. She had another job to do; find the divine artefacts, dethrone Batu, and bring the Steel Prince back from the dead. Yuu nodded and turned away, leaving the Hosan forces to their fate and following Natsuko over the rocks away from the battle.

Chapter 23

Yuu tripped over a rock and fell, bouncing her shin off the edge of the stone. She grazed her hand preventing herself from crashing face first to the ground and cried out at the pain and shock. It was the bloody mask's fault. With the Art of War's mask on, she could barely see up, down, or side to side. She hadn't seen the rock until it was too late. She reached up to take the mask off and froze, her hand hovering over the ceramic surface. She traced her finger along the crack she had given it at the battle of Jieshu. Her grandmother had worn the mask for nearly twenty years and not once had it been damaged. But then her grandmother had never actually seen battle. In all her stories, she was the consummate strategist. She made the plans, watched from the back lines. The closest her grandmother had ever come to an actual battle was the map. Yuu had been a different Art of War. She stood beside the Steel Prince on the battle lines. She didn't fight, but neither did she hide from the fight. At the battle of Jieshu, she had stood at the front, shoulder to shoulder with the soldiers of the Steel Prince's rebellion. Back to back with the fake Steel Prince himself. She committed everything she had to that battle, all her pieces, and herself.

"Come on," Natsuko said. "It can't hurt that bad. It's only a little scrape. You mortals are so fragile."

Yuu sat down on the rock she tripped over and stared at her scraped palm. The pain was necessary, a product of her failure, of her loss to the Cochtans. Proof of a lesson learned, never to be repeated. Blood welled from a hundred little cuts, oozing with grit. Something dark and viscous had oozed out of the Cochtans' broken engines. When the prince had slashed the soldier's throat, the pulsing light on the engine had faded as he bled out.

"Blood Engines," Yuu said.

"What's that now?"

Yuu looked up at Natsuko. "They're Blood Engines. There's been rumours for months that the Cochtans managed to resurrect their Blood Engine, but rumours are rarely the whole truth." She pointed back down toward the battle. "They haven't resurrected the Blood Engine — they've discovered a whole new type of engine that runs on blood. Their own blood!"

"So what?"

"It's a weakness!" Yuu said. Something inside her fluttered. Hope. Not hope for herself, but hope she could change the course of the battle. She could save the Hosans, save Roaring Tiger and all the others, even that annoying cock of a prince. She could save Hosa one more time. "One last time," she whispered to herself.

Yuu started scrambling over rocks down toward the pass.

"It doesn't sound like a weakness," Natsuko shouted. "Sounds like a strength."

Yuu was already breathless from the effort and excitement. "Every strength is a weakness waiting to be exploited," she shouted, quoting Chaoxiang as she continued her precarious flight down the rocks.

The goddess shouted something, but Yuu didn't hear it over the sound of battle below, the shuffling of her feet on the rocks, and the rushing of blood in her ears. She leapt over rocks and slipped down patches of scree. Cochtans and Hosans were fighting hand to hand, blades and spears whipping about as they split the air. She saw Roaring Tiger at the rear of the melee, a new spear in his hands. His body might be slowed by his age and size, but he wielded the spear like lightning, stabbing at the front lines of the Cochtans and driving them back. She needed to get to him. She had neither the voice, nor the presence to command the Hosan army, but he did.

Yuu charged into the battle, slipping between two Hosan soldiers fighting back to back. They didn't even notice her. A glowing Cochtan sword lashed out. Yuu leapt to the side, and the searing blade slashed through a fold of her robes, cutting a patch away and setting the fabric to sizzling. It might have sent her up in flames if not for the recent rain. She patted furiously at the flaming edge and ran on. All around her people were fighting, spears and swords slashing and stabbing, glowing blades searing flesh, filling the air with the stench of roasted meat and blood. Bodies and limbs lay strewn on the bamboo leaves, bleeding out. Yuu needed a drink now more than ever, but it would have to wait.

Another body fell in front of Yuu, a Cochtan soldier with a bushy black beard and only one eye staring at her, blue and full of terror. He shouted something in his own language and raised a hand just as a Hosan woman stabbed a spear down into his chest, twisted it and pulled it free again in a spurt of blood. The man's arm dropped, and his eye went vacant as death settled over him. The woman nodded once at Yuu, then turned away to find another enemy to fight. Yuu stepped over the body and continued. Hosans and Cochtans would kill each other no matter what she did or didn't do. But she had choreographed this dance of death. She had to see it through. If the Cochtans won, they would push further into Hosa and kill more Hosans.

She caught sight of Roaring Tiger clashing with a Cochtan soldier on the far side of the pass, close to the trees. "General!" Yuu screamed. A pair of soldiers locked in a deadly struggle stepped in front of her, blades pressed together, pushing at each other. One was a Lotus Guard, a thin woman with a harelip curled into a snarl. The other was a Cochtan soldier, a man with a youthful face twisted in hatred. The engine strapped to his back flared brighter for a moment and steam hissed out of the pipe behind his shoulder. He pushed the Lotus Guard back a step, then another. Yuu ducked around them and ran on toward Roaring Tiger.

Yuu shouted again for the general as she ran. Roaring Tiger stepped back from the Cochtan soldier and brought his spear down, bouncing the tip off the ground, then thrust it forward. The spear haft bent upward slightly and the blade slipped under the Cochtan's chest plate, driving into his gut and lifting him up, before throwing him back down to the ground. Roaring Tiger thrust his spear down into the man's neck, finishing him.

"What are you doing here, strategist?" Roaring Tiger snarled. "Why didn't you flee when you had the chance?" He stepped back from the fighting, and Yuu joined him. Blood was dripping steadily down his face, pooling in the flesh around his chins and dripping onto his chest plate. He was breathing heavily, holding his side with one hand and wincing.

"I did," Yuu said. "I came back."

Roaring Tiger grunted and leaned on the haft of his spear. "Yet more evidence that you're not the genius I thought you to be." She couldn't miss the implication of his words, even if she'd wanted to. The Hosans were losing, and it was Yuu's fault for underestimating the Cochtans.

"Tell your soldiers to aim for the pipes on the Cochtans' arms and legs, General," Yuu told him. She hoped she was right.

"Their armour?"

"Yes. They're connected to the engines on their backs, and to the soldiers as well, at least that's what it looks like. If you break the pipes, the engines lose pressure, that's the steam that hisses out of them. And it might cause them to bleed out, too… I'm not actually sure about that part yet."

"What?"

"The engines are powered by the soldiers' blood."

"That's…" the General started. His lip curled and he shook his head. Then it dawned on him. "Blood Engines."

"New Blood Engines, General. But the pipes are not as armoured as the soldiers' bodies."

Roaring Tiger grunted. "Hitting arms and legs are wasted attacks. Aim for the body or head to put a man down for good." One of the first things soldiers were taught when learning to fight. "Well, you're in it with us now, strategist. Find a sword or stay behind me." He pressed forward shouting commands to his men, telling them to strike at the Cochtan armour. His roaring voice carried over the battlefield, and the Hosan soldiers responded without question. Yuu realised then what they might achieve together. Her tactics and stratagems, and the general's raw command, the force of his personality projected around him as an indomitable will. They would be unstoppable.

With the new tactics spreading through the ranks, the battle started to turn. The pipes connected to the Cochtan engines were easy targets, and when they were damaged the soldier became a liability. A dead soldier was a loss to the force, but an injured soldier was a burden. The Crimson Tide was no fool and soon realised that cracking the engines on the soldiers' backs would cause them to explode. He swept through the enemy, explosions following like fire rockets in his wake. When the Hosan cavalry arrived, it was over. The Cochtans tried to fight back, their rifles crippling the cavalry, but they were slow and cumbersome to reload. Between the cavalry, the Lotus Guard, and the Crimson Tide, the Cochtan forces were slaughtered to a man.

Yuu leaned against a bamboo tree at the edge of the battlefield, running a thumb over her newest little statue and watching Roaring Tiger congratulate his troops. She was exhausted, but also invigorated. She'd won this battle at least, but there would be many more to come before the invasion was turned. They would have to do it without her though. Her path led back to Anding now. Hopefully in time to find the artefacts before another champion beat her to it.

Natsuko did not return. Yuu guessed the goddess went back to Tianmen again. Or maybe she was visiting her shrines, answering prayers. It seemed unlikely though. From what little she had seen, the gods spent more time fighting with one another than helping their worshippers. Natsuko claimed she wanted to end all the wars to avoid the missed opportunities they created, but she did not seem so enthusiastic about giving those opportunities back to the people who missed them.

As the light of the day began to fail, Yuu picked her way through the battlefield. The Hosan injured were being carted away. Those too wounded to go on would be taken back to Anding, and those with only minor injuries would be patched up and returned to their squads. The Hosan dead were collected, stripped of valuables, their names recorded, and then burned in pyres just outside of the forest limits. Some of the mourners said prayers to the gods, and others to the stars. Yuu was now sure neither were listening. The Cochtans were treated less respectfully. Hosan soldiers picked through the bodies, spearing them to make certain they were dead. Then their corpses were left to rot, a final insult. Yuu wasn't sure if the Cochtans believed in burial or burning, but they would receive neither here. Already the carrion feeders were gathering, crows cawing from above and shining eyes watching from the depths of the forest. Whether those eyes were animal or spirit, Yuu did not know.

She knelt to examine a battered engine on the back of a facedown corpse. The pipes were connected to the Cochtan's armour in several places along the arms and legs, but she could not see where it penetrated the skin. The broken engines leaked blood so dark it was almost black. They were bulky things, attached to the backs of the soldiers with a multitude of straps, pipes, and panels. Each had a round glass pane in its centre, and through it Yuu could see the same thick blood, glowing slightly with a crimson inner light. The workings of such machines were beyond her, though if she had time, she would gladly stop to study them. But time was short, and she couldn't stay.

Roaring Tiger stepped up beside her. He was limping, wincing with each step. He had a bandage wrapped around his head, covering his left eye. "The prince is in the infirmary," he said. "Will be for most of the night. He took a knock to the head and a slice across the thigh. Says he'll march with us to Sun Valley in the morning, though."

Yuu could take the hint. "I should go."

Roaring Tiger grunted. "You could stay. By the stars, I could use you, strategist. Hosa could use you. Emperor WuLong is certain to pardon you, and I'll happily protect you from the prince until then."

Yuu winced at that and gazed over the battlefield, at all the bodies. She could not deny a large part of her wanted to stay, to fight on. She loved being the strategist, developing plans, outwitting opponents. She loved seeing her orders carried out, the ploys she saw in her head wrought in truth as soldiers and heroes and generals deferred to her greater knowledge. She loved it. And she was good at it. Her grandmother had taught her well. From the moment the old woman had taken her in, a starving child with no family and no future, every aspect of Yuu's life had been dedicated to becoming the Art of War. Her grandmother's legacy. A strategist without equal. Years of studying history, geography, politics, philosophy, strategy. A decade of games played against the odds, the challenge almost unbeatable. Her mind had been sharpened keener than any sword or spear. Her grandmother forged Yuu into herself reborn. Then the old woman died, starved herself by degrees so Yuu could live. Her grandmother had given Yuu everything she had. She had given Yuu life. And now Yuu owed it to her grandmother to continue her legacy, to wear the mask and be the Art of War.

But now, looking at the consequences, at all the pain and blood, was it truly something she wanted? *Focus on the lessons. The pain is nothing but a tool to remember.* To most of Hosa, her grandmother's legacy was one of victory. But to Yuu, that legacy was one of pain. Of lessons with harsh consequences. Of guilt as lives were sacrificed like pieces of the chess board. Of grief for the loss of the one person who had ever truly mattered to her. She had left it all behind once for a reason. To be herself and not her grandmother. To find out who she was without the legacy.

Yuu drew in a deep breath and when she released it, it was a ragged thing that came with tears no one but she would ever know about. "My mask doesn't fit as well as it once did, general," she said. Roaring Tiger grunted.

They were both silent for a while. Then Yuu noticed a soldier standing at the edge of the forest, holding Lump, though staying clear of the old beast's mouth. The general really was more perceptive than she had given him credit for. They had even saddled the old monster. "Don't let Li Bang follow me, General," she said. "And don't let him join the infantry either. He deserves better."

"What am I to do with him then?"

"Use him," Yuu said. "He has a valuable technique. He can see things without being there. I imagine even you could find some use for that skill."

"An oracle?" He grunted. "Could be useful. Li Bang, you called him?"

"Yes," Yuu said. "But he'll need a better name. Blind Eye." He'd probably hate it. Or, knowing Li Bang, he'd just be happy to have one.

"Blind Eye Bang," the general said and nodded his head. "I'll stop him from following you. And I'll make sure the emperor pardons you, tells those bloody royals from Qing to drop the bounty." He snorted. "Or maybe jump off a bloody cliff."

Yuu smiled and shook her head. "I wouldn't bother, general. I don't think you or anyone will be seeing the Art of War again." She turned and bowed to him. "Goodbye, Roaring Tiger. It was a pleasure to fight *with* you for once."

Roaring Tiger returned the bow stiffly from injuries. "And to you, Art of War. And give my regards to the crone as well."

Yuu stood and walked away. She collected Lump from the waiting soldier and led the beast away through the battlefield.

Yuu rode into the outer boundaries of the Forest of Bamboo, away from the path at the bottom of the mountains. There were carts on the trail ferrying wounded back to Anding, and Yuu wanted isolation. She needed time to think.

The Art of War had not been as comfortable a mask as it once had. She couldn't deny a part of her enjoyed wearing it, poring over the maps, developing the strategy to defeat the Cochtans. It had been fun in the same way a game of chess was fun, though a lot more had been at stake than a few lien. It felt right, like coming home after years away. But something had changed, the home had changed hands. She no longer recognised the people who lived there. Seeing the battle up close, being a part of it, no longer held the same thrill it once had. No, *thrill* was not quite right. Battle had never been thrilling to Yuu. When she sat beside the Steel Prince at the head of his armies, her strategies playing out before them, she felt a sense of justification and purpose. She'd believed in his cause to overthrow the Emperor of Ten Kings with all her heart. Watching soldiers die, sacrificing pieces for the sake of the game, had never felt wrong before. It felt necessary. This was different. It wasn't that she didn't believe in protecting Hosa from the Cochtans. She just didn't believe in it enough. It was a war that served no purpose, and she could not be a part of it.

The truth had been her companion for the past five years, even if she hadn't bothered to listen to it until now. Daiyu Lingsen, the Art of War, died with the Steel Prince. Yuu was not her anymore.

She reached up and unfastened the Art of War's mask. She turned it around in her hands and stared down at its plain face. Entirely featureless save for the eye slits and the crack.

"I'm sorry, grandmother," she said. "I'm not you. I could not be you." She would be disappointed, but that was nothing new. Her grandmother had always been disappointed in her.

Yuu let the mask slip from her fingers. It landed on the leafy forest floor without a sound. She wiped tears on her sleeve and urged Lump to move a little faster. The Art of War was dead, again. This time, Yuu promised, she was dead for good.

Chapter 24

Yuu found Natsuko waiting for her at the gates of Anding. She walked Lump up the hill, falling in behind a cart of wounded troops. The old stallion flared his nostrils at the smell and Yuu patted his neck. She agreed with him: many of the men and women in the cart were too far gone to save. The city gates were open and its citizens were armed. Old men carried rusted swords or wooden clubs, trying their best to look threatening. Yuu spotted some women up on the walls, bows ready at their sides. There may not be any soldiers left in Anding, but the people were not about to let the Cochtans march in and retake their home. They were galvanised by the brief occupation, determined to defend themselves and their families. Yuu smiled at that.

"It's about time," Natsuko said as she stepped up beside Yuu. The goddess walked easily along on top of the muddy road while Yuu and Lump slogged through the muck. "Lost the mask, I see. Shame. These people would welcome the Art of War with open arms."

Yuu didn't want welcoming. She wanted to be ignored, forgotten. "Let's get this done," she said more sharply than she intended.

"Aren't we terse today," Natsuko said with a cackle. "Are you sleeping enough, dear?"

Yuu had slept just fine and in good company too. The soldiers carting the wounded set up camp and she joined them after leaving the Forest of Bamboo behind, sharing their rations, their fire, and their songs. There were dozens of carts on the roads, each carrying dozens of wounded. Anding was soon to become a hospice for the injured.

The cart ahead of them stopped at the gate as an old man set to inspecting the troops in the back. A woman of middling years, heavy with child yet still holding a wooden club, spoke quickly

with the soldier driving the cart and they were waved through.
Yuu and Natsuko were next.

"Travellers?" asked the pregnant woman.

"Of a sort," Yuu said with a bow, tilting her douli so the
woman could see her face.

The woman narrowed her eyes and made a suspicious
humming noise in the back of her throat.

"Got the look of a soldier about her," the old man said to the
woman. "It's in the eyes." Yuu glanced at the old fellow and
wondered what he saw. Whatever it was, one side of his mouth
lifted in a sad half-smile. "Might not be wearing a uniform, but
she's a soldier. No doubt."

The woman peered at Yuu a moment longer, then nodded.
"We don't have much, but there's shelters set up for you soldiers."
She lowered her voice. "And if you need to disappear, won't be so
hard here. Maybe find a new life." She turned her gaze to
Natsuko. "And what about you?"

"Oh, don't mind me," the goddess said with that inhuman
smile of hers. And they didn't. The woman waved them into
Anding without another word.

Anding was not a thriving city, not anymore. Evidence of its
recent occupation was everywhere, and despite Yuu's wishes the
citizens had not rebelled peacefully. They had burned their own
city rather than let the Cochtans remain in peace. Broken
buildings, some crumbling, others nothing but ash and timbers.
Discarded weapons lay strewn on the streets. An old man and
woman sifted through the rubble of their ruined house. A young
girl stood crying in the doorway of her home, a mangy puppy still
and lifeless in her arms, while a slightly older boy knelt before her
washing dried blood and ash from her spindly legs. A kindly-
looking woman and a limping soldier in cracked armour carried
buckets of water. Wars were always fought on two fronts. One is
the battlefield between soldiers. The other is back at home
between the loved ones and their grief. That was what Yuu saw in

Anding. Not a city in its death throes, wallowing in grief. But a city trying to rebuild, to reclaim what it had lost. A city brought together by tragedy, forged into a family by hardship, made strong by the support they showed each other and the determination they rallied around. Hope. That was what Yuu saw in Anding. Hope of a new start.

An old woman handed her a bowl of cold stew near the gate, and Yuu accepted it gratefully, bowing low, the only form of thanks she could offer. Then the woman directed her to the nearest shelter for soldiers.

"Do my eyes look so different?" Yuu asked Natsuko as they walked past a one-armed man holding a ladder against a building wall, while a woman at the top of the ladder hammered at the roof. Yuu spooned some of the stew into her mouth and swallowed it down. It was spicy, masking the lack of flavour, and greasy too. She appreciated it all the same.

Natsuko was quiet for a long moment, then said, "Yes, you mortals seem quite fragile at times. Many of you get a look about you after a hardship, a distant look to your eyes, as though you're looking through what's in front of you, seeing the past instead of the present." She sighed. "I hate that look. I see it every day at my shrines."

"Because it's not yours," Yuu said with a bitter smile. She felt gloomy, as though a heavy blanket had settled over her and was muting the world. She felt like she was watching herself move through life, detached, like a little version of herself sitting upon her own shoulder.

"Eh?"

"Some things are lost, but you can't touch them," Yuu said. "It's not like lost lien, or a spoon, or a child's favourite toy. Sometimes things are lost, and they're just gone. Things that are inside, rather than out. They're not yours to withhold or give back."

"Oh, don't be so melodramatic," Natsuko said. "You're not talking about loss. You haven't lost anything. You're talking about change. Well, you will never again be who you are right now. Change is as inevitable as time. So, you might as well get comfortable with who you're going to be and stop mourning who you were."

Yuu glanced at Natsuko, but the ancient goddess was staring straight ahead.

"Snap out of this maudlin mood," Natsuko continued. "Because we're not done. We've got a lot to do and a long way to go yet. Time is running out, and we are still far behind the leaders in this game."

A game. The goddess still considered the contest a game. But for the sake of the game, Batu started a war that was ravaging two empires. For the sake of the game, Yuu lured the Cochtans into a trap that killed thousands. Perhaps all the gods really were as bad as the others. But no. Surely the god of war was worse. Yuu may not be certain she could trust Natsuko, nor any of the gods, but she was certain the goddess would make a better tianjun than Batu.

"What are we looking for in Anding?" Yuu asked. She'd had enough of her spicy soup and held out the bowl for Lump to slurp up. The old stallion did so noisily and then snatched the bowl from Yuu's hand.

"A mirror, about so big," Natsuko held up a hand and splayed out her fingers. "It has a wooden handle faded from years of being held in perfumed hands, and the backplate is decorated with ornate gilding in a depiction of thorny vines. It belongs to Guangfai, the god of beauty."

Yuu suppressed a chuckle. "The most cherished artefact of the god of beauty is a mirror?"

Natsuko cackled. "He is a vain, insufferable fool. He checks his own reflection hundreds of times a day to make certain he is still pretty." She rolled her eyes. "He's a god. He can look however he damn well chooses. Too pampered for my liking. What he calls beautiful, I call false. A single shoe missing its partner, that is beauty. The look on a person's face as they watch their true love walk away without ever knowing the truth of their affection, that is beauty. Beauty is emotion, good or ill. Pain or happiness or fear or love. Beauty is in the experience. That mirror is nothing but Guangfai's vanity incarnate."

"You don't seem to like the other gods much," Yuu said.

Natsuko scoffed. "I like some of them well enough. I like my brother Fuyuko. But many of us are hateful creatures with no purpose. Do you know how many people worship Guangfai?"

"The god of beauty? I would expect many." Pleasure houses all over Hosa kept statues of the god, usually exaggerating how well-endowed he was. He was always pictured with a distinctly effeminate beauty, as though his gender were not nearly as defined as people would like to think.

"Many and more and more on top," Natsuko grumbled.

"More than worship you then?"

The goddess fell silent and doubled her pace, striding down the street with a renewed purpose. Yuu struggled to keep up despite her longer legs.

"In there," Natsuko said. She pointed at a rundown building that was only just managing to stay above the level of a hovel. A black cat sat beside the doorway, watching Yuu through yellow eyes, its tail flicking back and forth.

"Any idea what I can expect?" Yuu asked. As soon as they stopped walking, Lump took the opportunity to place the bowl he had been carrying on the ground and set about scraping it clean with his teeth.

"None," Natsuko snapped the word like a twig.

Yuu took a deep breath and let it out slowly. The goddess was impossible when she got like this. Tantrums like a child, only she was a god with the power and will to back up her temper. It made for a dangerous combination, Yuu was sure. The cat scattered away down an alley when she got close. She pulled the door open and glanced inside. "No corpses this time at least." Natsuko gave no reply, so Yuu stepped inside.

Despite its outward condition, the house was not entirely derelict. A purple rug covered the floor, thin, ratty and dust puffed up with every step Yuu took. Pale cobwebs gathered in the crooks and corners of the ceiling and fat black spiders crawled about them lethargically. A soft voice drifted from somewhere deeper inside the building. Yuu recognised it as singing, a lilting lullaby she could almost recognise. To the left of the door hung a large, ornate mirror, entirely at odds with the house it was in. Its surface was polished to a gleaming shine, but its gilded frame was tarnished and rusting in places. Yuu caught a look at herself, her first in quite some time. Her robes were no longer just patchwork and tatty; they were now filthy too. Her skin had an oily sheen, her hair lank and greasy, though mostly hidden by her douli. No wonder the people of Anding had taken such pity on her, she looked like a destitute vagabond.

Yuu followed the soft singing down a hallway. There were more mirrors on the walls, many of them, some large and some small. She could not help but glance at her reflection in them, seeing herself from different angles as she moved along. Given her current state, the reflections were not welcome. She tucked a few errant strands of hair behind her ears and tried not to look in any more of the mirrors. At the end of the hall, warm light spilled out from behind a paper door. The singing was coming from inside. Yuu still couldn't quite place the song. She reached for the door and her hand hovered before it. The skin between her shoulder blades tingled. She felt like she was being watched. She glanced back down the hall, but only saw her reflection staring back at her from a dozen different mirrors. There was something odd about this house, something wrong. Her stomach fluttered as she took hold of the door and slid it open.

Chapter 25

The room beyond was empty. Mirrors lined the walls, all shapes and sizes, dozens of them, maybe hundreds. So many Yuu could barely see the walls between them. Light was coming from inside the room, though there were no torches, lanterns, or windows. And the singing was louder now. The song tugged at her memories, yet she still couldn't quite place it. She took a step into the room, looking to either side of the door, but the room was empty.

Only it wasn't.

Yuu looked at the mirror ahead of her, a large rectangular thing that reflected much of the room. She saw herself standing in front of the doorway so black it looked like the void between stars. And there, in the mirror, a young girl sat on a chair, her back to Yuu. She was singing softly to herself, brushing her thick, raven hair. She was there. In the reflection, she was there. Yuu took another step forward. Another reflection caught her eye, in a different mirror on the same wall, this one round and smaller. It showed the same young girl, but this one showed her face. She was weeping tears of blood, her mouth screaming the words to the song. She had no tongue.

Yuu turned away from the reflection of the girl, her heart pounding in her ears. She was trembling, breathing rapidly, tears stinging her eyes. She glanced into another mirror, a large rectangular one almost as tall as she was. The same girl was there, pressed up against the mirror, face contorted with terror. She was screaming and pounding her hands against the mirror as though trying to smash it, to break her way out. Yuu took a step towards the mirror. Something flashed to her left, a small round mirror, the girl's face large in its shining glass, the face of a rotting corpse, eyes hollow, skin cracked and weeping thick yellow pus. Her mouth moved with the melody of the song.

Yuu spun away, caught sight of the girl in a square mirror a little smaller than the chess board in Xindu. The girl waved at Yuu, a frightened look on her face, then pointed at Yuu. No. Not at Yuu. Behind her. Yuu spun again and almost tripped on the tattered rug. On the wall in front of her, dozens of mirrors, dozens of versions of the same girl, some sitting and singing, others screaming, some mutilated almost beyond recognition, others terrified. And in one, a dressing mirror, Yuu saw the girl cowering on the floor, knees pulled up to her chest, arms wrapped around them. In that reflection Yuu stood behind the girl and behind her something dark and glistening, a distorted face with hollow eyes and teeth like knives. She screamed and spun again, tripping on her own feet and crashed to the floor in a puff of dust. Yet, there was no one there. Still Yuu scrabbled backward on her arse. Away from the terror.

Her heart pounded. She couldn't catch her breath. She rubbed tears from her eyes with her sleeves, and when she opened them all the mirrors showed the same image. The girl was no longer crying, no longer singing. She stood in front of the mirror, grinning, her eyes gone, the sockets nothing but a black void. She pointed. In all the mirrors, she pointed at Yuu. Then she sang again, louder. Uncomfortably loud. Deafeningly loud. Yuu clasped her hands over her ears, squeezed her eyes shut, and screamed. No words. No thought. Only a horrified shriek. Her terror clawed at her, tore at her, ripped her apart, and scattered what little sense remained at the girl's feet.

Yuu had to force her eyes open. She was trembling, rocking back and forth, her nose streaming. The girl watched her from the mirrors. In some she giggled. In others she raged, fists pounding, teeth gnashing as though she were trying to force her way through to bite Yuu. Yuu saw herself in some of them as well, cowering, terrified, beaten. She watched herself in a mirror in front of her, focused on the reflection of the mirror behind her. She watched the girl's fingers slowly break through the surface, slender, delicate, and wrap around the mirror frame. The girl slid from the mirror and crawled along the floor toward Yuu. All Yuu could do was watch, too frightened to move. The singing was so loud she couldn't hear anything else, couldn't hear herself crying. The girl rose behind her, dark hair, dark eyes. And Yuu watched. Watched her death close in on her.

It was a yokai. It had to be. An ungaikyo. A vengeful spirit possessing the mirror. Yuu squeezed her eyes shut again and forced her mind to work, to remember. Legend had it the ungaikyo were people who were staring into mirrors when they were murdered. They could manipulate reflections, make people see things. But they were trapped in the mirrors. Trapped unless someone else took their own life while staring into their mirror. Only then would they be released, their place taken by the unfortunate soul who had fallen into their trap.

Yuu forced her eyes open again. In the mirror in front of her, the girl laughed as she drew a knife across her face, skin splitting, blood oozing.

"It's not real," Yuu said. Or at least she thought she said it. She couldn't hear herself over the singing. "You're not real!" she screamed as loudly as she could, and this time she heard her own voice.

Another mirror showed the girl looking shocked, a hand over her mouth. She shook her head sadly, then glanced up a little, staring at something behind Yuu. Yuu refused to look. It took every scrap of will she could muster, but she refused to play this spirit's game any longer.

Yuu got her feet beneath her and rose on shaking legs, her breath ragged and her face wet with tears. "Not real," she whispered. "Not real. Not real. Not real." She looked at the mirrors on the walls, desperately trying not to look at the reflections in them, ignoring the girl as she screamed and threatened. "Not real. Not real. Not real." Square mirrors, round mirrors, rectangles. "Not real. Not real. Not real."

Yuu started toward the door, and there, hanging beside it was a small oval mirror the size of her hand, with a faded wooden handle. Yuu lurched forward, still telling herself the reflections were not real, desperately trying not to look into the glass. She snatched the mirror from the wall, clutched it to her chest, and ran from the room.

The mirrors in the hallway all showed the girl now, begging her to turn back, pleading, shaking her head, crying. "Not real. Not real. Not real." Yuu screamed over the song echoing around the hall and ran. She flung open the door and lurched into the cool afternoon air. She staggered three steps and collapsed onto wet cobblestones, hugging the mirror to her chest and crying tears of relief.

Natsuko coughed loudly to get her attention. "What's with all the screaming?"

Chapter 26

"You can get the next one," Yuu said, voice trembling, hands shaking. She tried to slow her breathing, to quiet her pulse. Fingers trailed across the back of her neck and she shivered and turned, expecting to see the girl standing in the doorway, but there was no one there.

"That's not how it works," Natsuko said so calmly Yuu wanted to scream. "I cannot…"

"You cannot help directly," Yuu snapped. "I know. I wasn't being… Did you know what was in there?"

The goddess shrugged. "A mirror."

A frantic giggle tore from inside of Yuu and she struggled to reign it in, to stop it from sounding like madness. She took another deep breath and closed her eyes. She could see the screaming girl's face staring back at her from the darkness. Hear the haunting song in the pulse of her blood.

"There was an ungaikyo in there," Yuu said. "In the mirrors. It…" She stopped and slowly pulled the mirror away from her chest, dreading what she might see in the reflection. When she finally mustered the courage to look into it, she saw only her own tired face, tear tracks down her dirty cheeks… and behind her was the girl, peering over her shoulder. Yuu screamed and threw the mirror away. It bounced on the path and skidded to a halt face down.

Natsuko tutted. "What was all that about? You could have broken it. Not that it would matter, I suppose. Broken or not, it's ours now. But I imagine Guangfai would be quite angry." A grin spread across her gnarled face. "Maybe we should smash it just to irk him."

Yuu glared at the mirror. An old man with a walking stick limped past, staring at her with something like pity in his eyes. No doubt she made for an odd sight, kneeling in the street, screaming at a mirror. But he had likely seen far more bizarre things recently. Grief, loss, and stress all had a way of pulling apart the threads of a person's sanity.

Yuu shook herself and scrabbled over to the mirror. She had a job to do. Natsuko needed her to win the challenge of the gods, and if she wanted to end the wars that plagued the world, Batu needed to be stopped. She picked up the mirror, careful not to turn it around and look into the reflection. It was such a delicate thing. A faded wooden handle with a sleeping dragon depicted on the bottom, a silver base with an intricate thorny patterning. She thrust the hateful thing out at Natsuko. "You take it."

"Oh no," Natsuko said. "That is against the rules. I am a guide and nothing else." The goddess had already been more than just a guide, whether she wanted to admit it or not. But Yuu doubted there was any use arguing with her. "Oh, will you look at that." The goddess peered into the mirror. "She is such a young one too. Murdered at the beginning of her life, so many opportunities snatched away." She stared at the girl in the mirror. "Kira Mirai was your name, dear. Do you remember it? Or has time and hatred made you forget you were once human? You could have been a singer. Your voice would have carried you to the emperor himself. You could have melted his frozen heart, brought joy to his sterile existence, changed all of Ipia."

"This girl could have married the emperor of Ipia?" Yuu asked.

"Yes," Natsuko said softly. "Not the current one. It's a missed opportunity eighty years old already. It was stolen from her. Kira Mirai was murdered by her uncle for a crime that was not hers. She made him feel things he should not." She sighed. "Not all opportunities are missed because of war." She glanced down at the mirror again. "Oh, do stop trying to scare me, girl. I am a goddess for heaven's sake. Even if you did convince someone to take their own life, your time is past. You are a yokai now and those opportunities are gone. They cannot be taken back.

There, there. I know. I am sorry for what was done to you. You didn't deserve it."

Yuu slowly turned the mirror back around and stared into the reflection. She saw the girl, Kira Mirai, sitting on the dusty street, her black kimono crumpled around her. She wept. Not tears of blood, not meant to scare. True tears for the life she lost. She remembered, no doubt about it. She remembered the person she had once been. The child she had been. "Is there anything we can do?" Yuu asked. Now that she knew the girl's story, she didn't seem quite so frightful. She seemed pitiful, tragic.

Natsuko shook her head slowly. "Yokai are the realm and governance of the shinigami. Only the tianjun can command those damned kami to do anything. No, the shinigami mostly just roam around causing mischief, fighting amongst themselves, and forgetting to do the one job that demands their existence, collecting the souls of the dead. Bloody useless things if you ask me."

Yuu sighed. "I mean, can we… help her?"

Natsuko knelt in front of Yuu and wrapped her gnarled hands around Yuu's. It was all the answer she needed.

Yuu stared at the girl in the mirror again for a few moments. "I'm sorry," she said softly, then turned the mirror around and slipped it into a hidden pocket in her robes. It felt strange carrying a possessed item so close to her. A yokai that had come so close to killing her, but she felt like the danger of the mirror was past. The girl's anger had turned to grief. It might turn back. She might become the vengeful spirit again, but even then, she was nothing but an illusion. A reflection of the past. Maybe when Natsuko was tianjun, she could free the girl somehow, but until then the only way for her to escape her mirror prison was for someone else to die and take her place. Yuu would not wish that punishment on anyone.

"Where next?" Yuu asked. She wanted to leave Anding as soon as possible. She felt guilty that the people of the city were busy rebuilding, reclaiming what the Cochtans had taken from them, and she wasn't there to help. She was a drain on their resources, and a danger to them all. The Ticking Clock was still out there, and might not be the only one after her.

"The next artefact should be quite simple," Natsuko said. "It is a sword. Esen, the god of dreams once used it to sever heaven from the world, which is why only Tianmen now exists in your world." Yuu never thought about it before, but supposed it made sense. The gates of heaven sat at the top of Long Mountain, but heaven itself was an entire world, according to legend. Perhaps heaven and earth had once been one.

"Is that a parable?" she asked.

Natsuko scoffed. "It would be nice and simple if it were, wouldn't it," she said. "You mortals are so eager to forget the truths of the world, and yet also so quick to cling to the past. You worship us still, but forget we used to walk among you as freely as I do now. Gods and humans and spirits lived alongside each other. Then Esen had to go and ruin it all with that damned sword." The goddess shrugged. "Anyway, he's dead now. But he left the sword for Khando, the god of dreams."

Natsuko started down the road. Yuu stood and walked after her, whistling for Lump to follow. The old stallion gave an annoyed whicker, picked up the empty stew bowl in his teeth, and started after them.

"Are you saying gods can die?" Yuu asked. She knew the Goddess had been hiding a lot from her, but that seemed a rather important thing to know.

"Well, of course we can," Natsuko said. "When gods go to war everyone loses. That is why we have this contest, and why the rules are so strict." She glanced over her shoulder at Yuu, a dark look in her fathomless eyes. "We used to run around fighting and killing each other all the time, but it made the world too chaotic. Spirits shuddered when we fought, and even the dragons fled from us. So, we decided to get you mortals to do it all for us. Much more civilised this way. Fewer earth-shattering cataclysms, which are really quite tiresome."

"So, you don't die anymore?" Yuu asked, still trying to wrap her head around it all.

Natsuko's face stretched into that inhuman smile. "I did not say that. It is just much rarer these days."

Yuu was missing something. She was certain of it. Natsuko was deliberately hiding something. "And you said Esen was the god of dreams, but then you said Khando was the god of dreams."

"One was, one is. We cannot *not* have a god of dreams, after all. You mortals need to worship someone."

A woman pulling a cart laden with straw passed them. She bowed her head a little by way of greeting, but Yuu could see her eyes lingering on Lump. Yuu wished she could give her the old beast, but she needed him. He might not be a lot faster than walking, but he was better than nothing. They were running out of time, and Long Mountain was still a long way away. And it would take days to climb even once she reached its base.

"So Esen died and Khando took his place?" Yuu asked.

"Yes," Natsuko said. "As I said, there has to be a god of dreams. It is all extremely complicated and not something you mortals need to concern yourself with."

Yuu couldn't deny it was a bit confusing, but was far from convinced it shouldn't concern her. "And Khando is in this contest?"

Natsuko cackled. "He was. He thought he could murder his way through the contest and chose the Leopard King as his champion. The Ticking Clock killed him first. You would not believe the mess."

"That's far from reassuring." One more reason she never wanted to see the Ticking Clock again. If he could kill both the Leopard King and the Laws of Hope, she doubted anyone could stop him. "But we're going to retrieve his sword? A sword that can sever earth from heaven?"

Again, the goddess cackled. "Scared you will break the world?"

"Yes!" Yuu said.

Natsuko led them to the city barracks. Once, it would have been full of soldiers, but they were all gone, conscripted to fight in Roaring Tiger's army. Now it was just a tall stone building, silent and grey, a monument to the general's mistake in leaving no one to defend the city. A few people were outside in the street, clearing away debris from a building across the narrow road. It had been set fire to and all that remained was a burnt-out husk of ash and scorched timbers. Two adjacent buildings had been torn down to stop the fire from spreading. It warmed Yuu's heart to know the rebuilding effort was underway already, but the feeling soured when she thought about how many lives had been lost and how few of the soldiers would return. Anding would rebuild, but many of its homes would likely stand empty for years, perhaps generations.

"Not much in there at the moment," said an old man shifting rubble onto a cart with a few other men. He approached Yuu and Natsuko, rubbing his ash-covered hands on his trousers. The left side of his face was bandaged, spots of blood showing through, but seemed hale enough. "If you're looking to report a crime, we have a setup in Stardew square by the main gate. Just a couple of old women acting as judge really, but they don't take any excuses. Su and Zhenzen have always been quicker to condemn than forgive." He chuckled, a noise that seemed out of place in the wreckage. "Sentence will likely be helping us rebuild though. Forced labour of a sort, I guess."

Yuu smiled at the old man. "I'm looking for a sword."

The old man frowned. "Plenty of those in there, but I'm not sure why you'd want one. We don't have much of a guard, but those that have taken up the role are more than up to the task."

No doubt the old man thought her a criminal. Sometimes a lie was easier to swallow than the truth, but sometimes the truth was easier to tell than a lie. "There's a sword in there that belongs to the god of dreams. I need to get it for the goddess of lost things."

The man's eyebrows shot up. He said nothing for a long moment as he looked between Yuu, Natsuko, and Lump. The horse set about snuffling at Yuu's robes while they waited. Eventually the old man rubbed at his chin, smearing it with ash. "You promise not to use it on anyone here? We've had enough trouble in Anding to last a dozen lifetimes."

"I promise," Yuu said. "I'm just here for the sword, then I'm bound for Long Mountain and Tianmen."

The old man barked out a laugh. "Well, you're clearly crazy, but we live in crazy times. Cochtan invasions, a leper emperor on the throne, and spirits flying about getting in everyone's business."

"Spirits?" Yuu asked.

He laughed again. "Would you believe it? Folk have been saying they've seen one of them Eeko'Ai swimming about the streets." He stopped and looked at her again. "Well, you probably would believe it. The thing is people keep saying they've seen different ones. Something big is coming, mark my words." He waved a hand and turned back to his fellows. "Take as many swords as you want."

"Thank you," Yuu said, bowing. "And good luck restoring Anding."

The old man glanced over his shoulder at her and snorted. "You really want to help? Forget the sword and lend a hand." He didn't wait for her reply, just walked back to the cart and bent his back to his task again.

"This is all Batu's doing," Natsuko said quietly. "A hundred years of war, chaos, and pain." She shook her head. "So much suffering, people have become used to it."

The goddess was right. All this pain and suffering could be traced back to Batu and his wars. Yuu wanted to help, not just the people of Anding, but all the people of Hosa. The best way she could do that was not by shifting rubble and restoring a city, but by helping Natsuko depose the god of war. "What does the sword look like?"

"A blade about as wide as a hand and broken halfway up its length." She caught Yuu's questioning look and cackled. "What? You didn't think a sword could cut through heaven and earth without breaking, did you?"

"Any more yokai in there?" Yuu asked. Most of the fear from earlier had worn away, but it left a raw numbness in her chest.

Predictably, the goddess did not answer. Yuu left her in the road to look after Lump and pushed open the heavy door into the barracks. The room beyond was large and gloomy and smelled of ceramic polish, oiled steel, sweat, and leather. It was a smell she was familiar with, comfortable with even. It reminded her of the years she served the Steel Prince, the camps they made and the armies that flocked to his banner. But those days were gone, and she wasn't sure she'd want them back even if she had the chance. She had just made the decision to give up war, to give up the Art of War for good. Everything her grandmother taught her, everything the old woman had done to her, Yuu wanted to leave it all behind. But what would that mean if Natsuko granted her wish and brought back the Steel Prince? Would he drag her back to war? Would she be able to say no to him?

Yuu picked her way between the furniture, desks and cots, cupboards and chairs. It was all untouched. The sword was not difficult to find. The armoury was full of weapons and armour, all untouched by the Cochtans. Yuu saw ceramic helms and breastplates stacked near to toppling, spears bundled into huge stacks against the walls, rack upon rack of serviceable dao swords, and in the centre of them, a broken sword with a blade far wider than the others, a sleeping gold dragon twisting around its crossguard, worn leather wrapping its hilt. Yuu reached out for the sword and paused, fingers just shy of touching it. She suspected a trap. The mirror had been guarded by a yokai, so too had the coin. The lantern had been at the very height of the false monks' power, and the ring had been in a triad stronghold. This sword must also be guarded, she supposed. It was in the Anding barracks, a place normally full of trained soldiers in a city that was nigh impregnable. Batu placed it here thinking it would be well protected, but his plan was foiled by his own need to spread war. Even so, Yuu glanced about the room to make sure no spirits or demons were hiding in the shadows, then she reached out and grasped the sword, wincing, expecting something horrible to happen.

Nothing happened.

She drew the sword from the rack and stared at it. It fit well in her hand, space enough to grip the hilt with both hands if she wanted to. The blade was uncannily well-balanced despite being broken halfway down, the steel ending in a series of jagged ridges. She had no doubt it would have been far too heavy for her if the blade had been whole, but as it was it seemed weighted specifically for her. A shame she barely had anything but the most rudimentary knowledge of sword play. Despite the Steel Prince's attempts to teach her, he had always been frustrated by Yuu's inability to learn to fight. He never suspected she held back on purpose. It was not an inability to fight, but an unwillingness to learn to fight. She fought as her grandmother had always taught her, as the old woman had beaten into her time and again. She fought with her mind. *The Art of War should never...* Yuu shook her head to clear it of her grandmother's influence.

"The sword that severed heaven from earth," Yuu said aloud, watching how the dim light reflected off the blade. She glanced around again. No one was watching, so she gave the sword a swing. It cut through the air with a mesmerising shimmer. She walked over to a desk in between two cots, shouted with effort, and chopped the sword down with all the strength she could muster. The blade bit into the wood with a *thunk* and stuck there. She had to wrench on it four times to pull it loose, feeling more and more foolish each time she jerked on it. It appeared the sword that severed heaven from earth was useless in useless hands.

Natsuko was sitting in the street, having a cup of tea with the men from outside by the time Yuu emerged from the barracks. Lump was also staring down at a cup of tea, watching the steam rise in wisps and fade away to nothing.

"You found it then?" called the old man with the bandaged face. He seemed far more jovial than before, but Yuu supposed a good cup of tea could do that. He frowned when she held up the sword. "Are you sure you don't want a better blade? That one is broken."

"That's the sword all right," Natsuko said, grinning her god's grin. "I'd know it anywhere. It will drive Esen mad to know you have it. I can't wait to tell him."

Yuu tied the hilt of the sword to Lump's saddle. The horse turned its head and snuffed at her robes, and she batted him away. "I've got nothing for you, beast," she said. Lump snorted and went back to staring at the cup of tea. "We'll try to find you some apples or something. Do you think it counts as being lost if an apple simply falls from a tree?" The horse did not reply.

"Go on then," Natsuko said to Lump. "But do not blame me if you burn your tongue." The horse quickly snatched up the cup and spilled more tea over his lips and chin than in his mouth.

The goddess shook her head and rolled her eyes all at once. "Tea?" she asked as Yuu picked a cobblestone clean of ash and sat down with Natsuko and the old men. "I'm afraid I don't have anything stronger."

Yuu took the tea and sipped at it. Now that she thought about it, it had been days since she'd had a drink.

One of the old men, a fellow with even more wrinkles than the goddess, raised his cup and said, "Your grandmother here was just telling us that the Art of War came back to save Anding. I wish I'd seen her. I was born just after she saved the city during the last invasion. Grew up on stories of her turning back the tide of Cochtans. Fitting she came back in our hour of need."

Yuu glanced at Natsuko and found the goddess watching her from the corner of her eye. "She rode out with Roaring Tiger," Yuu said. "I doubt she'll be coming back."

"Shame," said the old man. "She's a real hero, our Art of War."

Yuu wondered about that. The Art of War, her grandmother, had saved the city and gone on to lead the war effort against the Cochtans, bringing victory wherever she went and directing the united Hosan forces to beat the Cochtans back to their own lands. She was a hero. But Yuu had never known that woman. She had known the grandmother who was kind and cruel in equal measure. Who fed her, clothed her, housed her, and raised her. Handed her a legacy, whether Yuu wanted it or not.

The old men finished the tea and offered Yuu and Natsuko shelter for the night so the two women could avoid travelling dangerous roads in the dark. Yuu didn't want to stay in Anding — she wanted to be as far away as possible — but Natsuko accepted the offer. They slept that night in an old dojo filled with folk rendered homeless by the occupation and wounded soldiers. A hundred people all huddled together for warmth and protection. Tomorrow they would start the journey to Long Mountain and toward the gates of heaven.

Chapter 27

They left Anding the following morning heading south, and Yuu felt her spirits lift as the city shrank behind them. There was too much emotion attached to the city, too much history and pain, and much of it was inherited from a woman who was her grandmother only in name. The old woman would have likely condemned Yuu's decision to leave the Art of War without a successor. Without a way to continue her legacy. But the old woman was dead, so what the hell did it matter what she thought?

Lump was well rested so Yuu rode much of the morning, but the old horse tired easily and before long she had to walk to spare his weary bones. As soon as she slipped down from the saddle, Natsuko appeared as though she had been there all along.

"You should have asked that general friend of yours for a fresher horse," the Goddess said as she fell in beside Yuu.

"And get rid of Lump?" Yuu asked.

The goddess grumbled. "Two horses would be better than one."

"Would you like to ride Lump?"

Natsuko shot Yuu a scathing stare. "The beast is ugly, slow, and flatulent." Lump swished his tail through the air and ripped up a tuft of grass as he walked on. His nostrils flared, and he swung his big head toward Natsuko, lips twitching. The goddess reached inside the sleeve of her hanfu and pulled out a desiccated apple, long since withered past anything Yuu would consider eating. She held it out, and Lump greedily snatched it up and crunched it between his teeth.

Yuu smiled. The goddess could be kind. She gave Lump an apple, brewed tea for the men in Anding, cared enough to give up the one thing that mattered most to her to stop Batu's endless wars. Yet she could also be callous. Revelling in the prayers of people who lost so much, and never giving anything back. Was

257

that what it meant to be a god? Cruelty and kindness delivered hand in hand?

"Where to?" Yuu asked. Long Mountain was but a hazy smudge in the far distance, still many days travel away.

Natsuko was silent for a while then said, "There's an orphanage just over the border into Long province. We can pick up another artefact there. It might be our last chance before we reach Long."

"That'll make five artefacts," Yuu said. "Will that be enough?"

Natsuko didn't answer. "We will reach the orphanage by nightfall," she said eventually. "If you do not mind riding this smelly monster again."

"How does it work?" Yuu asked. "If you… we win."

"Eh?"

"From what you've said, becoming tianjun is a bit like becoming emperor." Yuu hadn't really thought about it much, but had no idea how the gods interacted with people, other than inspiring worship and seemingly offering nothing in return. After all, people prayed at Natsuko's shrines to ask for lost things to be returned, yet she never returned them. Yuu's hand found the little Pawn she had used to beat her grandmother so long ago. Well, maybe she only rarely returned things. "So, if we win the contest and you become tianjun, can you just stop the wars? Make the Cochtans retreat and never come back."

"That is not entirely how it works," Natsuko said. "The tianjun rules heaven. She can make laws to alter the world in subtle ways. Spirits like the shinigami are bound to follow the tianjun, obey her. But mortals are trickier. You resist control, yet offer fealty so readily. You hate injustice, yet heap it upon one another. You do not obey, but you ask us for guidance. The tianjun cannot control mortals, cannot force you to obey, but the tianjun sets policy. All those generals and emperors who pray to the gods for guidance are given what advice the tianjun commands, no matter which god is prayed to."

Yuu glanced at the sword attached to Lump's saddle. "Alter the world in *subtle* ways?" she asked. "You said the god of dreams used this sword to sever heaven and earth."

Natsuko grumbled. "Things were different back then. We ruled both heaven and earth. That's why Esen did it. He wanted to set mortals free from the whims of the gods, give you the strength to resist, to make of the earth what you wanted and not be beholden to us." She sighed. "Not everyone agreed with him, but some things can't be undone."

"But how?" Yuu asked. "How did he sever heaven and earth with a sword?"

Natsuko gave her a pitying smile. "He was a god, dear." An infuriating answer, but Yuu could tell it was the only one she was likely to receive.

They passed many travellers on the road, but none paid them much attention. Some were soldiers on their way to Anding to sign up with Roaring Tiger, not knowing the general had already moved on. Others were merchants on trade routes. A few asked for news, and Yuu was happy to provide what little she knew, but most ignored the lone woman on a worn-out old horse.

When she turned a bend around a hill and the orphanage came into view, Yuu was surprised. She expected it to be attached to a village or town, part of a larger settlement, but she was wrong. It stood alone, not a settlement in sight. It was a collection of squat wooden buildings, long but not tall with a well in the centre of a beautiful courtyard and shrines all around it. Fields surrounded the complex, some teeming with vegetables and others full of ankle-high yellow blade grass swaying in the breeze. It was almost picturesque, and looked old. Yuu could not understand how it survived the last emperor's rule, when bandits roamed the province and no unfortified town was safe. She pulled Lump to a

halt, slipped from the saddle, and rubbed the ache out of her
thighs. The horse gave her a long-suffering glance and lowered his
head to snuff around the ground for something to chew. Yuu
spotted a red hanfu on the other side of Lump, though again she
hadn't seen the goddess appear.

"Is this it?" she asked.

"Yes," Natsuko said in a quiet voice. "The… artefact is in
there."

A couple of children ran out of one of the buildings, a girl
chasing a boy, both no more than six or seven years old. They
didn't even seem to notice Yuu as they chased each other around
the well, giggling and squealing. She just watched them for a few
moments. This was a childhood she never had. Even before the
Seafolk had taken her father and her mother abandoned her in the
hope of bearing the Emperor of Ten Kings a child. Even with her
grandmother she never had a childhood like this. The other
children hated her, called her names and pushed her to the ground
when the adults weren't watching. Not that their parents would
have stopped them. Yuu wasn't even certain grandmother would
have stopped them, now that she thought about it. It was all a
lesson to be learned in pain, the manipulation of others to one's
own ends. She wondered how much of her childhood trauma was
by her grandmother's design.

"What are we looking for?" Yuu asked. "And who does it
belong to?"

Natsuko said nothing. She took a slow step forward, then
another, and Yuu fell in behind her, whistling at Lump to get
moving. He ignored her, but didn't seem likely to run off any time
soon, so Yuu left him.

All the other artefacts had been guarded in some way. Some
by humans not even knowing what they had in their possession,
and others by spirits placed there just for that purpose. Yuu
brushed her fingertips against the mirror hidden in her robes, and
thought just for a moment she could hear the song of the girl

trapped inside. All in her imagination, of course. Whatever this new artefact was, it too would be guarded. Perhaps the whole orphanage was nothing but a mirage to trick the unwary seeker. Another yokai. Or maybe something worse.

Natsuko maintained her ponderous pace, eyes fixed on the playing children. A small fence surrounded the entire orphanage, though it was little more than a boundary and would stop neither human nor animal determined to enter, and a single gate led into the grassy courtyard, a shrine on either side of it. One of the shrines, Yuu noticed, was dedicated to Natsuko. The other was to her brother, Fuyuko. Twin gods said to look after all children.

The door to the largest building swung open just as Yuu and Natsuko reached the gate. Three more children, even younger, barrelled out, giggling as they joined the others. A wrinkled woman with a kindly smile followed them out. She was wearing a black hanfu stained with paint of a dozen colours. She froze when she spotted them at the gate and said something Yuu couldn't hear. Then she started gathering up the children. The little ones clearly thought it some sort of game, running away from the woman and trying to trip each other up so their comrades might be caught first. Another game Yuu recognised, though she had never been allowed to play.

A second woman appeared at the door, tall, wearing a spotless green hanfu with red trim. She was older than Yuu, though not by much, with some wrinkles around her eyes but none around her mouth. She wore the years well and moved with elegance and strength. Raven hair cascaded down her back in thick braids, reaching just past her hips. Yuu knew with a certainty this woman was her opponent. Whoever she was, she was here to protect the artefact.

Yuu was already considering the possibilities. The woman did not appear to be armed, but that was far from an indication of how dangerous she might be. There was only twenty paces between them, and the courtyard was still full of children playing.

Yuu had only a carving knife and the small dagger the Ticking Clock had almost killed her with. The broken sword hung from Lump's saddle, but she was probably better off with the dagger. She had a few wood shavings imbued with qi, but none of her chess pieces were yet ready. None were finished. Her options were limited and without knowing what the woman was capable of, there was not much she could do to form a plan.

Another child emerged from the building, edging around the woman in the green hanfu. Yuu guessed the boy to be no more than eight or ten years old. He was small for it, hands held nervously by his side and eyeglasses pushed up the bridge of his nose. A dark mop of unruly hair made him seem half wild, but he clung to the woman's hanfu, and didn't join the other children.

Yuu met the woman's gaze and saw her tense just a little. They both knew what was coming.

"Fuyuko!" Natsuko said, her voice barely more than a breath. The goddess was grinning, a smile of pure joy. "I found you!"

Natsuko pushed through the gate and ran through the courtyard past the screaming, giggling children. Yuu watched the years fall from the goddess. By the time she stopped in front of the woman and the boy, Natsuko was a girl again, the same age as the boy. Yuu followed more slowly, picking her way forward cautiously. She had no doubt the goddess was beyond harm, but she certainly wasn't.

"Fuyuko," the goddess said. "It's me." The boy edged further behind the woman, hiding behind her hanfu. The smile fell from Natsuko's face and the wrinkles started to appear again. "It's me, Fuyuko. Your sister Natsuko." Within moments she was the ancient crone Yuu had come to know so well, and all trace of the young girl had vanished. "You don't recognise me," she said. Tears ran down the creases in her face.

As Yuu reached Natsuko's side, she saw the woman in the green hanfu eyeing them both. There was compassion in her eyes, but steel in her posture. "Batu said someone would come, and that it might be you," she said, her voice soft as petals brushing against skin.

Natsuko's face twisted with rage. "You're his creature?"

The woman didn't falter in the face of a goddess' anger; Yuu had to give her credit for that. She would have run screaming.

"I am no one's creature," the woman said. "But this boy is in my care, and I will protect him from any and all danger." Again, her eyes flicked to Yuu. "We should talk."

Yuu bowed her head in agreement. She was certain of one thing: she did not want to fight this woman. At least not without sufficient preparation. She placed a hand on Natsuko's shoulder. The goddess flinched but didn't move away. "I don't know what's going on here, Natsuko," Yuu said. "But I think I've pieced together a little. He's your brother, *and* he's your artefact. The one thing you cherish more than anything else. That's why you both couldn't enter the contest. Let's hear what the woman has to say. We shouldn't fight. Not here."

The goddess sniffed loudly and bowed her head.

The woman in green ushered Fuyuko back inside the building then turned to the courtyard again. "Mai, look after the children please." She gestured to one of the smaller houses nearby. "This way. I'll brew some tea, and we can talk."

The house was small and cosy, two rooms separated by a paper screen. There was a small table in the centre of the room, a stove to one side, and two bed rolls in the corner. Yuu knelt in front of the table while the woman busied herself about the stove. Natsuko grumbled. She appeared distracted. It was unnerving to see her in such distress.

"My name is Yanmei," the woman said as she set a kettle on the stove.

"I am Yuu," Yuu said, bowing her head. "This is Natsuko."

"The goddess of missed opportunities," Yanmei said softly, bowing respectfully to Natsuko. "I hope the shrine outside was to your liking. I—"

"Why doesn't Fuyuko recognise me?" Natsuko said sharply.

"I don't know," Yanmei said. She knelt at the table opposite Yuu and waited while Natsuko joined them. The goddess was tense, an unnerving presence in the room, setting Yuu on edge. If Yanmei felt it, it didn't show. She sat with a straight back, yet didn't appear uncomfortable. There was an undeniable elegance to her. "Let me explain what I can. What *I* know.

"I am a teacher at Heiwa Academy, an Ipian school for children with techniques. Along with teaching the children, it also my role to find new students. Children with gifts, potential. The mandate of Heiwa is to teach the strong, to raise children to power and knowledge and wisdom. I find those with techniques who could become dangerous if not trained correctly, or if trained by the wrong people. At Heiwa we teach them to use their techniques and to use their minds. We teach them to be strong and kind." She paused and smiled. "It's a work in progress. There is a lot of fighting. But we control it as best we can."

It certainly sounded like a worthy endeavour. Hosa was rife with tales of legendary bandits with techniques that made them feared among the people. How many of those might have taken more peaceful paths if they simply had the chance?

"I come here whenever I can," Yanmei continued, "to see the children Mai is raising. My father was a bandit, and he used to come here too. He took children who showed promise and forged them into monsters under his command. I hope to make what amends I can by leading similar children down a different path."

"Get to the point," Natsuko snapped.

Yanmei glanced at the goddess and bowed her head. "Some days ago, while I was visiting, the god of war appeared. He had a young boy with him. The boy remembered nothing, but Batu said his name was Fuyuko, the god of orphans. He said people would come for the boy, that they would try to take him by force, and they did not mean to be kind to him. He made me promise to protect the boy from everyone. I am to keep him here until the moon begins its next cycle. I am duty bound to protect him."

The kettle started to boil and Yanmei stood and walked back to the stove. She poured the tea and turned around, startled to find Natsuko was gone. Yuu hadn't even noticed the old goddess disappear. "She does that," Yuu said. "She'll be back eventually."

Yanmei returned to the table with just two cups of tea and again knelt opposite Yuu. "I won't let anyone take him," she said.

"Not even his sister?" Yuu asked. "I can guarantee she has his best interests at heart."

"Does she?" Yanmei asked. She raised the cup to her lips and sipped. Yuu did the same, but the tea was scalding hot, so she blew the steam away. They watched each other for a few moments.

"He's a God," Yuu said. "You know that?"

Yanmei bowed her head in acknowledgement.

"He belongs in heaven with his sister."

"Hmm." Yanmei sipped at the scalding tea again.

Clearly, Yuu needed a different approach. Something to convince Yanmei of the truth, because Yuu was certain of one thing, she did not want to fight this woman. Something in her bearing, in the way she spoke and moved, hinted at a strength of body and mind Yuu could not hope to match. Nor could she hope to trick her way to victory. But sometimes words could win a battle no amount of bloodshed could hope to. "She's his family," Yuu said. "Sister and brother. They should not be separated."

Yanmei was silent for a moment, lips drawing into a thin line. "I find it peculiar that people always consider familial bonds unbreakable. They like to believe family members are kind to each other. Loving and accepting." Her eyes flicked up and met Yuu's, and Yuu knew she had made a mistake. "It's a lie," Yanmei continued. She placed her cup on the table and began rolling up her sleeves. "As I said, my father was a bandit, quite a famous one. People called him Flaming Fist, but I called him father."

Of course, Yuu had heard of the Flaming Fist. He had been a terror in the west during the old Emperor of Ten Kings' reign. The bandit warlord was famous for wrapping his hands in oily chains and setting them on fire during battles. He disappeared a few years ago and no one seemed to know what happened to him, though Yuu had some suspicions. He was almost certainly dead.

"His hands were not the only things he liked to burn," Yanmei continued. She finished rolling up her sleeve and showed Yuu a muscular arm mottled with discoloured flesh. Burns long since healed, but indelible evidence all the same. In some places Yanmei's arm was smooth, melted flesh that never healed properly. In others it was rough and red, a different type of burn, but likely no less painful. Motley evidence of a tragic past. Yuu closed her eyes. It was all too familiar. Too uncomfortable. It stirred memories she didn't want to recall.

"He said I was a wilful child," Yanmei said, her voice even, unwavering, steel and fire. "When my mother passed, he told me I was all he had left of her, and he couldn't allow me to hurt myself. Every time he burned me, he said it was for my own good, so I would learn. If I left the camp, a burn to remind me that wasn't allowed. If I flirted with one of his men, a burn to warn me away. He called me his precious flower, the Last Bloom of Summer, to be protected at all costs. Protected against everything but him. He was allowed to hurt me because he was teaching me. So, you'll forgive me, if I don't trust the love of family or the protection of blood."

Yuu squeezed her eyes tighter but it was no good. She couldn't stop the tears. How could someone do that to a loved one? How could someone hurt their own family like that? But of course, she knew. She knew all too well. *Focus on the lessons and not the pain.* The lessons were what was important; the pain was nothing but a tool to remember them. *Focus on the lessons.* Focus on the lessons.

"Oh, I see," Yanmei said, kindly this time. "I'm sorry."

Yuu heard a rustle of fabric and felt Yanmei kneel beside her. Strong arms wrapped around her and pulled her close. Yuu clenched her teeth, squeezed her eyes shut, and tried to forget. But it was no good. The dam was breaking, and nothing could keep the truth from rushing out. She couldn't even remember the lessons anymore. All she could remember was the pain. It erupted from her throat as a strangled sob, tears falling like autumn rain, nails digging into palms. Seeing Yanmei's pain written bare on her skin had shaken something loose Yuu had been hiding. Broken down the walls she had built up around her past. It unearthed Yuu's own pain that she never had the strength or courage to deal with. The real reason she had wanted to leave behind the Art of War.

Her grandmother had been a hero, a legend in the history books of Hosa. She fed Yuu, clothed her, sheltered her. In the end she had died for her. Her grandmother had been all those things: hero, legend, grandmother, saviour, teacher. And also torturer. It started as nothing, a pinch on the back of a hand when Yuu's attention slipped. A kick to the shin when she moved the wrong piece. But as time went on, as Yuu grew and learned, the punishments became more severe. A needle stab to her wrist when she lost to a blatant deception. A week without food when she stared after the other children playing in the village.

Yuu came to expect the pain, came to dread it. Failure was pain. Loss was pain. How many times had Yuu felt the sting of the old woman's gnarled backhand when she found herself distracted during a game? How often had the Art of War tried to beat the compassion out of her young protégé? The expectations her grandmother set had always been too high, insurmountable, yet any time Yuu did not meet those expectations, any time she did not exceed them, she felt the pain.

Yuu's grandmother might have seen in her a protégé, a way to continue her legacy, but the rest of the family only saw another mouth to feed. An outsider. A young girl from Nash, smarter than all of them and didn't know well enough to hide it. The other children picked on her, pushed her down, stole what little she had; her mother's old scarf, the rest of her bao. The adults were no better. They might have called her grandmother family, but that didn't extend to the orphan she had taken in. Not a day went by when they failed to remind her she wasn't one of them. That she didn't belong. If she got in the way she was knocked aside. If she dared to talk out of turn, she was slapped into silence. Her grandmother saw it, played on it, played Yuu against her own family. Yuu saw it now for what it was. Her grandmother wanted Yuu to rely on her and her alone. Spend every moment with her learning to be the new Art of War. Distraction was pain. No choice but to focus. No friends save her grandmother. No family save her grandmother. No one. No one at all, save an old woman who showered her with torture as often as love.

Yuu learned everything her grandmother taught her. History, politics, geography, religion, economics, logistics. Anything and everything her grandmother had presented her with, in the hope it would please her. But it was never enough. And every time she was distracted, every time she failed, every time she lost. The pain. *Focus on the lessons. The pain is nothing but a tool to remember.* Words spoken with false kindness even as she pressed a blade to Yuu's arm and drew red lines along flesh because she lost a game to an old woman who had decades, a whole lifetime of experience more than her.

Yuu learned to trick the other children into fighting amongst themselves so they'd leave her alone. She'd take a toy from one and plant it on another to create dissension amongst the ranks. She learned to deflect the anger of the adults too, listening and watching, then revealing their secrets to each other so they would leave her alone and war amongst themselves. She learned to

survive. To push her compassion aside and treat people as pieces
in a game. She learned how to move them to her will. And it had
all been her grandmother's plan. To continue her legacy. A new
Art of War, forged in conflict and pain. Seeing people as pieces to
be played. To be sacrificed.

Yuu had almost forgotten the pain. Had made herself forget
it. *Focus on the lessons.* Focus on the lessons. But the lessons had
made her cold, indifferent. Her grandmother's lessons had allowed
her to kill her Steel Prince. His wounds were dire, but he might
have been saved. Yuu never gave him the chance. She killed him
and put another piece in his place. To win the war. And it worked.
But it left her with nothing. It left her *as* nothing.

Yanmei was still holding her, strong arms wrapped around
Yuu, making her feel safe. Protected. She had never felt safe and
protected, and felt her walls come tumbling down. All her pain
and repressed memories revealed themselves as surely as the sobs
shook her body and tears rolled down her face.

Eventually, Yuu sniffed and wiped a sleeve across her face.
The tears had stopped. Her eyes felt as raw as her insides. She
stirred, and Yanmei pulled away.

"You didn't deserve it," Yanmei said softly. "Neither of us
did. No matter what they told you, it was their pain, and they
should have kept it. You didn't deserve it."

Yuu nodded and sipped her tea. It had cooled.

Chapter 28

Natsuko stormed down the marble halls of Tianmen, fists balled at her sides, feet slapping the stone. She was angry. No, she was furious! She knew Batu was devious, knew he would take the opportunity to toy with Fuyuko's life, but this? He had gone too far. This time she would make him pay.

"Batu!" she screamed as she threw the doors to the throne room open and stepped inside. The throne was empty. "You conniving tyrant, show yourself!"

She heard a polite cough to her left and spun about to see the god of war standing by the wall of cloud that surrounded the throne room. Some of the cloud had peeled away to look out on heaven, showing emerald fields of grass, a sparkling azure snake of a river winding through the landscape, and colourful dashes as various spirits cavorted about. He stood next to an easel with a painting on it, a daring depiction of the Ruby Falls, a waterfall where the river ran red, pouring into a great cavern. There was no one else in the room. "Little Natsuko," Batu said. "I hear your champion is doing quite well."

Natsuko grit her teeth to stop from spitting at him and stalked over to the God. She didn't care if he *was* the god of war, nor the tianjun. She wanted to shout at him. To hurt him. She grabbed the painting, kicked the easel over, and threw the damned Ruby Falls out through the gap in the clouds. It landed on the grass and a little spirit in the shape of a blunt-faced hound quickly ran over to sniff at it.

Batu stared at Natsuko silently for a moment, then said, "You seem a little angry."

"What did you do to my brother?" Natsuko screamed.

"Ah, that," Batu said and turned toward the throne. The opening in the cloud closed, cutting off the sight of heaven. "There's no need to shout, Natsuko. We're both gods. We've seen how these sorts of things go. Maybe if you calm down, we can talk about it. I promise you'll want to hear what I have to say."

He sauntered away as though without a care in either world. As angry as Natsuko was, she knew it wouldn't serve her. She couldn't hope to fight Batu, he was the god of war, a powerhouse even among gods. And as tianjun he held her life in his hands just as surely as he did Fuyuko's. She stomped after him, stopping at the foot of the dais even as he climbed up to it and plopped down in the jade throne with an air of nonchalance.

"What did you do?" she demanded, managing to keep herself from shouting this time. At least outwardly. Inside she was screaming bloody murder.

"I couldn't allow Fuyuko to go and find you on his own," Batu said with infuriating aplomb. "That wouldn't be fair to the other gods. I had to make sure he stayed put." He leaned back and stared up at the drifting clouds above the throne room. "So, I took away his memory."

"And his godhood?"

"Yes, that too," Batu smiled. "It was all in the interest of fairness, little Natsuko." A grin flashed across his hairy face. "I suppose it must be quite maddening to know he has lost *so* much, and not be able to give any of it back."

Some things weren't just lost, they were gone. Gone beyond any hope of return. Gone beyond even her power to restore them. Some things, however, weren't lost at all. They were taken and held hostage.

"Why do you want to be tianjun, little Natsuko?" Batu asked. "You know what it means, don't you? You know what it entails. You have to oversee *everything*. Barely even have time for tea."

"To get rid of you," Natsuko snarled. "To change things."

Batu laughed. "Get rid of me? Do you really think anything will change if you're tianjun?"

"There is no greater cause of missed opportunities than war," Natsuko said firmly.

"You blame me for missed opportunities? How rich. I always knew you were idealistic, but can it really be, little Natsuko, that you don't understand your own nature?" He laughed, a full belly laugh that reverberated around the throne room like thunder. "Under your rule, there would be more opportunities missed than ever before." He leaned forward and snarled at her. "Mortals would suffer a plague of lost items, things going missing from right under their foolish noses. We do not define our worship, Natsuko. We are defined *by* it. Our very existence *demands* it. You would cause the very thing you seek to curtail." He leaned back in his throne and waved a lazy hand in the air. "Which is why I have caused so many wars."

"You love war!" Natsuko spat. "You revel in bloodshed, in the worship mortals heap at your feet with every corpse."

Batu grinned. "I do. But that doesn't mean it's all my fault. I tried peace. Thirty years ago, I tried to bring peace to all the empires of the world. I whispered in ears, constructed all the signs. Do you remember, little Natsuko? I even had you plant the idea."

Natsuko remembered all too well. "You had me take swords from warriors all over the world. Heirlooms lost with no clues as to how."

"And what happened? Hosa entered into its bloodiest period since the Cochtan invasion. The Emperor of Ten Kings began the unification wars, taking the opportunity he found in peace to bring all Hosa under his rule. The Ipians split their empire in two. Two royal families at war for the Serpent Throne. The Seafolk took to the calm waters not to embrace fishing, but to sail to Nash and raid the coastline. And the Cochtans used the peace to develop new weapons of war and resurrect old ones that should have been left dead. I tried for peace, little Natsuko, but I am the god of war. I am tianjun. And heaven and earth define themselves by this throne." He slammed a fist down onto the arm of the throne. "I tried peace and it led to war. So why not embrace it?"

"All the more reason to remove you." Natsuko knew Batu was telling the truth. He did seem to be trying peace a few decades ago, but not anymore. He said it himself, he intended to bathe the world in war, and was doing just that. "If you stay tianjun for another century, war is all the world will know."

"You miss the point, little Natsuko. I tried peace and it ended in war all the same. I am defined by worship, and I am worshipped for war, so war is what I bring whether I try to or not. You, Natsuko," he said, wagging a finger at her, "are defined by missed opportunities and lost items, and that is all your rule will bring to both heaven and earth. It will be a century of misery and loss the likes of which will make my time as tianjun seem glorious. War may be responsible for missed opportunities, as you say, but it also creates new opportunities. It brings people together against common enemies. It makes heroes out of mortals and keeps them worshipping us for protection and salvation and victory." He leaned forward, shedding his nonchalance, fire in his eyes. "War is glorious. It forges the mortals into ever stronger weapons.

"But with you on the throne," Batu continued, "what will there be but sorrow and misery and people cursing your name for the things they have lost?" He leaned back and half closed his eyes again. "A century defined by the things it could have been. By the opportunities missed, rather than those taken. An opportunity missed."

Natsuko stared at the god of war, speechless. She hadn't thought about it really. What heaven and earth might truly be like under her rule. She had been so focused on removing Batu. She assumed she could change things, reduce the number of missed opportunities. Use her power as tianjun to make mortals' lives better, return what they had lost, and set them all on the best paths available to them. That was what she had been fighting for. That was what she had sacrificed Fuyuko for.

"I can give your brother back to you," Batu said, as though he read her mind. "I'm the only one who can. Even *if* you somehow win and take my place on this throne, you cannot restore your brother's memories or godhood." He grinned savagely. "*I* took them. Only *I* can give them back. Depose me, and they're lost forever. He is not strictly mortal, but neither is he a god anymore. He'll age as a mortal, though, and he'll die as one. And he'll never ever" — he fixed her with a stare and sneered — "remember you."

He was telling the truth. Only the tianjun had the power to take away a god's power. If Batu lost the throne, Fuyuko would stay as he was, and a new god of orphans would be born. After all, there had to be a god of orphans. For as long as orphans would pray to be united with their parents, there would need to be a god to hear their prayers.

"Or you can drop out of the contest" Batu said with a shrug. "Tell your champion to discard her artefacts and go home. Do that and I will return Fuyuko to you. Things can be as they were, little Natsuko. You and your brother together. The twin gods, as it was always meant to be."

It would be easier, she knew. If Batu was telling the truth, then her time as tianjun might be worse than his, and without her brother by her side to help her, to guide her… Natsuko would be lost. She always relied on Fuyuko to be the voice of reason when she could not, and she did the same for him. They were twins, born to be gods together. Born to be together forever. She wished he were with her now, beside her, offering his advice. His belief. His will. His desire. No! Natsuko shook her head. Joining the contest this time had been Fuyuko's plan as much as her own. They had decided together, knowing they had the best chance of picking the right champion to unseat Batu. Fuyuko was the god of orphans, but like Natsuko he hated it. He hated knowing each and every child who was orphaned, and knowing that despite their prayers there was nothing he could do about it. And he hated war because nothing in the world created more orphans than war. Fuyuko would never agree to Batu's terms, and he wouldn't want Natsuko to either.

"No," Natsuko said firmly.

Batu shrugged, a smirk splitting his bearded face. "Suit yourself, little Natsuko. A shame you'll never get to say a proper goodbye to your brother."

Natsuko turned and stormed toward the great doorway. She made it two steps before faltering. When she glanced back, she saw Batu still watching her through heavy lidded eyes. "Are you scared, Batu?" she asked as sweetly as she could. "The god of war scared of a little girl?"

Batu frowned. "What would I have to be scared of?"

"Good question," Natsuko said, feeling her impishness returning. "But I can't imagine you'd offer me this deal unless you were scared I might beat you. That my champion might beat you." It made sense. This was exactly why she had chosen Daiyu. There was no warrior in the world, no matter how strong or skilled, who could beat the god of war. He was power personified, battle incarnate, general, soldier and hero all. But if Natsuko had learned one thing from Daiyu so far, it was that any enemy could be defeated, even at their own game, just as long as you understood the rules better than they did.

Natsuko grinned at the god of war over her shoulder. "My brother might not remember me, Batu, but in his name I will beat you." She hummed to herself and skipped from the throne room, leaving Batu seething.

While the older woman, Mai, was out in the garden busy trying to keep an eye on a dozen playing children, Natsuko snuck past her into the building where Fuyuko was being held. Her brother was sitting alone at a desk. There were desks and chairs set up in rows, a slate board at the far end of the room, some words scribbled on it in chalk. It was a classroom. They weren't

just looking after the children here, they were teaching them to
read and write, providing them with skills and knowledge they
could use to forge better lives for themselves once they were old
enough to leave the orphanage. Natsuko smiled at that. Fuyuko,
her Fuyuko, would have loved this place. They took orphans in,
cared for them and protected them, prepared them for the world
outside their protection. He really would have loved this place.
But that was who he was before, not who he was now. Not who he
might one day be.

Fuyuko had a book open in front of him. Reading while the
other children played outside. He always was a quiet, studious
type. Natsuko approached slowly, trying to decide what to say.
She glanced about the classroom, hoping for inspiration.
Bookshelves lined the side wall with a variety of texts, many far
too advanced for a normal child of his age. He had no doubt read
them all. Would he remember them now? Or had Batu stolen
those memories from him as well? Did he remember anything at
all? Natsuko gave up with caution, it had never been her way, and
ran down between the desks and slid to a stop in front of her
brother. She bowed quickly and straightened up, beaming at him.

"Hi. I'm Natsuko. I'm your sister," she said, forcing the
words out and not letting them choke her with sadness.

"Uh…" Fuyuko stared at her blankly for a moment, then
fumbled out of the chair, stood straight, and bowed as formally as
if she were an empress. "Hello, Natsuko. I'm Fuyuko."

"I know that, silly. You're my brother." Batu might have
taken his memories, but he hadn't taken her brother. Not really. He
was still there, in the way he was overly formal even with her, in
the way he wore his eyeglasses pushed up the bridge of his nose
even though he didn't need to wear them at all, in the way he
pushed back his mop of unruly hair, only for it to fall in his face
again. His memories were gone, but he was still Fuyuko.

"I'm sorry," Fuyuko said, still bowing. "I don't remember
you."

How much to tell him? How much did he know? Foolish questions Natsuko didn't care to consider. He was the considerate one, who sought to understand a situation long before encountering it. She had always been the impulsive one, wading in up to her knees before stopping to think.

"That's because the god of war stole your memories," Natsuko said as she hopped up onto one of the desks, scattering the paper and charcoal onto the floor. "He's an arsehole and we hate him."

"We do?" Fuyuko asked, finally straightening from his bow, and wincing at the mess Natsuko had made. He quickly went about picking up the scattered items, though he wouldn't find one of the charcoals. It was lost.

"We do!" Natsuko said. "You more so than I."

"Why?"

"Because he makes war, silly. And war makes orphans. And you hate orphans. Well, no, that's not true. You love orphans. You just don't like that there are orphans."

Fuyuko nodded at that. "Everyone should have parents. Do I… Do we have parents?"

Natsuko drew in a deep breath and paused. It was a far more complicated question than he knew. Perhaps it was best to stick to the basics. "No," she said, shaking her head.

"Oh. So, we are orphans?"

"Yes."

Fuyuko nodded as he finished tidying up and then returned to his desk. Sitting and idly running a hand over the book on his desk, even as he stared at Natsuko. "Will I ever remember?"

Natsuko felt her smile slip and fought a wave of grief. It threatened to wash away her innocence and leave her as the old crone once more, and she didn't want Fuyuko to see that. He had to see her as his sister, young and boundless. "No," she said, shaking her head to fling away the tears. "I don't think so. You'll have to make new memories."

"With you?"

"Of course!"

Fuyuko smiled. He smiled so rarely it broke Natsuko's heart. "You're staying then?" he asked.

By the time Natsuko reached the building where Yuu was having tea with the enemy, her youth had slipped away. She was the crone again. Her skin wrinkled beyond age, her hair grey as a winter sky. Fuyuko didn't want to return to Tianmen. He didn't understand. He was an artefact, her artefact, and she needed him to beat Batu and cast down the god of war. He didn't remember this was all his plan. They had just chosen her to compete because she was better suited to the contest, but it was *his* plan.

She stopped at the door and waited, listening through the crack.

"I'm sorry," Yuu said, her voice quiet and hoarse.

"You have nothing to be sorry for," said the other woman, Yanmei. "Do not think it is over. You have faced it, admitted it, but it will take more than tears to wash away your wounds."

Wounds? Had they fought? Natsuko thrust open the door, startling both women, and stormed in. Yuu had her back to the door and quickly wiped at her face with the sleeves of her patchwork robes. Yanmei stood, facing Natsuko impassively. The room didn't look like it had been at the epicentre of a fight.

"You're back," said Yanmei. "I assume you spoke to Fuyuko?"

Yuu sniffed and stood, turning to face Natsuko. Her eyes were red from tears, and her shoulders were slumped. "I assume you spoke to Batu," she said with a forced smile.

Natsuko looked between the two women. She wasn't sure what happened in her absence, but Yuu looked uninjured, though she had definitely been crying. "Both of you are right," she said. She stalked over to the stove and poured herself a cup of tea. She didn't need to drink, but it felt good to be doing something.

"Your brother's memories?" Yanmei asked softly.

"Gone. Gone and not coming back. Batu tried to leverage them, to get me to give up."

Yuu tucked an errant strand of hair behind her ear, a habit she had when she was nervous. Mortals were full of annoying habits. "I assume you told him to shove it up his own arse?"

Natsuko shrugged. "Words to that effect."

"And Fuyuko?" Yanmei asked.

Natsuko glared at the woman, but even in the face of a god's wrath Yanmei didn't back down. "Wants to stay. But he can't. I need him. We only have four artefacts. It's not enough. He has to come with us, or his sacrifice means nothing."

Yanmei shook her head. "I won't let you take him." She looked at Yuu. "I'm sorry. But I promised to protect him."

Natsuko balled up her fists. "You promised Batu," she said through clenched teeth. "The very monster Fuyuko sacrificed himself to get rid of. By stopping us from taking my brother, you are protecting Batu, and I guarantee that is the opposite of what Fuyuko wants."

Yanmei frowned and looked away. After a few moments she looked at Yuu, and there was an unspoken question in her eyes.

"May we stay the night?" Yuu asked. "I think… there are decisions to make that might be better made by fresh minds."

"Of course," Yanmei said. "This is a guest house. You may stay here, and I will move my things in with Mai." She looked at Natsuko. "You may see Fuyuko and speak with him, but do not try to take him against his will."

Natsuko bristled and took a menacing step forward. "Or what?"

Yuu slid between them. She gave Yanmei a slight bow, then turned to stare at Natsuko. "We are guests and will abide by their rules."

Natsuko threw up her hands and cackled. "Fine. Fine. It's not like I can take him anyway. It's against the rules." It was not entirely true.

Chapter 29

Yuu woke to a buzzing like thousands of bees in the distance. It took only a moment to recognise the sound.

She threw off the covers, startling Natsuko, and grabbed her robes from their pile on the floor. They felt itchy and grimy against her skin. She had taken the opportunity to wash herself in the orphanage's baths but had not time enough to wash her robes. She was also fairly certain the grime was now the only thing holding them together, it had been so long since they had been cleaned.

"What are you doing?" Natsuko asked. She cocked her head. "And what is that noise?"

"It's a thopter," Yuu said, pushing her arms through the sleeves and doing a quick check of the pockets. The mirror, the ring, and the coin were all still there. As was the carving knife and her little chess pieces, still works in progress. And finally, the dagger the Ticking Clock had almost killed her with. She hoped he would regret giving it to her.

Natsuko's face sagged, the wrinkles forming wrinkles of their own. "You have to run!" she hissed. "You can't fight him, Daiyu."

"I know," Yuu said, considering the possibilities. "I'm not prepared. If I'd known he was coming—"

"He's after *you*. He might not even know Fuyuko is here. You have to run, lead him away."

Yuu started for the door. "Thank you for your concern."

Natsuko snorted as she walked after Yuu. "I'll distract him. He can't harm me. You get Lump and go."

Yuu stopped at the doorway and turned back to the goddess. "I can't run, Natsuko. For a start, he has a thopter. Lump can't move faster than a trot on the best of days and I'm afraid if I push him, he'll just keel over... and nobody wants to smell that.

Second, he might be here to kill me, but he can't track me. Sarnai led him here, to Fuyuko. He knows your brother is here."

The Goddess frowned. "You can't run."

Yuu pulled the door open and stepped into the crisp night. The sky was lit with stars beyond counting, and a bright moon was waxing toward full. The buzzing was louder outside, and Yuu could just about see a light flickering above them, moving back and forth, the stars around it blotted out. She couldn't have the Ticking Clock land in the orphanage. She made for the gate and strode out into the field of grass beyond. A light wind whispered through the yellow blades, and the moonlight lit the gentle landscape in an ethereal blue. She looked around for some advantage. Perhaps she could make for the longer grass away from the path and hide, try to surprise the assassin. It seemed unlikely. There was the hill beyond the vegetable fields, but taking the high ground was not nearly as advantageous as people often think. It wouldn't improve her skill. It would merely ensure her legs were first to get cut off.

Lump sauntered over, chewing on something and eyeing her lazily. She couldn't imagine the old stallion would be much help, but he nuzzled against her, his nostrils flaring as he sniffed at her robes for something to eat. She pushed his head away and tried to shoo him off, but he wouldn't leave. Loyal and stoic to the end, it seemed. Or probably too dumb to understand what was about to happen.

"Go stand somewhere else," Yuu said, pushing the horse's head away. "You don't want to be in between me and him." Lump just sidled a little closer and snorted hot air at her.

"What's the plan then?" Natsuko asked. Lump swung his head around and sniffed at the goddess.

"I'm thinking," Yuu said. The thopter was descending. They had left the orphanage complex but not by far, hopefully it would be enough to protect the children. The Ticking Clock was an assassin, but surely even he would blanch at the senseless murder of children.

"Think faster?" Natsuko suggested helpfully.

The thopter touched down on the grass, its blades slowing, and the Ticking Clock climbed out. Yuu hadn't seen the assassin since his battle with the Laws of Hope. He still wore the long coat, and his body was entirely covered, not a patch of skin showing at all. His head was a metal helmet, his eyes glowing soft blue behind its goggles. And he had both arms again, which was something of a shame. Yuu braced herself, expecting an immediate attack. It didn't come.

A small ball of fire floated out of the thopter. It was orange at the centre, but the flames licking above it burned a searing white. It was detached from everything around it, but still somehow burning. Yuu watched it float next to the Cochtan assassin. Natsuko sighed.

The ball of fire flared blindingly bright for a moment. Yuu squinted. When the spots in her vision cleared, the fire was gone and in its place stood a tall woman with scales along her arms and face, legs drawn together in a thick snake tail that coiled beneath her. Light blazed from the woman's skin and behind her eyes. She smiled a predator's smile, flames dripping from her teeth, scorching the grass.

"Prepare for gloating," Natsuko said quietly. "The bitch loves to gloat."

"Natthuko," Sarnai lisped, fire spraying out of her mouth like spittle from a toothless old man. "I didn't exthpect you to make it thith far."

"Sarnai," Natsuko said, holding out her arms as if in welcome. "Fuck off."

"Distract her for a few minutes," Yuu whispered.

"And how should I do that?" the goddess grumbled. "Shadow puppetry?"

Yuu shrugged. "Throw her a tea party or something, sure. Whatever works."

Natsuko blinked a couple of times, then sighed and took a couple of steps forward. Sarnai slithered forward to meet her, the grass burning beneath her tail.

There had to be something Yuu could use to her advantage. Her chess pieces still weren't ready, and until they were, they would break apart almost as soon as they formed. She had plenty of wood shavings, and in the dark, they might surprise the Ticking Clock, but that was only if he came close enough. With those small pistols he had slung at his hip, he wouldn't even need to approach her. He could kill her where he stood. Perhaps she could use Lump as cover, but that was something her grandmother might suggest, and Yuu simply wasn't willing to do it. The old beast had carried her well since they left Ban Ping and deserved better than to be sacrificed like that. Perhaps she could use her technique with the wood shavings to create a series of shields, covering her approach as she closed on the assassin. But then what? All she would manage would be a hasty path to her demise.

She heard the crunch of footsteps on grass behind and turned to find Yanmei walking calmly toward her. The woman no longer wore a simple hanfu but was decked in loose trousers and a leather jerkin, a half breast of faded green scale covering her chest. In the crook of her arm she carried a naginata as long as she was tall and carved with crawling vines all the way up its length. The blade atop it was almost half as long as the pole, single edged, with a series of metal rings through holes drilled into the offside. A bronze counterweight moulded in the shape of a blooming lotus flower was attached to the other end of the pole. It was the type of weapon that would take both great skill and strength to wield properly.

Yanmei stopped at Yuu's side. "Is that who I think it is? Even my father feared the Ticking Clock, and he famously feared no one."

"I'm sorry," Yuu said. "I believe he's here for me."

"Not Fuyuko then?"

Yuu shrugged. "Well, he might be here for both of us."

Yanmei pursed her lips. "No chance he'll just leave?"

"Natsuko is negotiating but…"

"You insufferable, ignorant child!" Sarnai hissed.

"You pig-headed, foul-smelling snake!" the goddess shouted back.

Natsuko and Sarnai both turned and stalked away from each other. The god of fire flared brightly for a moment and became a small ball of floating flame once more. Natsuko was cackling as she approached, and Yuu had the feeling the negotiations had consisted mostly of insults.

"Pleasantries have broken down," the goddess said.

"That was not a few minutes," Yuu said. "Who broke them down?"

"Her," Natsuko said and then smiled. "She was being a bitchy little zit, so I told her to fuck off."

"I suppose it's my turn," Yanmei said calmly. A calm Yuu did not feel.

"You can't…"

"I promised to protect Fuyuko," Yanmei said. "From everyone."

"Not against him, you can't," Yuu said. "He's beyond… I think he killed the Laws of Hope."

Yanmei glanced at Yuu, and much of her confidence seemed to drain away. "Really?"

"I think so," Yuu said. She wondered what she was doing. This woman was clearly a warrior and willing to fight her enemy for her. She was a piece to be played. A piece Yuu hadn't even realised she had until she looked down and found it on the board. Yet she didn't want to sacrifice her. She didn't want to sacrifice anyone anymore. That was her grandmother acting through her, and she wasn't her anymore.

"What's the plan?" Natsuko asked.

"I am," Yanmei said, her voice wavering just a little. "It's important to remember that no matter the pain they gave us, there were gifts too. The hardest part is not realising what they did to you; it is learning to separate the good from the bad. My father was a vicious monster who beat me and burned me and tried to shelter me from the world. But he also taught me to fight. I hate what he was. I cannot forget what he did. But I am his daughter. I will not deny that."

The Ticking Clock started forward, each movement jerky like a bird's. When he spoke, his voice was a tinny rasp. "It is time, Art of War."

Yanmei stepped forward and lowered her naginata. "I will be your opponent today, Ticking Clock."

The Ticking Clock's head jerked toward her and then back to Yuu. "You send yet another to die in your place? So be it." The assassin's coat billowed as he reached down, grabbed one his pistols and pulled the trigger. Yanmei moved so fast Yuu barely saw her swing her naginata in front of her. The Ticking Clock's shot fell to the ground in two halves.

Yanmei winked at Yuu. "Stay back," she said, then launched forward into a sprint, closing the distance in moments.

Chapter 30

The Ticking Clock fired his other pistol just moments before Yanmei reached him, she threw herself to the side, swinging her naginata, and deflected the shot with the flower-shaped pommel. It hit the ground just a hand span from Yuu's feet and she took a step back. Then Yanmei leapt at the assassin. She twisted, pivoting her weapon around with blinding speed. The Ticking Clock lurched backwards, dodging the strike, and bending back into a handstand. When he gained his feet again, his jian was in hand.

Yanmei thrust out her pole arm and the Ticking Clock barely brushed the strike aside. Yanmei thrust again. The assassin nudged the strike away with his metal elbow and was already moving, lurching forward, scraping his blade down the haft of the naginata, keeping Yanmei from bringing the blade to bear. Yanmei spun the weapon around in her hands and jabbed the pommel into the Ticking Clock's breastplate. She shouted with effort and pushed him back, pushed herself back, feet skidding through the grass a dozen paces apart.

Yanmei twirled her naginata, a veritable whirlwind of movement cutting through the air. She advanced upon the assassin, using her weapon as a shield. The Ticking Clock backed up a step. His head swung around mechanically. Then it stopped and he whipped a small dagger at Yanmei. The throw was perfectly timed to find a gap in Yanmei's spinning shield. She lurched to the side but the dagger grazed her arm, finding not only a gap in her spinning naginata, but also in her scale armour. A few scales fell away with the dagger, blood trailing after them. Yanmei cried out and stumbled, and the Ticking Clock ran at her.

He struck at Yanmei, almost close enough to touch, and she barely managed to give ground. Yanmei backed up again and again, struggling to find space to bring her naginata to bear, but the assassin closed relentlessly. She feinted left, and the Ticking Clock swung his sword at thin air. Yanmei leapt away, twisting in mid-air, spinning her weapon to cover her aerial retreat. She landed lightly on her feet, lashing out at the Ticking Clock with the bladed edge, forcing the assassin back.

"She has him," Yuu said. At times the fighting was almost too fast to follow, but the longer it went on, the clearer the outcome became. She had underestimated Yanmei. And so had the Ticking Clock.

"You sure?" Natsuko asked. "Seems pretty even to me."

Yuu shook her head, smiling. "No. Yanmei has the speed, the power, and the reach. She's going to win."

"Let's hope so," the goddess grumbled. "You've bet your life on it. And my brother's."

Yanmei darted forward and attacked again with a barrage of lightning fast thrusts. The Ticking Clock jumped away, turned and ran. Yanmei chased after him, unwilling to give him the time he needed to reload his miniature rifles or plan his attack. It was the right move. It should have been the right move, but the Ticking Clock's torso whirled about as though disconnected from his legs and thrust his blade at her. Yanmei barely stopped in time to turn the strike away on the pole of her naginata, but it threw her off balance and she reeled back. The Ticking Clock's legs backstepped, and he closed on Yanmei, slashing at her, too close for her to do anything but block. Her pole arm was hard wood, prepared to take a beating, but with each sword strike, chips of wood flew into the air. Yanmei retreated and the Ticking Clock closed again, his legs swinging around to match his body. He chopped at Yanmei's naginata, hacking the wood.

"Looks like you were wrong," Natsuko said. It was not helpful.

Yuu had to do something. Had to help. None of her pieces were ready and she hadn't had time to seed the battlefield. The Ticking Clock pushed his sword against the pole of Yanmei's naginata, pressing it against her body, and drove forward. His other hand twisted unnaturally, the elbow bending back on itself, and he pulled out another dagger. He thrust at Yanmei. She screamed as the dagger bit into her side. Her scale armour had stopped it from digging deep into her, and its hilt hung from her midsection.

Yuu needed to help somehow. She didn't need to kill the Ticking Clock, just distract him. She rushed forward and picked up the little shot from the grass. She pushed as much qi into it as she could as quickly as she could, and felt her limbs grow heavy, the world dimming a little. Then she threw the shot at the combatants. Yuu fell to her knees, too weak to stand. The shot landed in the grass a few paces from Yanmei and the Ticking Clock, and Yuu activated it immediately. A boulder thrust out from the ground, a malformed thing of earth and rock, and already crumbling. The Ticking Clock glanced at it for just a moment.

Yanmei threw herself back, kicking and forcing herself away from the Ticking Clock as Yuu's boulder crumbled to dust and sand at their feet. The Ticking clock slid back on the grass, keeping his balance, but Yanmei went sprawling on the ground. She rolled quickly to her feet, clutching at her side, the dagger still sticking proudly out of her armour, blood running along its edge.

The Ticking Clock closed again and Yanmei staggered back, swinging her naginata to keep him at a distance. Her strikes were wild now, lacking precision, but more than making up for it with raw power. The assassin tried to deflect each one with his sword, looking for an opening. Yanmei slipped and went down on one knee. The assassin lunged in.

Yanmei jumped up with a scream of fury, twisting and pivoting her naginata so the blade whipped around toward the Ticking Clock. She caught the assassin off balance, unable to retreat. He raised his sword to block. Yanmei's naginata crushed it, shattering the blade and slicing through his arm. It spun away in a gush of dark fluid and landed heavily on the grass.

The Ticking Clock staggered away, clutching at the stump of his arm above the elbow. It wasn't blood leaking from the wound. It was black, viscous fluid. There was no flesh there. The wound was metal and wood and gears still churning though there was nothing left there to move. The assassin tumbled backwards and struggled to crawl away. Yanmei was breathing heavily. The dagger still stuck out of her left side. Blood dripped from the blade onto the grass as she slowly advanced toward the Ticking Clock. He crawled and scraped across the grass, and clambered back to his feet. Yanmei thrust her naginata and speared the Ticking Clock through his leg. The assassin collapsed to one knee. Yanmei twisted the blade, and the leg broke apart below the knee in a crash of gears, pistons, dark fluid and hissing pipes.

Yanmei stepped back and watched the assassin crawl across the ground toward his thopter, one leg a trailing wreckage, one arm missing. "Run away," she said. "Run back to Cochtan and get your enginseers to fix you. And know this, assassin. Fuyuko is under my protection. I won't let you, or anyone else, take him."

The Ticking Clock didn't look back. He crawled toward his thopter through the long grass, trailing sparking wires and dark fluid. Yanmei watched him go.

Natsuko arched her wrinkled brows at Yuu. "You were right."

Yuu smiled at her. "You should say that more often."

"Maybe if you were right more often."

The Ticking Clock reached his thopter and dragged himself into the cockpit. He flipped a switch, the engine buzzed, a hissing pipe spraying steam into the air. Yanmei finally turned and started back toward Yuu and Natsuko.

"You were amazing," Yuu said.

Yanmei grimaced as she fingered the dagger in her side. She decided to leave it where it was for the moment. "I hope you didn't miss my meaning," she said. "Fuyuko stays with me."

Natsuko grumbled but said nothing. She might be a goddess, but even she dared not argue with Yanmei. Yuu couldn't hope to beat her and had no intention of trying.

"We need to look at..." Yuu started to say. She looked past Yanmei toward the Ticking Clock and his thopter. The Cochtan assassin's flying engine was whirring noisily, pumping out steam, but its blades weren't moving. He pulled himself out of the cockpit and swung himself to the side of the thopter. Then he sat on a small ledge on the side of the engine. The whole thing started to move around him.

Yuu, Natsuko, Yanmei, and Lump all stared, caught between shock and horror, as the thopter seemed almost to come alive around the Ticking Clock. Shining black metal rods like chopsticks extended from the engine and began repairing him on the spot. New sections were torn from the thopter and grafted onto his metal armour. His broken leg was ripped away and replaced with a shiny new metal cylinder much larger than before. Within a mass of whirring gears, hissing steam and clinking metal, the thopter unmade itself and was rebuilt around the Cochtan assassin.

"Shit," Yuu said.

Natsuko nodded, gaping.

When the engine stopped whirring, only a skeleton of the thopter remained. The Ticking Clock stood and took a slow, heavy step forward, testing out his new form. He was taller now, towering, like a giant ripped with muscle and coated in metal armour. His arms and legs were as thick as tree trunks, and his chest bulged. On his back was a metal barrel with plated tubes running into his arms and legs. A Blood Engine. The Ticking Clock took two steps forward, his feet thudding down and crushing the grass. He clenched both new hands into fists and punched them together in a shower of sparks.

Yanmei sighed and her shoulders sagged. She drew in a deep breath and stepped forward to meet the Ticking Clock reborn.

"Aim for the tubes connected to the barrel on his back," Yuu said. "If you can cut through them, you might disable him."

Yanmei paused. "Might?"

"Hopefully," Yuu said. The engine did not look nearly so fragile as the ones the Cochtan soldiers had worn.

Yanmei strode forward to meet the Ticking Clock in battle once more. Yuu scattered a few wood shavings on the ground around them. She doubted they'd do much, if anything, against the monster, but it was the only preparation she could make.

Yanmei launched into a sprint and the Ticking Clock held his ground. She thrust her naginata at him with as much power as she could. The Ticking Clock was too bulky now to dodge it. He raised his hands, and the blade bit into his new gauntlets with a clang of metal. But the Ticking Clock didn't budge. He pushed forward and threw Yanmei back on to the grass. She rolled and bounced up in a crouch, leapt forward again, slashing left then right. The Ticking Clock blocked the strikes with his gauntlets. Sparks and metal shavings flew into the air, but the damage was minor. He threw a punch, far faster than his size should allow, and Yanmei barely stepped out of the way. He followed with another punch, and Yanmei leapt aside, pivoted her naginata around herself and struck the Ticking Clock's chest plate with the flower pommel. The metal cracked with a screech that made Yuu wince. The chest plate was weak, a chink in his armour. If Yanmei could break through his defences again, thrust her blade through the crack, perhaps she could pierce the assassin's heart. Assuming he had a heart.

The Ticking Clock let out a tinny whine and thumped back a step, but his hand shot out and Yanmei was too close to get away. He clamped his huge fist on her shoulder and started crushing it. Her scream cut across the field like breaking glass. The Ticking Clock raised his other hand, and Yuu saw a spark of fire glowing under his fist. A gout of flame shot out of a tube on his wrist. Yanmei lit up like a torch.

Chapter 31

"No!" Yuu breathed the word and took a step forward, as though she could somehow rush to Yanmei's aid. But even if she could fight off the Ticking Clock, it was too late.

"Shit," Natsuko said.

"Can't you do something?" Yuu asked, frantically searching her face. "Can't you…"

Natsuko just shook her head. Of course not. There was nothing to be done.

The Ticking Clock held the burning corpse up for a moment, then flung it to the side and focused his goggled eyes on Yuu. Yuu knew she should do something, try anything. Even if it was just jumping on Lump's back and riding away. But she couldn't take her eyes from Yanmei's flaming corpse, the smoking, charred embers of her armour floating into the air. Yuu had known the woman less than a day, but it felt like years. Yanmei had seen the pain Yuu was hiding and given her no judgments, only compassion. And she had died protecting her, protecting Fuyuko. Another pawn in a contest between gods.

The Ticking Clock took a thunderous step forward, then another. He was moving slowly, maybe because his swollen metal body required it, maybe because he expected a trap. Yuu wiped away her tears and felt a tug at her arm. Natsuko stared up at her.

"Run," the goddess said. "I'll slow him down."

Yuu shook her head. "You can't get involved. It's against the rules."

"If you die, I lose either way," Natsuko said. "I might as well try."

Yuu wasn't sure she had any more running left in her. The Ticking Clock had found her twice now; he'd find her again. She looked at him, a monstrosity of machine and man, and focused on the crack in his breastplate. If only she could find a way to use it.

Maybe some wood shavings. But no, they wouldn't have enough force to penetrate the metal chest plate, even with the crack. Perhaps the broken sword. It was back at the orphanage, but it had once severed heaven and earth, surely it could...

She was so busy trying to strategize that she almost missed the movement behind the Ticking Clock.

Yanmei's burning body moved. She pushed to her knees, the grass incinerating at her touch, and then staggered upright. She was a blazing inferno. Her clothes fell away in ash and cinders. Her hair was loose, the thongs tying it together burned away, it floated around her head like dark veins snaking through the fire. Her eyes were black, dark voids amidst the flames. She carried her naginata, and that too was aflame, the wooden pole sizzling in her grip. Yanmei burned, but she did not fall.

"How?" Natsuko whispered.

"It's a bloodline technique," Yuu said. She remembered something Yanmei had said the day before, about her father. "It's Flaming Fist's bloodline technique!" The bandit warlord had famously been able to set his own fists alight, wrapped in oily chains, and not suffer any burns. Yanmei had evidently inherited the technique, but it was not just her fists that were alight. It was all of her. The technique was stronger in her than ever it had been in her father. *She* was stronger than he had ever been!

The Ticking Clock slowed his advance, apparently realising something was wrong. He looked back over his shoulder, and even through his mask Yuu heard his tinny gasp.

Yanmei's burning form lowered into a crouch, her eyes so dark and full of malice Yuu was transfixed. "We're not done yet, assassin," the flaming woman hissed. She launched forward, faster than before and trailing fire behind her. The Ticking Clock barely got his hands up before Yanmei's naginata scraped across them, scorching the metal, embers pluming in his face. The assassin reached for Yanmei, but she leapt to the side and struck again, carving a blazing gash in the Ticking Clock's armour, then again in the other direction, each time leaping aside before he could counter.

They danced back and forth, Yanmei a flickering flame darting about and striking with blistering force, the Ticking Clock staggering about on the grass, desperately trying to keep her in front of him. Yet still she failed to stop the assassin, and how long could she continue to burn?

"The barrel on his back," Yuu shouted. "Aim for the barrel."

Yanmei glanced her way, coal black eyes locking on her. Yuu could see her snarling face in the flames, her rage as hot as her fires.

The Ticking Clock tried to capitalise on Yanmei's distraction. He surged forward, arms wide, ready to grab the flaming woman. No matter how hot her flames, she was still skin and bone beneath them. He could crush her. Yanmei, rather than dodging his flailing grasp, leapt up and flipped over the hulking assassin in a blazing arc. She landed, her feet sizzling on the grass, and struck, the blade of her naginata crunching on the metal barrel even as her pole finally burned through and splintered apart. Dark fluid gushed out of the hole in the assassin's barrel, spurted onto Yanmei's flames, and lit.

The Ticking Clock exploded.

The explosion knocked Yuu on her arse. Her ears rang from the noise and spots swirled in front of her eyes. Fire and smoke billowed into the air, and the top half of the Ticking Clock's body came crashing down on the grass, a sizzling, steaming mass of metal. Natsuko stood there. The explosion hadn't affected her at all. She peered toward the patch of fire that Yuu assumed was Yanmei, lying in the grass still covered in flames, unmoving.

Lump got back to his feet, blew out his lips, stamped his feet, then bent his head and started chewing grass. A giant, metal assassin exploding in flames only bothered the horse in so much as it had interrupted his meal. Yuu pulled herself up on his shoulder, and Lump glanced at her and began snuffling her robes.

"Is he dead?" Yuu asked. Her voice sounded muffled, as though she were speaking through a door.

Natsuko shook her head slowly. "Neither of them are." Her voice was muffled too.

Yuu started forward and her vision swam, her legs giving way beneath her. She caught herself on the goddess' shoulder. The little goddess didn't even budge. Yuu closed her eyes until the spinning stopped, then stood straight again.

The Ticking Clock's lower half was a smoking wreckage sitting at the bottom of a scorched crater in the earth. There wasn't much left, and every piece seemed more engine than man. His upper half wasn't much better. It was still alive, but barely clinging to what little was left to him. One arm was gone, a shattered mess of gears and pistons, the other bent, broken, and charred. His hand clawed feebly at the dirt as he tried to drag himself to his thopter again. Judging by the look of the engine, there wasn't enough left of it to fly away.

A dozen paces away, flames rose into the night as Yanmei struggled back to her feet. She was still burning, dark hair whipping about on the heat, untouched by the flames. Her eyes were cold and damning amidst the fire. She staggered forward and the grass burned beneath her. "Is he dead?" she asked.

"Close enough," Yuu said. She could feel Yanmei's heat a few paces away. "He's no danger anymore."

"Good," Yanmei breathed. The flames guttered out and she collapsed onto her hands and knees. She was naked, her clothes burned away, and her skin steamed in the cool air. Yuu rushed forward to help, but Yanmei shook her head. "Don't! I'll burn you. I need to... to cool."

Yuu nodded and backed away, staring at Yanmei. The grass sizzled and scorched beneath her. Her skin was red, but not burned, and her old scars given to her by her father stood out. Her shoulder was bloody where the Ticking Clock had grabbed her, and the dagger wound in her side was trickling blood.

"We should… finish him off… this time," Yanmei said as she climbed back to her feet. She hugged herself, but Yuu was certain if they tried to cover her with a robe or blanket it would catch fire.

The Ticking Clock's attached arm still flailed at the ground. It was missing two fingers, and there seemed no strength left in it. Perhaps he could survive the damage, Yuu was not certain how much of the man was really left underneath the engine, but they would not give him the chance.

Yuu fished the Ticking Clock's dagger from her robes. It seemed fitting that they kill him with his own weapon.

"Give it to me," Yanmei said. "It was my fight. He should die by my hand."

Yuu nodded and flipped the dagger around, holding the hilt out to Yanmei. She felt the heat coming from the woman as she drew close. Yanmei took the dagger and staggered over to the Ticking Clock.

"You fought well," she said as pried open the damaged breastplate with the dagger. A beating heart lay inside, connected to pipes and surrounded by a silken cushion. "Now rest."

The tenderness Yanmei showed the assassin made Yuu a little uncomfortable. She fidgeted in her robes, and her hand brushed against something cold and hard and smooth.

"Stop!" Yuu shouted even as Yanmei thrust down the dagger and held it, poised above the assassin's heart. "I want to try something."

"I gave him a reprieve once," Yanmei said wearily, "and it almost cost us everything."

"This isn't a reprieve," Yuu said. She knelt next to the Ticking Clock's head. His hand flailed uselessly at her until Yanmei grabbed it. With a wrench and a twist, she snapped the last of its wires and pistons and threw the appendage away. The assassin's eyes darted about beneath his cracked goggles, and his breathing became a rapid, tinny whistle. He was dying, whether they helped him along or not. Yuu ripped the goggles from his face. His eyes were the blue of a washed-out sky after a violent storm, the skin around them withered and brown as old leather.

Yuu pulled the mirror from her robe and glanced into its glass. She saw the girl sitting on the ground, her kimono rumpled beneath her. She seemed bored, but when she looked up at Yuu, her face broke into a grin. Not a malicious smile, just a little girl's wild grin.

"I hope this works," Yuu said to the mirror, unsure if the girl could hear her. She flipped the mirror around and held it in front of the Ticking Clock's eyes. "Now, Yanmei."

Yanmei thrust the dagger into the heart of the Cochtan assassin, and the Ticking Clock died with a final rattle.

Chapter 32

Yuu held her breath, waiting for something to happen. She glanced at Yanmei, but the woman merely shrugged. She left the knife in the assassin's heart and stood, holding herself against the chill. Yuu flipped the mirror around again and saw the Ticking Clock, no longer broken and dying, sitting on the grass. He jerked his head up and saw Yuu, drew his pistol and fired at her. She saw the flash, but nothing happened. He was trapped in the mirror. Dead. A yokai. Just as the girl had been.

Natsuko cleared her throat, and Yuu spun around. The old goddess was standing over a young Ipian girl in a black kimono. It had worked! Kira Mirai sat before them free of the mirror that had trapped her. Exactly what that meant, Yuu couldn't be sure. Had she just freed a young girl, or a vengeful spirit? There were rules at play Yuu was not familiar with.

Kira looked up wide-eyed and grinned at Yuu. The girl had terrified her from that mirror space, tried to get her to kill herself, and Yuu had set her free. Now that she really thought about it, she wondered if it was a good move. Kira lurched to her feet and ran at Yuu. Yuu stood awkwardly, frozen, and the girl barrelled into her. Yuu staggered back, but Kira gripped hold of her robes and hugged her.

"Thank you thank you thank you thank you thank you," the girl sputtered, her face buried in Yuu's robes.

"What just happened?" Yanmei asked.

Yuu drew in a breath to answer, but sighed it out. "Perhaps we should discuss it over a pot of tea." She smiled. "Once you're dressed."

They returned to the orphanage. Mai was in with the children, keeping them as quiet as possible. Yuu thought about leaving Kira with them while she discussed the child with Yanmei, but was not yet sure what the girl was, and would not risk putting a potentially dangerous yokai around innocent children. She took Kira back to the small guest house with them and sat around at table. Yanmei disappeared into the other room to dress. Yuu brewed some tea while Kira chatted endlessly about how boring it had been inside the mirror.

"I used to have friends," the girl said. "They would come, and we would play while mother worked in the kitchen with the other adults. Kameyo never really liked me, she always thought she had a better singing voice, but we all knew she couldn't hold a note past two seconds and…" She paused for a moment and pouted. "They're all dead now, aren't they?"

"Yes," Natsuko said, reaching over and patting the girl on the knee. Yuu saw Kira flinch at the contact. The old goddess had barely taken her eyes from the girl. "It's been eighty-two years since you died, Kira."

The girl smiled sadly. "Please call me Mirai. My friends all call me Mirai."

"We're not your friends," Natsuko said.

"But we could be," Yuu said quickly. "I would be happy to call you a friend, Mirai."

The girl smiled so wide it brightened up the room. "You heard me singing, didn't you," she said, her dark eyes fixed on Yuu. There was something unnerving about that stare, her eyes were too dark. "I'm so sorry about, um, trying to kill you."

Yuu returned to the table with the tea and knelt.

Yanmei returned in a clean robe, a bandage showing under the collar. "Would someone mind explaining?"

Natsuko rolled her eyes and huffed. "The girl was murdered eighty years ago while staring into a mirror. She came back as a yokai, trapped in the mirror until she could trick some other fool into dying while looking into the mirror at her, and swap places. My guess is Batu offered her a deal — swap mirrors and have a good chance at winning her freedom."

Mirai frowned and pursed her lips. "I don't remember."

"And you freed her," Yanmei said. "Why?"

Yuu thought about that for a moment. It was a question she was struggling to find an answer for. "Do you remember how you died?" she asked the girl.

"No," Mirai said. "I…" She frowned and her dark eyes welled with tears. "No. It hurt though. And it wasn't fair. I didn't want to die. There was something around my neck and… I didn't want to die. I didn't want…" Tears started to fall in earnest. Before Yuu knew what to do, Yanmei was there, holding the girl and stroking her hair softly. Mirai went rigid at first, but soon relaxed, clutching at Yanmei's clothing as she sobbed.

Yuu decided to tell Yanmei about the girl's death in private. If Mirai truly didn't remember, then that was probably for the best. And if she did remember, then there was probably nobody better to help her through the trauma. "I freed her," she said at last, "because it was an innocent life traded for one soaking in blood. The world is definitely better off without the Ticking Clock, and I think it is also better off having Mirai in it."

"Is she still a yokai?" Yanmei asked. Yuu saw the girl stiffen in the woman's arms.

"Yes," Natsuko said. "Freed of the mirror, an ungaikyo will live and age and die just as a mortal. She is now both human and spirit." The goddess rubbed her temples. "What that means exactly is something only she can determine."

Yanmei looked at Yuu. "I'll take her. Heiwa is set up to teach children just like Mirai, children with nowhere else to go and power even they don't understand." Yuu was glad for that. She had hoped Yanmei would take the girl. She might have freed Mirai from the mirror, but had no idea what else to do with her.

"Will you take Fuyuko as well?" Natsuko asked almost in a whisper.

"Of course," Yanmei said.

"Are you sure?" Yuu asked the goddess. Fuyuko wasn't just Natsuko's brother. He was a god in his own right, and Natsuko's artefact. "Don't we need him to beat Batu?"

Natsuko glanced at Yuu. There was grief in the lines of her face. She shrugged. "We have the artefacts that Sarnai and the Ticking Clock collected now. Four of them out in that contraption he was flying. That makes eight in total. It will have to be enough." She paused to sip her tea. "My brother is a god no longer, Batu stripped that from him along with his memories, and he'll only restore them if I give up. I can either save my brother and give up on the very dream he fought for, or I can sacrifice him to see that dream made manifest. At least if he's here with this woman, I know he'll be well protected."

"I swear it," Yanmei said. "You say Fuyuko has been stripped of his godhood, but like Mirai here, he is not entirely mortal either."

"No," Natsuko said. "He isn't. I don't know what that means for him, either."

"He'll have a home at Heiwa," Yanmei said. "I promise."

Natsuko nodded, and Yuu took the goddess' hand and gave it a squeeze. Natsuko didn't pull away.

There seemed little else to say after that. It was mid-morning when Yuu said goodbye to the orphanage, to Mirai, and to Yanmei. The woman had saved her, though that wasn't nearly giving her the credit she deserved. With new supplies for the last leg of the journey and eight godly artefacts, Yuu mounted Lump, and continued toward Long Mountain.

Chapter 33

As Long Mountain grew larger in the distance, stretching across the horizon, Yuu worked on finishing her chess pieces. One by one, they took shape in her hands, and she infused the wooden miniatures with her qi with every scrape and chisel. Li Bang was the first one she finished. Blind Eye Bang, as she was certain he would come to be known. She gave him a broad smile and a heroic pose, his chui resting on his shoulder. The accidental gouge carved into his stomach was an irritating flaw, but she supposed all the best pieces had a few of those. Li Bang would be her Shintei piece, moving only in straight lines, the solid backbone of any offence.

Next was the Thief, moving so uniquely, always both forward and then sideways. Yuu had considered Fang for the piece. He fit, of course, being a thief himself. But he had stolen from her, and she needed her pieces to be loyal. So instead she carved Lump out of the wood block. The horse was old, always ravenous, and smelled like a misused outhouse, but he was loyal and hardworking, and there was a strange slyness to his milky eyes. She carved his piece as she imagined the beast would want, head down and snuffling about the ground for something to eat.

For her Monk, Yuu chose Roaring Tiger in his ceramic armour ornately decorated in crashing waves, snarling tiger heads leaping from the waters. She posed him sitting down, dao in hand with its point towards the ground, other hand on his knee, ready to stand up and spring into motion. He had a deep red smudge down his back where Yuu's blood had soaked into the wood. Another imperfection for a perfect piece. He was a peculiar choice for a Monk. But the Monk was also often the first to be let loose to conquer the battlefield, and that suited the general.

She spent some time deliberating on the Hero. Arguably the most powerful piece in the game, able to move in any direction, cross any distance. Powerful enough to strike deep into the heart of enemy territory, but important enough to hold back until absolutely necessary. Yuu chose Yanmei for the piece, and on the way from the orphanage to Long Mountain, she spent many hours deciding on which of Yanmei's forms to use. She was the kind tutor, caring for children, standing up to anyone who might do them harm, even gods. She was the warrior, naginata in hand, scale armour across her chest, powerful enough to face down a legend. And she was the fire, a raging torrent of flame, the daughter of Flaming Fist and stronger than he had ever been. Yuu knew which form Yanmei would prefer, but carved her as the warrior instead, decked out in her faded scale armour and wielding the naginata in both hands.

And that left only her own piece, her Emperor. A carving of herself she had started back in Ban Ping. Tattered robes of a pauper, hands buried in hidden pockets, a douli on her head. She spent some time considering the face. What face to give to her piece? Daiyu Lingsen, the woman she had once been. Or Yuu, the woman she had become. In the end she chose the former; Daiyu Lingsen, the Art of War, her mask undamaged. For all the hurt she had caused, her grandmother had given Yuu a gift as well as a curse. She taught her the ways of the world and how to thrive in it. Had given her the wisdom to see beneath the lies and rules, and a technique to protect herself. She had given Yuu the Steel Prince.

The day Yuu met the prince, she had been attacked by bandits. She had been turned out by the people she had never considered her family and set adrift with nothing but the clothes on her back and a legacy several sizes too big. She wandered aimlessly for days, lamenting her poor fortune, before she came upon the Forest of Qing. That was where they found her. Six of them, dressed in rags, armed with clubs, crude spears, and the desire to take something from someone, anyone. For many, banditry was a way to survive, to eat. For others, it was a way to inflict pain. They ran her down not for her possessions, for she had little of those, but for the thrill of it. Yuu fought them off as best she could, but she had yet to carve her first chess set and was still new to her technique. She left her possessions along with the bleeding bandit she had stabbed in the arm, and ran for the forest edge. They were faster and caught her easily. But the moment they threw her to the ground, a man in silver armour burst out of the forest, swinging a huge sword. The bandits were slaughtered in moments. Then the Steel Prince turned to Daiyu with a scarred smile. He picked her up and carried her back to her things. The chess board was still there, the Art of War's mask secreted away inside with the pieces, but everything else was lost, taken by the bandit she had stabbed in the arm. Daiyu had cried, inconsolable and in shock, and the Steel Prince had led her back to his camp.

In the end he had quieted her by setting up the chess board, laying out the pieces. Daiyu woke from her stupor and sat down to play him. Twelve times they played and twelve times she won. And slowly, Daiyu found comfort in the man, in his conversation, in his kindness. They talked over chess, over wine, over campfire and over food. The prince had an unquenchable fire inside him, a desire for justice. To see the Emperor of Ten Kings pulled down from his throne, not to take it for himself, but to free the people of Hosa from the peace of the sword. He had only a dozen soldiers with him at the time, hardly an army. He was an idealist. But he was a man others would line up to follow. A man others would lay down their lives for. Daiyu fell in love. Not with the man, but with the ideal. With what he represented and, she realised now, with his desire. From that first day, Daiyu knew the Steel Prince meant to fight a war. To raise an army and march it against his enemy. He meant to fight a war, though he had no idea how. He was a warrior of great skill, but knew nothing of troop movements, supply lines, tactics or strategy. His men would follow him into the jaws of hell, wage a war against an immortal emperor, but he would not let even one fall in his name. And that was why he would lose. That was why he was doomed to failure. Unless she helped him. Unless she took up the legacy her grandmother had beaten into her. Unless she became the Art of War.

The mask had been his idea. The only thing other than the chess set to survive the bandit attack. The Steel Prince had not known who Daiyu was at first, who her grandmother had been, but saw in her an opportunity. She was clearly a skilled strategist, he had learned that from their conversations as they played, and he thought if they put the mask on her, if they told others she was the Art of War come back to help him fight a just war, others would flock not just to him but to his cause. To *their* cause. He was right. When it came to the hearts of men, he was always right. Just as she was always right when it came to their minds. With his leadership and her strategies, their forces swelled, and they won every battle they fought. He laughed when, two years later, she finally told him the truth of who she was. He laughed and looked to the stars, and claimed it was fate.

Yuu carved her own piece with the Art of War's mask on its face, undamaged. A tribute to the woman who shaped her life. And a reminder that even the Art of War was but another piece in the game. But Yuu was not a piece. She was the player.

At the base of the mountain there was a small village, little more than a dozen houses clustered around a stream that ran down from the snowy top of Long Mountain. It was the village of the keepers, attendants who spent their lives trekking up the mountain to tend to the thousand shrines studded along its face. According the legend, every god, living or dead, had a shrine on Long Mountain. Spirits, too, those of any significance at least, had shrines. Some were grand things, ornately decorated and standing the test of time and weather. Others were broken, worn away by accident or design. The gods fought amongst themselves; the spirits fought amongst themselves. They were ever willing to deface a rival's shrine if it meant an advantage in power. But the keepers were neutral. They tended all the shrines without bias. In days of old there was no more honourable a profession, but these days the keepers were all but forgotten by anyone who mattered. Yet still they performed their task. Thankless, forsaken, yet devout to the end.

Yuu slipped from Lump's back as she approached the village, and the horse gave a grateful whinny, dipping its head to snatch up a mouthful of grass. "This is why you smell so bad," Yuu said to the horse. "You never stop eating." The beast whipped his tail from side to side, and Yuu backed away a few steps, expecting the beast to let loose another blast of virulent wind. It had not been the most pleasant of journeys, yet she wouldn't trade Lump for any other horse, no matter how young or ambrosial it might be. She patted him on the neck and apologised that she had no more apples to give him. Lump snuffed about her robes all the same.

"You'll find food and water in the village," Natsuko said, appearing on the other side of Lump. It never failed to startle Yuu when she appeared like that, but the horse didn't seem to care. "Supplies for the trip up the mountain. They're expecting you. Well, they're expecting all the champions." They had three days left before the full moon. Three days left to trek up the mountain to Tianmen. "They might even have some wine, too." The goddess shot Yuu a knowing look. She hadn't thought about wine for days, maybe even longer. Now that she did though, she wouldn't mind a drink. But it didn't seem quite as imperative as it once had.

Yuu approached the village. "Have any of the others arrived yet?"

"How should I know? For all I can tell, the horse could be a champion. If only you hadn't lost the lantern."

Yuu shrugged. "Not sure I lost it considering I never had it. And I doubt Lump is a champion. Unless he is the most cunning actor ever to take a stage." The horse swung his head to look at Yuu, turned his glassy stare on Natsuko, then bent his head and ripped up another tuft of grass and lethargically chewed away.

Most of the buildings in the village of the keepers appeared to be homes. They had stone walls and wooden roofs with characterful awnings in the shape of undulating dragons or crashing waves. There was one much larger building, an inn with a stable attached, proving the village had once been a popular place of pilgrimage before the worship of the stars had become so dominant. Behind and above them all loomed Long Mountain, dominating horizon and sky. A snaking path started at a grand torii, and led up the mountain, disappearing into the snowy reaches.

As soon as they reached the village, a man and a woman rushed along to greet them. She was young, wearing an apron dusted with flour, and flushed from the morning's labour. He was older, leaning on a wooden cane, back bent, fingers stained with ink. His climbing days were long past, but it appeared everyone in the village of keepers worked, no matter their ability. No doubt the old man wrote the prayers the climbers took up the mountain to place on the shrines. They both bowed low as they met Yuu where the dirt road gave way to stone.

"Goddess," the woman said, her voice a savage rasp from some long-ago illness. "We knew you would come."

Natsuko nodded, her hands on her hips. "Take note," she said to Yuu. "This is how a god should be treated."

Yuu cocked an eyebrow at the old crone. "You want me to bow to you every time you appear?"

"Yes," Natsuko said firmly.

"What about Lump?" Yuu asked. "Should he bow to you too?"

Natsuko glared at her, and a smile broke across her weathered face. "My champion will require food and water and a bed to rest in for the night. We will begin the climb tomorrow."

"Of course, Goddess," the old man said.

"This way, Chosen," said the woman. She stood and helped the old man straighten, and they turned back to the village, gesturing for Yuu to follow.

They led Yuu to the inn. She stabled Lump, giving him a bag of proper feed to eat, and took the bag of artefacts with her. So close to their goal, she was not about to let them out of her sight. Chaonan's ring, Yang Yang's coin, Guangfai's mirror, and Khando's broken sword. From the Ticking Clock, she had taken four artefacts: Sarnai's scale, the first she had ever shed according to Natsuko, for Sarnai had once been human before becoming the god of fire, and her transformation into the snake-like creature was a gradual thing. Fung Hao's barbed whip. The god of labour loved nothing more than to use it to spur his worshippers on to greater effort. Champa, the god of laughter's smile. In truth the artefact was just a small statue of the chubby god bent over in uproarious laughter, but Natsuko said the god was unable to smile without it, and there was nothing the god of laughter loved more than to smile. And Bayarmaa, the goddess of beasts' artefact was a necklace of teeth, each one taken from a different animal, with a dragon's huge tooth in the centre. Yuu wondered what sort of world the goddess of beasts would bring about if she managed to win and become tianjun, but Natsuko assured her Bayarmaa was out of the running, her champion the second killed by the Ticking Clock.

Yuu froze as soon as she stepped inside the inn. It was not empty. A big man with arms like tree trunks sat at one of the tables. He was bald save for a long tail of hair trailing from the base of his skull, and his shirt was a ragged thing with the sleeves torn off. On his left arm was a scrawl Yuu recognised, a contract between man and god. The man turned his head and looked at her. He had a chubby face with bulging cheeks and soft wrinkles at the corner of his eyes. A small stringed instrument Yuu was not familiar with sat on the table, but she could see no weapons about the man. She chose a table far away from him and kept a wary eye out for danger.

She ate well, a soup of rice and vegetables, then retired to the room the keepers provided. She knew she'd need to be well rested to climb the mountain the following morning when she would knock on the gates of heaven and throw the god of war from his throne.

Chapter 34

The next morning Yuu said goodbye to Lump at the base of the trail up Long Mountain. The old stallion tried to follow her, starting up the dirt path after her, but she knew he'd never make it. He was tough as old leather and proved it every day since Ban Ping, but the trail was too steep, the footing too treacherous. And he was just too old. In the end, the keepers had to hold him back to stop him from following, and more than one took a nip for their troubles. Yuu made them promise to look after the beast and feed him as many withered apples as he wanted.

The climb was hard and Yuu was breathing heavily and sweating long before she took her first break. The trail split here and there, different paths to visit different shrines, but all roads led to the top. All paths led to Tianmen. Occasionally she caught sight of the other champion she'd seen at the inn. He was big and powerful, but struggled up the mountain just as she did. They locked gazes once or twice, but he made no threatening moves, and Yuu was glad to keep her distance. She would not be safe until she reached Tianmen. There was nothing to stop the man from trying to take her artefacts here at the last stretch.

When the sun went down on that first night, Yuu decided to stop and take shelter under an old crumbling shrine. The name had long since been worn away, and the roof had mostly fallen in, but it was shelter in case of snow. Natsuko came to her, and they spent a few hours talking about her brother. Strange spirits danced across the mountain at night, streaks of colour and sounds Yuu couldn't quite make out. She watched them for a while, a growing sense of unease churning in her gut. It wasn't until she recognised the spirits, that the cause of that unease dawned on her. They were the Eeko'Ai. Five spirits, great in legend yet small in size, each with the face of a different animal. They were known to appear at times of great importance. Seeing all five Eeko'Ai at once was considered to be terrible luck, a portent of calamity to come.

The second day of her trek up the mountain was even tougher. The paths grew steeper, the footing more unstable. Yuu found herself scrambling up patches of loose rock or coming across dead ends and having to double back to find the trail again. The ground grew thick with snow that never melted, and the air was so cold she was shivering despite the effort of the climb. The shrines so far up were older, yet still well-tended. A few were broken, the names of their gods eroded beyond understanding, but most were whole and declared their patron proudly. Many had candles burning on small steps leading up to the shrines, and Yuu wondered how they stayed lit in the wind and freezing cold. She passed one keeper, a young woman wearing so many layers of clothing she looked enormous, like a bear with a human face, weathered by so many days spent in the cold wind and snow. The keeper bowed to Yuu as she passed and called her *Chosen*, but said nothing else. Yuu kept going, her feet cold and numb in the snow. She saw no one else that second day.

The second night was depressing. Natsuko did not appear, and Yuu spent the night shivering, hugging herself against the cold, huddled up in a shrine dedicated to Sarnai. It seemed warm from the outside, and given that she was the god of fire, Yuu had hoped for a toasty night. Then again, the goddess had good reason to be spiteful, so perhaps she made her shrine cold to mock Yuu.

Come the third day, Yuu was stiff and exhausted. She had barely slept, and the cold crept into her bones. Every step was an agony of aching limbs and pain like needles driving into her feet. Even so, she continued to climb. She wished Natsuko would appear for the company if nothing else.

High up, the snow swirled around her into a blinding blizzard. The wind bit through her robes in mocking gusts. More than once, she stumbled to her knees in the powdery snow. It seemed like it would be so easy just to stop. To lie down in the

cold and drift off to sleep. But that would not end Batu's wars.
That would not depose the god of war and place Natsuko on the
jade throne. It would not bring back the Steel Prince. So Yuu
struggled back to her feet and plodded on. Her mind felt thick,
waves of exhaustion pounding her thoughts. It was like wading
out to sea, each step tougher than the one before and the current
always trying to drag your feet from under you.

Yuu was surprised when she finally saw Tianmen above her.
She had no idea how far she had climbed, how close to the
summit she was. One moment the snow was a swirling blanket of
whites and greys obscuring everything, and the next it settled to
big, lethargic flakes drifting against a bright, cloudy sky. A large
torii stood in front of her, two redwood trunks rising and twisting
in a mesmerising tangle with a golden beam across them, forming
the portal. Beyond the arch was a palace of marble floors, jade
pillars, and churning cloud. Tianmen, the gates of heaven, the
kingdom where gods and spirits were born. She had arrived.
Scholars the world over would kill for a chance to see this.
Philosophers had spent lifetimes ruminating on what truly lay past
that arch.

"You made it," Natsuko said stepping up next to Yuu. Her
feet did not sink into the snow like Yuu's. She stood above it. Of
course, this was still the mortal world.

"No thanks to you," Yuu said, her voice trembling with
shivers.

"Needed to make certain you were committed," Natsuko
said. "That you wouldn't turn back."

"Another test?"

The goddess cackled. "The last one. Now we wait until
tonight, count everyone's artefacts, and..."

"And kick Batu's arse off his throne," Yuu said, feeling the
excitement rising. "Can we at least wait inside? It looks warmer in
there."

Natsuko nodded and smiled. "It is. Time for some food and a bath. Half a day before the moon completes its cycle."

"Good," Yuu forced the word through chattering teeth and pushed her foot forward. Only twenty paces and she would be standing in the halls of heaven itself.

"Long time no see." A figure detached itself from a small stone shrine by the twisted red portal and stepped forward.

"Fang," Yuu spat. The handsome thief was still wearing his red leather jerkin, but he had a long fur coat over it. Yuu wished she'd had the sense to bring a coat like that.

"It is I. Fang, King of Thieves," he said loudly. The grin that stretched his face looked genuine enough, but she couldn't forget he had stolen from her.

Yuu kept plodding toward the gate. "Ignore him," Natsuko said. "One last ditch attempt to steal the victory from us."

"I thought you were the Prince of Thieves." Yuu said.

"Was I?" Fang frowned and shrugged his shoulders. "The old king must have abdicated. So, how have you been since Ban Ping?" He strode forward easily, despite the snow, and fell in beside Yuu. She quickly checked all the pockets in her robes and then took a half step away from him. She noticed his little red fox sitting on the snow, watching them through mismatched eyes, one green and one golden.

"Since you stole the artefact I was after and left me to die at the hands of the Ticking Clock and the Laws of Hope, you mean?"

Fang scoffed. "You hired a notorious thief, Fang, King of Thieves. What did you expect?"

Yuu glared at him for a moment. Tianmen was just a few steps away now. So close. "A little professionalism?"

"I was the very epitome of professionalism," Fang said warmly. "My profession is stealing things. I stole it from them, and I stole it from you. Two throats with one knife. How could I be any more professional?" He finished with that wide, handsome smile of his. She knew she should hate him, should be angry at him, but after all she had been through, and given how close she was to the end, Yuu just didn't have any anger left in her. Besides, he hadn't tried to kill her. At least not directly. She knew it was a poor scale on which to measure him.

"So, you're a champion too?" Yuu asked.

"I'm afraid so," Fang said. "I noticed that tattoo on your hand when we were… ahem… at the inn."

"Kept your own covered though."

Fang held up his gloved hands and shrugged. "So how many artefacts have you got?"

Yuu stopped. She was so close to Tianmen she could feel the heat of the palace.

"What are you doing?" Natsuko said. "Get inside. You're protected in there. He can't take anything from you."

"How many do *you* have?" Yuu asked Fang.

The thief grinned and took a step back. "I asked you first. But let's just say my hunt has been outrageously successful and my victory is no gamble. I'm reliably assured that no other champion has ever collected so many artefacts themselves."

Themselves. Yuu considered the word. Words were like rules. They mattered far more than most people realised. Their meaning could be abstract or exact, and the contest might depend on the various connotation of the word *themselves*. She had collected only four artefacts herself, but she had eight. How many, then, did Fang have? Was it possible to change things, so late in the game? She glanced at the little red fox sitting on the snow, its head cocked slightly to one side.

"Yang Yang," Yuu said. "I have a wager for you."

315

Chapter 35

"What are you doing?" Natsuko hissed.

Yuu glanced down at the goddess. "Trust me," she whispered so no one else would hear. Now if she could only trust herself. Her plan would work. She was sure of it. Mostly sure. Pretty sure. She tucked a few strands of hair behind her ear.

The fox stood up and stepped forward, growing and changing as it did, slowly taking human form. By the time the fox took its third step, it had turned into a man. Yang Yang was taller than Yuu and stood sidelong to her, staring at her out of the corner of his eye. He was handsome, even more so than Fang, with a dusting of stubble outlining a chiselled chin, and a wide, golden eye. He took a swaying step forward and turned quickly so his other side was to Yuu. He was no longer man, but a beautiful woman with sharp features and ruby-red lips, her green eye glowing as it peered sideways at her. She wore a black-on-red robe that barely covered her bust and was slit down the side from the waist showing a smooth leg. Another swinging step and the God was a man again. He wore trousers, and an open, long fox fur coat, but nothing underneath. His chest was sculpted with muscle and entirely hairless. Yang Yang, the dual god. God of gambling, and goddess of lies, all rolled into one.

"Your champion is a fool, Natsuko," Yang Yang said, smiling, his voice deep and mocking. He took another step forward, changing sides so the goddess of lies stared at Yuu. "But why would I bet anything against you, when I have nothing to gain?" Her voice was silken and alluring.

"What are you doing, Yuu?" Fang asked. His smile had vanished. "You can't bet against the god of gambling."

"Listen to him, Daiyu" Natsuko said.

Yang Yang hissed, "Quiet," and took another step forward, switching again to her male side. He stared at Yuu hard, his voice deep and resonant as a struck gong. "Why should I take your bet?"

Yuu swallowed and fought the urge to take a step back. There was something disconcerting about Yang Yang. The duplicity of the god made Yuu tense. "As I understand it, the artefacts are kept by the god who collected them," she said. "Even if you win. Even if Fang wins. You won't get your coin back."

The god of gambling went still as stone. "You have my coin?"

Yuu fished inside her robes and pulled out the jade coin, holding it up for Yang Yang to see, then closing her fist around it.

"Terms?" Yang Yang asked.

Yuu wondered how far she could push him. Would he accept an outrageous bet? All his artefacts for the coin. He was sure to win, after all. The god of gambling never lost a bet. But then the god might be too savvy for such a thing. Not all battles were won decisively. Sometimes all that was needed was a gentle tipping of the scale.

"One of yours for one of ours," Yuu said. "The coin for the lantern."

Yang Yang grinned through his stubble. "The game?"

"A flick of the coin," Yuu said. "I'll flick and call the side. If you win, you get the coin. If you don't win, I get the lantern."

"You're giving away our hard-won artefacts!" Natsuko howled. Yuu could have kissed her for playing her part so well without even knowing the game she was playing.

Yang Yang turned her female side to Fang. "Fetch the lantern, dear," she said sweetly.

"But…"

"Now!" There was iron underneath her silky purr. When Yang Yang turned back to Yuu his male side was showing again. "I accept the terms. Now give me my coin."

Yuu waited until Fang brought out the lantern and placed it on the ground between them. Her heart was racing. The more she thought about it, the less likely it seemed her plan would succeed. It was the one rule she had never tested. They were all waiting for her.

Yuu took a deep breath and flicked the coin in the air. Yang Yang grinned. "Edge," Yuu said. The jade coin hung in the air, spinning, but not falling. Yang Yang glanced at Yuu, then back to the coin. It was gaining speed, spinning faster.

"That's not..." Yang Yang said, angry. A snarl formed on his lips. "You can't..."

Yuu shrugged. "You had the coin crafted, imbued with qi by a master craftsman," she said. "Whichever side was called, it would land with losing side up. But it has no will, no mind. I called edge, and it cannot decide which is the losing side. It has not the will to make the decision."

Yang Yang switched faces, showing Yuu the goddess of lies, seething behind her blazing green eyes. "Both sides are losing sides, so it does not matter," she snarled. "You still lose."

Facing down an angry goddess might be something Yuu had become used to, but that made it no less daunting. She felt a little buoyed by Natsuko cackling behind her even as the coin still hung spinning in the crisp air. "Whether I win or lose doesn't matter," Yuu said. "The terms of the bet were clear, and you accepted them. If you win, you get the coin. If you don't win, I get the lantern."

"But you lose no matter what, so I win," Yang Yang hissed.

Yuu shook her head. "The coin has yet to land. It can't land since it can't choose a face to land on. You cannot win, and by the terms you agreed to, if you don't win then I get the lantern."

Yang Yang reached out and closed her hand around the coin, clenching her beautiful pearlescent teeth as she tried to stop it from spinning. After a few seconds she hissed and pulled her hand back, shaking it like she'd just been burned. The coin continued to spin, hanging in the air between them. Yang Yang's male side was already facing Fang, opposite Yuu. "Kill her!" He snapped, his voice like a struck anvil. "Take her artefacts."

Fang took a step back, slipping in the snow, and held up his hands. "Ooh, that's not really my thing. I'm a thief, not a murderer."

"You're a master swordsman!"

Fang nodded. "The King of Thieves knows how to duel." He grinned and lowered his hands, flicking his fingers by his sides. "But I don't fight."

"You were always going to have to fight. Kill her!"

"Now?" Fang asked, his fingers still fidgeting. "Before she steps through the archway, you mean."

Yuu snatched up the lantern and leapt between the twisted wooden pillars. The warmth of the palace hit her the moment she was through the torii. A pleasant heat that brought feeling back to her numb fingers. She was in a marble hallway, gold veins running through the fissures in the stone. Pillars of jade lined the corridor, which seemed to run forever in both directions, and the walls were made of churning white cloud. She turned to look back out at the frigid mountain top. Natsuko was cackling, almost bent over, holding her stomach. Fang was grinning, handsome as ever. But Yang Yang was furious. She fixed a cold green eye at Yuu.

"Looks like I missed my chance," Fang said. He shrugged. "Guess we'll just have to do it the honourable way and see who won without all the pesky violence." He stepped past his snarling patron god and through the archway to stand next to Yuu in Tianmen. "That's much better. I was freezing my scars off out there."

"Thank you," Yuu said quietly.

Yang Yang turned back to the spinning coin, apparently trying to figure out how to make it stop. Natsuko strode past her fellow god and entered Tianmen. "We should go and get some

food while we have time," the old goddess said to Yuu. "And...
that was very clever."

"So how many artefacts *do* you have?" Fang asked. The
three of them were watching the god of gambling fretting over his
coin, but Yuu looked past him at a dark figure trudging toward
them through the blizzard.

"Well, I personally collected four artefacts," she said.

Fang frowned, but there was a smile playing on his lips.
"That's not an answer."

Yuu just smiled. The dark figure stepped through the
swirling snow, resolving into the large man she had seen in the
tavern at the base of the mountain. Like Yuu, he had not thought
to wear a coat, and his huge arms looked pale as the grave and he
was shivering from the cold. He glanced about quickly, then
started forward again, hurrying toward the torii and giving Yang
Yang a wide berth.

"Hello there, fellow chosen," Fang said to the big man
stepping into Tianmen. "Good to see at least three of us made it."

The big man carefully placed his stringed instrument on the
ground and shook the snow from his shoulders. He rubbed his
hands together and nodded to each of them. "Xin Fai," he said by
way of greeting.

"Yuu," Yuu said with a slight bow of her head.

"And I am Fang, Emperor of Thieves."

"Emperor now?" Yuu asked.

Fang winked at her. "How does it feel to have bedded an
emperor?"

Yuu rolled her eyes. "Who is your patron?" she asked Xin
Fai.

"Champa," Xin Fai said.

Fang leaned against a jade pillar and yawned. "Never heard
of him."

"God of Laughter," Yuu said. "I have his artefact."

Xin Fai nodded slowly.

"I'd be willing to trade it for one of yours," she said.

Fang laughed. "Don't take that deal, friend," he said. "I present to you the last fool who tried." He gestured to the god of gambling still studying his spinning coin.

Natsuko stepped between them. "Artefacts can no longer change hands until after the counting." She eyed all three of them. "You're in Tianmen. I would recommend you observe the rules."

Yuu shrugged. "Afterwards then," she said.

Xin Fai nodded again. He was shivering, but now, surrounded by warmth, he smiled. "I am certain Champa will be pleased." He rolled his eyes. "He has not stopped complaining since we met."

Natsuko cackled. "This way to the feast hall, Daiyu. The spirits will bring food... and spirits"

Yuu turned to the others once more. "Will you come with me?" she asked. "We no longer have anything to fear from each other, and I'd kill for some company." She glanced at Natsuko. "Mortal company."

Fang glanced back at his god and sighed. "Why not? Better than watching Yang Yang skin his hands on the coin."

Xin Fai bowed, and when he straightened, he had his instrument in hand again. "I'd be honoured."

They spent the next few hours swapping stories about how they obtained some of their artefacts. Yuu was glad of the camaraderie for as long as it would last. She was certain Fang embellished his stories of his dashing heists and daring duels. She didn't mind the falsities as they made for exciting escapades. Xin Fai was a natural storyteller, and though his stories seemed bland compared to Fang's boasts, he told them in such a way that Yuu ached to hear more. For her own part, she told them about playing cards against a corpse for the coin and stealing the ring from the triad boss. That last one made Fang roar with laughter and spill his wine. Yuu, for her part, drank only water. Despite how much she wanted a drink, she needed a clear head for what was to come.

The moon rose all too quickly, and almost without warning, it was time to count the artefacts and declare the next tianjun.

Chapter 36

Batu summoned them, and there was no mistaking it. His voice echoed down the halls of Tianmen, and the spirits fled at the sound. Yuu shared one last drink with the other champions. They toasted to the victor, whoever it may be then made their way to the throne room. Yuu knew the way without being told, as though something was guiding her feet along the marble halls. One glance at the bewildered expression on Fang's face, and she was certain she was not the only one.

The throne room was busier than she would have thought possible. Hundreds of gods all standing around, waiting to find out who would be their next tianjun. Some were tall, others short. Some appeared human, others as animals. And some, like Sarnai, were something entirely different. Hundreds of gods, and three mortals amongst them. Natsuko told her no mortal set foot in Tianmen apart from this one occasion every century. The gods all watched them with eager interest.

Yuu went to stand before Natsuko, and Xin Fai before the obese Champa. Fang sauntered over to where Yang Yang stood with her female side glaring at Yuu. She tried to ignore the hostile stare, but it bore into her. Yuu realised she missed her mask. It had been a sort of shield, protecting her and bolstering her courage. But no, she lost the mask for a reason. She would face this final part of her task without it. She would face it as Yuu, rather than the Art of War.

Batu sat his throne lazily, lounging with a leg over one of the arms. He was bare chested with tufts of golden hair on his shoulders and chest, with golden sideburns that ran down to his chin. His half-lidded eyes roved lethargically over the gathering. It was an act that did not fool Yuu for a moment. He gave the impression of casual nonchalance, but was a coiled snake ready to strike. A tall redwood, iron-bound staff rested against the throne, and by the scars, it had seen its fair share of combat. Natsuko said the gods warred amongst themselves from time to time, but why would he need his staff now? Here? He was tianjun, lord of all the gods. Surely, he had nothing to fear.

"Is it time?" Batu asked in a slow drawl.

A goddess in a deep blue robe shuffled forward on slippered feet and bowed her head to Batu. "It is, tianjun. The moon has risen." She gestured with a flourish and the clouds shrouding the sky above parted to show the full moon glaring down at them.

"Hikaru," Natsuko whispered. "Cowardly god of the moon." Her inhuman smile crept across her face.

Batu sat up suddenly and clapped his hands with a slap that echoed about the throne room. "Excellent!" His lazy demeanour was entirely gone now, replaced by energetic fervour. "How many of our foolish mortals still live to face the tianjun?"

Silence descended upon the gods as they searched the crowd for the mortals. Natsuko coughed quietly and nudged Yuu in the back. She took a step forward and then another, breaking from the crowd and moving to stand before Batu at the foot of the throne. She glanced left at Fang; his usual grin had deserted him. On her right Xin Fai crept forward step by step, clearly uneasy in front of the divine audience.

"Just three of you?" Batu asked with a laugh that none of the other gods joined him in. "Must have been a bloody contest this time around." He swept his gaze over them, lingering on Fang and longer still on Xin Fai. Yuu had the feeling she was being dismissed out of hand. "Well, go on then, let's see which of you has the honour of challenging the god of war."

Yuu glanced back to Natsuko even as Fang and Xin Fai started reaching into packs and pulling things out of their pockets, dumping divine artefacts on the marble floor. She had that feeling she was once again missing something. Natsuko didn't meet her gaze. Yuu was suddenly certain there was more to the contest than collecting a bunch of artefacts. Natsuko had been deliberately hiding something from her, and perhaps the other gods had been hiding it from their champions also.

"What's this?" Batu said, chuckling and slapping his hand on the arm of the throne. "Little Natsuko, don't tell me your champion collected no artefacts at all. Did you truly choose so poorly?"

"What are you doing, Daiyu?" Natsuko hissed.

Yuu tucked some hair behind her ear as she considered, her mind a whirl of possibilities, putting together things Natsuko had said, things Yang Yang had said. Batu's supreme confidence even as they were deciding who would replace him. She glanced down at the contract scrawled on her skin. "Why did you choose me as your champion?" Yuu asked, heedless of all the whispering gods with eyes fixed upon her.

Natsuko glanced about at the other gods, wringing her gnarled hands together, then grimaced and hurried forward to stand in front of Yuu. "What are you talking about?"

"I'm no thief who could steal artefacts, nor a warrior able to take them from others," Yuu said.

"Yet here you stand with enough artefacts to win," Natsuko said. "I think."

"By chance and luck," Yuu said. "If not for Li Bang, I would have failed back in Ban Ping twice. The coin I secured on my own, yes. The sword and mirror would have been beyond me if not for Roaring Tiger's army. And if I had not met Yanmei, the Ticking Clock would stand here instead of me. My achievements are those of others."

"Quickly now, little Natsuko," Batu said. Yuu ignored him, and all the other gods and champions. This was a truth she would chase to the end.

Natsuko grumbled and stared up at Yuu. "I chose you because you have the sense to secure allies to make up for your failings. I chose you because you see the steps ahead as well as behind. Everyone, mortal and god alike, has a weakness, and you see them. You just proved this again with Yang Yang and his coin."

"Which of us has the honour of challenging the god of war," Yuu said, repeating Batu's words.

"Little Natsuko…" Batu said.

Natsuko leaned to the side, glancing past Yuu. "Oh, shut up, you insufferable arse. Unless you're in a rush to lose your throne, you will give me a minute here."

Batu chuckled again. "One more minute then, little Natsuko." The way he said her name made Yuu seethe.

"The contest is only the first part," Natsuko said. "The winner then has to duel the tianjun. If the tianjun dies… well, then I take the throne."

"A mortal duelling a god?" Yuu asked.

"The rules are different here, Daiyu," Natsuko said. "We're not protected here. gods can die."

Yuu shook her head, then pushed hair out of her face. "But…"

Natsuko took Yuu's arm and tried to turn her back to face Batu. Yuu refused to budge. "I picked you, because no warrior can best the god of war in a fight. Batu is the god of war. He is made of it, built of battle. He is the fight incarnate. No mortal warrior could hope to win. But you… you're not a warrior. Your skills don't lie in the fight, they lie in the structure of the fight. You counter martial skill with strategic understanding. You see the rules of the games and how to bend or break them. You—" Natsuko paused and poked Yuu hard in the chest "—are the only one who can beat Batu."

Yuu shook her head. The realisation of what the goddess wanted from her was terrifying. "You expect me to beat the god of war in a duel. How?"

Natsuko smiled her godly smile. "By outplaying him. By outthinking him. Why else have you been carving all those chess pieces if not for this?"

"Time is up, little Natsuko," Batu said.

Yuu stared down at Natsuko for another second. She had been played. They had all been played. She looked down at the contract scrawled upon her arm.

"You can't bring him back, can you?" Yuu asked.

"What?"

"The Steel Prince." She wondered if Natsuko even remembered her promise. "You can't bring him back, even if you do become tianjun." Strangely, she didn't feel sad or angry or betrayed. She felt relieved.

Natsuko sighed as though Yuu were a disobedient child. "Of course not. He's been dead five years. And I never agreed to. I said I'd give you back what you have lost, what you cherish most, which I already have done." She took hold of Yuu's hand and squeezed it firmly. "It was never some foolish prince who got himself killed. What you lost was far more personal. You lost your purpose. I gave that back to you the moment you agreed to be my champion. This is your purpose, Yuu. This is your meaning. And don't you dare try to tell me it's not a whole lot better than having a prince to snuggle up to. You were never meant to be some ghost drifting from village to village, robbing old men of their pocket money. You were meant to do great things. You have the potential to be great. But you lost the drive, your purpose. Your will to be more." Her smile slipped, and Yuu saw the old goddess' eyes filling with tears. "Tell me, aren't you happier now than when I found you? Don't think for a moment my wonderful company has done that for you. You have a reason to live again, a reason to fight again, and a goal to test yourself against again."

She was right. Of course she was right. Yuu knew the truth long ago, from the first moment she met the Steel Prince. She never really loved him, not the man. She loved the name, the ideal. She loved the purpose he represented and the justification he gave her to put her skills to practical use. The goddess had kept her promise. She had given Yuu back her Steel Prince, the true Steel Prince. She had given Yuu back her reason to live and to fight. To stop Batu. To end war, all war.

"Do you really think I can win?" Yuu asked in a whisper. Batu was powerful, that much was obvious. She could outplay just about anyone in a game, but she was no warrior.

"Of course I do," Natsuko snapped. "I wouldn't have dragged your sorry arse halfway across the Hosan empire if I didn't. But what I think doesn't matter. Do you think you can do it?"

"Last chance, little Natsuko," Batu said. "I grow bored. Does your champion have artefacts or not?"

Yuu thought of the people of Anding, their city ravaged by war. Of the soldiers under Roaring Tiger's command, dying to protect Hosa. Of the children Yanmei protected, orphans of war. She didn't know if she could beat Batu — the task seemed impossible — but she knew she had to try. If no warrior could beat him, then maybe she could, for she was certainly no warrior.

Yuu stepped around Natsuko, already reaching inside her robes. She pulled out the lantern, the sword, the statue of Champa laughing, the ring, the scale, the whip, and the necklace of teeth. Finally, she pulled out the mirror and glanced into its glass. The Ticking Clock stared back at her. She laid them all on the ground in front of Batu.

Fang laughed, a truly joyous sound. "This must really sting, Yang Yang," he said, mocking his own patron God. Yuu glanced at the thief. Seven artefacts lay on the ground in front of him. He caught her eye and winked at her. "Well done."

She looked the other way at Xin Fai also standing in front of seven artefacts. "Good luck," he said with a bow of his head. "I believe you will need it."

Batu was silently grinning at her. The gods behind her were whispering to each other. She heard a few laughs, some others scoffed. None of the voices seemed to think she had a chance against the god of war.

"Well, well, little Natsuko," Batu said eventually. "It appears I underestimated you."

Natsuko cackled. "Only a fool sees a necklace in place of a noose, Batu."

Batu grinned as he stood from his throne and reached for his staff. "Mindless ramblings," he said. "Now you underestimate me. Come, mortal. It's time we ended this foolish charade."

"Now?" Yuu asked.

"Yes, now!" Batu snapped. He stalked down the steps like a predator on the hunt, all pretense at lethargy gone. He stopped in front of her, and Yuu took a step back, unsure of what to do, her legs trembling. Should she strike now or wait until he made the first move?

Batu reached out and Yuu flinched away, already reaching for one of her chess pieces and wishing she had more time to formulate a plan. "Such a jittery one," Batu said. "Give me your hand, mortal."

Yuu glanced at Natsuko and the goddess nodded. She extended her tattooed right hand slowly. Batu rolled his eyes at her. "The other hand." Yuu dropped her right hand with an embarrassed cough. It really wasn't fair; she had no idea what was going on and was desperately trying to concentrate while also trying to think of a strategy. She could flee into the gathered gods, use them as cover, and then strike out at Batu from the crowd. Batu grabbed her left hand, his large fingers encompassing hers, and her right arm started to itch. Her tattoos were glowing. The scrawled letters shone with a bright luminescence and lifted from her skin, floating in the air for a moment and then fading into nothing. Then her left arm began to itch also, and she saw new tattoos writing themselves upon her skin. Words snaked up and around her arm, crawled around the manacle still clamped on her wrist. It felt like ants scurrying through her veins, but she fought the urge to scratch. Batu was staring at her, eyes dark and intense, and Yuu realised the same tattoos were writing themselves on his arm. One contract began, even as the last one ended. Yet she still could not read it.

As soon as the last contract vanished and the new one stopped scratching its way up her arm, Batu dropped her hand, looked up at the gathered gods, and roared, "It's time you all realised the truth. *I* am tianjun!" Yuu staggered back. "I took this throne a hundred years ago, and I will not relinquish it. No mortal can beat me. *I* am tianjun, and *I* will always be tianjun."

The murmuring of the gods grew louder, but none of them rose to challenge Batu. None except Natsuko. "Prove it," she said, her voice old and paper thin compared to his. "All this bluster. My champion stands before you, Batu." Yuu wasn't sure she wanted Natsuko taunting the god of war. She needed time to prepare. She needed a plan.

"Here?" Yuu asked, already glancing about, assessing the battleground.

Batu glanced at her and grinned, his golden sideburns framing his face like a monkey's mane. "Of course not. This is the throne room. We have a place set up just for the battle." He waved a hand to the side and another torii, like the one she used to enter Tianmen, opened. Beyond it was a huge square arena, open to the elements, the sun shining down upon its gleaming stone floor. There was a row of stone pillars on each side of the arena and beyond it raised wooden benches all around. This wouldn't be just a duel — it would be a spectacle. Batu wanted all the gods there to witness him defend his reign. To be there when he secured his throne once and for all.

"When did you build this?" Natsuko asked.

Batu glanced down at Natsuko. "While you and your little champion were out fetching divine junk. I thought it was time we gave the contest the ceremony it deserves. After all, it's the last one we'll ever hold."

Again, the gods murmured amongst themselves, yet none dared contradict him.

"After you, champion," Batu said, waving toward the archway. He smiled at her but his eyes blazed with malice.

Yuu drew in a deep breath, stepped forward, then stopped. She turned to the gods moving to file in behind her. "To any of you whose artefacts I collected, I give them back to you." She didn't need them anymore, and if they meant so much to the gods who cherished them, then they should have them. Yuu stepped through the torii into the arena.

Chapter 37

Natsuko was one of the last to pass into the dojo. She even held up a few of the other gods in idle conversation. Batu wouldn't begin the duel until she was there, until all of them were there, especially her. This was his way of sending a message, of showing them he was not going to be deposed, not now, not ever. He wouldn't begin until they were all watching, and the longer she could give Daiyu to prepare, the better.

At last, she stepped into the dojo. Batu was showing off, twirling his staff around in fanciful patterns. It looked extremely dangerous, and she wagered that was his point. Yuu was walking between the pillars on the arena floor, probably counting steps, committing the battleground to memory. She stopped by a marble pillar and rested a hand against it, then continued walking. She knelt near the centre and brushed a small stone away from the floor. A strategist needed to know the terrain. Natsuko walked toward the benches, clutching Daiyu's mask. White and featureless save for the two eye-slits and the crack running from the right eye to the chin, almost like the track of a tear.

"Natsuko," Yuu said as the goddess reached the stands. Champa and Khando were there. They had always been among Natsuko and Fuyuko's closest friends.

Natsuko hid the Art of War's mask away inside her hanfu and fixed a grin on her face she didn't feel. "Don't you have more important things to be doing?" she said. "You have a god to kill, girl."

"Thank you," Yuu said, smiling. She looked younger than she had when they first met. She looked her age. Guilt and self-pity had added a decade of creases to her face, but they had fallen away over the past few days.

"Eh? What for? Getting you into this" — she grinned — "god-awful situation."

"For trusting me," Yuu said. "And for getting me to trust myself again." She stepped over the lowest bench and grasped Natsuko's hands in her own. "I finally understand what all the pieces mean, and where I fit into the game." She pulled away and strode off to battle the god of war.

Natsuko looked down at her hands as she climbed up to sit between Champa and Khando. She had a sour feeling in her stomach as she looked down on the little Empress chess piece of herself. It was expertly carved with two separate sides, one a grimacing old woman, the other a smiling young girl. On the bottom Yuu had etched a message. *We are never more vulnerable than in the moment of victory.*

Natsuko sat down, a scowl settling on her face. She pulled out the mask once more and stared down at it in one hand, the chess piece of herself in the other. "That poor girl," she said.

"What's that, Natsuko?" Champa said, smiling.

"She has no idea what I've done to her," Natsuko said.

Khando patted her lightly on the shoulder. "We never do." Of course, he had been through it before. "Do you think she'll win?"

Natsuko cackled. "I bet my brother on it," she said confidently, then lowered her voice to a whisper. "She has to bloody win."

Yuu stood about four paces opposite Batu at the centre of the dojo, her hands tucked into her sleeves, her douli hiding half her face from view. She looked at ease, but Natsuko knew her better than that. She knew her champion would be trembling. She had never quite managed to rid herself of all emotion.

Batu slammed one end of his staff down on the floor, shattering the stone slab. "Let this be an end to it then," he shouted. He turned to Yuu. "Come then, mortal. Take your shot, you will have only one."

Yuu did not move.

Natsuko grinned. "There is a propensity to confuse heroism with rash action. They are not the same. A true hero acts not on impulse, but on rationale and consideration."

"Sounds like philosophy," Champa said with a smile, the one Yuu had so recently returned to him.

Natsuko glanced at the god of laughter. "It is. Written by the Art of War."

Yuu watched Batu showboating, his arms wide open as if welcoming an attack. She didn't budge. Her strategy was set, her plan in motion. She needed him to make the first move.

Batu gazed around at the watching gods, a wide grin on his face, finally spotting Natsuko. "Your champion is frozen in fear, little Natsuko," he shouted. "Then I will end this!"

The god of war lurched forward into a run, crossing the distance between them in four bounding strides, his staff raised to strike. Yuu focused on the central pillar and activated her first piece. Roaring Tiger crashed out of the pillar looking just like the general himself but made of stone. He collided with Batu, shoving him away. The god of war's staff whipped past Yuu's head so close its breeze ruffled her hair. Her heart raced in her chest, thundered in her ears, but still she didn't move.

"What is this?" Batu shouted at the stone general. But of course, Roaring Tiger didn't answer. He was made of marble, a wooden chess piece at his core, animated and controlled by Yuu's qi and her technique. A perfect replica, even down to the red smudge along his back.

Yuu was not fool enough to believe one piece could hold the god of war at bay for long. She focused on the floor behind Batu and activated her second piece. Li Bang dragged his bulky form out of the stone behind Batu, his chui already swinging before his back foot had formed. He thumped the head of his mace into Batu's stomach, and the god of war stumbled away coughing, blood spattering his lips. He staggered back a step, straightened up, and wagged a finger at Yuu. She watched him from beneath the rim of her douli and refused to move. It wasn't time for her to join the fight yet.

Batu recovered and whipped his staff around at the stone Li Bang's head, but Roaring Tiger parried it with his stone dao and deflected it into a pillar. Batu leapt away, twisting in mid-air and landing nimbly on his feet. Fighting two opponents, he was more reserved, stalking them, testing his reach with the tip of his staff.

Roaring Tiger circled left as Li Bang charged the god of war. Batu's staff shot out with lightning speed, catching Li Bang in the stomach and cracking the stone along the gouge there. Bits of Li Bang's gut crumbled away, dusting the floor, but he continued forward and grabbed hold of the staff even as Roaring Tiger closed on Batu, dao swinging. The god of war roared and whirled his staff, driving the stone Li Bang off his feet and into the path of Roaring Tiger. The two crashed together and went down in a pile of stone limbs, chips of both rolling and skidding across the stone floor. Batu turned from the struggling statues and ran for Yuu once more.

Now it was time for Yuu to move. She activated her third piece and a stallion charged out from the stone beneath her. But unlike old Lump, this one was not slow or tired. Yuu squeaked in alarm as the stone stallion rose between her legs and she slid into position on his back. The god of war stepped toward them. But Roaring Tiger had regained his feet and leapt in his way. Li Bang also clambered to his feet with a great crunching noise, and both statues stood side by side, blocking Batu from Yuu as Lump galloped away.

Yuu clung to Lump's stone mane for dear life as he galloped around the outside of the arena. She bounced painfully, her legs and arse banging against the stone, and reached into her robes with her free hand, grabbing handfuls of wooden shavings and scattering them about the arena floor. The gods all around her were a blur of colour and staring faces. The noise of their shouts and cheers mixed with the clamour of Lump's hooves pounding stone into a messy cacophony.

Batu pushed Li Bang back with the butt of his staff, then spun away, swinging the weapon around and shattering Roaring Tiger's arm. Chips of stone flew into the air and the stone dao fell to the ground. Li Bang recovered and lunged at Batu, but the god of war ducked the clumsy strike, leapt up, and smashed the end of his staff down on Roaring Tiger's head. Roaring Tiger exploded in a shower of stone and dust, the little wooden chess piece spinning across the floor. Batu stared at it for a moment, and a grin spread across his hairy face. He crushed the statue with his heel. Pain lanced through Yuu's chest like a dagger thrust into her heart as the qi connection to her piece was severed. She sagged over on Lump's back, struggling to hold on and breathe. Her grandmother might have been able to separate herself from the consequences, but it was something Yuu had never been able to do.

"Nothing but toys!" Batu shouted. He stared at Yuu as she trotted around the arena on Lump's back, struggling to sit straight once more. "Is this how you hoped to win? By throwing toys at me?" He leapt forward, and slammed Li Bang in the chest with his staff, cracking stone and sending chips flying. He twirled his staff about and delivered another crushing strike to Li Bang's head.

She couldn't lose Li Bang. Not yet. It wasn't time. Yuu leapt from Lump's back and hit the floor in an undignified tumbling sprawl, bashing her knee and elbow. She swallowed down the pain and struggled back to her feet as the horse statue galloped into the fray. Batu stepped back from Li Bang and swung his staff around. Its iron tip bashed the horse's face, shattering its jaw, and spinning it about, but Lump's momentum carried the statue forward. It slammed into Batu, knocked him down, and rolled on top of him. A mortal would have been crushed under the stone horse's weight and for a moment Yuu hoped it would be an end to the fight.

Yuu limped on, grimacing at the spiky needles crunching in her knee with every step. Batu rose shakily from under the weight of Lump. Lump struggled too, kicking out his powerful stone legs and striking the god of war in the face with a flailing hoof. Batu roared and lifted the massive stone horse as he straightened up. Then he slammed the stone Lump down headfirst on the floor. The statue of Lump fell apart, stone and dust crumbling away leaving Batu clutching a small wooden chess piece of a horse. He gripped it in both hands and snapped it in two as easily as a child would a twig. Another knife plunged into Yuu's heart as the connection was shattered, and she staggered, clutching at her chest. Tears blurred her vision and she stumbled to one knee.

"You look done, mortal," Batu said, grinning bloody teeth at her.

Li Bang rose from behind Batu and swung his chui, the head crunching into Batu's side. The god of war staggered from the force, crying out and spun about, swinging his staff.

Yuu staggered upright and leaned against one of the marble pillars for support. Her heart was hammering fit to burst and she couldn't catch her breath. Every statue lost was like a part of herself carved away.

Batu hammered Li Bang again with a weighty strike of his staff, bits of the statue skimming across the floor. Li Bang grabbed for the staff, getting one stone hand around it, but the god of war punched him in the face, heedless that he was punching solid stone, crushing Li Bang's nose and shattering his cheek. Batu punched him again, and Li Bang's jaw fell away in a solid chunk.

Yuu was running out of pieces far too quickly and though Batu was wounded, he seemed to be growing stronger with each blow dealt and received. Yuu pushed away from the pillar and took a steadying breath. One more piece to play, her strongest piece. She flung out a hand toward the pillar behind Batu and activated her Hero.

Yanmei erupted from the pillar, written in solid stone, dressed in scale armour, and wielding her naginata. The statue showed none of the woman's colour or fury, but it moved with her grace and strength and skill. Batu turned from Li Bang just in time to catch the blade of Yanmei's naginata in full swing. He howled as the pole arm smashed into his hand but held on all the same. Li Bang, his face a crumbling ruin, lurched forward and wrapped his chipped and disintegrating arms around the god of war, holding him long enough for Yanmei to jerk her naginata free, twirl, and smash Batu's head with its flower pommel. Batu rolled with the blow, using the momentum to flip Li Bang over, crashing the statue on his back onto the stone floor. The god of war leapt backwards, raising his staff over his head in both hands, and brought it down on the remains of Li Bang's face. The statue crumbled to gravel and dust.

Yuu collapsed to her knees again, both hands clutching her chest. She choked on her breath and wheezed past the pain. She didn't have time to waste. She had to get into position.

Batu laughed as he and Yanmei traded blows and Yuu staggered upright, all but forgotten as all eyes in the arena were drawn to the real conflict of hero versus god. She found the pillar Yanmei had burst out of and collapsed against it.

"What is she doing?" Khando asked. "This isn't fighting. She's just annoying Batu with tricks while she runs away."

Champa laughed. "You should have chosen a warrior like I did, Natsuko. Xin Fai would have put up a good fight."

Natsuko scoffed. "He would have lost."

Again, the god of laughter smiled. "Probably. But I think Batu is right. No one can depose him now."

Natsuko watched Yanmei move in a whirling dance of blade and stone, her naginata spinning around her stone body with hypnotic grace. Batu was bleeding from a head wound above his eye, and his lips were bloody, but he was smiling, grinning as he danced with Yanmei, matching her speed, and deflecting her attacks. He was enjoying the battle, Natsuko realised, so much so he had all but forgotten Yuu was even there. "So, we should just give up?" she asked bitterly "Let Batu Keep the throne?"

"Yes," Khando said. "What else can we do?"

"What a worthless god of dreams you are, Khando," Natsuko said. "Your predecessor would be ashamed."

Khando sighed. "What does that matter? Esen is dead."

"Yes," Natsuko hissed. "You killed him."

"Oh," Khando was silent for a moment. "Is that why you chose her?"

Champa laughed. "She still has to win, Natsuko."

Yuu struggled back to her feet once more. Beneath her douli, she was now wearing her Art of War mask, though it was undamaged, the crack missing. Natsuko glanced down at her own hands, at the chess piece she held in one, and the mask she still held in the other.

The stone Yanmei leapt back and darted around a pillar, forcing Batu to follow her. She gave ground across the dojo in measured steps toward the centre, spinning her naginata before her, catching and deflecting Batu's staff strikes. He thrust his staff low, and its iron-shod tip cracked into Yanmei's leg, shattering the stone. She went down onto one knee. Batu leapt forward, dropped his staff, grabbed the statue's head in both hands, wrenching it off her shoulder with a crack of splitting stone. Yanmei crumbled, stone rubble skittering across the floor. Batu stared down at the wooden Hero piece as he plucked up his staff once more, then crushed the Yanmei chess piece with the end of his staff. Yuu took a step back, but showed none of the pain she had at the destruction of the other pieces.

Batu rested his staff in the crook of his arm, wiped the dust from his hands and glanced about the arena before finally settling his gaze on Yuu. "Is that it, Champion?" he shouted to her across the detritus-strewn floor. "No more toys to throw at me?"

Yuu took another step back but said nothing.

"It has been fun," Batu said with a bloody smile as he approached her slowly. "But ultimately predictable. Give up and I will let you surrender. This is your one chance."

Yuu raised her hands and stretched out her fingers, and the arena floor erupted in stone shards as sharp as wood shavings. Batu shouted as stone slivers punched into him, knocking him off his feet. But almost as soon as the stone shards erupted, they began to crumble, leaving nothing but fragments of rock on the floor, and dust hanging in the air.

Batu rose again, using his staff as a crutch. Blood dripped from two shallow wounds in his chest. He grimaced as he got back to his feet, then roared a bellowing laugh. "So be it!" He leapt into the air and landed just two paces away from Yuu, swung his staff at her in a blur of motion and shattered Yuu's head. Her decapitated stone body stood there and started to crack.

Batu's eyes went wide. "What the—"

Yuu's stone statue crumbled away, and a stone Hosan soldier holding a broken spear, the Pawn Yuu had used to beat her grandmother, burst from the shell of the stone Yuu and plunged its stone spear up into Batu's chest, and out his back in a spray of blood.

Batu swayed on his feet. He reached up with one hand and gripped hold of the spear shaft as his blood trickled down it. He snarled, then choked and retched blood over the Pawn. His hand fell to his side and the god of war toppled sideways to the dusty stone floor.

The gods fell silent, gaping at the dead god of war. Natsuko looked down at the chess piece in her hands and read the words on the bottom again. *We are never more vulnerable than in the moment of victory.* In her other hand she still held the Art of War's mask. The silence broke all at once as the gods started talking and shouting at one another. Some were incredulous, others ecstatic, some furious. Natsuko sighed, but the sound was swallowed by the tumult. Apologies would do no good, but they were all she could offer her champion.

Chapter 38

Yuu emerged from the pillar, from the hollow Yanmei's statue had ripped out when she entered the battle. As her Hero piece had drawn the attention of the god of war, she had slipped inside, replacing herself with her own piece. Her Pawn, with another Pawn hiding inside. The entire fight had gone according to plan, but it had still been close, and the price of failure would have been so high. She picked her way across the arena floor to where her final piece waited and pulled her qi from it. The stone soldier crumbled away leaving only the little chess piece on the floor. Used so long ago to secure her very first victory, and now again to secure her most important victory. She scooped up the piece and smiled as she ran her thumb along its familiar surfaces. Then she pocketed it inside her robes and stared down at the body of Batu, the god of war.

His skin was glowing softly, a golden haze rising from him almost like steam. But he was definitely dead. His eyes were lifeless, distant. The hole through his chest had pierced his heart and blood pooled beneath him. She had done it. Somehow it didn't feel real. But she had done it. A wild giggle burst from her lips and she quickly clapped a hand over her mouth to stifle it. She had killed the god of war, pulled him down from his throne. Now, Natsuko could take his place and finally end the constant conflicts that had plagued the world for a hundred years. Hosa and Nash and Ipia and Cochtan could know peace at last. True peace. Without a god whispering promises of power or battle plans or inciting jealousies and hatred. Maybe now, the four empires could heal, enjoy a time of prosperity instead of violence. In the world Natsuko could help to create, could guide into being, there would be no need for the Art of War. That, Yuu decided, was a more fitting tribute to her grandmother than any battle she could win. A fitting finale to the legacy she had wished to leave behind. An end to war, and an end to the need for strategists like her. She had done it.

The tattoos scrawled on Batu's arm began to glow. They rose from his flesh, shining brightly for a moment before fading into embers and then nothing. She glanced down at the contract written on her own arm. It was still there, unchanged.

"Daiyu," Natsuko called from behind Yuu. The goddess wasn't perfect, far from it. She could be grumpy, capricious, offensive, and even a little vindictive, but she was better than Batu. She would be a better tianjun than Batu. "I'm sorry."

Yuu banished the mystery of the contract on her arm and turned to congratulate the goddess, a smile still on her face. She felt a sharp pain in her chest. Natsuko stood in front of her, the lines of her face drawn down into a frown. Yuu glanced down to see a hilt sticking out of her chest, her little carving knife. Somehow it was in her, its blade biting into her, piercing her. The pain rushed in and burned inside her chest and Yuu gasped, knowing it would be the last breath she'd ever take. She toppled backward, her vision already fading, and Natsuko caught her, lowered her to the floor. In her other hand, the goddess held a mask. She gently placed it on Yuu's face and she had not the strength to resist. It felt so familiar. It felt like betrayal. But Yuu was already too far gone to fight it.

As Natsuko laid her down on the arena floor, the last thing Yuu saw was the goddess staring at her, mouthing words she couldn't hear. Words written in golden light. She died with an itch on her arm.

Natsuko stepped through the torii, leaving the arena behind, ahead of a nervous, chattering throng of gods. Before her sat the throne of the tianjun. A throne no one other than Batu had sat in for a hundred years. The throne itself held no power, yet it was more than just a symbol. It signalled to all heaven and earth, to mortal, god, and spirit alike, that whoever sat upon it was lord of heaven. Their mandate was supreme, their wishes would be fulfilled. Natsuko's desires would take form. Fuyuko's vision of the world.

She stepped forward, straightening her back as she strode toward the throne. The other gods pushed and jostled their way through the archway behind her, dragging Yuu's corpse with them. Natsuko was truly sorry for what had to be done to the strategist, to her champion. But it did have to be done. It was the law. The rules of the contest. Fang and Xin Fai waited just inside the throne room, watching. She would decide what to do with them later. They could be useful, carry the word of the new tianjun to the world, or perhaps they knew too much about the gods and the struggle for the throne. But for now, they simply weren't important.

Natsuko rolled a few kinks out of her neck. Her feet stepped lighter; her bones felt less weary. Her skin shrunk, the wrinkles receding, and her hair grew darker, the grey fading to black. By the time she reached the foot of the throne, she was a girl again. She giggled as she skipped up the steps. When she reached the top, she turned to stare down at the gods arrayed before her. She saw friends and enemies, cohorts and conspirators, brothers and sisters. They were all her subjects. Whether they liked it or not. Slowly, Natsuko sat down on her throne. It dwarfed her, but then it was built for men, and she was a child goddess.

"Batu is dead," Natsuko shouted over the clamour of the gods. One by one, they fell silent and stared up at her. "His regime of war is at an end. All of you must inform your worshippers, your monks, the people who visit your shrines, that war is no longer the mandate of heaven. It is time for peace."

Changang, the god of life, stepped forward, apart from the whispering gods. He bowed his head deeply. "Tianjun," he said in a voice like crackling paper. "Before any such wishes can be carried out, there is a matter that cannot wait." He straightened up and stared at Natsuko. "We must have a god of war."

Natsuko nodded even as all the other gods voiced their agreement. It was true. The rules of the contest were clear. She had just been waiting, putting it off for as long as possible. It felt like a betrayal. It *was* a betrayal, and she hated doing it. She stood and held up her hands, waiting for the gods to fall silent.

"Batu is dead," Natsuko announced, her voice trembling. "Rise, Yuu, God of War."

Epilogue

Emperor WuLong limped into the temple with General
Roaring Tiger at his back. The old general was a moving
cacophony. When he wasn't grunting, growling, or swearing, his
armour clicked and clacked against itself. Emperor WuLong was
also informed that the general smelled of horse and battle and
sweat, but he couldn't tell. He'd long since lost the ability to smell.
Behind his porcelain mask, he didn't even have a nose anymore.
The Leper Emperor, they called him. His body ravaged by a
disease that had eaten away at him piece by piece. He still felt the
pain of it, though it was less than it had once been.

"We have five hundred soldiers stationed on the western side
of Shin, ready to make the climb," Roaring Tiger growled even as
Emperor WuLong lowered himself onto his knees before the
shrine of Batu. "We also have a hundred wushu masters from Sun
Valley ready to climb the cliffs under nightfall. We will surprise
those Cochtan bastards and throw them out of Shin and out of
Hosa."

He made it sound so simple. But Emperor WuLong knew it
would be a difficult and bloody battle. The Cochtans had an
elevated, highly defensible position in Shin. They had the range
with their rifles and a tactical advantage with their thopters. Add
to that the new Blood Engines, and Emperor WuLong was far
from certain his superior numbers could carry the day. No. If they
wanted to win, they would need more than numbers, more than
techniques, more than strategy. They would need the gods. They
needed Batu's favour.

"Leave me, General," Emperor WuLong rasped. The disease
had ravaged his lungs along with the rest of him, and words were
ever painful things. He was glad no one could see the pain behind
his gilded mask.

Roaring Tiger grunted. "May Batu grant us victory." A brief nod of his head, then he turned and clinked and clacked his way out of the temple, leaving Emperor WuLong alone with the gods.

WuLong sagged as soon as the general left the temple, and a groan of pain escaped his lips unbidden. No one else could know how he suffered. They could call him the Leper Emperor as much as they liked, as long as they still thought him strong enough to hold Hosa. To hold the throne and keep the other provinces in line.

It was customary to pray on the eve of a battle: for fortune, for victory, for mercy. The list of things to pray for was almost endless. Some people might shun the favour of the gods, but they were usually the fools who thought themselves above worship. The gods were real, WuLong knew this personally, and only a fool sought to anger them. There were a dozen shrines in the temple, each one dedicated to a different god, but Batu's shrine was front and centre. He was the god of war and tianjun, his place was highest among heaven. It was his favour the Hosan forces needed if they were to take back Shin province. A statue of Batu on his throne took up most of the shrine, housed in a small wooden pagoda. The god of war lounged on the throne, staring straight ahead, and sporting a half smile. Worshipers had scattered several old weapons about the foot of the shrine, gifts given freely to the god of war to curry his favour. WuLong brought no such gift with him now, but had a much greater one to give. Hosan soldiers would die in battle later that night, and Batu loved nothing more than the spilled blood of warriors.

"Hear me, Batu," WuLong whispered, placing his hands on the ground and bowing low, his mask touching the stone floor. "God of War, Lord of Battle, Ruler of Heaven. Your children need your blessings. We are forged in your likeness, made whole by your worship. We march to war in your name."

He heard the crumbling of stone. Shards of rock scattered the floor about his hands. A sandaled foot broke free of the shrine.

Batu had never come before him as such. WuLong had seen
shinigami, spirits, the ghosts of heroes. But never before had the
Lord of Heaven graced him with his presence. It was always in
whispers and glimpses from the corner of his one remaining eye.

The sound of crumbling rock faded away and WuLong could
hear his own laboured breathing and the distant sounds of his
army camped outside. "Batu..." he started only to be interrupted
by the sound of a polite cough. It was certainly not a man's cough.

WuLong looked up from the floor to see a robed figure
sitting on the ruin of Batu's shrine. She wore patchwork robes of
myriad colours, an old bamboo douli, a steel manacle on her left
wrist, and a plain white mask he recognised well. Her feet dangled
over the edge of the little shrine, and in her hand she held a chess
piece, a Hosan soldier in full armour with a broken spear.

WuLong struggled to sit. His arms and legs and even his rear
hurt. "Daiyu Lingsen," he said haltingly. "Why are you here?
How? Where is Batu?"

The Art of War slid off the shrine and bent backwards a
little, stretching her back. "Sorry about the mess," she said. "I'm
still getting used to... everything."

WuLong rose from his knees and stood up slowly, painfully.
He faced the strategist, mask to mask. "You should not have
come. The Qing family..."

She held up a hand to stop him. "That no longer matters. I'm
here on behalf of the tianjun."

"Batu?"

Silence stretched between them, and WuLong realised Daiyu
Lingsen's eyes were two dark voids, as though there was nothing
but darkness behind the mask. But through the crack running
down from her right eye, he could see her lips quirked up into a
smile. "Batu is dead," she said eventually. "Natsuko rules in his
place now."

WuLong frowned as he tried to remember a Natsuko. He had
once spent a long time amongst the temples on Long Mountain,

but those memories were slow to return to him. "God of Missed Opportunities?"

"She has — deposed Batu," Daiyu Lingsen continued. "And I'm here with a message." Through the crack of her mask, he saw her smile vanish. "Make peace, Leper Emperor. Go to the Cochtans and make peace. Whatever it costs."

"This is madness! They have invaded Hosa. We stand here at the edge of victory, of pushing them from our borders. Batu said to make war, to—"

"I really don't care what Batu said," she interrupted him. "The fool is dead. Natsuko rules in his place. She has declared a new age of peace for Hosa, Cochtan, Ipia, Nash, and even heaven. And what the tianjun wants, the tianjun gets."

WuLong felt pressure on his teeth and realised he was close to grinding them, and he had few enough of them to spare.

"Ooh," Daiyu Lingsen turned and approached a shrine dedicated to Zhenzhen, the goddess of booze. A small cup of wine was laid out for the goddess, but the Art of War scooped it up, lifted her mask a little, and slurped it down in one, then sighed. "I am going to miss getting drunk."

"What if I don't?" WuLong asked. "What if I don't make peace with the Cochtans?"

Daiyu Lingsen slipped her mask back down over her chin and turned to face him again. She stepped close and held up the chess piece between them. It was unmistakably a Pawn.

"Do as she says, Leper Emperor," Daiyu Lingsen said as she stepped around him and walked back to the god of war's shrine. "Trust me when I tell you not to get on the wrong side of this tianjun. Make peace, Emperor WuLong." She dusted a few loose stones away from the shrine, clearing off the last bits of evidence the statue of Batu had ever existed. "But prepare for war." She turned and sat down on the shrine again.

"What war?"

Daiyu Lingsen chuckled. "*The* war." As her voice died away, she went still and silent.

WuLong approached the woman on the shrine and peered at her through his mask. She had turned to stone. Perched on top of the shrine, with the debris of its previous inhabitant scattered among old swords and daggers on the floor before her, sat a statue of the Art of War. Her douli and mask gave her an oddly threatening look. In her hand, instead of the Pawn, she held a different piece. Emperor WuLong stared down at it, at himself made miniature.

Acknowledgements

First and foremost I want to say a big ol' thank you to everyone who read Never Die and demanded more, both those of you who got in touch directly and those of you mentioned it in reviews. I heard you! Your requests gave me the kick up the arse I needed to get moving on a vague idea I had for a sequel that was not a sequel. Without you all, the Mortal Techniques series would not exist.

I'd also like to thank my sister, Rhian, for giving me the idea of expanding the Art of War's story. Just remember, every time you ask for more information about a character, you might be inspiring a whole new story. And another big thank you to Mihir who poked and poked and poked until I agreed to turn the whole thing into a series. I blame you for many sleepless nights!

A shout out to NoCabal for being a wonderfully supportive community. Not that I'm admitting there is a secretive cabal of authors, there definitely is NoCabal. But if there was, they would be lovely people always willing to lend a hand, an ear, an eye, or many other disembodied parts.

My undying respect and awe go out to Felix Ortiz for his artwork, which is nothing short of mind boggling. And to Shawn T. King for working his black magic and making book covers work. With the outstanding work they both have put into the Mortal Techniques, I feel the series is as much theirs as mine. And another bow of respect goes to the angriest editor I know, Mike Myers for kicking the crap out of my manuscript and making it SO much better.

Lastly I want to thank my fiance Vicki for listening to my mad ramblings and pretending they make sense, and for keeping the house well stocked in whiskey. And also to Korra T. BeagleFace for dragging me away from my desk every day for walkies.

Books by Rob J. Hayes

The War Eternal
Along the Razor's Edge
The Lessons Never Learned
From Cold Ashes Risen

The Mortal Techniques novels
Never Die
Pawn's Gambit
Spirits of Vengeance (coming September 28th 2021)

The First Earth Saga
The Heresy Within (The Ties that Bind #1)
The Colour of Vengeance (The Ties that Bind #2)
The Price of Faith (The Ties that Bind #3)
Where Loyalties Lie (Best Laid Plans #1)
The Fifth Empire of Man (Best Laid Plans #2)
City of Kings

It Takes a Thief...
It Takes a Thief to Catch a Sunrise
It Takes a Thief to Start a Fire

Science Fiction
Drones